ANIMAL'S REFORMATION

AN INSURGENTS MC ROMANCE

CHIAH WILDER

PROLOGUE

STREAMS OF WARM water ran over Melanie Eaton's bare back as she stood beneath the shower spray in hopes that it would calm her fraying nerves. She slowly let out a breath, fighting back the bile burning her throat. She couldn't believe that she'd agreed to meet Hunter Lewis.

What the hell was I thinking? I'm not ready for this. The slight tingle between her legs was an evident reminder of exactly why she'd agreed to meet her online boyfriend. It'd been so long since she'd enjoyed any male attention, and the loneliness that had permeated her life was unbearable. When Hunter had shown an interest in her, Melanie had been flattered, and over the course of four months she'd fallen in love with him. *And now we'll be spending the weekend together.* As much as the thought thrilled Melanie, if she wasn't careful, her nerves would get the better of her, and Hunter would see a trembling mess of insecurities instead of the confident and flirty woman she'd pretended to be.

Melanie closed her eyes and leaned back against the slick tiles. Everything would be all right because Hunter was the man she'd been yearning for, and the things he said to her made her believe she was the perfect woman for him. *It'll be nice to have someone to go out with, to cook for, and to make love to.* She smiled as shivers skated across her skin. *But ... you don't know if he's really who he says he is.* Melanie shushed the small voice in the back of her mind—the one that had been thwarting all spontaneity in her life ever since she was a little girl. For once, she ignored it and made plans to spend a wonderful weekend with the man she loved.

The day before, Hunter's strong, deep, and sexy voice silenced the faint warning bells in her brain, and she'd be damned if she was going to pay attention to them now—not when she was *this* close to a life of happiness and love. She sighed and brushed her fingers across her breasts while she pictured Hunter's full lips wrapped around her nipples.

Then she heard it, a sharp indistinguishable noise over the rush of water. Her eyes snapped open and she wiped the steam off the glass doors and peered through them. Nothing. But then again, it was hard to see through the mist. *These damn nerves of mine!* Melanie shook her head and watched the drops of water trickle down the shower doors. *Oh God!* Her wet hands flattened on the tiles in an attempt to hold her balance. Did she see a shadow dart by the open doorway? A shiver sneaked up her spine. Eyes blinking, she opened the shower door a tiny bit and stared at the patch of light spilling from the bathroom onto the camel carpet in the hallway. *I'm just being silly. No one's out there. I'm sure I locked the dead bolt.* For a long second, panic gripped her. *Didn't I lock it?* Melanie squeezed her eyes shut, frantically trying to remember her earlier actions. *I'm sure I did. Get a hold of yourself. Relax. Hunter will be here soon.* The thought of meeting him for the first time helped to divert her attention from irrational fear to contained excitement.

After turning off the water, Melanie stepped out of the stall and wrapped the large plush towel around her. When Hunter had asked her to find a small hotel for them, she'd decided to splurge and booked a small suite at one of the finer boutique hotels in Green Mountain Falls. The only requirements he'd had was that the place be small, secluded, and romantic, and she succeeded on all three points.

Melanie ran her fingers through her long brunette hair and looked into her blue eyes reflecting in the mirror. She was pretty sure Hunter would like what he saw because she'd made it a point to send real pictures of herself, and the way he complimented her made her feel special and cherished—something she'd never felt from a man before meeting Hunter.

She slipped on her robe then towel dried her hair, glancing at the time on the cell phone every few seconds. Hunter would be there in twenty minutes so she had to speed it up. She turned on the blowdryer, and as she ran the warm air through her hair, she heard something coming from the other room. Turning off the dryer, she stood silent and alert, her ears straining to pick up any unusual sound. There was nothing. Just the muted voices across the hall, the soft blowing of the heater fan, and the low rumble of the elevator as the doors shut. That was all … nothing out of the ordinary.

Cinching the belt tighter around her small waist, Melanie sucked in a deep breath, grasped on to the doorjamb, and tried to look into the small living area—but all she saw was darkness. Cursing herself for not leaving a light on, she put one foot in front of the other as she made her way toward a pretty crystal floor lamp she'd seen when she'd first arrived. Groping the smooth glass base, she tried to find the switch as icy fear pebbled her skin. A sigh of relief escaped from her lips when her fingers finally turned it on. She held her breath in anticipation of a warm flood of light, but nothing happened. *Dammit!* Melanie kept turning the switch over and over as if by some miracle light would appear. Nothing. Groaning, she looked around the dim room trying to find another lamp and spotted one by the sliding glass doors. Earlier she'd gone out on the balcony and watched the town's twinkling lights sparkle in the distance. *Maybe I forgot to lock the balcony door.* Of course she was being paranoid again—something that her friends and family accused her of far too often. Who would want to climb up three stories to come into her room? When she thought of it that way, it really *did* sound paranoid and crazy.

Throwing her shoulders back and her head held high, she strode toward the second lamp in the room and switched it on. A golden glow filled the room, washing over the floral paintings on the sable-colored walls, the overstuffed sofa, and the glass-topped coffee table. Everything appeared normal, but why did she sense that something was out of place?

Folding her arms around herself, she turned to look out through the sliding glass door. The lights in the distance winked at her and she focused on them in a vain attempt to alleviate the eerie feeling that someone was in the room with her.

A wisp of warm air caressed the back of her neck and she stiffened. In the glass's reflection, she saw someone behind her. *Oh God!*

"Melanie?" a deep voice whispered.

I know that voice. It's ... "Hunter?" She whirled around and met the penetrating gaze of the man she loved. "What the hell are you doing here?"

He let out a rumbling chuckle and gently touched her cheek with his warm fingers, then spoke, "Is that anyway to greet your boyfriend?" A glint flashed in his eyes ... or was it a twinkle?

Something was off, but Melanie was so relieved to see him that she pushed the nagging feeling aside and grasped his hands. "I'm sorry, but you startled me. How did you get into the room?"

"You left the door unlocked. I wanted to surprise you, so I came in." Hunter's gaze ran over her, and all of a sudden she felt self-conscious.

Melanie stepped back and smoothed down her frizzing hair. "I look a mess. I lost track of the time and haven't finished getting ready yet."

Hunter pulled her into him, hugging her tightly. "You look beautiful just as you are." He backed away a bit, then cupped her chin and tilted her head back so she looked directly into his eyes. "You're perfect. I've been waiting a long time for someone like you." He dipped his head and pressed his lips on hers.

Melanie closed her eyes and got lost in the warmth spreading through her body. She wrapped her arms around his narrow waist and relished the feel of his mouth pleasuring hers. Suddenly, he broke away and turned her toward the balcony.

"You're too much, my sweet. I want to take this a bit slower."

"Me too," she whispered. For the longest time she'd fantasized being in his arms, feeling his lips on hers, and now that he was here, her body was tingling with desire.

For a few seconds, she waited for him to reclaim her and pull her against him. Then he was behind her again and she leaned into him, loving the hardness of his chest, the warmth of his body against hers.

One of Hunter's arms went around her neck and she ran her fingers over it, gently tugging at the hair on his forearm. He pressed tighter across her neck and she coughed slightly, a single thread of panic weaving through her.

"You're hurting me," she rasped, trying to push him away.

"Am I, my sweet?"

Tears streaked down her face as her throat constricted. "Please."

"This will calm you," he whispered.

A sweet medicinal smell invaded her nostrils, and before Melanie could process it, a white cloth covered her nose and mouth. *What's going on? I can't breathe!* With muffled cries, she twisted and squirmed to break free, but Hunter was too strong. She struggled to get her breath, but the more she fought, the more she breathed in the sweet substance. *Chloroform? Probably.* How had something so right turned into something so horribly wrong?

As Melanie clawed at his arms, he rubbed his face against her hair. "You're so beautiful. You're just perfect. I love you, my sweet angel," he kept saying as the fight in her began to wane.

After what seemed like an eternity, the spinning room began to shrink as blackness spread in front of her vision and blocked out the lights. Her knees felt like rubber and her hands fell down by her side as she slowly slipped away.

Melanie's lids fluttered open. The room was dark except for the light peeking out from the bathroom. Her eyes darted around in search of Hunter but smudged outlines of the furniture were all that she could see. A warm rush of air played over her body, and she turned to stare at the rumbling heater in the corner of the room. Goosebumps prickled Melanie's skin, and she gasped in horror realizing that she was lying on the bed naked. She tried to cover herself, but her arms wouldn't move, and it was at *that* moment she knew she was in big trouble. Hunter had secured her wrists to the posts of the bed, and when she tried to move her legs, her heart sank—they were also tied up.

"Hunter? Where are you? Why are you doing this to me?" Tears laced her quivering voice, and then she saw him emerge from the shadows. With a furrowed brow and a penetrating gaze, he moved toward her until he stopped at the side of the bed. He was naked also, and his eyes roamed up and down her body. She turned her head away in embarrassment.

"You're just like I pictured you would be. So beautiful. So tempting." Hunter reached out and buried his fingers in her hair. "So soft." He grasped her chin with his other hand and turned her face to him. Dipping his head down, he pressed his lips against hers.

Melanie recoiled from his touch and tried to move away from him, but she couldn't; she was helpless ... and scared out of her mind.

"Why do you rebuke me?" he whispered as he ran his hand down the length of her body then back up until it rested on her breasts. "So fucking tempting," he muttered as he pinched her nipple. "You belong to me ... body and soul. I've waited so long for this."

Melanie saw lust and evilness in his eyes. She cried out "Help! Help me!" but he quickly cupped his hand over her mouth then slapped a piece of tape over it. Her insides trembled as tears streaked her face, and then she saw it—a long knife with an ivory handle. *No! This can't be happening! Hunter loves me. Why's he doing this? No!*

The blade of the knife was smooth and cool against her flesh. She stared at Hunter, silently pleading with him to untie her, but if he noticed her fear or discomfort, he didn't acknowledge it. Instead, he hovered over her, his handsome face not more than an inch or two from hers. "You smell like an English garden, my sweet." He peppered her face with feathery kisses while the knife moved across her skin.

Melanie moaned and struggled, but each movement she made seemed to fuel his depraved lust even more, so she stopped and lay there, waiting for the inevitable. Hunter positioned himself between her legs and ran the tip of the knife gently over her private parts. Terror filled her lungs and her breathing became labored. All she could do was pray that her death would be quick.

"I can't get over how beautiful you are. You're my favorite one so far." He pressed his mouth over her nipple and sucked it tenderly.

Melanie's eyes widened. *So far? How many women has he done this to?*

Hunter pulled away, his gleaming eyes bored into hers. "It's time, my sweet." He held his shaft in his hand then plunged it into her. The pain seared through her and she shut her eyes and clenched her teeth while he violently raped her. His heavy breathing filled up the room until he grunted then stopped moving. She could still feel him inside her, and she peeked out from under her barely opened eyelids as he knelt between her legs with his head thrown back.

"So fucking good," he mumbled.

A silver glint shone in front of her; a sliver of moonlight seemed to make the knife's blade glow. *Oh, God, no!* Even though she tried to look away, she couldn't. The shimmering blade rested on the side of her neck. Her gaze snapped up to Hunter, but he wasn't looking at her. His focus was on the knife and a slow grin spread over his face.

There was no pain. Just a sudden warm stream running down her skin. A metallic scent assaulted her nostrils as the blood filled her lungs. Melanie tried to cough, to scream, but her voice had been silenced forever. As the life drained out of her, she heard a feral cry coming from Hunter. He slammed into her again as his warm release spilled inside her.

"We are now one, my sweet."

The pressure of his lips on hers was the last thing Melanie felt as she slipped into darkness.

CHAPTER ONE

OLIVIA OPENED THE door to Kory's apartment, and her heart sunk as she heard high-pitched moans greeting her. *Dammit ... not porn again.*

"Oh, yeah, baby ... yeah ... ohhh ..."

After a long day filled with screaming kids and irate parents, the last thing she wanted was to play out some porn fantasy Kory was watching. All she wanted to do was change into her comfy pajamas, make a grilled cheese sandwich, and get lost in a corny romantic comedy. Donning handcuffs and stilettos were not in her Thursday night plans. Not. At. All.

Olivia dropped her briefcase with a *thud* on the kitchen table and shrugged out of her parka. She'd build a fire, curl up in front of it, and pretend not to hear all of the lusty moans blasting from Kory's—now *their*—bedroom.

"Olivia?" Kory said. From the sound of it, she could tell he was excited and that her plans for a quiet night had just been crushed.

Fuck! "Yeah?"

"Come on up here." She heard more short pants and squeaks.

Yeah ... he's excited all right. Olivia's mouth turned downward. Since she'd moved in a month before, they'd screwed more times than they'd talked. Kory was insatiable, and half the time she was rubbing sore muscles from all the positions he kept twisting her in. It was ridiculous and it made her rethink her rashness in setting up house with him after only a few weeks of dating.

"Are you coming? I'm in the bedroom."

"Baby ... yeah ... ohhh ... fuck ..."

Yep, it's porn. All of a sudden Olivia had a throbbing headache, and she massaged her temples and looked longingly at the cold fireplace as she passed through the family room.

"Ahh …" Kory groaned.

She sighed, knowing that he'd be raring to go the minute she opened the bedroom door. Standing before it, she sucked in a deep breath then slowly exhaled. "Here we go," she mumbled and opened the door, her eyes landing on the blank TV screen.

"Yeah … uh-huh … baby …!"

Her gaze darted to the bed and she stood there blinking as she tried to process what she was seeing—a woman with washed-out blue hair, pendulous breasts, and a wide ass straddled her boyfriend.

"Oh … yeah … baby. Uh-huh …"

It seemed like the skank who was riding her boyfriend had a limited vocabulary.

Kory turned his head and looked at her, his face red and contorted. "Hey, babe," he grunted between pants. "I've been waiting for you. Take off your clothes and come join us."

Olivia stood rooted to the spot, watching Kory's fingers dig into the bucking bronco's hips. "Are you fucking serious?" she asked.

"Come on. Champagne's real good at this. She'll make you feel comfortable."

Champagne? Is this for real?

The woman glanced over at her. "I know this is your first time, but don't be shy," she said as she continued to bounce on Kory's dick.

"Get the fuck over here," he ordered, gyrating his hips.

The blue-haired woman threw her head back and moaned. "Fuck, baby. Oh … yeah."

"It'll be fun, honey," Kory said, a crease starting to form over his forehead. "Don't ruin this, okay?"

"Ruin your fucking session? I wouldn't dream of it," Olivia replied.

"I tried to wait for you to come home, but we kinda got carried away. Remember I told you I was planning a surprise for you?" He thrust upward as the wild bronco squealed in glee. "Well, this is it. It's gonna be so hot. You'll love it."

"Stupid me … I thought the surprise was going to be a romantic dinner at Greystone's."

"This is better. Get the hell over here … you're breaking the mood." Irritation laced his voice.

"Yeah … you're kind of a downer," the woman added.

"If you loved me, you'd already have joined in," Kory said as he rolled Champagne off him, then sat up. "Do you want me to make out with you a bit to warm you up?" He pulled the sheet over his still erect dick.

Why am I not a screaming lunatic about this? My boyfriend is fucking another woman and I'm still standing here calmly discussing the options with him. Olivia pursed her lips and ran her eyes over Kory, then over Champagne, who lay flat on her back holding her phone over her face. "I think that's the problem, Kory … I don't love you." From the way Kory's head hit the back of the headboard, she knew her words had stunned him, and they'd surprised her too. *Don't I? I thought I was in love with him.* But if she were, wouldn't she be feeling awful and more devastated than she was?

"You're just being mean because you're mad I started before you got home. I'll make it up to you, baby. Come on over here." He held his hand out.

She went to the closet and pulled out her suitcase then started filling it with enough clothes that would get her through the weekend and part of next week.

"Don't be this way, baby." Kory started to get up, but the death stare she shot at him must've worked because he slumped back and watched as she gathered her clothes and toiletries.

"So I guess she's not gonna join in?" Champagne said, her eyes still fixed on her phone.

"Why're you being so bitchy about this?" Kory asked as if she'd caught him leaving the toilet seat up again instead of fucking a woman with faded butterflies tattooed on her butt cheeks.

Rage bit at the back of her throat, and she kept the urge to throw something at him in check. He didn't deserve any indication that he'd hurt and humiliated her. He didn't deserve *any* attention from her.

Olivia zipped up her suitcase and wheeled it toward the door. "I'll be back for the rest of my things next week."

"Olivia … Don't be this way. You're overreacting." Kory threw off the sheet and swung his feet off the edge of the mattress. His dick was still straight as an arrow. "I love you, honey."

Unbelievable. She glanced at Champagne—*God, that name is beyond ridiculous*—and shook her head. "He's all yours. Just to cue you in, though—he doesn't have a clue how to give a woman an orgasm." Kory's face fell and he opened his mouth but nothing came out. "That's right, *baby*, all of it was just good acting and faking on my part. You're not the stud you think you are."

Olivia walked out of the room and closed the door against Kory's angry retorts. Grabbing her briefcase from the kitchen table, she went into the garage, threw her suitcase in the back seat of her car, and took off.

"All I wanted was a damn grilled cheese sandwich," she said out loud as she thrummed her fingers on the steering wheel while waiting for the light to change to green. The snow fell at a quick pace, and the back and forth motion of the windshield wipers mesmerized her. A horn blared from behind, making her jump, then the driver swerved around her, throwing glares before speeding away.

For the fifth time since she'd left the house, Kory called and Olivia ignored it. He was the last person she wanted to speak to … ever. "You sure know how to pick them," she muttered, turning onto Willow Lane Drive. She pulled in front of a three-story apartment building, switched off the ignition, and rested her forehead on the steering wheel. Olivia couldn't believe she was back at her old apartment. She'd really thought that Kory would be the one to give her a sense of security and keep her grounded, but she was so wrong, *again.*

Olivia slid out of the car and wheeled her suitcase into the vestibule of the building then pressed the button for 3C. Harper buzzed her in, and with a resigned sigh, Olivia pulled open the glass doors and headed to the elevator.

"A glass of white wine is already on the coffee table." Harper stood in the hallway as Olivia walked over to her. "Alice just got here."

Warmth spread all over Olivia—her friends always came through for her. Even though she'd only moved to Pinewood Springs the year before, Olivia liked Harper and Alice immediately after she'd met them on her first day at Slavens Elementary School. Harper was a third grade teacher, and Alice and Olivia were teaching assistants. Olivia was assigned to Harper's classroom as well as Kennedy's, another teacher at the school.

Alice and Harper had an apartment together, and when they'd found out Olivia was looking for a roommate, they had suggested she move in with them, which pleased her immensely. The three of them got along so well, and Olivia couldn't believe her good luck in meeting such great friends. After running away from her native San Diego, she felt like a fish out of water when she'd arrived in Denver to stay with an old school friend. But once she decided to accept the teaching job in Pinewood Springs, things seemed to be falling into place in her life, well, except in the man department. That was still a disaster just like it had been back home. *I guess some things never change.*

"Let me take your suitcase." Harper wheeled it into Olivia's old room, came back to the family room, and sank down on the couch. "What the hell happened?" she asked while picking up her wineglass.

Olivia kicked off her boots, tucked her stockinged feet under her legs, and shook her head slightly before she leaned over and curled her fingers around the wineglass. "Remember I told you about the surprise Kory promised me?"

"Wait … I want to hear," Alice said padding into the kitchen. "Let me get a vodka cooler first." She walked into the family room and sank down in the chair across from the couch. "We all thought the surprise was going to be either some sexy lingerie, which would really have been for *him,* or a steak dinner at Greystone's." Alice twisted the top off the bottle and brought it to her plum-glossed lips.

"I said it'd be lingerie, but from what you've mentioned about his sexual likes, I'm starting to suspect he bought you a butt plug or a St. Andrew's cross or something." Harper took a sip of wine.

"A butt plug would definitely be up his alley but not a St. Andrew's cross. From what you told us, Kory didn't seem to be *that* extreme," Alice said.

"We were all wrong," Olivia said as her finger ran around the rim of the glass.

"A romantic weekend getaway?" Harper offered.

"It couldn't have been that, otherwise Olivia wouldn't be here with a packed suitcase. What did the jerk give you?" Alice asked.

"My boyfriend brought a woman home for us to have a threesome, only he started before I walked in the door."

"No!" Harper's eyes widened.

"That's despicable, even for him." Alice leaned forward and extended her hand. "I'm so sorry. I knew you thought he could've been the one."

"Yeah ... well, he's definitely *not* the one. The skank had a really bad dye job—her blue hair was all faded with a couple of inches of dark roots."

"Sounds awful." Harper patted Olivia's knee.

"And when I walked into the room all I saw were dull butterfly tattoos flying across her ass as she rode him. It was horrifying." Olivia shuddered at the memory.

"Who puts butterfly tattoos on their ass?" Alice asked.

"That's not really the point of the story, is it?" Harper threw a stern look at her.

Olivia busted out laughing. "Alice is right—who the fuck does that? And if you're gonna ink a swarm of them all over your butt then at least keep them touched up, you know? Her fuzzy, blurred ones just looked like shit." Thoughts of the flowered vine curling down her spine swirled around in her head, but she'd made sure to touch it up over the years.

"Okay, but what the hell did you do when you saw them together? What did Kory say?" Harper sometimes ran their conversations like she did her classroom—always cutting through the fluff and wanting to get to the point.

"He asked me to join them." Olivia leaned back against the cushion, the recitation of his words still stinging her.

"What an asshole!" Alice covered her mouth.

"Did he really mean it?" Harper asked.

"Oh, yeah. He thought I'd like to have a threesome. I guess he thought our sex life needed spicing up. I don't know. I can't believe I even slept with that sonofabitch." Olivia poured more wine into her glass.

"I tried to warn you," Harper whispered.

"I know." Olivia took a big gulp. "When am I going to break the loser streak I seem to have going on since I started dating?" She sank her fist into the cushion.

"We've all had bad boyfriends," Alice said soothingly.

"True, but you at least found a good one. Jonathan adores you, and you feel the same about him. My problem is, I never get a fucking break," Olivia replied.

"You'll find the right one. I never thought I would and then Jonathan just came into my life. It'll happen."

"I'm just tired of waiting. I mean, I took the advice you both had given me and accepted a date with Nathan a few months ago, even though I'm not really into cops. I thought maybe if I go out with someone I wouldn't normally dream of dating, it might work out. Total disaster. He wound up going crazy possessive on me after we'd dated for only a few weeks, and now he's stalking me. Then Kory enters my life, and he was so different from Nathan that I thought he was what I was looking for ... until he goes and does this crap tonight. That's what I'm saying—I've got shitty luck with guys."

"My problem is that I keep having crushes on guys that I find out are already taken. Take Jim Farley. He's so handsome and sexy, and I thought that maybe we could've had something, but then I find out he's married and has two kids. Why can't I find a decent *single* guy?" Harper said.

"Farley's a jerk," Olivia said. "He's always looking to get laid." On her first day of work at the elementary school, she'd bumped into the seventh and eighth grade science teacher. Jim Farley was more than friendly and even suggested that they go out for a drink that night. With his clean-cut good looks, he wasn't really her type—she tended to go for the rugged, bad boy look—so she declined the invitation. When she'd later found out he was married, it pissed Olivia off and she stayed away from him. She knew Harper had a major crush on Jim, but her friend would never date an attached man.

"I've decided to try online dating. A lot of people I know are doing it, and several of them have found the right person. You never know." Harper glanced over at Olivia. "You should try it. I put up my dating profile a few days ago, and I already have a few guys wanting to chat with me. Who knows?"

"Isn't that dangerous as hell? I mean … you don't know if the person, or what he's telling you, is even real. It's so easy to lie online. A lot of people get catfished." Olivia poured more wine in both her and Harper's glasses. "Anyway, I'm too busy with working at school, my part-time receptionist job, and taking two online classes to go through messages and decide who's legit or not. After what happened tonight, I'm done with men. I want to concentrate on finishing my degree so I can be a school counselor. Men and I don't do well together, so I'm placing a moratorium on dating and relationships and men." She lifted her glass up in a mock toast and then took a sip.

"We'll see how long that lasts," Alice said.

"It's time to finally break the fucking cycle, and the only way I can do it is to stay far away from men." Olivia guzzled the rest of her drink and leaned back, suddenly feeling lightheaded.

"Maybe it is a good idea to take a break from dating. I did, and then

I met Jonathan." The corners of Alice's mouth twitched.

"I just want to get married and have a family. How can it be so hard to find someone?" Harper ran her fingers through her hair.

As if on cue Olivia's phone buzzed; she glanced down, then groaned. "Does he *really* think I want to talk to him? How could I have gone out with such an idiot? And ... he wasn't even my type, at least not in the looks department." Exasperated, she clicked off her phone.

"I wondered about that. You like the scary-looking guys—the ones who ride big Harleys, wear leather jackets, and have a lot of chains dangling from their pockets." Alice laughed.

"That I do." Olivia closed her eyes and images of her dad and his friends decked out in leather floated through her mind. Her dad was a member of East Bay Dogs—a motorcycle club in San Diego county. The club wore their one-percenter patches with pride. Her dad's club, his brothers, his motorcycle, and even the club whores meant more to him than his own family. They always had. Her lids fluttered open. "But I'm not into bikers."

"I hope not," Harper said. "You don't want someone like that. When those Insurgents walk down the street, they scare the hell out of everyone. They act so cocky, yet they're nothing but criminals. Haven't you seen them around?"

"Not close up." *I've avoided them. I'm done with that life.* "Anyway, there're good and bad people in every walk of life." *Leo was a good person who Dad sucked into his club. Mom begged him to leave Leo alone, but he didn't give a shit. I guess I'm lucky to be a girl, otherwise I'd be a member of the East Bay Dogs.*

"Kennedy's taken an interest in going to their parties with a few of her other friends," Alice said.

"I didn't know she was doing that. She's asking for trouble. The parties can get pretty wild, and not all bikers play nice," Olivia said. Kennedy was a mutual friend of theirs and she taught sixth grade at the school. She had a real wild side and a reckless disregard for danger—a lethal combination.

more business during the slow season."

Klutch leaned over and grabbed a few pretzels. "When's Diesel getting out?" he asked between bites.

"Should be in a few more months," Wheelie replied.

Animal shook his head. "If he'd stop getting into fights, his ass would've been outta the pen last year. I went up to see him last week and told him Banger's pissed as shit at him for fuckin' up."

"How'd that go over?" Wheelie asked.

"He wasn't too happy to hear it, but he knows his ass is needed here. I told him to hold his damn temper in check until he gets paroled," Animal answered.

"Seems like he'd be missing pussy too much to fuck up like he's been doing," Klutch said.

"That's all he talks about when we speak. Who the hell knows what goes through his head? I just tell him to get his ass home 'cause I need help with the business." Wheelie brought the beer bottle to his mouth.

"She's all yours," Smokey said as he clasped his shoulder on Klutch's. "I Icy, bro. It's been a while since I've seen you at the club. You good?" he asked Wheelie.

"Yeah. I've been busy with the carwash and … Sofia."

"I bet," Animal said while Klutch chuckled.

Smokey pointed his finger at Animal. "I don't wanna hear shit from you about me coming back so fast. I gotta get over to Blue's Belly. Freddy just called and he's real pissed about something. *Fuck*."

Animal held up his hands. "I wasn't gonna say a damn thing, but now that you mention it…" He grinned.

"Who the hell's that?" Klutch asked as he looked toward the door.

Smokey and Wheelie's gaze drifted to the front, and Animal looked over his shoulder.

"Fuck," Animal muttered.

"You know her?" Smokey asked.

"Yeah." Animal turned around in his chair and locked eyes with Emerald. She threw him a small smile then walked toward him, tugging a little girl behind her. "Lucy?" Animal said, standing up. The girl cast her gaze downward and followed her mother until Emerald stopped abruptly in front of him.

"Long time no see," Emerald snarled.

"How the fuck did you get in here?" Animal asked as his eyes ran quickly over her. He had to admit, she looked damn good, and the way she smirked told him that she knew it. Emerald was one of many one-night stands he'd had over the years, but the night they'd spent together had produced the small girl hiding behind her. At first he hadn't believed Emerald when she told him she was pregnant, and then he questioned whether he was the father or not. But once paternity was established, Animal had stepped up to the plate and took responsibility for his daughter. Although Emerald had taken Lucy and left Colorado, Animal sent monthly child-support checks, cards, and presents, and called from time to time. The fact that Emerald would never put Lucy on the phone never stopped him from reaching out. Now, Emerald was standing in front of him with Lucy, and he didn't have a damn clue as to why the hell she was there.

"The guy at the front gate let me in because he was thinking with his dick." She darted her eyes around the room. "Just like all of you do."

Animal made a note to tear the prospect a new asshole once he figured out what the hell Emerald wanted. "Why the fuck are you here?" he asked.

"It's nice to see you too," she said coolly. She glanced at the empty chair beside him. "Can I sit down? My feet are killing me." Emerald slid onto the seat before he had a chance to answer, and Lucy scrambled on a chair at the table next to them.

Animal stared at the seven-year-old as she focused her gaze away from his. Two dark braids fell down over her shoulders, and she kept clasping and unclasping her hands while her left leg bounced up and down.

"Hey, kid," Animal said. "How've you been?" Lucy's leg moved faster and she wouldn't even glance up at him. He sucked in air through his teeth and averted his eyes to Emerald's. "What's going on?"

"Stop gawking at me and get me a drink." She crossed her legs and the light bounced off her silver stiletto boots.

"Whaddaya want?" Animal asked, his mind still trying to grasp that his daughter was only a few feet away from him. The last time he'd seen her she'd just turned one. *Damn, it's been too long.*

"A gin and tonic." A seductive smile spread across her lips. "Please."

"Do you want something to drink, Lucy?" Animal asked. Her braids swayed as she shook her head *no*. He motioned the prospect over and told him he needed a gin and tonic and a double Jack.

Smokey's mouth had been hanging open since Animal had acknowledged Emerald, and if his gut wasn't burning as bad as it was, Animal would've been laughing over that as well as the expressions of Wheelie, Klutch, and most of his brothers. Suddenly all the attention was on him, and he knew their damn tongues would be wagging for days over this one. Sometimes the guys were way worse with the gossip than the club women.

"You still haven't told me why you're here." Animal eased himself back into the chair.

"I was passing through and wanted to come by to say hi. Aren't you glad to see me ... *us?*"

"Fuckin' shocked is more like it." Animal scrubbed the side of his face. "Where're you headed to?"

"I'm going to join my fiancé in Illinois." Her gaze skimmed over him. "You're looking real fine, baby. How do you find me?" She smiled at Rusty when he set the drinks down.

Ignoring her question, Animal picked up his glass and threw it back, enjoying the smooth burn as it spilled down his throat. "How's Lucy?"

"Who? Oh ... *our* daughter." Emerald glanced sideways at the girl. "Ask her."

"Fuck, bro," Smokey muttered. "That's your kid?"

"Damn," Wheelie said.

"Shit," Klutch added.

"You comin', baby?" Charlotte asked Klutch as she padded over to the table.

"In a minute," he said. "Just chill for a bit."

"Okay," the club girl said as she turned around and headed for the couch.

Animal went over and sat on his haunches in front of the small girl, his elbows resting on his thighs. "I'm your dad, Lucy."

"I know," she said without looking at him.

"I'm real glad to see you."

No answer.

"How've you been?"

Lucy shrugged as both legs started bouncing.

Animal spread his hands and pursed his lips. "I know this is awkward as fuck, but I want you to know that I'm really happy to see you. It's been a long time … too long."

Lucy wiped her nose with the sleeve of her red turtleneck sweater.

For a few seconds, Animal just watched her, but Lucy never met his gaze or said a word to him. With an audible sigh, he stood up and raised his hand, signaling for another drink.

The ringtone of a phone broke through the crazy-ass vibe that swirled around the table, and Smokey took out his cell and cursed. "Fuck. It's Freddy again. I gotta go. I'll call you, bro," he said to Animal as he reluctantly put away his phone and walked out.

Wheelie cleared his throat as he stood up. "I better get going too. Sofia wanted me to take her to some furniture store. I'll see you around." He bumped fists with Animal then turned around and headed out of the clubhouse.

Animal jerked his head toward Charlotte while staring at Klutch. "Don't you gotta be somewhere too?" he said after the biker didn't budge.

"Not really," he replied.

"Charlotte's waiting," Animal said, his eyes narrowing.

"Oh … yeah … fuck. I guess I better go." Regret washed over his face as Klutch slowly rose to his feet. He kept looking over his shoulder at Animal as he shuffled over to the couch.

Animal took a deep breath and let it out before he sat down opposite Emerald. Leaning forward, he splayed his hands on the table, staring at her as she sipped her drink. "Now tell me what the hell's going on. There's no fucking way you're driving through Colorado to get to Illinois from Minnesota." He took the drink Rusty brought over and pressed the rim of the glass against his bottom lip. "What's the *real* reason you're here?" He took a gulp and put down the tumbler.

Emerald shook her head and looked at his hands. "I'm done. Finished. Enough. I have to live my life. I'm still young. Do you remember how old I am?"

Animal pulled at his brain, but for the life of him he couldn't remember, so he just sat there watching her lips flattened into a straight line. "Twenty something?"

"You're so fucking pathetic," she hissed, her fingers growing white as she tightened them around the glass.

"I don't remember shit like that. Anyway, what does your age have to do with any of this?"

"I'm twenty-seven, asshole." Emerald glared at him.

Anger pricked his skin. "Watch your mouth. If you wanna keep sitting in *my* clubhouse, you show me respect. Next time you don't, your ass is outta here."

His words seemed to have worried her because she leaned back and threw him a weak smile. "I just brought up my age to remind you that I was only twenty when Lucy was born. It wasn't planned at all and it took me totally by surprise."

Animal's gaze darted over to his daughter, and the only sign that she understood what her mother just implied was the way she wiped the corners of her eyes. Something inside him twisted like barbwire and he shook his head. "Don't be saying this shit in front of Lucy."

"Why not? She knows she was the result of a one-night stand with a good-looking biker who didn't want to settle down. She knows that her

CHAPTER THREE

Three months later

THE HEAT BLASTED through the vents making the small room even stuffier. Olivia pulled her dark hair back and secured it with a tie she wore around her wrist, welcoming the weight off of her neck.

Mr. Rinker, the title officer, shuffled through the papers before inserting them into a large folder and handing it to her.

"Congratulations on the purchase of your new home." He smiled and the lines around his eyes deepened.

Olivia ran her fingers over the smooth portfolio. "Thanks. I've never owned anything before, so this is really exciting." *More like terrifying.* She pushed her chair back and its wooden legs caught briefly on the plush carpet.

The title officer stood up and shook her hand. "Is there anything I can get you before you leave?" he asked, handing her a pen with the name of the company emblazoned on it.

Olivia rose to her feet and slung her purse strap over her shoulder. "I'm good, thank you."

"It was a pleasure doing business with you, young lady." Mr. Rinker smiled again, then walked out of the room.

Olivia went over to the large window and stared at the craggy, snow-covered peaks in the distance. "It's final now—I'm a homeowner," she said under her breath. After scrimping and saving for over a year and working two jobs, she was finally able to lay down some permanent roots in this quaint mountain town she now called home. Buying a house was huge for her, and it didn't matter that her new residence was only nine hundred square feet—it was all hers.

Olivia took out her cell phone and debated whether to call her mother and tell her the good news, but changed her mind and slipped the phone back into her coat pocket. Her mother wouldn't give a shit and that thought pained her. For a split second, Olivia wondered if she should call her dad, but that idea left her head as quickly as it had entered it. To say that she and her dad had a strained relationship was an understatement, but sometimes when she was really happy or even sad, she wished that they had a normal one. Hell ... Olivia wished she had a normal relationship with either of her parents, but she didn't, and had accepted that it would never happen. That's just the way it had been ever since she was in junior high—the year her dad walked out on them for one of the club girls he'd screwed around with for better than a year. As long as she could remember, her father always had a woman on the side, and her mother had accepted it as long as he came home—and then one day he didn't.

"Is there anything else we can help you with?" a cheerful woman in her early twenties asked from the doorway of the conference room.

Startled, Olivia turned around and the thoughts from her past scurried to the corners of her mind. "Uh ... no. I was just looking at the beautiful view." She shuffled toward the door.

"Take your time—I'm not rushing you."

"No ... it's okay—I really do need to go." Olivia smiled at the woman, then walked by and headed out of the office.

Frosty air whipped around her and she rushed over to her car. As she slid into the driver's seat, the familiar tune on her cellphone filled the empty space, and she fished it out from her purse.

"Hello?" she said, switching on the ignition.

"So ... is it a done deal?" Kennedy asked.

"Yes! I'm a homeowner now. Damn, that sounds scary as hell." Olivia giggled.

"We have to celebrate. Let's go to Star Bar—they've got the best martinis ever and a pretty decent happy hour."

A grin spread over Olivia's face. Kennedy was always looking for an excuse to drink, eat cheaply, and scope out guys. She was the one friend Olivia could count on to be available to party any day of the week. "Why the hell not? I'll call Harper and Alice and see if they can join us. When do you want to meet up?"

"I'm still stuck at school, filling out paperwork. I hate it! I stupidly thought teaching was about *teaching*, but it's really about all the damn reports and forms. I want to go home and change, so let's meet up in about an hour and a half. Happy hour goes until six thirty."

"Sounds good. Do you want me to pick you up?" Olivia exited the parking garage.

"Thanks, but no. Who knows? I may meet a guy I want to get to know."

Olivia shook her head; Kennedy was always on the prowl for men. "Then I'll meet you there. Later." She tossed the phone on the passenger seat then cranked up the heat; she still wasn't used to the cold after being a Southern California girl her whole life.

Sometimes Olivia worried about Kennedy because her friend seemed too trusting with men, believing anything they told her. Some of the guys she homed in on made Olivia a bit nervous and she'd tell Kennedy about her concerns, but even though her friend listened to her worries, Kennedy did what she wanted anyway. Despite the fact that Olivia was only one year older than the twenty-four-year-old teacher, she was way more seasoned and experienced than her friend, but she figured it was because of the way she'd grown up with the motorcycle club always looming in the background.

Looking in the rearview mirror, her heart sank when she saw Nathan's patrol car pull in behind her. "When the hell is this jerk going to stop this?" she said out loud while braking for the red light. Refusing to look at him, she focused on the people crossing the street. A tooting horn next to her made her jump in the seat, and she quickly turned to look over at the car—it was Nathan. Groaning, she rolled down the window, determined to tell him off—once and for all.

"Hi, beautiful," he said, leaning toward the passenger side.

"If you don't stop following me, I'm going to call your supervisor. You need to move on, Nathan. Just leave me alone."

His brown eyes narrowed and Olivia could see his body grow rigid. "Don't flatter yourself—I'm not following you, I'm working." He pointed his finger at her. "And don't ever threaten me. People who do that live to regret it."

Before she could reply, Nathan rolled up the window and switched on his overhead lights then went through the light. Olivia watched the patrol car disappear into the distance and a cold shiver ran down her spine. Cursing herself for getting involved with the crazy cop, she turned at the next right and drove to her apartment with her eyes fixed on the rearview mirror.

SATURDAY MORNING HAD a nip in the air, but no snow, which Olivia was grateful for since it was moving day. She glanced around her room to make sure all of her things were packed. She shut the door and headed to her packed car. A wave of excitement flooded over her as she drove toward the storage unit to meet up with the movers.

"Is that it, miss?" one of the movers asked.

"Yeah," she replied to the lean and wiry man.

"We'll meet you at your new house." He marked something off a piece of paper securely held in the clipboard in his hands, then closed the door to the storage unit.

My new house.

When Olivia turned into the cul-de-sac of her new neighborhood, she smiled as soon as she saw the yellow-painted cottage amid the larger homes. It seemed as though her house was one of the few remaining from when the neighborhood had first been developed in the mid-1950s, and she loved it.

Pulling into her driveway, she waved at the two moving men who smiled at her as they carried her newly purchased queen-sized mattress into the house. It felt good to finally have all of her things in one place after having them in storage for such a long time. The apartment she'd shared with Harper had been basically furnished and the few small pieces of furniture she'd purchased she had left behind. For the better part of an hour, the two men unpacked the truck while Olivia directed them where to put the pieces of furniture and numerous boxes she'd had in storage.

"We're all done," the wiry guy said as he handed the clipboard to Olivia. "Just sign here." He wiped his hand on his jeans then pointed to the bottom of a form.

"You didn't bring everything in," she replied, perusing the document.

"The cabinet didn't fit through the door," he answered.

"What does *that* mean?" She walked outside and stared at the antique china cabinet on the sidewalk leading to her house.

"It won't clear the doorway—it's too tall." The mover darted his eyes from Olivia to his cellphone then back to her. "We got another job to do, so just sign the form and we'll be on our way."

"What am I supposed to do? I can't possibly carry that in by myself. You have to bring it inside." Olivia hugged the clipboard to her chest.

"I just told you we can't do that, lady. It won't work and we don't wanna be responsible if it breaks." He sighed in apparent frustration.

"Can't you take it apart? I think if you just unscrew the top half, that would work." Olivia went over and examined the back of the piece. "I see some screws here."

"We're not allowed to take apart furniture—it's not in the contract. Just sign here." The worker stood next to her, his hand running over his shaved head.

"But—"

"No buts, lady. We just can't do it. You'll have to deal with it on your own." He tapped his dirty finger on the piece of paper. "We did our job. You should've measured it before you bought it."

"I thought a moving company would *move* my things, not leave them on the damn sidewalk." She grabbed the pen out of his hand.

back to a box on the counter. "Would you like some water?"

"Okay." Lucy stepped into the kitchen. "Your kitchen's smaller than ours."

Olivia took out two tall plastic glasses. "I'm sure it is. Your house is a lot bigger than mine. How long have you lived in the neighborhood?" she asked while filling one of the tall tumblers with water from the faucet.

"Not that long." Lucy leaned against the refrigerator.

"We gotta go, kiddo," a deep voice said from behind Olivia.

"Lemme finish my water," Lucy replied.

Olivia turned around and held out her hand to Lucy's father. "Thanks so much for helping me. I never introduced myself—I'm Olivia."

The man glanced at her hand, then at his daughter, then back at Olivia. "No problem."

Olivia dropped her hand. "Would you like some water? I'm afraid that's all I have to offer at the moment." Olivia's laugh came out too shrill, and she wanted to slap herself silly for being so damn nervous around a man she didn't even know.

"I'm good, but thanks." He shoved his hands into the front pockets of his jeans. "Ready?" he asked his daughter.

The girl bobbed her head and handed the half full glass to Olivia. "Bye." She scurried out of the kitchen and her father turned to follow her.

"Wait," Olivia said. He paused and looked over his shoulder at her. All of a sudden she felt like a damn fool.

"Yeah?"

"Uh … I just wanted to say thanks again."

"Sure." He headed toward the front door.

When he walked out, Olivia stood in the doorjamb and watched him swagger across the grass to the house next door. The cold, crisp air blew through her, rustling her hair and numbing her cheeks, yet she stayed rooted to the spot, staring at the door Lucy's father had just shut.

All of a sudden a group of children shattered the quiet as they ran and whooped in the frigid air, their red, yellow, and bright blue jackets garish against the gray winter afternoon.

Olivia stepped back and closed the door slowly, her gaze still glued on the house next door. "He's probably married," she said under her breath even though she hadn't seen a wedding band on his finger. Her dad had never worn one, but then he was a skirt-chasing bastard. *Aren't most men?* Kory's face floated in front of her mind. "Ugh!" she breathed out. The last thing Olivia wanted to do was think about that loser, or any of the other losers who had littered her past.

"No more men, remember?" she said aloud. With a strong shot of determination coursing through her body, Olivia switched on the ceiling light, walked over to a stack of boxes, and began to unpack them, banishing all thoughts of the opposite sex from her brain.

CHAPTER FOUR

THE FLAMES CURLED and swayed, crackling as they burned the dry wood in the fireplace. Animal sat on the couch, feet plopped on the coffee table, watching the wisps of silver-gray smoke dance their way up the chimney. He brought a bottle of beer to his lips and took a long pull. Lucy was in her room playing LEGO Jurassic World that his sister had given her the week before. He'd offered to play with her, but Lucy had shot him down, preferring to hole herself up in her room and play it alone.

Since Emerald had left Lucy in Animal's care, his daughter seemed to grow angrier and more withdrawn as the weeks rolled by. He attributed part of it to the fact that Emerald hadn't made one fucking phone call to Lucy in almost three months. She'd called when she arrived in Illinois, and then nothing. Not even a damn postcard. And to make matters worse, Animal was fighting a seven-year bashing campaign that Emerald had instigated against him. He couldn't blame Lucy for hating his guts.

Animal took another gulp of beer and leaned his head against the back of the couch. Lucy drove him fucking crazy most of the time, and he had to keep his anger in check when she'd give him attitude, but he loved having her in his life, and that surprised the hell out of him. The only problem was that he didn't know how to reach her.

When Animal saw the *SOLD* sign in front of the yellow cottage, he'd hoped the new buyer had a kid around Lucy's age who she could play with since it seemed his daughter hadn't made many friends at her new school. That was about as much thought that he'd given to the new potential neighbors until that afternoon.

When Lucy had first come running into the house, telling him that he had to help carry some furniture, his first reaction was "Fuck, no." But one look at his daughter's sparkling eyes and he was out of the chair. Animal snapped off the football game, grabbed a couple of screwdrivers and his work gloves, and followed Lucy out the door.

The china cabinet stood out like a sore thumb, and as Animal had walked toward it, a shot of lust buzzed through him after he'd seen Olivia bent over, her killer ass facing him. For a split second he just stood there and admired the view, then Lucy tugged on his arm and snapped him out of his sexual fog. But when she'd straightened and turned around from the piece of furniture, Animal hadn't expected her to be such a knockout, and if Lucy hadn't been in his life, he would've laid it on thick. Animal was on his best behavior even though he'd stolen a couple of long sideways glances toward her as he worked on taking the cabinet apart.

And, *damn*, if she wasn't a looker with long dark-chocolate brown hair that would make any man long to wrap the tresses around his hands, green eyes the color of spring leaves on an aspen tree, and a pert nose that twitched when she'd pretended not to have checked him out, which had been often. And her lips. *Fuck.* They had him betting they were as soft as they looked. Her full tits, which made a groan rumble up from his chest and get stuck in his throat, a small waist, and rounded hips filled out the package quite nicely.

Animal kicked his feet off the table and put the empty beer bottle on top of it. Ever since Lucy had come to live with him, he'd been as good as a fucking choirboy, and he couldn't afford to blow it, especially with the tempting next-door neighbor. Lucy was his focus now. She was his daughter and she deserved his care and attention. Her bitch-of-a-mom had abandoned her, and Animal knew Lucy was hurting something awful because of it; he had to try and ease her pain—to make her whole again. And pretty Olivia was a dangerous distraction he didn't need.

Animal pushed up from the couch and glanced at the time: 6:30 p.m. He smoothed back his hair, climbed the stairs to Lucy's room, then knocked on her door.

"What?" A thread of irritation wove through her soft voice.

He turned the knob and swung the door open. Lucy sat cross-legged on the bed with her eyes fixed on the television screen, a black control in her hands.

"You kicking ass?" he asked, entering the room.

A small shrug. "I guess."

"How 'bout getting some dinner?"

Another shrug. "I guess."

Animal wiped the corners of his mouth with his thumb and index finger. "Whaddya feel like?"

Another damn shrug. *Fuck!*

"Work with me, kiddo. Do you wanna go out or order in?"

Lucy paused the game then turned toward him, her eyes narrowed, her body tense. "Why don't you know how to cook?"

He jerked his head back. "Never had to do it. I've lived at the club since I patched in twelve years ago."

"So we're gonna have pizza all the time?"

"Guess that's the plan until you're old enough to cook. Now, what the hell do you wanna eat?"

"I don't care." Lucy turned away and restarted the game.

His stomach hardened as he watched her grip the control. "You gotta give me a fuckin' break here," he said, scrubbing a hand over his face. "I know this is hard for you, but I'm tryin' to find the way for us, you know?"

Lucy didn't say a word, her gaze still glued to the screen as her fingers pushed various buttons on the game device.

"Just fuck it," Animal muttered under his breath as he stalked out of the room and walked down the hall to his bedroom.

Perched on the edge of the bed, he tapped in his sister's phone number and stared out the window at the snowflakes that had begun to fall.

"Hey, Jada," he said.

"Hey. How're you and Lucy doing?"

"Not so good. I don't know how the fuck to reach her." Animal pushed up from the bed, walked over to the window, and looked out. A sharp wind swept the trees, blowing snow into crystalline clouds. He glanced at Olivia's house, hoping to catch a glimpse of her. Some windows were uncovered, the light spilling out in golden squares and rectangles across the frost-nipped lawn, but there was no sight of her.

"You need to give it time, Animal. You and Lucy are still getting to know each other."

"I know, but I can't seem to communicate with her. She's so fucking pissed at me because her mom has been trashing me for years."

"Just be patient with her. I know patience isn't one of your finer qualities." Jada laughed.

"It's not." Animal blew out, his breath faintly steaming up the windowpane.

"How can I help you?"

He smiled—good ol' Jada was always willing to lend a helping hand. That was a lot more than he could say about his mother. "You cooking dinner tonight for Dad?"

"I am. Do you and Lucy want to come over? I'm just making chili and cornbread."

"Sounds better than pizza or that boxed macaroni and cheese shit I've been feeding us for the last couple of weeks."

"Dad would love to see Lucy, and so would I."

"Is Mom home?"

A long pause. "No … she went out."

"Out? Where to?"

"With some friends. So you guys can come over anytime."

"I'll tell Lucy and we'll see you in a few. Thanks."

"You're welcome, but you know you don't have to wait for an invitation to come over for dinner. I cook at least four times a week."

"I'm surprised you're home on a Saturday night. I thought you'd be out dancing with Veronica and Lori."

"I didn't feel like it tonight. We were super busy at the carwash because it was so warm most of the day, but it's really cold out there now."

"Yeah—it's snowing."

Then he saw Olivia in the middle of her living room. Her long hair fell over her shoulders and down her back—*untamed* crossed his mind—and she wore a long-sleeved T-shirt that ended a few inches above her knees. The shirt hugged her rounded hips so damn nicely. When she bent over a box, which was sitting on top of what looked like a coffee table, her shirt rode up, and he had to wipe the steam off the window to see out.

"Are you still there?" Jada's voice brought him back to the phone call.

"Yeah … uh, sorry about that. So, we'll be by in a bit. Later."

"Bye."

Animal held the phone in his hand and watched as Olivia unpacked the box, her lovely ass moving so damn perfectly. All of a sudden, as if she sensed him watching her, she stood up, tugged the hem of the T-shirt down, and gazed out into the dusk. He pulled away from the window quickly, but—he was sure, given the illumination in his room—not fast enough. He switched off the lamp then looked out again and saw Olivia standing in the middle of the large living room window staring right at his house. After a few seconds passed she moved away, then turned out all the lights in the room.

Animal cursed his lameness under his breath as he pulled down the blinds. He'd bet that come morning, Olivia would have coverings on all her windows. He sauntered into the bathroom and splashed cool water on his face several times. *Get a fucking grip and stop acting like some damn perverted Peeping Tom.* There was no doubt that Olivia was a pretty woman who piqued his sexual interest, but he had the club girls to scratch an itch if he needed it that badly. A nice woman like Olivia was bad news. Women like that wanted the whole fucking package: love, marriage, and babies. He had his hands more than full with an angry, mouthy seven-year-old, so a woman looking for the damn Cinderella dream was something he definitely didn't need. In his experience, the nice girls always wanted the fairytale endings. He saw that with his sister, Jada, and all her friends, and he'd been pressured more than a few times by women he'd dated to settle down and start a family. Hell, he *already* had a family, and he was fucking that up big time.

Animal hung up the towel and walked back to Lucy's room. She was standing by the window looking out, and turned around quickly when he cleared his throat.

"It's really coming down," he said.

"If I was at home, I'd be out playing in it with my friends," she said, her gaze fixed on the pale brown carpet.

"How 'bout I ask Jax to bring Paisley over tomorrow and the two of you can play? You remember her from the rally we went to last month. She's around your age and she told her mom that she'd like to hang out with you."

Lucy glanced up. "Really?"

"Yeah." It wasn't entirely true, but he knew Jax, a fellow Insurgent, would bring Paisley over, and Animal was pretty sure the two girls would hit it off. "Does that sound good?"

"I guess."

"Great—I'll arrange it. But right now we're going over to Grandma and Grandpa's house. Aunt Jada's making chili with cornbread, and it's all from scratch."

The corners of her mouth twitched a little, but he caught it, and that small movement made his fucking day.

"I guess that sounds good," she mumbled.

"Then we'll go as soon as you're ready."

Lucy walked over and turned off the television then looked at him. "I'm ready now."

"Then grab your jacket and let's head out."

Minutes later, they were backing out of the garage, and Animal flicked on the windshield wipers. He glanced over at Olivia's house and noticed a large sheet covering the living room window, and he grimaced.

"That snowflake's the biggest," Lucy said, pressing her finger against the passenger window.

"Yeah, that one kills all the others."

The wipers squeaked across the slightly icy windshield, and he cranked up the defroster as the SUV headed toward his parents' house.

"Do you think Paisley would like to build a snowman tomorrow?" Lucy asked as her finger traced a thin trickle of water that ran down the window.

"I'm sure she would." Animal glanced over at her, then reached out and ruffled her hair, resting his hand on top of her head.

Lucy turned, her eyes wide and startled, and he withdrew his hand and gripped the steering wheel, his gaze fixed forward. They drove in silence the rest of the way, and when he killed the engine, she scrambled out of the car and ran up the sidewalk to the porch. Jada flung the door open and pulled Lucy into a tight hug, and Animal lifted his chin to his sister as he walked up the concrete steps.

"I'm so glad you came over," Jada said to Lucy as she led her into the house. "I'm glad to see you too." She looked behind her shoulder at Animal and smiled.

He grunted and stomped his boots on the outdoor mat then entered the foyer. Heat circulated around him as he shrugged off his leather jacket and gloves. Jada and Lucy had disappeared, and he hung up his coat then strode into the family room. Overstuffed chairs and a long couch filled the space, and a stone fireplace held a crackling fire, making the room warm and cozy. His father sat in his wheelchair close to the hearth and in front of the TV. The sound was low and it looked like he had on some kind of crime drama. A colorful afghan fell about his shoulders, and as Animal watched his father doze, his head jerking at intervals onto his chest, he noticed how thin and frail he had become. Before his dad had stepped on a land mine and blew off his legs during a tour in Iraq, he had been a robust and healthy man. But after numerous surgeries, skin grafts, and physical therapy sessions, his dad was just a shell of his former self.

Animal rubbed the heel of his palm against his tightening chest as he moved toward his father. He crouched down on his haunches and plucked out two tissues from the Kleenex box on the TV tray next to the wheelchair. With the tissue, he gently wiped the spittle from his father's chin. The gesture must've woken his dad, because the older man's head bounced up and his bleary eyes stared at Animal.

"Hey, Dad. I didn't mean to wake you," Animal said, running the back of his fingers across the old man's cheeks.

A wide smile spread across his father's face. He cleared his throat then grasped Animal's wrist. "It's good to see you. How long have you been here?"

"Lucy and I just got here. How've you been? You look like you lost some weight."

His dad shook his head. "Don't go worrying about me—your sister does enough of that for all of us." He chuckled, which rippled into a coughing fit that made tears stream down his cheeks.

Animal handed his dad the glass of water from the tray, then gave him a few tissues that he promptly swiped across his eyes, cheeks, and then his mouth. He put the water back on the tray and settled back in the wheelchair.

"Do you wanna sit on the couch? I can help you with that," Animal said.

"I'm good. I smell chili—your sister's a good fucking cook. We'll be eating soon. How're you getting along with Lucy?"

Animal rose to his feet then dragged one of the armchairs close to his father and plopped down in it. "We're still at an impasse, but I don't think it's as bad as it was in the beginning. It's just gonna take time, I guess."

"It will—it's all still pretty new to her."

"Yeah. I'm gonna have Jax bring Paisley over tomorrow so they can play together. Paisley's a friendly kid, so it should work out. Although, Lucy can be sorta snarky and shit, but I think she reserves most of that just for me."

His dad snickered and patted Animal's hand. "She'll come around. You did. Remember what a hell-raising pain in the ass you were at around eight or nine years old? And I'm not gonna even mention your damn teenage years."

Animal scrunched his face. "So what you're saying is, Lucy's attitude is payback?"

The old man shook his head. "Nope. I'm saying it only gets worse."

"Fuck … That's something to look forward to." Animal laughed. "You wanna a beer?" he asked his dad as he rose to his feet.

"I could go for one."

"Where's Mom?" Animal walked into the kitchen and took out two cans of Coors.

"Out with some friends. She has it hard with me like … this." His dad shifted in the chair.

"Bullshit." Animal popped the top and handed the beer to his dad. "Look at Savannah and Ryder. They're together all the time. They go out to dinner, even to nightclubs, and on the weekends, they're always doing something with Timmy. Don't think that Mom never being around is your fault. She's always put herself first—you were the one there for us, Dad … not Mom."

"Watch what you say about your mother. She had a hard time grow-ing up with that crazy mother of hers and no dad. Anyway, we got it figured out, and I'm glad she's able to enjoy herself—that's what I want for her."

Flashes of anger streaked through Animal, but he held his tongue and guzzled half his beer instead. For as long as he could remember, his father had been the one to read bedtime stories to him and Jada, take them to the park, on hikes, help with their homework—the whole nine fucking yards. His old man had been both mother and father to them, and he never once complained. All Animal remembered about his mother was how she'd loved creating drama, craving to be the center of attention all the time. When Jada had entered high school and had all the guys panting after her, his mom had the fucking gall to be jealous of her. *Her own fucking daughter—what kind of a damn mom is* that?

"There's my sweet granddaughter." His dad's voice broke through Animal's thoughts, and he looked over and saw Lucy standing next to Jada, smiling. "Come on over here, sweetheart, and let your grandpa see you better."

Lucy darted her eyes from the older man to Jada then to her dad. Animal winked at her and tilted his head toward his dad. "Do as Grandpa says."

The girl walked over very slowly, and once she was close enough, her grandfather held out his weathered hand and she placed hers in his palm. Warmth spread through Animal as he watched his dad and daughter holding hands without her flinching or scurrying away as she'd done on numerous visits to his parents' house. Maybe Lucy was beginning to trust them all a bit more.

"The cornbread will be out of the oven in fifteen minutes. Why don't you watch some TV with Grandpa?" Jada asked as she shuffled to the kitchen.

"What should we watch?" Lucy asked.

"Whatever you want," Animal's dad replied.

"While you two figure it out, I gotta make a phone call." Animal pulled out his phone and ambled to the den and closed the door. When he was young, the den had been his favorite room in the house. He used to close the door, then take out all the maps his dad had of almost every state in the country. Animal would sit in the leather wingback chair and imagine riding a motorcycle on all the back roads depicted in the maps. For as long as he could remember, his dad had owned a Harley, and as soon as Animal had been old enough, his father would nestle him safely on the back of his bike and they'd go for long rides in the mountains and valleys. So it'd just been natural that when Animal had turned eighteen, his dad had bought him a used Harley for his birthday. And once he'd slid onto the smooth leather seat, Animal knew he'd found his calling—to ride and live the biker lifestyle.

Animal called Jax and asked if he'd like to come by the following day with Paisley to hang out with him and Lucy. Jax readily agreed, and even offered to bring over enchiladas for lunch made by Cherri, his old lady. After he'd hung up the phone, Animal flipped open the laptop and clicked on the screen. He wanted to check out one of the games Jax had mentioned that Paisley was crazy about. Animal thought Lucy might like it, too, so he decided to order it before it slipped out of his mind.

He blinked as the brightness of the screen hit him right between the eyes, and then squinted as he became accustomed to the light. Then, a sultry, smoky background greeted him, replete with a sexy woman standing behind a bare-chested, buffed guy. The woman's body was pressed against the man with her hands on his chiseled pecs and her stockinged leg on his hip, held firmly in place by his hand. *Discreet Passion* highlighted in red blazed across the top of the image. *What the fuck?* Animal's gaze darted to the right of the screen and landed on a drop-down menu box with several categories: woman seeking man; man seeking woman; one-night stand; friends with benefits; boy-friend/girlfriend; husband/wife. There was a place to sign up for a free membership and one to log in. He clicked the log in button and it instantly brought him to a profile page—his mother's to be exact. Animal ground his teeth together and clenched his fists as he skimmed over the page. Pictures of his mother in various seductive poses assaulted him, and he sucked in a sharp breath.

"How the fuck can you do this?" he gritted under his breath. The pictures of his mother were not accurate. She'd photoshopped her face from when she was in her twenties onto a body that was lean, slightly curvy, and pretty stacked—*definitely not hers*. He grabbed a piece of paper and pen from the middle desk drawer and jotted down the name of the site and his mother's profile name and ID number, then he snapped the cover shut and leaned his head back against the chair.

Animal couldn't even process all of it at that moment, and when he thought of his dad sitting in the wheelchair by the fire while his wife was out carousing with some fucking douchebag, it made Animal want to smash the computer to smithereens. He wondered if his dad knew about his mother's fucking extramarital activities, or if—

"Dinner's ready," Jada said, opening the door wider.

Animal scrubbed his face with his fist and stood up.

"Wow … you look super pissed right now. What's wrong?" Jada stepped into the room and closed the door behind her.

"Do you know where *Mom*"—he grimaced when he said the word— "is right now?"

Jada folded her arms over her chest. "I told you, she's out with friends."

"Where?"

"I don't know. Maybe dinner?"

"You're bullshitting." He held his hand up in the air. "Don't say you're not. I can tell by the way you're clutching the shit outta your arms."

A strained silence stretched between them for several seconds until Animal broke it.

"You know, don't you?' he asked.

Jada nodded. "I'm guessing, so do you."

"Just found out. What the fuck? Does Dad know she's whoring around?"

Jada's arms dropped to her sides and she stepped back. "Don't be so crude."

"I chose words that describe things accurately. *Whoring* was *me* being polite." He cracked his knuckles. "So what about Dad?"

His sister shrugged. "I'm not sure, but I think he does, or at least suspects it. I mean, she leaves here in short dresses and so much perfume that I can smell it for hours. I guess Dad and Mom have an agreement."

"That's a crock of shit. She's fuckin' cuckolding him. I can't believe he'd stand for that bullshit."

"Maybe he's okay with it because he knows Mom still needs what he can't give her. When they're together, they laugh, talk, and joke around with each other. Not everything's black and white all the time."

"This is for me, and I'm gonna talk to her about it."

"We eating or what? Lucy and I are starving." Their dad's booming voice was muffled through the shut door.

"Coming," Jada said as she opened it, then glanced over at Animal. "Are you going to eat with us?"

"Yeah." He stomped across the room.

"Please don't let your anger spill out during dinner. Lucy and Dad aren't responsible for what Mom does, so don't take it out on them." Jada walked out into the hallway.

"No worries," he answered, but inside a raging volcano was ready to explode. When he got home, he'd go down to the basement and do a round with the punching bag, but for now, he'd have to forget what he'd just learned and focus on having a nice time with his family. Animal would look into the shit site, then have a long, overdue talk with his mother about respect and loyalty. His dad and Jada may be okay with what was going on, but Animal wasn't. Not. At. All.

"Can you pass the sour cream, Son?" A voice sliced through Animal's angered haze.

He looked up and stared at the container for a second before registering what his dad wanted. Lucy giggled and as Animal glanced over at her twinkling eyes, all the fury swirling inside him subsided. He winked at her then picked up the sour cream and handed it to his father.

"How do you like the chili?" Animal asked his daughter.

She stuffed a piece of cornbread in her mouth and nodded enthusiastically. Her long, thick braids swayed with the motion.

He laughed and reached over to pat her shoulder, and surprisingly, she didn't jerk away.

"Jada's a damn good cook," he said, throwing a half-crooked smile at his sister. "I talked to Jax, and he and Paisley are gonna come over tomorrow for sure."

"What time?" Lucy asked.

"Around noon. He's gonna bring lunch—enchiladas. I know you like those." Animal buttered a piece of cornbread.

Lucy nodded again, then wiped her mouth with the back of her hand. "I do."

"Paisley's a sweetheart," Jada said as she scooped more chili into Animal's bowl. "Want some more, Dad?"

The older man shook his head. "I'm good, thanks."

As they ate and chatted a sense of peace that Animal hadn't felt since Emerald had dropped Lucy in his lap descended on him. If only he could freeze this moment with his daughter, everything would be all right, but he knew it wouldn't last. Deciding to enjoy the first real father-daughter bonding they'd had, he picked up his fork and dug into the steaming bowl of chili, his gaze fixed on his sweet little girl.

CHAPTER FIVE

"ARE YOU SURE you'll be all right? I know how debilitating your migraines are," his wife said.

"I'll be fine, but thank you. You and the kids go out and enjoy yourselves. Tell Roger and Maribel I'll catch them the next time around." He helped her with her coat.

Two young boys raced down the stairs, whooping and laughing, until they stopped at the back door. He handed them each a blue and gray scarf.

"It's freezing out there—you don't want to catch a cold."

"You're not coming, Daddy?" the younger boy asked.

"Your father has one of his bad headaches, so he has to stay home."

"I wish I felt better." He ruffled the boy's blond hair.

His wife stroked his cheek. "I guess we'll be going now."

He grasped her hand and brought it to his lips and kissed it. "I'm sorry about spoiling your night."

"Oh … honey, don't even worry about that. I'm just sorry you don't feel well. We won't be home too late." She opened the door and the boys dashed out into the garage.

The tall man stood in the doorway and watched the SUV pull out of the garage. He waved to his family, then waited until the car disappeared before closing the door. He ran his hands over his clean-shaven face then walked over to one of the cupboards and reached for a wineglass. After pouring himself a good amount of Chardonnay, he shuffled out of the kitchen and down the hall to his office. As he swung open the door and looked into the darkness, relief spread over him. *I'm alone at last.* The man walked inside and switched on the small lamp that sat on top of a large mahogany desk. Papers and several books were strewn across it, but his gaze landed on his computer—his most prized possession. It was a gateway to the darkness that lived inside him, the beast that he kept concealed most of the time ... until he couldn't. Then, the dark passenger did terrible things before he was sated.

The office was his haven—his sanctuary from having to pretend all the time, which could be damn exhausting.

The troubled man slipped into the worn leather chair and moved it closer to the desk. On the top left corner, a framed photograph of his lovely wife adorned the space. Frou-Frou—his pet name for her—was the best wife a man could have. She kept a clean and orderly home, was fussy about her appearance, and was a wonderful mother to their two boys. He loved her dearly, but she knew nothing about the depravities buried deep within him. Sometimes when they made love, it would come out to play, but Frou-Frou had freaked out the few times it did, and he had to shut it off and be content with ordinary lovemaking.

Frou-Frou loved being intimate with him, but in the last few years, he'd found himself inventing excuses as to why he wasn't in the mood more often than he liked. Frou-Frou had brought it up to him, the fear of him having an affair etched on her face. When the man had reassured her there was no other woman, she'd relaxed—even giggled, and after that, he made love to her more often, the dark images always front and center in his head.

In this room he was "Hunter Lewis"—unmarried and hungry. Hunter clicked on the computer, enabled his IP address blocker, and logged in to *Discreet Passion*. He'd created several phony profiles across many different dating and hookup sites, but he'd had the best luck on this one.

"Hunter" switched on the messenger program and scrolled through the list of women, his eyes searching for a woman in her twenties, with long dark hair, a nice curvy body, pale skin, and a fresh face—totally the opposite of his wife. Frou-Frou was attractive in a severe, organized way. With short blonde hair, a lean body that was perpetually dark thanks to the tanning salon, and a face that showed a bit too many lines for his taste, he was definitely aging better than his wonderful wife. Frou-Frou wasn't as sexually attractive to him as she'd been when they'd first met back in college. Of course, he didn't expect her to look like a twenty-five-year-old again, but he did miss her long hair, the soft curves she used to have before she became obsessed with eating lean and working out all the time, and her smooth, sun-kissed complexion. Too many hours spent sunbathing in the high-altitude sunshine was making its mark on her skin almost weekly, or so it seemed.

A small jingle interrupted his reflections, and he glanced at the screen and smiled. Hunter opened up the message. *"Hi. Do you want to talk?"* came across the screen. A small circular picture of a white kitten was in the profile photo space. A rush of adrenaline surged through him when he read the words.

With fingers flying, he typed *"Hi, I'm Hunter. What's your name?"*

Less than a second passed and the words *"Katie. I'm sort of new to this"* came back. Hunter leaned back and stared at the message. He liked it when the women were new to the game, it made them more vulnerable and intriguing. After playing the seduction game for the past several years, he was a pro at it. First, there'd be gentlemanly flirtations and compliments, then an exchange of pictures, interest in her day-to-day life and her problems, and finally, the sweet little thing would be putty in his hands. At that point, getting her phone number would be child's play, and after several long conversations, they'd make a date to meet. Just thinking about the way she'd offer herself to him made his mouth go dry and his hands sweaty.

Another jingle brought him out of his reverie. *"Are you still there?"* Then there was an attachment. Hunter quickly opened it and the photograph of a luscious young woman sitting on a chair in what looked like a formal living room filled up his screen. Long dark hair—check. Pale skin—check. Very enticing breasts—double check.

He stared at the smiling twenty-something for several seconds, then placed his fingers on the keyboard. *"What a treat. You are so beautiful with an air of mystery and sensuality about you. I can't help but wonder why you're on this site. You must have a line of men wanting to go out with you."*

Another jingle. *"Thank you—you're too kind. The men I've met have all lacked that certain refinement I hope to find here. The way you write makes me think you're not just the average guy."*

Hunter laughed then typed *"You're right—I've never been accused of being average."*

For the next hour, he and Katie "talked" about everything, and with each sentence and word, Hunter knew he was reeling her in. Frou-Frou often told him that he was a charmer and that's why all her lady friends were smitten with him.

"I give my sweet Katie two weeks or so before she'll belong to me … body and soul," he muttered under his breath.

A wicked smile spread across his lips, and evil glints of dark passion flashed in his eyes. Soon the hunger that threatened to devour him would be fed, and life would be calm again until the next time.

CHAPTER SIX

CLUTCHING A PILE of books in her arms, Olivia glanced at the clock above the principal's office and cursed under her breath. The locker-lined hallway, usually teeming with students rushing off to their classes, was quiet and still. Even though she'd given herself an extra thirty minutes earlier that morning, Olivia was still late. The shower-head had inexplicably fallen off while she was washing her hair, so she had to finish the job in the small sink in her bathroom.

Olivia rushed down the hall, her heels tapping on the waxed floor and bouncing off the white walls. One of the Junie B. Jones books she used for her remedial reading students slid loose and fell to the floor with a resounding *thud*.

"Oh shit," she mumbled.

She stopped and bent over to scoop up the fallen book. With it now secured in her free hand, Olivia dashed forward, her attention focused on the reading materials in her arms.

Bam! She plowed into something hard and immovable.

"Oh, crap!" Her shriek echoed all the way down the hall as she hit the floor, books and folders sprawled out around her. "What the hell?" Olivia looked up and met the dark eyes of her sexy next-door neighbor.

"Sorry." The tall, dark, and deliciously handsome man held out his hand to her.

Olivia took it and as he helped her up, she tried to ignore the zing of energy and spark of something sensual that his touch had caused. She withdrew her hand quickly, then brushed off her black pencil skirt. He bent down and picked up the folders in one hand and a couple of books in the other.

"Thanks," she mumbled when he handed them to her, and then he scooped up the rest of the books off the floor.

"No problem," he replied while handing her the last of the hardbacks.

Olivia scraped her fingers through her hair and willed the crazed butterflies fluttering in her stomach to stop.

"I guess I'm always thanking you for something."

"Seems that way," he replied in a low, deep voice.

The corners of his mouth turned up and he cocked his head to the side; slowly and thoroughly, his dark gaze traveled up and down her body, seeping into her pores like melting chocolate, until it landed on her breasts.

Heat rushed through Olivia's body and her mouth went dry as cotton as she attempted to think of something to say.

"Uh … do you need something?" she sputtered.

He looked up, his eyes moving to her mouth. "What're you suggesting?"

Olivia knew her face was neon red just from the way it felt, and she turned away from his searing gaze and smashed the pile of books against her chest, shielding it from him.

"You're wandering in the hallway, so I was just wondering if you're looking for someone." When she glanced back up, his stare remained.

"I'm good."

Not able to contain her curiosity, Olivia shifted in place. "Why are you here—at the school?"

"I dropped off Lucy. Why're you here?" He glanced at her books, then back at her. "You a teacher?"

"Lucy goes here?"

"I just said that."

A nervous giggle slipped past her lips. "Right. I'm actually a teacher's assistant. I work with students who have reading problems and help to bring them up to speed for their grade level."

"Lucy's got some problems, but her fuckin' teacher doesn't agree with me."

"Who's her teacher?"

"The older lady—reddish hair. I don't remember her name, but it's some color."

"Mrs. White?"

Her neighbor snapped his fingers. "That's it. I want Lucy to get some extra help with that, but the bitch doesn't agree. I talked to the principal about it too."

"What did Mr. Lorry say?" she asked.

He narrowed his eyes and jerked his head back. "Said the bitch teacher makes the assessment. Fuck that."

Olivia licked her dry lips. "Mrs. White is an excellent teacher. If she doesn't think—"

"I fucking know what my daughter needs. I read with Lucy every night—she's got some problems."

"What does your wife think?" *What the hell? Did I just ask that?*

"I'm not married," he said, a smirk ghosting his lips.

Olivia cringed, still kicking herself for asking the question. "Well then, her mother?"

"She's not involved."

Heavy footsteps thumped across the waxed floor, and Olivia looked behind her shoulder and saw Marcus Thurber—also known as the "Casanova of Slavens Elementary"—walking toward her. The seventh and eighth grade teacher wore one his disarming smiles on his face as he came over and stood beside her.

"Playing hooky?" he said, nudging her with his elbow.

A low rumble of sound—almost like a growl, came from her neighbor's direction, and Olivia snapped her gaze to him. A small gasp broke from her throat: his face darkened into a scowl and his eyes glittered like sharpened knives. She glanced at his clenched fists and froze in place. Marcus must've picked up the menacing vibe emanating from Lucy's father because he quickly stepped away from her as a nervous laugh escaped her lips.

"I didn't mean to interrupt you," he said, only looking at Olivia. "I'll catch you later." He sauntered away and disappeared into one of the classrooms.

"Who the fuck is he?"

Startled by the harshness of his voice, she jumped and almost dropped the books on the floor all over again.

"He's the English teacher for the upper classes," she said, her voice sounding like sandpaper.

"I don't like him."

A simple statement that held so much threat. A chill snaked its way down her spine.

"Okay, but you don't even know him."

"I know his *type*."

If she closed her eyes while having this conversation, Olivia would swear she was talking to one of the bikers in her dad's MC. It was too crazy.

"Uh … I have to get to my classroom. I'm so late right now."

There was a pause while black eyes bored into her.

"Go on. I'm not stopping you, am I?" His voice held a glint of amusement. The tone slid over her skin like a lingering caress, setting every nerve ending alive.

Olivia groaned inwardly, hating the way her body was reacting to him. She took a hesitant step backward, which made him smile and run his tongue over his bottom lip. Another silent groan. *Dammit!*

"Am I stopping you, Olivia?" he asked in a low voice.

"No," she whispered, her heartbeat roaring in her ears.

"Then …?" He moved closer.

"There you are, Olivia." Clara White's voice broke the spellbinding hold he had on her, and she let out a relieved breath and shifted the load in her arms.

"How are you, Mr. Walsh?" Clara's voice was stern.

Without answering, Lucy's father pressed his lips together then swaggered down the hallway until he pushed open the steel door with his foot and disappeared into the bright morning light.

"He's such a rude man," Clara huffed. "I hope he wasn't bothering you."

"No, he wasn't," Olivia replied, her gaze still fixed on the closed door.

"The best thing for you to do is stay far away from him. He's bad news, and it isn't any wonder that his daughter, Lucy, is so snippy and morose." The teacher waved her hand toward the end of the hallway. "Look who she has as a role model." She rolled her eyes.

"Mr. Walsh told me Lucy's struggling with her reading. I wouldn't mind helping her out." Olivia ignored the older woman's snide remarks about her neighbor.

"Lucy's reading is only a little below standard. Nothing that more concentration can't solve. She doesn't need to spend time with you or any other assistant. I have students in my class who need more help than she does. Men like him"—another wave of her hand toward the closed door—"are used to bullying people to get their own way. I already told him that Lucy is doing just fine. Don't let him push you into doing something that isn't needed."

"He didn't push me at all. He just mentioned that Lucy is having some problems."

Clara pushed the wire-framed glasses up the bridge of her nose. "Well, she's not. Remember to stay away from him—he's bad news."

Olivia was ready to ask her why when Neil, one of the second graders, rushed out into the hall holding one hand over his mouth and another on his belly.

"Are you sick?" Clara asked, scurrying over to the boy.

Neil nodded as he hurried toward the bathroom with his teacher on his heels. Olivia glanced at the clock again and her stomach knotted. *I should've already been in my classroom.* Instead she'd been frozen to the spot, captivated by her neighbor who, according to Clara's estimation, was bad news and should be avoided at all costs. *Why does that intrigue me even more?* Olivia shook her head as she hurried to the third grade classroom.

When she entered the room, Harper gave her a concerned look and motioned for her to come over. Multiplication problems littered the whiteboard and several students were in front of it, figuring out the answers to the equations.

"I'm so sorry I'm late. I had a mishap with the shower-head this morning. Just one more thing I need to repair. How's it going with the lesson?"

Harper chuckled. "You're going to have to find yourself a man just to help you out around your place."

Her neighbor's rugged face flashed in her mind. "It's less complicated for me to learn how to do the repairs than to be involved with any guy."

"Still holding strong to your *no man* rule?"

"Yep." *I'm trying. No … I* am.

"Good for you. Last night's date was a disaster. I'll tell you all about it at lunch," Harper whispered.

"I can't wait to hear—I need something to fortify my resolve." Olivia snickered.

"Believe me—this'll do it." Harper glanced over at the whiteboard. "Estella, double-check your addition." She turned back to Olivia. "Aaron, Lucas, Emily, and Riley need help with the lesson."

"All right." Olivia put away the reading books in one of the cupboards then took out the math book. "I'm on it." She walked over to the four students and led them out of the room to a smaller, adjacent one that had a round table surrounded by six chairs. The students plopped down on the plastic chairs, and Olivia opened a folder, handed out a worksheet filled with multiplication problems, and began to work with the children.

The minutes turned into hours, and before Olivia knew it, the last school bell rang and students poured out into the hallway from every room. She navigated toward the front door through the sea of children, and the din of the halls began to subside as the students rushed out of the building.

Standing on the corner, Olivia watched out for the children as parents and guardians picked them up.

"There he is," she heard one of the third-grade mothers say to another one.

"Damn ... he's so *hot*," the other one replied.

Olivia looked over her shoulder and saw Jenny Pierson and Ashley Tarleton staring across the street. She darted her gaze in that direction and sucked in a sharp breath: Lucy's father. *Of course, because he is fucking hot.* As he crossed the street, she was acutely aware of his narrow hips and the corded power in his thighs and legs that molded around his tight blue jeans. *Oops!* He caught her looking at him, and not at his face. Damn. His lips tucked into a smug smile, and she bent down, pretending to pick up something from the ground.

"Hiya, Animal," Ashley Tarleton said in a breathy voice that pricked Olivia's nerves.

"Hey," he replied stopping in front of the two mothers.

Ashley scooted closer to him and said something in a low voice that Olivia couldn't hear. Animal—*was that his actual name, or a pet name Ashley had invented for him?*—chuckled and whispered something back. From a sideways glance, she watched him laugh and talk with the perky blonde in black yoga pants and a low-cut sweater.

Olivia felt a twinge of something like jealousy, which was ridiculous because she didn't even know him. And she definitely wanted to keep it that way. She moved away and focused on the kids, refusing to give him, Ashley Tarleton, or any other sexed-up mother another thought.

"Olivia!" someone called out.

She turned around in the direction of the voice and saw Lucy skipping toward her. Her dark braids bounced against her red quilted jacket. Olivia smiled and waved at the young girl.

"Hi, Lucy."

A rosy flush to the cheeks from the chilly air illuminated the girl's face. "What're you doing here?"

"I teach here. I help out in Ms. Porter's classroom."

"She's gonna be my teacher next year." A wide smile revealed a lost tooth on the bottom.

"You'll love her—she's wonderful. How do you like your class?"

Lucy shrugged. "It's okay. I wish I went to Paisley's school. She's my new friend."

"That's great."

"Hey, kiddo." There was that deep voice that made Olivia's insides jump.

She willed herself not to turn around.

"Hi." The gaiety in Lucy's demeanor plummeted.

"Hey, Teach." A sliver of mockery laced his voice.

Plastering a too-broad-of-a-smile on her face, Olivia pivoted and lifted her chin. "Hello, Mr. Walsh."

He leaned in close … too close. "Fuck that, *Olivia*, call me Animal." The warm breath of his whisper fanned over her neck.

She stepped away from him. "That's an unusual name."

"It's not his real one," Lucy grumbled, seemingly upset that Olivia's attention had shifted from her to her father.

Olivia focused back on the girl, refusing to let *him* pull her in again like he had earlier that day. "I kind of thought it wasn't. Do you have a nickname?"

Lucy shook her head. "My mom called me Lucy"—her face grew pale and she looked down at the sidewalk—"or stupid brat."

The last three words were barely audible but Olivia caught them and they pierced her heart. She knew too well how verbal abuse could hurt just as much, if not more, as a punch in the face, or a strap to the back. Her mother's weapon of choice had never been; her hands, like her father's, but her tongue was sharper than a razor blade, and cut much deeper.

"I don't have a nickname either," Olivia said, tugging at one of Lucy's braids.

Lucy looked up. "You don't?"

"Nope, and it's okay. I like my name just fine. You have a very pretty name too."

"I do? No one's told me that."

"I named you after Grandpa's mom. You got your great-grandma's name," Animal said as he moved away from Olivia and stood beside Lucy. "Her full name was Lucille, but everyone called her Lucy. She was a strong woman who didn't let anyone get away with shit. You have her dark hair and spirit."

Lucy's eyes widened. "I didn't know that."

"I got pictures of her. Do you wanna see them?"

The girl nodded so hard that her braids swayed as if a strong wind had just blown through.

Warmth spread through Olivia as she watched Animal try and connect with his fragile daughter. From the first day she'd met the young girl, Olivia had picked up a strain of sadness and loneliness within the child. Then, when she'd seen how standoffish Lucy was with her father, Olivia suspected something had happened to crush the girl's trust in him.

"We gotta get going, kiddo." Animal's deep voice pulled Olivia from her thoughts. "We need to go to the grocery store before we head home."

"Okay." Lucy looked over at Olivia. "My dad doesn't know how to cook."

"Hey, I make killer bacon and eggs." He chuckled.

"I mean like Aunt Jada." A small smile danced across the girl's lips. "She's my aunt. I never had an aunt before," she said to Olivia.

"Aunts and grandmothers are awesome," she replied, fully aware of Animal's piercing gaze on her.

"Do you cook?" the girl asked.

Taken aback, Olivia just nodded.

"See ..." she said, looking at her dad.

"What's your point?" he asked. "She's a woman—of course she can cook."

Olivia laughed dryly. "I don't think there's a cooking gene in women, but I could be wrong."

Lucy giggled and Animal's forehead furrowed as he rocked back on the heel of his boots.

"I was going to bring over dinner to you and your dad as a thank you for helping me out on Saturday. What's your favorite food?"

The girl scrunched her face and tilted her head as if deep in thought.

"You don't have to do that," he said, irritation apparent in his voice.

Olivia threw him a sidelong glance. "I know that, but I want to. If you hadn't come along, my cabinet would've been ruined in the snowstorm that night."

"Spaghetti," Lucy said.

"I didn't know that." Animal rammed his hands in the pockets of his jacket.

"I love spaghetti too. How about I make up a batch and bring it by on Wednesday night?"

Lucy looked over at her father. "Will that work?"

"Yeah." His gaze fixed on Olivia. "That'll work just fine."

Animal was doing that thing again with his eyes, drawing Olivia in and captivating her, yet making her a nervous wreck.

Olivia pulled up the collar of her sweater and glanced away. "I'll let you two get going." She smiled at Lucy.

For several seconds the three of them stood in silence, but Animal's gaze on her never wavered. Breaking the quiet, Olivia waved at Lucy then walked away, very much aware of his eyes on her behind as she walked back into the school.

Once inside, she leaned against the concrete wall and took a few deep breaths in an attempt to calm her nerves. *Why do I let him get to me?* There was something oddly familiar about Animal, but she couldn't pinpoint exactly what it was. Also, an aura of danger surrounded him, and from the way Ashley and Jenny acted toward him, she knew women picked up on it. Many women were drawn to that—bad boys, a walk on the wild side—but Olivia wasn't one of them. Growing up with a dad in an outlaw club, she'd had her fill of danger and recklessness and all the women who'd thrown themselves at her father without even giving a damn that he was married with children. Then again, he hadn't given a shit about that either. *Why am I thinking about all of that right now? And what's up with that dumb nickname—Animal. His buddies probably gave it to him because of the way he parties or something equally juvenile.*

"Are we still coming over to see your house?" Alice asked, jarring Olivia out of her musings.

"Uh … yeah. Is Harper still down for it?" she replied.

"She is. We thought we'd christen your house with Chinese food and a good bottle of Chardonnay. I already bought the wine." Alice shifted her large tote from one hand to the other.

"I insist on paying for dinner. Does delivery from Twin Dragons sound good?"

"Works for me, and you know Harper loves that place," Alice said.

"Then it's a plan. Come on over around six."

"Okay, I'll tell Harper. See you soon." Alice opened the front doors. "Are you leaving now?"

"No. I have to finish up a report before I head home. Later." Olivia pushed away from the wall and scampered down the hall toward her classroom.

OLIVIA SAT CROSS-LEGGED on a chair, wrapped in her favorite fuzzy green nightshirt. Strewn across the coffee table laid empty Chinese food cartons. She picked up her glass of wine and leaned back against the soft cushion.

"I'm so stuffed," she said before taking a sip.

"Me too, but then I'll be starved in about an hour. It's always like that with me and Chinese food," Alice said.

"It was so good," Harper said. "And just what I needed after that disastrous date last night."

Olivia shook her head. "I still can't believe what an asshole that guy was. What kind of a guy talks about ways he could get his ex-girlfriend back? And this was your first date."

Harper sat up straighter on the couch. "I know! And … to add insult to injury, the idiot wanted me to help him come up with ideas on how to win her back." She groaned and sank back into the cushion. "Why can't I find a normal guy?"

"Where did you meet this jerk?" Alice asked as she broke open her fortune cookie.

"Online. I'm definitely done with that dating site. I'm thinking of checking out another one. Kennedy keeps talking about *Discreet Passion*. I've stayed away from it based on the name alone, but I may check it out. She says it's for hookups, one-nighters, but also for people looking for relationships and even marriage. At this point, what do I have to lose?"

"Your life," Olivia said.

"I'm with her on this one," Alice added.

"I'm real careful when I meet a guy. I always go to public places for a while, I never give them my address, and I do background checks to make sure they aren't on parole or have anything creepy out there. Too bad there aren't ways to check out if a guy's a jerk before you waste your time on him."

The women laughed, and Olivia pushed the second bottle of wine toward Harper. "As long as you're careful then I guess it's okay. I'm gonna go on one of those sites as research for a paper in my psych class."

Alice giggled. "That's a new one, Olivia. Come on, you're with friends. You can tell us if you're getting back out there."

"I'm not, and I'd totally tell you if I were. This really is for my psychology class that I'm taking online. Just one more semester and I'll have my degree. I can't wait."

"You'd make a great teacher. I think you should do that instead of being a school counselor," Harper said as she filled her wineglass.

"I love teaching, but I'm drawn to guiding and working with troubled kids," Olivia replied. "Anyway, I'm thinking of setting up a fake profile on *Discreet Passion* because it isn't just the run-of-the-mill dating site."

All of a sudden a deafening roar rattled the windows and sliced through the night air.

"What the hell?" Harper said jumping off the couch.

"It's a bike," Olivia said, rising up from the chair.

"A bike? Impossible," said Alice as she followed Harper to the window.

"A motorcycle—not a regular bike." Olivia pulled the sheet away from the window and peered out.

Sure enough, chrome gleamed under the soft streetlights, and a big-ass Harley swung onto the driveway of Animal and Lucy's house. The biker killed the engine and quietness descended once again over the cul-de-sac. Olivia watched as the man walked up the sidewalk, then sucked in a small breath when she saw Animal walk out on the porch. He bumped fists with the man, talked for a few seconds, then the biker went into the house. Before following the visitor, Animal turned around and stared right at her. Olivia's heart pounded and she tried to move away, but she couldn't. Instead, she stood transfixed, her gaze locked with his until Harper and Alice's voice broke the hold. She slowly let the sheet slip from her fingers, shutting out the outside world.

"He's a biker," she muttered under her breath. Suddenly it all made sense: his road name, the odd familiarity, the danger he exuded, the swagger—*oh, the damn biker swagger*—and the attitude.

"That was one loud-as-hell motorcycle," Alice said as she grabbed the bottle of wine and settled back down on the couch.

"I wonder what makes them so noisy. My uncle had one when I was a kid, but it didn't sound like that at all."

Still standing at the window, Olivia slowly turned around. "Illegal aftermarket pipes. Bikers replace the industry exhaust pipes with the aftermarket ones. They say the noise keeps them safe, but a lot of them just like the sound. It's like holding up the middle finger to the establishment." She shuffled over to the kitchen and took out another bottle of white wine from the refrigerator, ignoring the surprised expressions on her friends' faces.

"How in the hell do you know all that?" Harper asked.

"My brother and dad rode bikes. I guess I just learned it along the way." Olivia refilled all their glasses with Chardonnay.

"The bigger question is, why is that biker coming over to your neighbor's house?" Alice said as she picked up her glass.

"I don't know. Probably a friend of his," Olivia said.

"Do you know your neighbors?" Harper asked.

"The one to my left is a nice young couple with two adorable kids—a boy and girl, both under the age of five. The couple across from me is in their late thirties, maybe early forties, and have three kids—two teenagers and one in grade school. Actually, I think the boy goes to Slavens. I'm pretty sure I saw him in the hall the other day."

A second or two passed and Alice and Harper looked at her expectantly. Olivia took a gulp of wine, set the glass down, and ran her fingers through the fuzzy fabric of her nightshirt.

"And who lives next door?" Alice said. "The house that the biker just went into?"

"Uh ... a guy and his daughter, Lucy. She goes to Slavens too. She's in Clara's classroom."

"I know her," Harper said. "She's the new girl. She's just been here for a couple of months—after the Christmas break. Clara said she keeps to herself a lot, but has a real temper on her. She also told me her dad is a royal pain in the ass and is a member of the Insurgents."

Olivia's stomach knotted. "Insurgents?" she whispered.

"Yeah—the outlaw motorcycle gang. You've seen them around town." Harper picked up a fortune cookie and ripped open the cellophane wrapper.

"I have, but I didn't know he was in that club." *That just figures.*

"Those are the guys Kennedy parties with sometimes at their club. I bet she knows him," Alice said.

For reasons Olivia couldn't figure out, that tidbit of information made her stomach sour and her body flush with anger at the same time. The thought of Kennedy and Animal together really pissed her off, but if she were being totally honest, the thought of Animal with *any* woman made her blood boil. *But it shouldn't. Maybe I need to start dating again.*

"Your neighbor's hot, though. He's got a great body on him, and he comes off as real dangerous and exciting." Harper giggled. "He's not my type, but I do think he's got a real sexy vibe going for him."

"I'd agree with that, but I could never see myself going out with him. I never was into bad boys. I like a stable, kind, and sweet man. That's why Jonathan's so perfect," Alice said.

"I like guys like Jim Farley." Harper groaned.

Olivia smiled and shook her head. "It's too bad he's already taken."

"It seems like the good ones always are. And Jim's such a good husband and father. He's nothing like that creep, Marcus Thurber. That idiot is always hitting on all the young teachers and mothers. I don't know how his wife puts up with him. I heard he's having an affair with Samantha Paulson. Can you believe it? What a louse." Harper broke open the cookie and took out the small white banner that held her fortune.

"Isn't that Daniel's mother?" Alice asked.

"Uh-huh." Harper waved the paper ribbon in the air. "So this says, 'The love of your life will appear in front of you unexpectedly.' Yeah … Right."

"Jonathan did. It does happen." Alice picked up her fortune again and re-read it. "Mine says, 'You should definitely go for it.' That says a lot." Alice laughed.

"Who writes these?" Harper rolled her eyes.

Olivia shrugged but her mind was on her sexy neighbor. She still couldn't believe he was a member of the Insurgents. As hard as she tried, it seemed like she could never shake off her damn past.

"I have to get going," Alice said standing up. "This was so much fun. I really love your house."

Olivia rose to her feet. "Thanks—I do too. It needs some work, but I bought it at a great price, so I don't mind using some elbow grease."

"When are you going to get some window coverings, or are sheets your go-to?" Harper chuckled.

"I've been looking online for some, but they're so damn expensive." Memories of Animal watching her from his second floor room when she'd first moved in flashed through her mind. "I definitely want to cover the windows."

"I don't blame you, especially now with having an Insurgent living next to you." Harper shuddered then walked over to the front door. "You remember Perry, right?" Olivia nodded. "I can ask him if he can get you a deal on blinds or something. He gets all that stuff either at cost or at a steep discount on account that he's a decorator."

"I forgot about that. It'd be great if you could ask him. I would love to get rid of the sheets. It's such a pain to have to tape them back all the time to let the light in." Olivia opened the front door.

"I'll call him during lunch tomorrow. See you in the morning." Harper stepped out onto the porch.

"I'll see you in the teachers' lounge for lunch," Alice said as she zipped up her jacket.

Wintry air swirled around Olivia as she stood on the porch watching her friends pull away from the curb. She wrapped her arms tighter around herself, tucking her chin downward into the soft fabric of her nightshirt. Above, clouds the color of wet ash covered the night sky, providing a modicum of warmth. Olivia glanced over at the Harley-Davidson Ultra-Classic Limited parked on Animal's driveway, and a sudden sadness rushed over her with the force of a wave, tumbling her emotions. She closed her eyes, remembering how Leo used to take her to the corner drugstore when they were kids to buy her Starburst candy when all the yelling and screaming got to be too much in the house. He'd always take out the leather wallet Grandma Betty had given him—*it made him feel so grown up*—and put down a five-dollar bill on the counter. No matter how much the candies cost, Leo would always give a five.

Tears seeped out of her closed lids and trickled down her face and off her chin. Memories flooded her mind—from Leo's infectious laughter, his crooked smile, and the way he'd always had her back—to the bikers who filled the crowded church and Leo's picture on an easel next to his steel-gray coffin. A chill ran through her. That night—the one when she'd lost her brother to a barroom brawl—had plunged her into a pit so dark, she was still recovering from it. It'd been over two years since Leo had been killed, but at times, it didn't even feel like a minute had passed.

The din of voices dragged her out of past memories, and Olivia wiped her cheeks and looked toward the noise. Animal and his friend stood by the motorcycle talking and laughing. She watched them even as her body shivered and her teeth chattered. Then his eyes found hers and locked on. For a long moment, they just stared at each other, oblivious to their surroundings, and something passed between them. Animal's friend punched his arm, breaking their connection, and he turned away.

A strong gust of wind whipped around her, tousling her hair, and Olivia opened the screen door and walked inside. She closed the door and leaned her forward against the smooth wood. The screaming cams from the Harley were like music to her ears, and she stayed there long after the roar of the exhaust pipes faded away.

After what seemed like endless minutes, Olivia locked the door, switched off the porch light, and made her way to the bedroom. Suddenly she was very tired, and all she wanted to do was crawl into bed and fall into oblivion.

CHAPTER SEVEN

INSIDE DREAM HOUSE, Animal sat at a table with Bones, Smokey, and Rags close to the edge of the stage where Diamond crawled across the floor until she was right in front of them. Loud, shuddering music blasted from the stage in the dimly-lit club. The place was packed, and a round of whistles and applauses egged Diamond on as she writhed and rolled around on the ground.

"Full house," Bones shouted to Animal.

"Yeah. I'm sort of surprised since it's a Tuesday night," he replied.

Animal hadn't planned to hang out with his brothers at the MC's strip club, but Banger wanted him and Bones to check out the new dancers and help out Emma, the GM, if she needed it. Jada had agreed to watch Lucy, and his daughter seemed happy to spend a night without him around. The whole situation with Lucy was aggravating as fuck. Just when he thought he was making some inroads with her, she'd shut down and freeze him out. He wasn't sure if she'd ever come around despite assurances from his dad and Jada that she would.

"Diamond's giving you the eye," Rags said, nudging Animal's side with his elbow.

He looked up and saw the dancer on her knees, her legs spread wide. The pretty brunette was topless, and she looped two fingers around the elastic on her thong then slipped out of it with the ease of an expert. Her gaze fixed on his as she crawled closer to the edge of the stage. She was naked except for thigh-high stockings and a pink sequined garter belt, where she stuffed the bills that men gave her. Diamond's hips humped the air in a sensually circular way, and Animal stared at the toned muscles in her ass and thought of Olivia. Since the sexy neighbor had moved in next door, she'd been on his mind way more than he liked.

"Too bad we can't fuck the help," Rags said. "Diamond looks like she wants to jump you right here and now." He guffawed.

Animal nodded, his eyes straight ahead, but the only woman he saw in his mind's eye was the pretty teacher's assistant. Like a fucking school boy, he was looking forward to the following night when she'd bring the dinner she'd promised Lucy. How fucking pathetic was *that*?

The thumping bass of the music pulled his attention back to the stage, and Animal watched Diamond wriggle around in all her sexy nakedness for the audience, but he knew she was really dancing for him. She had the hots for him in a big way and had even told him she'd quit Dream House so they could get together. Animal had been flattered— she was one of the top dancers at the club, but he'd told her he wasn't in the market for a girlfriend, and he didn't want her to lose out on making money for a few nights of fucking. To her credit, Diamond hadn't held his rebuff against him, but that didn't mean she didn't keep trying.

Twenty minutes later, Diamond exited the stage, blowing kisses to a group of businessmen before disappearing behind the black curtain. Sparkling red and pink lights cast swirling patterns across the stage. The poles gleamed and the music flowing out of the ceiling's speakers wasn't as hard hitting. When the next dancer took the stage, the tunes would be amped up and the stripper would entertain the mostly male audience for another set of four songs.

Rinse and repeat. Animal stood up and stretched his back, cracking his neck in the process.

"Where're these new chicks we're supposed to be checking out?" he asked Bones.

"The next one up is one of them. You in a hurry or something?" Bones replied.

"Probably wants to check out his neighbor again," Smokey said as he picked up his shot of Jack.

"Neighbor? Whaddaya mean?" Bones said while Rags leaned in to hear.

"No one. You're full of shit, dude." Animal picked up the beer bottle and took a long drink.

"You're the one who's full of it." Smokey looked at Bones and Rags. "Last night I stopped over at his place, and when I was leaving, there was this chick next door on the porch … and lover boy here went ape-shit over her. I was talking and all he was doing was staring just like some lovesick pussy."

Bones and Rags guffawed, and Animal clenched his fists.

"Fuck, man, you never mentioned you had a sweet piece living next door to you," Bones said.

"It's a damn good setup—easy access and all, you know?" Rags laughed and leaned back in the chair.

"You're all fuckin' assholes. She works at Lucy's school, that's all."

"You're gonna fuck Lucy's teacher? All right, dude!" Bones high-fived it with Smokey and Rags, but just laughed when Animal refused to lift his arm one inch.

"That's damn hot. I always wanted to bang a teacher. Ms. Carlson was hot as fuck. She taught English at Pinewood Springs High when I was a sophomore." A wide grin spread across Smokey's face. "Damn … she had a starring role in so many of my dirty-as-fuck fantasies. I'd love to bump into her again."

"You're all full of shit. There's nothing going on with Olivia—"

"*Olivia.* Sounds like you're pretty cozy already," Smokey said. Bones and Rags busted out laughing.

"Grow the fuck up. She's just a chick who lives next door. Hell, she's not even my type—she's a good girl."

All of a sudden, the three men nodded and grew somber.

"I hear you, dude," Rags said.

"Good girls have stars in their damn eyes. Fuck, man, stay clear from that one." Bones motioned the waitress for another round.

"Even so, you sure were giving her the eye, and it wasn't like the way you look at Charlotte or even Diamond. You better be careful, bro, or she'll have you tied and locked down," Smokey said.

Animal sank back down on the chair, a scowl deepening the fine lines in his forehead. "No chick's tying me down."

"I'll drink to that." Smokey clinked his glass against Animal's beer bottle.

"Me too." Bones held up his empty glass.

"Fuck, yeah," Rags said picking up his tumbler.

The conversation switched to the latest Harley-Davidson of their vice president, Hawk, and the way he customized the hell out of it.

By the time midnight rolled around, Animal had had it with the loud music and gyrating dancers. He had to interview job applicants the following day for his appliance repair business. He started Mountain Appliance Repair a few years before, and it had really taken off due to the fact that he didn't gouge customers and knew what the hell he was doing. Since it'd grown so fast, Animal had to hire some employees, and finding people who had strong work ethics and knew what the fuck they were doing was a difficult task. He'd had to let Tyler go because the dude smoked too much weed on the job, and it was screwing up his ability to be reliable.

"I'm outta here. The redheaded chick's a go, but the blonde with the humungous fake tits and the other one with the two left feet are a no. Do you agree with me?" he asked Bones.

"Yes, for the two, but the big-titted blonde should stay. Let's see how she does with the guys," Bones replied.

"Yeah—she's pretty hot," Rags said.

"I'm with Animal on this one. The chick didn't know how to dance or flirt. I dunno, she didn't have sex appeal, and that's something a dancer needs, especially for booking private rooms. I don't see her as a money maker for the club," Smokey said.

"We should give her a chance. If she doesn't do well in a month, then we'll let her go," Bones replied.

Animal pushed his chair back and rose to his feet. "I told you what I think. Prez will be the one who'll decide."

"Banger *and* Hawk," Rags said.

"Right. Hawk usually has the final say since he's more involved in running the gentlemen's club. Either way, I did my part and now I'm outta here."

The men bumped fists and Animal headed toward the exit. The cold air wisped inside as he opened the front doors and stepped out into the night. The frigid wind iced his cheeks as he made his way across the parking lot. Settled into the SUV, Animal switched on the engine, cranked up the heat, and pulled out of the lot.

When Animal turned into the cul-de-sac, he glanced at Olivia's house and saw that there was a light on in one of the back rooms he guessed was her bedroom. The bullshit he told his brothers at Dream House about Olivia not being his type was so not true. Olivia was exactly his type: dark long hair, stacked nicely, sweet ass. The truth was, he could find that with Charlotte or some of the other club girls, even the hangarounds, so those physical traits alone weren't the only things that attracted him to her. It was the blush of high color on her cheeks anytime she was nervous, the way her pert nose crinkled while she laughed, and how those sweet lips made her face light up when she smiled.

"Fuckin' pussy," he mumbled, dragging his gaze away from her house. He pulled into the garage, closed the door, and went inside.

"Hey," he said as he entered the family room.

Jada lay on the couch in front of a crackling fire, watching the television. She pushed up into a sitting position and swung her legs off the sofa.

"Hey. I thought you'd be later."

"I gotta get to the office early tomorrow morning. You wanna crash here? I don't like you driving alone this late."

Jada laughed as she slipped on her shoes. "It's just a little past midnight. Believe me, I'm out way later than this on weekends. I'm good." She rose to her feet and scooped up her backpack.

"How was Lucy?"

"Great. After she finished her homework, we played a video game then watched some TV. She had a good time. I made tacos for dinner—she loved them."

"I'm glad. Was she distant with you?"

"A little, but I'm pretty sure she still misses her mom. Has Emerald called her at all?"

"Nope. She's such a fuckin' bitch. I tried calling her but the slut just won't answer the damn phone." Anger bubbled just beneath the surface of his skin.

"I guess you'll have to reconcile the fact that she's turned her back on Lucy. I can't even begin to believe a mother could do that, but she has."

"I figured that out the day the bitch left Lucy with me. I gotta admit though, I love having Lucy around."

"And I love the way you are when you're with her." Jada walked over to him and playfully poked him in the ribs. "All soft and vulnerable, and you get this warm glow in your eyes when you look at her. It's so sweet. You really are a good dad, you know?"

Animal wrapped his arm around his sister's shoulders and kissed the top of her head. "Thanks for being such a good liar—you almost have me believing it."

"You are. Lucy just needs a lot of patience, and she also needs some work with her reading. She was struggling with a book that should've been a cinch."

Animal moved away and pounded his fist into his hand. "I told that shit for a teacher that Lucy needed a reading tutor, and she acted like I was a fuckin' moron. *Bitch.* I even talked to that sorry excuse for a principal and got the same reaction. Those fuckin' assholes."

Jada chuckled. "Parenting is loads of fun, isn't it?" He glared at her and she held up her hands. "Sorry—bad timing for a joke. Okay ... so you could hire a tutor on your own. Schools are cheap and don't want to spend the money. I mean Lucy's not horrible at reading, it's just that she needs some help, otherwise she'll fall further behind each grade."

Olivia. And Lucy likes her. "I know someone I can ask."

"There you go." Jada slipped on her jacket and gloves then wrapped her scarf around her neck. "I'll see you later."

Animal pulled out his wallet and took out sixty dollars and handed it to Jada.

"You don't have to pay me," she said. "I love spending time with Lucy."

"I know, but you helped me out tonight, and I know you could use the cash. Wheelie doesn't pay you that well at the carwash."

Jada tucked it into her pocket then zipped it up. "Thanks." She smiled at him and walked to the door.

Animal opened it up for her. "Call or text me when you get home."

"I will. See you soon." She ambled down the sidewalk toward her Chevrolet Tahoe.

He stayed on the porch and watched the red tail lights of the car fade into the night. Animal turned and looked in the direction of Olivia's house; it was dark and quiet. He slowly turned away and went into his home.

CHAPTER EIGHT

OKAY, SO SHE was a coward. Olivia would be the first one to admit it. Instead of delivering the spaghetti dinner in person, she'd bought—and spent way too much money on—an insulated food container that kept the spaghetti, garlic bread, and meatballs hot. She left a little bit early from school in order to put it on the front porch before Animal or Lucy came home. A ridiculous move for a professional twenty-five-year-old who owned her own home? Of course, and she cursed herself for doing it as she taped a note to the container then sneaked away.

Now Olivia hid in the shadows of her unlit house, peeking out the living room window, watching vehicles coming and going. Soon the encroaching nightfall swallowed up all the lingering shadows of the day, lending an eeriness to the bare trees and darkened houses.

Olivia saw several windows illuminate intermittently at Animal's house and figured they were security lights. The porch light switched on, bathing the container she'd left earlier in a warm glow. Doubts began to creep through her until Olivia decided to walk over and grab the food then bring it back when Animal and Lucy came home. Just as she began to push away from the window, two headlights lit up the street like moonbeams. She grimaced when she recognized Animal's dark blue SUV and slinked back a bit farther from the window. Olivia watched the vehicle pull into the garage and stayed rooted after the door had shut.

"This is so fucking juvenile," she said aloud, yet Olivia couldn't pull away from the window.

The front door opened and she saw Lucy push on the screen door. It looked like she said something because in less than a few seconds,

Animal appeared on the porch and picked up the food container. Olivia watched as he read the note. Then, as if he could sense her watching him, he looked over, straight at her window. Blood rushed to her head and Olivia held her breath as she ducked out of the way. Her heart banged like crazy against her ribcage, and she sat on the floor plastered against the wall for what seemed like hours. Olivia slowly rose to her feet and shuffled to her kitchen for a much-needed glass of wine. She glanced at her phone and realized that forty-five minutes had passed since she'd first seen his car pull into the garage.

A low growl in her stomach reminded her that she hadn't eaten anything since that morning. Switching on the lights, she took out a bowl of extra spaghetti and meatballs from the fridge and put it in a pot on the stove. As Olivia waited for her dinner to heat up, she jumped when her cellphone vibrated across the countertop. She reached out and grabbed it as a web of apprehension wove through her. When Olivia saw Kennedy's name on the screen, she let out a sigh of relief and put the phone to her ear.

"Hi, Kennedy."

"Hey there, girl. What do you have going on tonight?"

Weariness wrapped around her like a heavy blanket, and the only way she wanted to spend her night was on the couch watching a mindless show.

"Just staying in. Why?"

"You *have* to come out with me. There's this mixer at Moonshine Flats. I heard there's going to be a lot of attractive men."

"I've sworn off men, remember?"

"Are you still serious about that?" An exasperated sigh came through the phone. "When are you lifting the fucking ban?"

"Not tonight. I'm beat. Sorry. Maybe Harper would like to go. She's looking for a nice guy."

"I already called her and she has a date with some guy her sister fixed her up with. I told her blind dates are the worst, but she sounded giddy to me."

"Maybe it'll work out. A friend of mine met her husband on a blind date." Olivia walked over to the stove and stirred the spaghetti and meatballs.

"I don't want a husband yet. We're all too young to even think of settling down. You know thirty comes real fast, so we might as well live it up some before we have to give it up for the fucking 'American dream.'"

"You don't have to sell me. I don't even want a date right now." Olivia turned down the heat.

"I don't know how you do it. I get all pissy if I haven't had sex in a few days. Why are you doing this again?" Kennedy clucked her tongue.

"Because I confuse sex with love, and I fall too damn hard for a man. I'm sure it goes back to my childhood—I had a douche for a dad and a mother who stood by her man no matter what humiliating things he did to her. I'm definitely fucked up, but at least I know that. They say the first step is acknowledgement of a problem."

"You're too into your psychology classes. We all mistake sex for love—we're women."

"You don't seem to." Olivia took down a plate from the cupboard.

"I used to, but then I started thinking like a man, and life has been great. That's what you need to do—date like a man."

"Maybe. Anyway, there's no one around I'm really interested in." Animal flashed into her mind. "No one at all," she said as if trying to convince herself.

"So I can't talk you into joining me tonight?" Kennedy asked.

"No. I really just want to veg. Another time. Let me know how it goes though."

"I will."

"Oh, Kennedy? I need to pick your brain about that dating site you were telling me about—*Discreet Passion*. I'm writing a research paper for one of my psych classes, and it's about online dating and interconnections."

"Are you actually going to go out on a *date* with one of the guys you connect with?" Kennedy asked.

"I'm not planning on it. I just want to see how the courting relationship is via a computer. Talking with people and interacting with the opposite sex has become so impersonal thanks to electronic devices. At least that's one of my premises of the research paper."

"Interesting. Okay, I can come over and help you set up a profile that'll be sure to get you plenty of hits. I haven't been over to your house yet, so I'm looking forward to it."

"Thanks. Have fun tonight, and I hope you meet someone perfect for you."

"Perfection is a nebulous word. We'll talk tomorrow."

Olivia put the phone down, filled her plate, soaked the pan in hot water and dish soap, then padded into the living room and sank down on the couch. She picked up the remote and clicked on the TV, channel surfing until she found a cooking competition, then settled back and ate her food.

The insistent ringing of her doorbell woke her, and Olivia realized that she must've dozed off. The chimes kept sounding in rapid succession, and she sat up, wiped the drool from the corner of her mouth, and ran her fingers through her mussed-up hair.

"Hang on a minute, will you?" she called, scurrying toward the door.

Olivia looked through the peephole and her stomach lurched when she saw Animal filling the space. *Shit!* She glanced at the mirror on the wall and groaned. *I look a mess. What the hell does he want anyway?* Sorry she'd called out, she fluffed her hair once more, pinched her pale cheeks a few times, and yanked open the door.

"Why are you ringing my doorbell like a lunatic?"

Animal ran his gaze over her, making her feel weird, angry, and vulnerable all at the same time.

"I came over to thank you for the dinner. Lucy thought you were gonna bring it over yourself and eat with us, but she liked it."

"That's good. I was real busy after work so I just dropped it off."

For a long pause he stared intensely at her. "Yeah … Right."

Feeling exposed, she wrapped her arms around herself and shivered. "It's cold out there. Do you want to come in for a minute?" *Why did I ask that? I just want him to go away.*

"I normally would, but I gotta get back. Lucy's alone."

"Of course." *Now I really feel like a doofus.* "I won't keep you then."

"I wanted to ask you something," he said, moving closer to her.

Butterflies fluttered in her stomach and she leaned in toward him. "What is it?" Her gaze fell on his mouth—on those perfectly shaped lips that looked so smooth and tempting.

"My sister looked after Lucy last night …"

His voice faded away as Olivia wondered what he did last night. Was he out with a woman? Probably. He was a good-looking guy and a biker to boot. Women flocked to those types of men.

"So how about it? I can pay you pretty well."

Pay me? What the hell is he asking me? "Uh … I'm not—"

"Lucy likes you and that's a huge plus, but if you can't do it, then, maybe you can recommend someone to help her."

"Lucy? Help her with what?"

"Reading." Animal looked at her like she was a space cadet.

"Oh, right. Sorry, I've had a really long day, and I was dozing when you rang the bell. So you want me to tutor Lucy?"

"Yeah—she's got a problem even if her teacher doesn't agree. My sister's noticed it too." A frown knitted his brows. "But I already told you that."

"Sorry," she mumbled. In that instant Olivia got the impression that he didn't like to repeat himself. "I can assess her if you'd like. I'm super busy right now with working at Slavens part-time and then at a dental clinic the other days. I'm also in college. I really don't have a lot of free time."

"I was thinking just once or twice a week. I can pay you seventy-five an hour." He glanced over at his house for the umpteenth time.

"That's too much," she said as she calculated the extra money per week. She could apply it to buying window coverings.

"Lucy's worth it. I want her to have any advantage I can give her. So, what do you say?"

"I'll come over and assess her, and depending on where she's at, I'll be able to tell how much work she needs. That's the best I can give right now."

"That's all I'm asking." He tilted his head to one side and smiled, a slow, seductive smile.

Heat flushed beneath her skin as she looked up at him and met his intense gaze. Swallowing, Olivia forced herself to break contact, but before she could, a low chuckle rumbled from his chest as he winked at her then turned around.

"I gotta get back. Can you come over tomorrow to check out Lucy?"

"Uh … yeah. What about six o'clock?"

Animal looked over his shoulder and nodded. "See you then, *Teach*."

The intense black gaze moved over her, almost insolently, making her flesh tingle. He then jumped off the porch and swaggered across the lawn to his house. Olivia retreated back into her home, hating the way Animal made her feel so vulnerable.

She padded over to the couch and plopped down as she replayed their conversation. Agreeing to tutor Lucy was just asking for trouble, but Olivia hated to think of Lucy struggling with her reading. From experience, she knew that a child who had reading problems was usually stressed and embarrassed about the difficulty, and Olivia couldn't deny Lucy a chance just because her dad was hot and Olivia couldn't grow the fuck up.

I'll assess her and then I can recommend a tutor. Happy that she'd come up with a plan, Olivia poured more wine into her glass and slowly sipped it as she stared at the TV screen.

CHAPTER NINE

BLUE'S BELLY WAS packed with people, almost shoulder to shoulder. Loud voices competed with the live rock music that dominated the atmosphere. Along the wall behind the hand-carved wooden bar, bottles with every hue of amber liquid lined the glass shelves. Patrons sat perched on barstools, gesturing to the three bartenders while putting plastic cards and money on the counter. The sallow light of street lamps trickled in through the thick leaded windows, and the scent of beer, whiskey, and smoky barbecue wafted in the air.

"This place is crazy packed," Olivia said, tugging down the hem of her short black skirt as she wound her way through a labyrinth of warm bodies.

"The place was remodeled, so tonight's the grand re-opening," Kennedy said. "I've been dying to see what it was going to look like."

"How do you like it?" Olivia had never been to Blue's Belly even though she'd heard good things about it. The place was known for their burgers and good local live music. Occasionally, the owner would book a national act, but the majority of the bands came from the county and other cities and towns around Colorado.

"I love it!" Kennedy pushed her way to the bar and leaned against it.

Olivia filled the tiny space between her friend and a tall, broad-shouldered man. "It's not what I expected. I thought it'd be like some underground bar you see in old movies. You know, the ones that have small spaces for lovers to disappear into, and jazz notes floating on the streams of cigarette smoke billowing from tall, dark, and good-looking men."

Kennedy laughed. "Sounds like a bar I'd love to go to. Blue's used to be more of a dive than a mysterious one like the movies from the 1960s."

Olivia darted her eyes around the place. "It's now shabby chic with a real rock and roll vibe going for it."

"I definitely love what Freddy's done with it."

"Freddy?"

Kennedy tossed her light brown hair over her shoulder. "He's the owner. I have to find him at some point and tell him that the new Blue's kicks ass. What're you drinking?" She gestured to one of the bartenders.

"A vodka martini. Ivy wants me to bring her back a white wine spritzer," Olivia replied. Ivy, a cute blonde with freckles and a cherubic face, was a dental technician at the clinic Olivia worked at two days a week. Over the past year, they'd become good friends.

"I'm still shocked that sleazeball Brady let her go out without him tonight." Kennedy sighed in frustration when the bartender took someone else's order.

"I know. I don't get what she sees in him. She told me that he likes rough sex." Olivia shuddered as she thought of the Slavens' Elementary gym teacher. Brady Sickles had always given her the creeps from day one, and when Ivy began dating him a few months ago, Olivia had told Ivy she could do much better. Her friend said that she liked him, but Olivia couldn't figure out why.

"I can see that. I heard from some of the students that he's real tough on them in gym class. Does she like it, and what do you mean by 'rough'?" Kennedy waved her hand vigorously at the bartender. He turned in her direction and fixed his eyes on her large breasts then smiled.

"He'll be coming over to take our drink order." Olivia laughed.

"He better, or I'm returning this blouse," Kennedy said, fingering the hem of her low-cut, form-fitting red top.

Olivia giggled. "I'd be so self-conscious wearing that. I wish I had your confidence." She pushed up the spaghetti strap on her blue jewel-toned silky top.

Kennedy shrugged. "I like the attention. I never had much of it growing up—busy parents obsessed with their careers. Boo-hoo … poor me." She patted her shoulder in mock comfort. "I'm sure your psych prof would have a field day with that one." She laughed.

Too loudly, Olivia thought. Kennedy always acted like she was immune to falling in love, getting hurt, or caring if a guy ghosted her, but Olivia had suspected it was an armor she'd put on to protect herself from heartache and feelings. She was so worried about her friend's reckless and destructive behavior with men, but whenever she tried to broach the subject with Kennedy, her friend would make a joke of it, masking the vulnerable little girl inside her.

"So, what does Ivy mean by 'rough sex'?" Kennedy asked again.

"Yeah, that's what we were talking about. Now you can't say anything to anyone." Olivia knew Kennedy would keep a secret until death, but she still felt the need to say it.

"Of course." Her friend leaned in closer to her.

"Sickles likes Ivy to be immobile, like totally tied up with a belt around her neck."

"That's fucking kinky. I didn't think Ivy was into that."

"She's not. She told me that Sickles will just stand back and watch her like that for a long time, then he flips her around and fucks her like a madman—her words, not mine." Olivia shuddered.

"Does he tighten the belt around her neck?"

Olivia shook her head. "No. It seems that he's just into the visual image of something around her throat and her not being able to move. Total weirdo."

"Why the fuck does she let him do that if she's not enjoying it?" Kennedy asked.

"The better question is, why the fuck is she with him?"

"Why *is* she?"

Olivia shrugged. "Any time I've asked her that, she simply tells me that the kinky sex is just a small part of their relationship, and that he's a very nice and caring man."

"She's got to dump him. I *knew* something was off with that guy."

"What can I get you ladies?" The bartender focused his gaze on Kennedy's cleavage.

She moved in further over the counter. "A black Russian, a vodka martini, and a white wine spritzer." Kennedy ran the tip of her tongue over her top lip. "Please."

A wide grin cracked the sandy-haired bartender's face. "Anything for you, babe."

Olivia rolled her eyes and shifted where she stood, trying to ease the ache in the balls of her feet. The strappy black stilettos were an extravagant purchase, but they were definitely sitting shoes only. Teetering on them, she leaned to the side and bumped against the man standing next to her.

"Sorry," she mumbled.

When he turned to look at her, his eyes widened as they lingered on her chest. Self-conscious, Olivia folded her arms across her breasts. The man's chuckle pricked her nerves and she pivoted away from him.

"Can I buy you a drink?" he asked, now fully facing her.

"No thanks," she said, looking at the bottles on the shelves behind the bar.

"Why not?"

Olivia gave him a sidelong glance. "Because I don't want one."

"Then why the fuck are you standing by the bar?"

"I should've said that I don't want one *from you*."

"Feisty, aren't you? I've never seen you in here before," the dark-haired man said.

Olivia ignored him and picked up one of the cocktail napkins the bartender had put in front of her and Kennedy, and began tearing it into little pieces. A clean-cut guy in black pants and a silver button-down shirt with black pinstripes was talking up a storm with Kennedy. Olivia glanced over at the bartender, wondering how long it could possibly take to make three simple drinks.

She tugged at the hem of her skirt again, wishing she would've worn pants instead. The man next to her was looking, his head to one side, into the mirror above the bar. Olivia noticed he was wearing a leather cut with the all-too-familiar one-percenter patch on it. She caught his blue gaze and held it, then he broke away and turned back to her.

"Hey, I know you," he said.

"That's a clever line," she replied, grateful that the slowpoke bartender finally brought their drinks.

"I don't feed chicks lines, baby. You're a neighbor to my brother—Animal."

When Olivia heard his name, her entire body tingled, much to her chagrin, and her mind raced as she wondered if he was in the bar. Not wanting to sound desperate or pathetic, she coolly nodded.

"Yes, I live next door to your friend." She didn't dare say his name for fear her voice would tremble. What the hell was the matter with her? If the mere mention of her sexy neighbor's name threw her in a tizzy, it was obvious that she needed to get back out on the circuit. But there was no way her circuit was going to include bikers—she'd had a lifetime fill of them.

"I saw you a few nights ago—you were on the porch giving my buddy the eye."

"What?" Olivia replied in a strangled voice, her face heating to the roots of her hairline.

The biker laughed. "Don't sweat it, babe, Animal was eyeing you too."

At that moment, she wished the floor would just open up and swallow her whole.

"Smokey!" Kennedy's voice danced above the music.

The biker shifted his attention from her to Kennedy and a loud boom of laughter burst through his lips. "Fuck, you're a tempting sight," he said moving away from Olivia. He wrapped his arms around her friend and hugged her quickly. "You look fuckin' good, baby."

"You too." Kennedy ran her hands up and down the biker's muscular arms. "Are any other Insurgents here?"

Olivia cocked her head to the left and strained to hear his answer.

"Yeah. How do you like the remodel? My company did the renovations."

"I love it! You did an awesome job." Kennedy leaned into him and he crushed his mouth against hers.

Olivia picked up her drink and Ivy's and turned away from the counter. "I'm going back to the table," she said to her friend who, at that moment, was totally preoccupied with Smokey.

Grimacing with each aching step, Olivia's gaze scanned the room full of people in search of Animal. She saw several men wearing their leather cuts with the three-piece Insurgents rocker on the back of them, and she felt a small, but real, stab of disappointment that Animal wasn't among them. Sighing, she weaved through the crowd to her table and put the drinks on top of it.

"That took forever," Harper said when Olivia sat down.

"It was so damn crowded at the bar," she replied as she picked up her drink and took a sip.

"The waitress came by twice since you guys went to get drinks." Harper looked around. "Where's Kennedy?"

"She bumped into a friend. Who knows when she'll be back," Olivia replied.

"How much do I owe you?" Ivy asked.

"Don't worry about it. You saved my ass big-time last week when I came in late after my morning class."

Ivy nodded. "I had to do some fancy footwork for sure. Dr. Linney's always so punctual, but it's Dr. Canty who can be a Nazi about it."

"And of course he was the one who was there. I've always had bad timing, especially with men." Olivia lifted her glass and clinked it with Ivy's and Harper's.

Kennedy came back to the table with two drinks in her hands, and Olivia suspected one of them was from Smokey.

"Did you lose your friend already?" Olivia asked as she sat down.

"Smokey's a great kisser, but he's a major player. He's looking for someone new tonight and so am I." Kennedy brought her tumbler to her lips.

"How do you know him?" Olivia asked.

Her friend put her drink down and leaned over and whispered in her ear, "I met him at one of the Insurgents' parties and we hit it off. We've gotten together a few times."

Olivia jerked her head back. "Like on dates?" That was an anomaly with most outlaw bikers.

"No, like just hooking up—usually at the clubhouse, but he came to my apartment one time. He's very good." She hitched up her brows in an exaggerated fashion. "I mean *v-e-r-y* good."

She laughed and smacked Kennedy's arm playfully. "You're so bad. Just be careful—a lot of bikers don't play so nice."

"Smokey plays real nice in a very wicked way. Anyway, we're just in it for the fun. It's not like we call each other or go out to dinner or anything like that—we just hook up."

As they all laughed and talked, Olivia couldn't help but look around the bar for one particular face. Every time she scoped out the place and didn't find who she was searching for, her stomach would clench slightly.

It was ridiculous, really. She hardly knew her neighbor, and when she'd gone over to his house to assess Lucy's reading a few nights before, he hadn't even stayed in the room. He was nowhere to be found during the hour she'd spent with the girl. When their time together had finished, Animal had simply led her to the door, thanked her, and that was that. Olivia wasn't sure what she'd expected from that night, but it'd seemed that he wasn't interested in getting to know her. She'd been there for a job—determining Lucy's reading ability. She knew that going in, but what puzzled and irritated Olivia was why the hell she'd been bothered when he treated it that way.

He's not interested, that's all. Of course he looks at me—he's a man ... and a biker—a double whammy. It means nothing. I know that. Her dad had a different woman every weekend, and her brother had embraced the biker lifestyle when he'd patched in, especially the partying with so many women. *That's the way they are. Anyway ... I'd never get mixed up with him.* That should've been the end of it but it wasn't, because for reasons she couldn't understand why, Olivia kept hoping Animal would walk into the tavern. Forcing herself to concentrate on the conversation at the table, she drew in a deep breath and joined in on it.

After several minutes passed, Harper glanced around. "Where's the waitress?"

"I don't know." Olivia joined in on the search.

"It's easier to just get your drinks at the bar," Kennedy said.

"Says you," Olivia replied.

Ivy glanced at her phone, the fine lines around her mouth growing taut. She pushed away from the table. "I have to go," she said as she rose from her chair.

"What's up?" Olivia pointed at Ivy's phone.

"Nothing. It's just that Brady has some free time and wants to come over." Ivy slung the strap of her purse over her shoulder. "Lately he's been really busy, and we haven't had much time together."

"I thought he was cool with you going out tonight," Olivia said.

"He is ... but he misses me." A slight blush colored her cheeks. "I really have to go. It was fun."

Before Olivia could say anything, Ivy rushed away and disappeared into the crowd.

"Why the hell does she put up with that weirdo?" Harper asked, looking at her empty glass.

Olivia shook her head. "Who knows. They never go out, and he only comes over to her place."

"She's never been to his house?" Kennedy asked.

"No—strange, huh?" Olivia replied.

"Maybe he lives with a woman, or he could be married. I heard the creep has a couple of kids. Maybe he has a wife too," Harper said.

"Wouldn't we know that? I mean, Slavens is a small school and Pinewood Springs is far from being a big city," Olivia replied.

Harper picked up her empty tumbler, then set it back on the table. "He keeps to himself a lot at school. He rarely comes into the teachers' lounge, and then when he does, he doesn't speak to anyone."

"Just leers at the younger women." Kennedy rolled her eyes. "He's such a jerk. I still can't believe a nice woman like Ivy is involved with him."

"Well … to each her own. Olivia, do you want to come with me to get a drink from the bar?" Harper picked up her empty glass again.

She reached down and massaged her aching foot. Olivia had kicked off her shoes the minute she'd returned to the table earlier that night. Grimacing as she slipped them back on, she nodded.

"Cute shoes are always the most tortuous," Kennedy said.

"I know," Olivia groaned then stood up. "Let's go. Do you want anything?" she asked Kennedy.

"I'm good. I see that clean-cut guy I was talking to at the bar before Smokey pushed him away heading right to me. Take your time." She chuckled and sat straighter in the chair.

"Will do. I'm so damn thirsty—it must've been the cheesy tots. I bet I'll gain five pounds just from retaining water," Harper said.

Olivia laughed then followed her friend and, once again, pushed her way through the crowd until she found a space at the corner of the bar and leaned against it. That was when she saw *him.*

Animal reclined against the bar with his elbows propped on the counter behind him, and his head cocked to the side as he pretended to listen to what a redhead with big breasts was telling him while he kept throwing sidelong glances at Olivia. She stood staring at Animal's sexy self, laughing and flirting with the woman. The redhead reached up and touched his lightly stubbled chin, but he pushed it away then turned toward Olivia and their eyes met. The woman pulled his face toward hers, and he allowed it, but he kept checking Olivia out from the corner of his eyes.

In that instant, Olivia knew that Animal was the man she needed to keep at a distance. She didn't like the tremors he put in her stomach and the prickle of heat he caused on her skin. The lustful throbs deep between her legs and her quick intakes of breath were all warning signs that her body was ignoring the rule her heart and brain had imposed: don't get involved with any man. Her body wanted to get very close and personal with Animal, and it had nothing to do with looking for temporary intimacy and sex. This was about so much more. That's what made it so dangerous and scared the hell out of her.

Damn, she could feel her panties melting into her flesh from the look in his dark eyes. Those hot, furtive glances had Olivia licking her lips. She wanted to sashay over and push the redhead out of the way so she could run her hands under his tight T-shirt and let her fingers touch the corded muscles of his chest.

"Did you want another drink?" Harper asked.

"What?" she answered, her eyes fixed on Animal's mouth.

"A drink. *Hello?*"

Animal stared straight at her, his lips arrogantly curving up.

Turn the hell away. But she couldn't. She sat there locking gazes with him, the noise and people fading away and leaving only the two of them. His mouth softened and his stare grew more intense. A fire burned there, drawing her in until she was lost in the depths of his ebony gaze.

"Oh God, Olivia, don't go *there.*" Harper's loud and caustic voice drilled into her ear, dragging her out of the fervid moment she and Animal were sharing.

Olivia broke contact with the biker and looked at her friend. "Did you order?"

"Don't change the subject. Okay … Lucy's dad is hot—I'll give you that, but he's off limits for two big reasons." Harper moved in front of Olivia, blocking her view of Animal. "Number one—" She held up a finger. "He's a student's dad, and if you start messing around with him you'll get fired, and number two—" She held up another finger. "He's in an outlaw biker gang. *C'mon, really?* Even Kennedy wouldn't risk her job over a hot dad."

Olivia lightly swatted away her friend's hand that was in front of her face. "You're being a little overdramatic."

"From the way you two were looking at each other, I'd say I wasn't."

"Looking at some sexy eye-candy isn't the same as getting involved with him. Like I said, 'overdramatic.' Did you ever get the bartender's attention? I think we have to show some cleavage." Olivia laughed and stepped to the side of Harper, refusing to even glance for one millisecond at Animal. She'd acted like a lovestruck school girl instead of a mature woman, and that was unacceptable. There was something about her neighbor that made her behave out of character.

"Do you want another vodka martini?" Harper's voice broke into her thoughts.

The sandy-haired bartender tapped his index finger on the counter. "What'll you have, lady?"

Olivia blinked several times. "I guess I'll go with a cranberry vodka." The barman rushed away.

The two women chatted while they waited for their drinks, and Olivia kept her gaze focused on Harper the entire time.

"It looks like another band is ready to take the stage. The way they're dressed, I'd say they'll be playing hair metal songs," Harper said.

Olivia looked over her shoulder and saw five guys setting up their instruments, then she glanced over to where Animal and the redhead had been talking and noticed they were gone. Jealously pricked, which was irrational.

"Here you go. Are these together?" the sandy-haired man asked as he placed their drinks in front of them.

"Separate," Harper said.

"Do you want to open a tab?" he said.

"I don't," Harper replied as she looked at Olivia. "Do you?"

Olivia shook her head and handed him her credit card. Once they were all paid up, they headed back to their table. The band on stage was just about finished with its sound check when Olivia slid into her chair. Austin, the preppy-looking guy Kennedy had been talking to earlier had taken over Ivy's seat and was conversing with her, and another guy, who looked like he'd been cut from the same mold as Mr. Preppy, sat in a chair next to Harper. He immediately extended his hand and introduced himself as Darcy to both Olivia and Harper. Her friend smiled widely while she just kept a straight face. Darcy turned to Harper and began talking with her.

"Austin has another friend. He just went to get him," Kennedy said into Olivia's ear.

"No ... I'm not interested," she mumbled.

"How do you know—you haven't seen him. Anyway, no one's asking you to make a lifetime commitment to him." Kennedy picked up her glass and brought it to her mouth.

"I'm not in the mood to make small talk. The band's going to be starting, and I really don't want some guy shouting in my ear while I'm wondering what the hell he's saying."

"I'm definitely getting worried about you. Look at Harper—she's enjoying Darcy's company."

The lead singer announced his band, then a burst of electric guitars and drums filled the place. Suddenly the room seemed too small, too hot. Olivia felt like she was suffocating—she needed some air. She stood up and pointed toward the bathrooms and Kennedy nodded, her eyes sparkling as Austin and another cookie-cutter guy came over to the table.

Olivia grabbed her purse and made her way to the door, weaving through the throng of people yelling to each other over the blaring music.

Outside, the air felt cold and sweet. She stumbled away from a group of patrons smoking cigarettes and leaned against the brick wall, drawing in a deep breath. Olivia looked up into the night sky studded with stars, and suddenly realized that she had never been with a man who treated her well. So afraid of being alone, she'd settled for men who'd paid her compliments and attention while mistaking their carnal lust for love. All the men in her life had been different variations of her father: a bully, philanderer, and egotist.

"I'm perfect fodder for the psych couch. A fucking cliché," Olivia muttered under her breath, puffing out clouds that dissolved into nothing.

She shivered as goosebumps rose on her arms and rubbed her hands up and down them for warmth.

"Was the music too loud?" the deep, familiar voice murmured close to her ear.

Warm tingles shot through her traitorous body, and Olivia didn't like it one bit. Lost in her thoughts, she hadn't even heard Animal approach. She looked up and the soft expression on his face mesmerized her.

"You're fucking freezing," he said as his warm, strong arms slipped around her.

"I'm good," she answered through chattering teeth.

"The fuck you are."

"No, really." Another shiver racked her.

Without a word, Animal pulled open his leather jacket. In seconds she was wrapped inside, his body heat warming her skin. Her heart jumped and plummeted straight down to the pit of her stomach. Something she'd never felt in all her life ached inside her. Olivia shivered, but this time the cold had nothing to do with it.

"I didn't expect to see you tonight," he said, his breath hot on her skin.

She looked up at him and noticed a small silver hoop dangling from his right ear. A strong urge to suck his lobe into her mouth and run her tongue across the metal overwhelmed her.

"You don't look like a schoolteacher tonight," he added in a low voice. His dark eyes were on fire.

Heat stole up her neck and spread across her cheeks. "Is that a compliment?"

"Fuck, yeah." Animal's arms wrapped tighter around her.

He's Lucy's dad. What the hell is wrong with you? Her rational mind yelled at her, but her lascivious body leaned closer to him. Olivia knew that she should push him away and go back inside to join her friends, but it felt so right being in his arms. Yeah … totally nuts.

She pulled back just a bit. "Won't your date wonder where you are?"

Confusion marked his face, then a smirk curled up his lips. "The redhead? She was just some chick trying to get it on with me. Were you jealous?" Animal's intense stare bored into her.

Olivia cast her eyes downward. "No, why would I be? You can date whomever you like."

"You're not a very good liar." He chuckled. "Why the hell are you out here in the cold?"

"I needed a breather. There're too many people inside."

"Aren't you gonna keep *your* date waiting?"

This time it was her turn to be confused. "Date? I came with my girlfriends." Then she remembered the friend that Austin had brought over to the table. *So Animal was watching me.* A schoolgirl thrill rushed through her. "Oh, you mean that—"

"Suit and tie at your table."

"He's a friend of the guy who's hitting on my friend Kennedy. I don't know any of them." She tilted her head back and met his gaze. "Were *you* jealous?" She ran her tongue across her bottom lip and his eyes watched the movement.

Filled with lust and desire, the heat of Animal's gaze met hers, burning holes straight through her body and making her gasp. Before Olivia could react, he yanked her closer and crushed his mouth on hers. He tasted like whiskey and smelled of leather and something clean—like snow falling on evergreens.

Animal tangled his hand in her hair and jerked her head back slightly, intensifying the kiss. A low moan escaped from her parted lips and their breaths mingled before he slipped his tongue deep inside her mouth. Fiery. Passionate. Demanding.

Bright warning lights flashed in her brain, and Olivia wanted to pull away before she lost herself, but her body wouldn't let her. It was like all her senses had been seduced and she felt as if she were floating in a haze of sensual heat.

"Olivia," he whispered slowly, prolonging each syllable as if he were savoring them.

Never before had her name sounded so beautiful, so sexy, so wonderful as it did at that moment. Another moan broke from her lips as she leaned in for another kiss.

His cellphone rang loudly, jarring both of them, and he pulled back. "I need to get this."

When he slid the phone out of the front pocket of his jeans, she could see the word *HOME* on the screen, along with a picture of Lucy. Olivia groaned inwardly and the sexual fog enveloping her evaporated into the frigid night air. She pushed away from him, and he held up his hand gesturing her to wait a minute.

Animal spoke in a low voice on the phone, and Olivia only heard snippets of the conversation, which she gathered was about Lucy staying up later than her prescribed bedtime. As father and daughter hashed it out, humiliation pricked at Olivia's cheeks as she berated her reckless behavior with a student's father. *How could I let that happen? Kissing him in public in front of a bar.* She brought her shaking fingers to her temples and massaged the dull throbbing that would inevitably lead to a doozy of a headache.

The cold breeze brought on another onslaught of goosebumps, and without Animal's warmth, she shivered profusely. Deciding that her best move would be to go home, Olivia turned around and headed back to the bar to retrieve her coat and say goodnight to her friends. To say she was mortified by her actions would be the understatement of the year.

"Olivia," Animal called out to her.

Heavy footsteps came from behind her and she stopped. "I need to get back inside."

"Yeah, it's cold as fuck out here. I'll buy you a drink."

"No, thank you. I'm going home," she answered.

He grabbed her arm and spun her around so that she faced him. A faint scowl marred his perfectly shaped eyebrows.

"What the fuck?" he said.

"I'm tired, although I don't really owe you an explanation."

Animal shook his head. "Yeah, you do. Are you pissed off about the kiss?"

"Yes." She held her hand up to stop him from speaking. "Not at you, but at me. I overstepped the boundaries."

"What fuckin' boundaries? Yours?"

"Yes, and the school's as well. You're Lucy's dad and she's a student at Slavens. It should be pretty obvious why I'm upset at myself."

A smile whispered across his lips. "I'm not gonna tell, so there's no problem. Anyway, you're not Lucy's teacher."

A jolt of pain stabbed into the back of her skull like an ice pick. *Shit!* "This really isn't open for debate. I had too much to drink and I acted foolishly—end of story." She pressed the heel of her palm against the side of her head.

Animal glared, unblinking. "There's no fucking way you're believing that 'I'm drunk' bullshit. You don't wanna have some fun? That's cool with me. I got a hot redhead in there who's more than willing." He jammed his hands into the pockets of his leather jacket, and she saw a muscle jump in his jaw.

His words affected her like a slap in the face, and she was annoyed by it. "You're free to do whatever you like," she said through clenched teeth before stomping away from him.

A tidal wave of heat washed over Olivia when she entered the tavern. Another band was on stage setting up as she made her way to her table. Harper and Darcy were still talking with each other, and Austin had his tongue halfway down Kennedy's mouth as they clung to each other. *At least he's not a student's father. Shit.*

"Olivia did you get lost?" Harper asked, a rosy glow lighting her face.

"I just stepped out for some air. I've got a splitting headache, so I'm going to take off. Are you good?" She glanced at Darcy then back at Harper.

"I'm very good." Harper smiled broadly. "I'll call you tomorrow."

"Okay, great." Olivia slipped her arms through the sleeves of her coat then pointed at Kennedy. "Tell her I said bye—I don't want to disturb her."

Harper laughed and leaned in a bit closer to Darcy, who snaked his arm across the back of her chair. "I will. Drive safely. I hope you feel better."

"Thanks. I just need to get some aspirin in me."

Olivia walked through the tavern toward the front door, very much aware of Animal's penetrating stare on her. Outside, the cold night air circled around her bare legs as she strode across the parking lot. She slid into her car, locked the doors, and cranked up the heat. Leaning over, she took out a pair of gloves from the glovebox and slowly put them on. Her head was a throbbing mess, and all she wanted to do was wash the makeup off her face, change into her comfy pajamas, and go to bed.

The night had been a disaster, but what had made it the absolute worst was that Animal's kiss had showed her that every other one she'd had in her life had been wrong. *And I loved every single minute of it.*

Large white flakes began to fall as Olivia pulled out of the lot, and she switched on the windshield wipers. She stared straight ahead at the snow swirling in the headlights of the oncoming cars as she slowly made her way home.

CHAPTER TEN

FOR THE PAST two weeks, Animal had closed shutters and pulled blinds on the windows that faced south, essentially shutting out the view of Olivia's house. The way he figured it, he didn't need any fucked-up princess messing with his dick, so the less he saw of her, the better it was for the both of them.

Olivia had made it abundantly clear that she'd regretted their kiss, and the last damn thing he'd ever do was chase a chick who didn't want what he had to offer—a great fuck. The lame BS excuse about being Lucy's teacher didn't cut it with him, and she'd had the damn gall to blame the way she responded on being drunk that night. Animal decided that the good teacher had been scared of the passions he'd aroused in her when they'd kissed. And by the way she'd responded, there was no fucking doubt in his mind that he'd turned her the hell on.

Animal went to the sink and washed the breakfast dishes then reached for a dish towel. He briefly shook his head, then went about drying the plates and coffee mug and putting them into the heavy old cupboard his dad had given him when he'd bought the house. The wooden cupboard had belonged to his paternal grandmother who'd brought it back from her small village in Ireland.

He slid the dish towel off his shoulder and hung it over the oven door handle. "Fuck her," he muttered under his breath.

Anyway, Animal wasn't interested in her *type*: one who always played by the rules, believed sex equaled love, and drooled over the thought of being Mrs. Prince Charming. Give him a woman who held up her middle finger to authority and that's the one who got his blood pumping and his dick hard. Nah ... he didn't need the goody-goody next-door neighbor. There were too many other chicks to mess around with—willing, available women who didn't give a flying fuck what people thought.

Animal went into the family room and walked over to the coffee table strewn with magazines and books of motorcycles. He straightened up the stacks and set them on a bookshelf next to the fireplace. A blaring car alarm pierced the quiet, and Animal walked over to the window to see if there was any trouble. Olivia's car was parked on the driveway, and he could see the back of her head in the driver's seat, her arms moving like a frenzied bird flapping its wings. A few neighbors rushed out to see what the commotion was in the normally peaceful cul-de-sac.

Finally the noise stopped and Olivia stayed in the car for a long moment before she opened the door. Instead of turning away, Animal propped an elbow on the window frame and watched as she stepped out onto the driveway. He sucked in a sharp breath and stayed still for several seconds, staring at her.

She wore skinny jeans, short boots, and an oversized sweater that came right to her waist. Olivia popped open the trunk and leaned inside, showing off that luscious ass, and pulled out a large canvas bag filled with what looked like groceries. He watched her try to balance the bag on her knee while she grabbed for something else inside the trunk.

The sunlight filtering through the leaves dappled her skin, highlighting her hair. She straightened up, a sack of food in one hand and a plastic gallon of water in the other, and she looked up at the trees with her head tipped back. As sun rays shone on her face, and her long hair cascaded down her back, he wanted nothing more than to kiss her. *Fuck, she's beautiful.*

As if sensing his scrutiny, Olivia glanced his way. For a long second, they looked at each other. Animal noticed her green eyes, wide and startled, and the pinkish flush on her cheeks. Seeing her that way—surprised, rattled, and aware—went straight to his dick.

Olivia put the items in her arms down and turned to face him square on, a smile tugging at her lips, her chin lifting up in defiance, and her eyes sparkling ... with desire? Maybe, but whatever it was, it made him want to plummet himself into her, to touch and smell and taste her. *Fuck.* Animal took a deep, ragged breath and kept his gaze fixed on Olivia even after she turned around, picked up the groceries, and faded away into her house. He stayed and watched, hoping Olivia would come back out again. The seconds turned into long minutes, and still, he stood against the window just to catch a glimpse of her, but she never appeared.

The cellphone in his pocket vibrated just before he pushed away from the window. It was Jax letting him know that Lucy was having a good time at his house. Cherri had arranged a slumber party for their daughter, Paisley, and Lucy had been glowing from excitement for the past two days about the sleepover. Animal pretended not to notice, but whenever his daughter wasn't looking, a big grin broke out over his face. The best thing that had happened since Lucy had come to live with him was how Paisley had become her best friend. Sometimes, though, Lucy would come home after spending an afternoon at Jax's house and she'd be more sullen than usual. From some of the things Lucy had said about Paisley having "the best mother in the world," Animal surmised that when his daughter saw her new best friend and Cherri together, it reminded her that her own mother had abandoned her. Animal didn't know how to deal with those emotions any time they'd come up, so he usually tried to distract her. Video games and Legos seemed to do the trick.

He slid the phone back into his pocket, closed the blinds, and stared around the quiet house. This was the first time in five months that he was alone. It was liberating and Animal decided to make the most of it. It'd been way too long since he'd gone to a club party and hung out with his brothers. A night of booze, rock and roll, and sex sounded good to him. The memory of his kiss with Olivia and the way she looked at him earlier that day played through his mind. Animal rolled his neck and then his shoulders, the muscles tight. Maybe he just needed to get laid to thwart the tension that had been building since the sexy neighbor moved in next door.

He scooped up his jacket from the back of the chair and thrust his arms through the sleeves. Animal just needed an outlet for his sexual tension, and the club girls would be more than willing. It was about time he lived it up a little; he'd missed the parties, playing pool with his buddies, and being a damn bachelor. With Lucy gone for the night, he had every intention of living up to his road name. Animal had earned it with every chick he banged and every bottle of Jack he downed, and it was time—if only for a night—to reclaim his reputation.

Animal tossed the keys to his bike in the air and caught them as he made his way to the garage. He threw one leg over his black Harley-Davidson Fat Boy then rolled the bike to release the kickstand. The motorcycle roared to life then lurched forward as he sped down the street. He threaded through the streets until he hit the old highway road, then increased his speed. Cool air carrying the sweet scent of pine engulfed Animal while mountain streams, forests, and wildlife blurred past him as he swayed around tight curves. Animal had taken the long route to the club, enjoying the sun on his skin, the drone of the engine, and the *feel* of the ride. The past few weeks had been snowy, and busy, so he hadn't been able to take out his bike, which had driven him crazy. Now, with the temperature in the high 50s, Animal relished the opportunity to go for a long ride before he headed to the clubhouse.

Two hours later, he pushed down the kickstand, removed his sunglasses, and walked across the lot, the gravel crunching under his boots. It was still early in the afternoon and most of the brothers would be either passed out or still snoozing from the previous night's party.

Before he could pull out a chair, Hog, a prospect, rushed over and placed a shot of whiskey and a bottle of beer in front of Animal. Staring into the distance, he tilted his head back and let the whiskey burn down his throat, feeling—for the first time in two weeks—the sweet unknotting of relief.

"Hey, bro," Throttle said as he pulled out a chair and sat down. "I haven't seen you in a long time."

"Been busy," Animal replied.

"Yeah … How's the parenting thing going?"

He shrugged. "Okay. Are you staying for the party?"

"Nah … Kimber and I are heading to Vail in about an hour." Throttle tented his fingers in front of him.

"Are you guys taking the back roads?" Animal asked.

"Yep. We've been itching to go for the last damn month, but the weather's been for shit. We're gonna go over Canyon Way."

"Those backroads kick ass. I need to do something like that, but it's kinda hard now with the kid and all." He took a long pull on his beer.

"I haven't ridden them in a long time, and it'll be a first for my old lady. Where's Lucy tonight?"

"A sleepover at Jax's."

"Well, fuck you!" Smokey cried as he walked into the main room. "Are you just here for a pit stop, or are you gonna party tonight?"

"Party. You look like you did a bit of that last night." Animal chuckled.

"Damn—it was wild. Some of the guys from the Night Rebels stopped over on their way to Wyoming for the bike rally. Shit—I'm so damn hungover." Smokey sank down in the chair and put his head in his hands.

Throttle laughed then rose to his feet and patted Smokey on the shoulder. "I don't envy you, dude. I gotta go. Kimber and me are riding to Vail."

Smokey nodded and waved away the shot of Jack the prospect brought over. Hog then put it in front of Animal and asked Smokey what he wanted.

"A fuckin' Bloody Mary. I always have that when I'm fuckin' wasted," he replied, and Hog scurried off to make the drink.

Bones and Klutch walked in just after Throttle left. Animal bumped fists with them, then they plopped down on the chairs, joining him and Smokey.

"How's your dad?" Bones asked. His facial muscles were taut, and he kept fidgeting with his keyring.

"Good. What's going on?" Animal said.

"Just got some shit news. A friend of my sister's was found murdered in a small hotel just outside of Pinewood Springs. She was found tied up and stabbed. Fuck, she didn't deserve that. You met her," Bones said to Animal.

"Who was she?" he asked.

"Katie Sellers. Jada knows her. My kid sister's been freaked out and crying all day." Bones picked up the shot of tequila and swallowed it.

"That's fucked. I better give Jada a call. Do the damn badges have any idea who did it?"

"Not a clue." Bones gestured for another shot.

"As usual." Klutch snorted. "They couldn't find their asses with both hands."

"What was she doing at the hotel?" Animal asked.

"Anna said she didn't know. I guess Katie didn't tell anyone she was going." Bones picked up the second shot and threw it back.

"A woman goes to a hotel to get fucked," Smokey grumbled. "Find out who she was meeting and you got your goddamn killer. It fuckin' pisses me off when men do that shit. They're nothing but pussies who can't get it up without hurting a woman. Fuck!" He slammed his fist on the table then groaned and put his hand back on his head.

Animal couldn't help but think of his sister, and a stab of icy fear hit him in the gut. "Maybe it's an ex." He took out his phone, then rose. "I'll be right back—I gotta make a call."

He walked through the hallway and out onto the back porch, then tapped in Jada's number.

"Hey, Animal." Jada's voice was thick, as if she'd been crying.

His heart squeezed. "Bones just told me about your friend, Katie. That fuckin' sucks," he said in a low voice.

"I can't believe it." A few sniffles echoed through the phone. "You've met her a few times, remember?"

Animal couldn't place her. "Not really."

"She came to my birthday party last year, and she was at the carwash a few weeks ago when you came by to talk with Wheelie. The girl with the dark brown hair down to her shoulders. She was kind of freaked out by all your tats, remember?"

Katie's face became clearer in his mind and he nodded. "Oh, yeah. That was her? Fuck. She seemed like a real nice girl."

"She was. Why would anyone want to do this to her?" Her voice hitched and then she went quiet, and he could hear her crying.

"People are fucked up assholes." Each sob and gasp made him flinch. "I wish I knew what the fuck to say," he muttered.

"It's okay. Thanks for calling me. I'll be all right."

"Be careful. Don't ever go anywhere with a guy unless you really know him well, and even then, let me know."

Jada let out a soft laugh. "Yeah, that'll really work. I have a hard enough time with Dad screening my dates. I can't imagine what it'll be like if you get involved."

He chuckled. "I probably don't wanna know everything about your dates. But on a serious note, just let me know the name of the guys so I can screen them. There're too many twisted fuckers out there that it isn't enough to just be careful—you gotta be smart, armed, *and* careful."

"I know. Okay, if I'm really interested in a guy, I'll let you do a background check on him."

"That's all I'm asking." Silence fell between them, then he cleared his throat. "I gotta get going. You good?" he asked.

"I will be. Thanks for caring."

"Fuck, you're my little sister. Call me if you need anything."

"I will."

"Later."

Animal clicked off the connection and stared at the blank screen for a long time. Katie's face kept floating through his mind. He'd just seen her and now she was dead—brutally murdered by some fucked-up excuse for a human being. It wasn't like violence or brutal atrocities were alien to him. Living in an outlaw world, he'd learned to appreciate each day and look behind his back constantly. Death was always imminent, but that was the price each member of the Insurgents paid to live their life by their own rules—a lifestyle they were prepared for and would fight to the death for—but poor Katie was like a lamb going to the slaughter. She wasn't in tune with the dangers that lurked in the shadows, always waiting to seek and destroy the unwary. Life could be so fucked up.

Animal slid his phone back into his pocket and made his way back to the main room. He'd have to make sure Lucy was always safe, and he could already anticipate the fights they'd have when she started dating. Thankfully that was many years from now, but no matter what, he'd always keep his daughter safe. He had to—that's what fathers did. For a brief moment, Animal wondered if Katie's father felt like he failed her because he wasn't able to protect her.

Bones, Smokey, and Klutch were still at the table, but Charlotte and Lola had joined them. The women waved at Animal when he approached, and Lola grabbed his hand and pulled him down on the chair.

"Long time, baby," she cooed into his ear.

Moving away, he nodded. "Yeah—been busy."

Undaunted, Lola scooted closer. "Then you must be real tense, baby. I can relax you real good, you know that." She pressed her lips against his cheek.

Animal gently pushed her away. "Not now. Maybe later—I'm staying for the party."

Smokey raised his head up and stared at him. "What the fuck?"

Without answering, Animal took out his phone again and started fiddling with it, ignoring Smokey's hard gaze on him.

Lola raked her fingers through his hair. "Okay, baby. I'll look for you tonight." She turned to Klutch and brushed up against him.

Animal just wasn't feeling it. After all the bravado talk he'd given himself back at the house, he just wasn't down for it. *Maybe tonight. The thing about Katie killed it.* But he knew that was BS. What had killed it was his pretty neighbor who looked so beautiful and sexy in the sunlight.

Wanting to get a head start on his plan to get good and drunk that night, Animal motioned to Hog for another shot.

CHAPTER ELEVEN

LIGHT FROM THE computer screen glowed bluish-white in the darkened den as he scrolled through profiles of women who'd expressed interest in him. It'd been two weeks since he'd united body and soul with his lovely Katie and sated the hungry darkness inside him. That should have kept the beast at bay for a few months at least, but it didn't. The evil urge clawed its way up from his depths, craving and demanding more.

It's too soon. Taking off his glasses, he pinched the bridge of his nose. In the past six months, the darkness had been surfacing too frequently, and from the quarter-page article he'd read in the *Pinewood Springs Tribune*, he knew the police from the surrounding counties were comparing notes.

The man slammed his fist on the desk, angry at the sloppiness of his last kill. There had to be some way for him to control his impulse, to keep it under wraps for a longer time, but he knew he was only kidding himself. The darkness had a mind of its own, and it was so damn relentless.

Shaking his head, the killer focused his attention back to the screen. A frustrated sigh pushed through his pursed lips while a carousel of different women's pictures blurred by as he clicked the mouse. Not one of them was even remotely satisfactory, let alone perfect. A thin film of sweat beaded along his hairline and he ground his teeth. He'd been slouched over the computer for the past two hours and nothing to show for it. The thought of searching for a new dating site crossed his mind, but he quickly dismissed it. One of the main reasons he'd chosen *Discreet Passion* was the messaging system. He could conduct all his chats through instant messenger in live time and not leave a record of his conversations. A lot of the women wanted to exchange emails, but he'd have none of that. Once the beast had been fed, he deleted the women's profiles from his hard drive, and then go in search of another perfect lady.

But tonight is a bust. Closing his eyes, he tipped his head back and dug his fingers into the back of his neck, massaging a growing headache. It seemed like it was getting harder to find the perfect woman.

Suddenly the door pushed open, and the light from the hallway spilled into the room. His eyes snapped open and heat flushed through his body.

"What're you doing in the dark, honey?" his wife asked as she switched on the floor lamp next to the leather wingback chair.

Nostrils flaring, he quickly clicked out of the open window and closed the lid of the laptop.

"I've told you to never come in here while I'm working," he gritted.

His wife brought her hand to the base of her throat and shook her head. "I'm sorry, but Tristan wants you to read him the story you started last night."

His wife stood tall and lean, her arms folded across her small breasts, her lips red from the matte lipstick he hated, and her too-tanned face looked so fucking earnest. For a fleeting moment, she disgusted him, and he wanted to reach across the room and pummel her with a ferocity that scared him. This was his Frou-Frou ... what was he thinking?

"He doesn't want me to read it," she said, taking a few steps back toward the door. It was as if she could sense his thoughts.

Ashamed of himself, he pushed up from the chair. "Of course I'll read to him. Reading is so important in the education of a child. Did you have Aaron read aloud for you?"

Frou-Frou nodded. "He's doing so much better since Olivia's been working with him."

"Olivia is very good at what she does." The image of the teacher's assistant with her captivating green eyes, curvy body, and long brown hair sent a rush of heat to his groin.

In the past six months, he'd found himself avoiding her as much as he could at work. He couldn't risk doing something stupid with someone he knew, but it'd become increasingly hard to keep the urge to be with her at bay.

"What are you thinking?" His wife laughed. "You seem so … distracted."

The killer slipped his arm around his wife's neck and pulled her to him, brushing his lips against hers. "Nothing really. I just have a full week of meetings. I'm looking forward to the weekend. Maybe we can all go to Silverton for lunch and take a ride on the train."

A smile spread across her face. "Tristan and Aaron would love that—they're crazy for the steam engine. I'd enjoy it too." She pecked his cheek lightly.

"Then it's settled."

They walked out of the den and climbed the stairs to the second-floor bedrooms.

Thirty minutes later, he switched off Tristan's light and closed the door halfway, then sauntered down the hall to the master bedroom. He walked into the room, shutting the door behind him, and found Frou-Frou propped up in bed with two pillows behind her back, reading a magazine.

She glanced up at him. "Did you finish the book?"

"Yes. Tomorrow night he wants you to start a new one with him." He unbuttoned his shirt.

His wife stared at him as he took off his clothes, and the desire in her gaze rushed through him. The man had been holding his hunger at an arm's length for the past week, and it had grown even more since his disappointment in not connecting with the right girl that evening.

Frou-Frou put the magazine down on the nightstand and slipped out of bed and padded into the bathroom. By the time she came out, he'd stripped down to his boxers. She threw him a small smile, and he watched her move over to the walk-in closet and hang up her robe. *She could never just throw it on the floor, or on a goddamn chair.*

"Did you close the door tightly?" she asked as she walked over to one of the lamps on the nightstand and switched it off.

The brown-haired man softly walked up behind her. "Yes." He gently squeezed her shoulders and let his hands fall down to her pert breasts. He pressed her closer to him and brushed his lips against her ear. "I need you," he whispered.

His wife turned around in his arms and faced him. Leaning into him, she pressed her mouth against his, but he stepped back as anger pricked his nerves.

"I'm sorry," she mumbled. "I got caught up in the moment and forgot."

He didn't say anything but his gaze stayed on her as she ambled over to the other lamp on the nightstand by her side of the bed. An aggressive lover appalled him, and he'd made it quite clear to his wife from the beginning of their marriage that he'd have none of it. *He* was the hunter, and his wife was the ... well ... she was the prey, and that's the way he liked it. To be in control at all times and the one to do most of the touching during lovemaking was what he required and *needed*.

The light went out and moonlight poured in from the window, illuminating his wife's body. In the alabaster glow, his wife's skin appeared pale, almost ghostly, and beckoned him. As he walked over to her, images of Katie, Melanie, and so many other lovely women entombed in his brain flashed through his mind.

He reached over and yanked Frou-Frou to him, and a startled gasp flew from her parted lips as she landed against him with a *thud*.

"Honey, I—"

Two fingers rested on her mouth. "Don't say anything," he said in a low voice.

She wore a red satin gown that clung to her body, and he slowly slipped the straps down, peppering kisses across her neck and shoulders as he did so. He watched as the gown slid down to the floor and she stepped out of it, her nakedness glowing in the soft white light.

For a long moment he stayed there, immobile, drinking in her love-liness, imagining the softness of her skin, relishing the dark craving rising to the surface. Then he pushed her down on the bed and took off his boxers. Satisfaction coursed through him when his wife gasped at his erection.

At that moment, he was Hunter and she was one of the young beau-ties he met online. He ran his hands up and down her trembling body, then lowered his head and slipped her nipple into his mouth and bit hard … very hard. She cried out in pain. It was the sound Hunter had been waiting for—it was music to his ears. He grabbed her legs and bent them at the knees, forcing them open wide—oh, so wide. He tuned out her whimpers, her soft pleas, and rammed into her so hard that it took the breath out of him.

The beast had come to life.

It was his wife's strangled gasps and her nails clawing at his hands that dragged him out of his climax, and his eyelids flew open. Horror spread through him when he saw his hands around his beloved Frou-Frou's neck choking the life out of her. The man immediately let go and rolled away, then pulled her into a loving embrace as she coughed and gulped air into her lungs.

Mortified, he stroked her upper back and murmured sweet and loving words to her. How could he let the darkness do this to his wonderful and patient wife? A lump of fear coiled in the pit of his stomach, and his heartbeat pounded like a train barreling down the tracks. *What would've happened if I hadn't stopped?* The answer to that chilled him to the bone. He had to find another beauty very soon; otherwise the beast would devour Frou-Frou and destroy his life.

With his wife now peaceful in his arms, he fell into a troubled sleep.

CHAPTER TWELVE

OLIVIA READ OVER her profile on *Discreet Passion*, made sure the blurred image of her face was concealed enough so she wasn't recognizable to someone who'd know her, and pushed the *PUBLISH* button. She inhaled and exhaled deeply as she stared at the screen. Within a few seconds of her profile going live, several men had sent her messages and many "winks"—a way of flirting in cyberspace. The whole thing kind of creeped her out, but her psychology professor, Dr. Davison, loved the premise of her research paper and was looking forward to seeing what her data turned up.

Olivia knew she'd lucked out in having Dr. Davison as her advisor, and even though the classes were online, she'd meet with him several times over the past few months. The professor was good-looking, had two cute kids, and was totally devoted to his wife.

Some women get all the luck with men ... unlike her, who kept attracting abusive, egotistical jerks, or bikers. Animal came to mind, right in front of Iceman. She shivered at the thought of the big, brooding biker in her dad's MC. For reasons she still didn't understand, her dad had gotten it into his drug-induced mind that Iceman would be the perfect man for her. He even went as far as to arrange a marriage with the biker. Yeah ... It was like her dad and Iceman were frozen in a medieval time warp. Leo and Iceman had been tight, so her brother was no help in dissuading the dude that she was most definitely not old lady material.

Leo ... I miss you so much. Learning that her neighbor was a member of an MC stirred up all sorts of things from her past. Even though most of the memories of her dad's MC were bad, the times she spent with Leo at the clubhouse, riding on his bike, going to motorcycle rallies, and even having a blast at a few of their wild parties were all good times, and she missed them. Even though she had some close friends in Pinewood Springs, a good job, and a new house, she still felt like a fish out of water sometimes. She missed San Diego, the beach, her friends, and the familiarity that comes from being a native of a city. And she especially missed Leo.

Her cellphone rang, bringing her out of her thoughts, and she grabbed it off the desk.

"Hello?"

"Didn't you know it was me?" Kennedy asked.

"I didn't look at the caller ID."

"Whatcha doing?"

"I just finished putting up my profile," Olivia answered.

"Awesome! Has anyone poked you yet?"

"Yeah, it's unbelievable. I was going to look them over, but I'm not feeling it right now. I think I'll get back to it tomorrow. What're you up to?"

"Going to a party in a bit."

"That sounds like fun. Who's throwing it? Anyone I know?"

Kennedy laughed. "Not really. I'd ask you to come along only I don't think it's up your alley."

"Try me. I'm sitting here with nothing to do, and it's a Saturday night. Pathetic, huh?"

"I thought you and Harper do stuff on Saturdays," Kennedy said.

"We usually do, but she's got a date with that guy we met at Blue's Belly a couple of weeks ago."

"Really? That's good. What was his name?"

"Darcy. She's gone out with him a couple of times. So far she says he seems decent. Are you still seeing Austin?" Olivia asked.

"No way. He was fun for a few times, but neither of us wants anything serious, and he wasn't *that* good to have a friends-with-benefits type of situation."

"Well, at least you know what you want. So why won't I like this party you're going to?"

"It's a biker party at the Insurgents' clubhouse. Remember I told you I go there sometimes? Well, seeing Smokey at the bar that night we were all there made me want to go back for a wild time. It's not your style."

Olivia walked over to the window and peeked out through the sheet at her neighbor's house. The lights in the family room and kitchen were on as well as in one of the bedrooms upstairs—Lucy's, she supposed. *Animal won't be at the party.* A tendril of disappointment curled through her, making her antsy.

During the past two weeks, she'd worked hard on avoiding Animal, even ducking into classrooms when she'd see him come into the school to drop off Lucy. Olivia had felt like a damn criminal who was evading arrest, but she couldn't risk being in contact with him. Each time she had, he'd pulled her into his web, and it was getting harder and harder to break away from it. The kiss they'd share touched something inside Olivia that scared the living crap out of her. *So, why do I wish Animal would be at this party?* Her body was the ultimate betrayer, that's why.

"Hello?"

Olivia cleared her throat. "I'm here," she said.

"I thought maybe the call went into a dark cyber-hole." Kennedy chuckled. "From your silence, I think you may be considering going to the party."

"Maybe. Is it just the local club or will other chapters be there?"

"Look at you … I'm guessing you've been watching too many *Sons of Anarchy* reruns."

Olivia stomach tightened. "Guess so. Will there be any other chapters or affiliate clubs there?"

"I don't think so. I'm really not sure what an affiliate club is, but I think it's just a regular Saturday night party."

"Are the guys cool or do they force themselves on women not wearing a patch?" Olivia glanced out the window again. Everything was the same. Usually, when she was spying, she'd see Lucy's silhouette by the window or crossing by it, and Animal usually stepped on the front porch for a joint at least a couple of times a night, especially when it was dark like it was now. *Maybe he is at the party and Lucy's at her grandparents' house.*

"The guys aren't like some biker clubs, but you will get hit on a lot. It's a definite boost to a woman's confidence." Kennedy giggled. "A perfect place to be after getting dumped by a boyfriend."

"If I decide to go, I'll follow you. I don't want to stay long, and if things gets dicey, I'll be able to leave. I'm pretty sure you'll be busy." *Why am I even considering this?* Something was drawing her to it—had been for a while now.

"That's cool. A friend of mine, Gertie, she's coming with me. She *loves* biker boys."

"I don't think I've ever met her," Olivia said.

"You haven't. She's my wild-side friend. She's even crazier than I am … a lot crazier. So, are you in?"

Olivia blew out a big breath. "Yeah, I guess so."

"I *never* thought you'd go to a biker party. This is so surprisingly refreshing, Olivia. Oh, don't wear anything too revealing unless you want to do nothing but fight off a bunch of horny guys." Kennedy sniggered.

I know the rules all too well. "Okay, thanks for the tip. What time are you heading over there?"

"I've got to pick Gertie up first, then I'll swing over to your place at around nine o'clock. Does that sound good?"

"I'll be ready."

"Great. See you then."

The minute Olivia ended the call, she regretted her decision. Going to an outlaw biker party on a Saturday night? "Are you fucking nuts?" she said aloud. She glanced again at Animal's house. "Just say hello the next time you see him, but going to a party at his clubhouse is insane." Rationally, Olivia knew that, but she had a strong desire to watch the men in leather from her perch on a barstool just like she'd done many times at the East Bay Dogs MC. Although, at those parties, she'd had the protection of her father and Leo, and the other members kept their distance from her.

Technically, Olivia was a rival of the Insurgents since her dad's club was aligned with the Grim Henchmen out of Oakland, and the Insurgents' San Diego chapter was aligned with the Angry Disciples in L.A. The Henchmen and the Disciples were sworn enemies, but none of that mattered to Olivia.

She would have a couple of beers and then go home and enjoy a romantic comedy—maybe *Legally Blonde.* That was her go-to movie whenever she didn't know what to watch. Glancing at her phone, Olivia saw that she had plenty of time for a leisurely shower and a bite to eat before readying herself for the night ahead. She drew in a deep breath and blew it out, then headed to the bathroom.

OLIVIA SAT IN the clubhouse's parking lot struggling to calm the fluttering in her stomach. "Everything's going to be all right," she muttered as she pretended to look for something in her glove box. Kennedy and Gertie were standing beside the passenger door, and the latter didn't look too pleased to be kept waiting.

Kennedy rapped on the window. "Did you find what you're looking for?"

"We have to get in there," Gertie said, rolling her eyes as she spritzed another dose of hairspray over her locks.

Going through the screening process at the front gate had been bad enough with three bikers raking their eyes over her to see whether she would be a good addition to the party. Wearing black jeans and a loose button-up purple blouse, Olivia had stuck out like a sore thumb amid all the women in micro miniskirts and barely-there tops, and she honestly thought the men were going to turn her away, but they'd jerked their head and she'd passed through.

Now she was only feet away from entering the clubhouse, and she wanted to throw up. Willing herself to calm the hell down, Olivia slammed the glove box, shoved her keys into her small crossbody purse, and slid out of the car.

"It's about time," Gertie huffed as she readjusted her breasts in her tiny top. "Let's go."

She marched ahead, and Olivia grabbed Kennedy's arm. "Stay with me for a while at the bar, okay?"

"Of course. I wouldn't leave a newbie to all the wolves." Her friend giggled, looping her arm through Olivia's, and they walked toward the club.

The strong smell of weed and cigarettes mixed with cheap perfume, curled around Olivia when she entered the crowded room. As she tagged behind Kennedy and pushed through the mob of men in denim and leather, Olivia kept her eyes downcast, refusing to meet those of any of the bikers'. When Olivia reached the bar, she was acutely aware of the stares and comments of the male onlookers. Not paying them any attention, she slipped onto a barstool and propped her elbows on the counter.

"What'll you have, sweet piece?" a buffed man asked from behind the bar.

From the absence of patches on the front of his cut, she knew he was a prospect. "A Coors Light is good."

The biker threw his head back and laughed. "We don't got any piss beer here, baby."

"A Coors then." Olivia had forgotten that light beer was akin to poison to outlaws.

Kennedy was already talking to a couple of good-looking men, who, every once in a while, stared blatantly at Olivia. Shifting her focus, she looked out over the crowd and could easily spot the club girls. With their dyed hair, short skirts, ample cleavage, heavy makeup, and stilettos, they all looked the same. Most of the hangarounds looked like women who came out to party with a bunch of testosterone-driven men who promised them a night they'd never forget. *Everything's the same, except the MC's name is different.* The club parties were played out in thousands of clubhouses across the country, and she'd bet all the men and women looked the same.

"Are you having a good time?" Kennedy asked as she glanced at Olivia over her shoulder.

"Yeah." She picked up the beer bottle and brought it to her lips.

This was all so familiar. She could almost hear Leo's rumbling laugh and smell the lingering cigarette smoke on his cut. Amid the cacophony of noise: blaring rock music, women's laughter, men's voices, clinking bottles, and the roar of bikes mingling together, Olivia swore she could feel the presence of her brother. Tears welled up in her eyes, and she lowered her head and quickly brushed them away with her hand.

"Hey, baby," a voice said behind her.

Olivia swiveled around on the stool and met the pale blue eyes of a ruggedly handsome biker. Her fingers curled tighter around the beer bottle.

"I haven't seen you around here before." He leaned in closer as she scooted near the edge of the barstool.

"I came with a friend," she replied. Her gaze landed on his cut; his road name, Hubcap, was displayed right above the diamond-shaped one-percenter patch.

"You're mighty fine-looking." Hubcap winked at her and snaked his arm around her waist.

Olivia gently pushed it away. "Thanks, but I'm just here for a drink then I'm heading home."

The blond-haired biker jerked his head back. "What the fuck? Why the hell did you come here if you're not gonna have some fun?"

Knowing this situation was a bit sticky, Olivia waved her hand nonchalantly. "I just came by to say hi to my friend, Animal."

"Animal? You his sweet piece for tonight?"

"Not exactly—we're friends, like I said."

Hubcap motioned the prospect to get a drink for him and Olivia, then ran his eyes up and down her body, slowly. Nodding, he handed her another bottle of beer. "Yeah—you're his neighbor. Fuck, Smokey wasn't shitting—you're one helluva sexy woman."

Smokey's got a fucking big mouth. "Right. Anyway, since he's not here, I'm going to probably leave after this drink." Olivia hoped Hubcap got the hint, and with her naming a club member, she hoped the biker would respect that and back the hell off.

"He's around. You better sit tight and wait 'til you see him since you're not wearing his patch. Dudes around here will think you're fair game."

"I know the score." The beer mixed with her nerves turned her stomach.

Hubcap nodded, but his gaze was fixed on a curvy brunette swaying to the music next to the bar. Without saying another word, he walked away. Less than a few seconds later, he had his arm wrapped around the woman and they were kissing up a storm.

Olivia looked away and glanced around the room, feeling self-conscious and desperate. When she didn't think Animal was there, she felt okay, but now that Hubcap confirmed he was, she felt like a fool. Pushing away the half-empty bottle, Olivia tapped Kennedy on the shoulder.

"I'm going to head out."

Kennedy's eyes widened. "Why? We just got here."

"Not really—we've been here for about forty minutes. Anyway, you were right—this isn't my scene. I shouldn't have come."

"If you're sure. Do you want me to get Smokey to walk you to your car?"

Olivia shook her head. "I'll be fine. See you at school on Monday."

Kennedy nodded then turned back to the two men she was talking with, and Olivia wiped her sweaty hands on her jeans and fished for her car keys in her bag.

"What the fuck are you doing here, Teach?" Animal's voice poured over her like warm melted chocolate.

Hubcap. These guys are like a bunch of cackling hens! Olivia spun around, a snappy retort on the tip of her tongue, but his burning eyes held her still.

"Do you fucking know how stupid it is to be in here?" Anger rippled off him as he took a step closer to her.

Olivia dragged her gaze away and shook her head. "I don't know why *what I do* is any of your damn business."

"Because I know the danger you're in, *Teach*. You think this is some college frat party?"

Refusing to look at him, she glanced over at the jukebox and saw Kennedy dancing very close to one of the guys she was talking to earlier. Hubcap and the brunette were fused at the hip, and several couples and trios were going full force in sexual explorations.

"Again ... why the *fuck* are you here? Did you come to see me?" His face softened and he leaned enough that their shoulders kissed. "I'm down for that, but you should've let me know you were coming. I thought you were fucking pissed at me."

"I am." She moved away and propped her elbow on the bar.

Animal waved his hand around the room. "You could've fooled me."

The smugness in his voice irked her and, for the umpteenth time, she regretted her decision to show up that night. But of course he'd think that—anyone would, and the fact that a part of her had come in hopes of seeing him niggled at her. Olivia knew she was giving Animal mixed signals, but that was because her brain and her body weren't acting in concert—they were giving *her* mixed signals.

"The truth is, my friend asked me to come, and I had nothing better to do, so here I am. I quickly realized that I made a mistake." She took out her car keys. "I was just ready to leave when you came over." Olivia slid off the stool. "Goodnight."

Animal's fingers wound around her upper arm, and as he put his mouth close to her ear, warm breath sent sparks through her body. "I'll walk you out, and saying no isn't an option."

She nodded and relaxed in his grip. As he guided Olivia through the maze of people toward the entrance, some of the bikers and a few of the women openly stared at her, then at Animal, and then back at her.

Animal opened the door and Olivia stepped through it. The night's cold air was especially refreshing after having spent time in the hot and stuffy clubhouse. Groups of men huddled in front of the brick walls, smoking joints and cigarettes, several of them calling out to Animal. He raised his fist in the air as he continued walking, his other hand still around her arm.

The two of them moved in silence, and she could hear needles and gravel crunch beneath their feet and smell pine in the air. When they arrived at her black Ford Fiesta, he took the keys from her hand and unlocked the door.

"Thanks for watching out for me," she said, her breath coming out in wisps of steam that dissipated rapidly in the frosty air. Olivia turned away to open the car door.

"No problem," he said in a low voice.

As she pulled open the door, Animal shut it, then placed his hands on her shoulders and swung her around to face him. His dark eyes held her gaze, and the ground crunched beneath him as he stepped closer. When she backed up, her butt bumped against the side of the car.

"I have to get going," she whispered.

He blocked her movements as she tried again to open the car door. He leaned closer, his scent twisting around her. Olivia's stomach did a somersault, and internally, she cursed it. Why did she have to be so damn attracted to him?

Animal's finger lightly tapped against her scalp. "What's going on in that pretty head of yours?" His intense gaze heated her skin, and the air between them seemed electrified.

"Just … that this is wrong," she managed to get out.

"Is it?" His eyes drifted to Olivia's lips and her breath caught in her throat.

In one swift movement, Animal yanked her close, her soft curves molding to the contours of his hard, muscled body. He crushed his mouth to hers, devouring her while his tongue plundered.

Olivia's hands slipped under his jacket and moved up his back; her fingers dug into his shoulder blades as she hung on, barely able to stand upright on her wobbly legs. A quiver ran through her as his hands swept down past her hips, cupped her ass, squeezing with urgency.

"Fuck, you're beautiful," he murmured.

His ran his tongue against her lips, nipping them and arousal washed over her, hot and thick and seductive. Olivia leaned into Animal and kissed him back with all the desire she felt for him at that moment.

As his hands slid up her blouse and curved around her breast, Olivia softly moaned into his mouth and sank her fingers in his hair. He rubbed her nipple through the purple top, the scraping fabric making it ache and harden. With his other hand, Animal moved her hair aside and lightly nibbled on the sensitive pulse beneath her ear. She groaned and lolled her head to the side, giving him better access. His lips peppered kisses over her skin, trailing a path down to her collarbone.

"I shouldn't be doing this," she whispered without budging. She licked her lips and tasted him.

He tweaked her nipple as she uttered the words, and she tipped her head back and moaned.

"What we do is between us alone—fuck everything else," he said as lips moved further down.

"But Slavens—Lucy." Olivia closed her eyes, relishing in the sensations burning through her.

"Stop overthinking this. Go with your gut—logic's fucking overrated."

Animal's mouth replaced his hand and he kissed her through the blouse, wetting the fabric with his tongue as he flicked her pebbled bud. With each burst of desire, she tugged at his hair, squirming against him. It had been a long time since Olivia had been with a man, and the way Animal woke up her body in such a short time was unlike anything she'd ever experienced.

A groan rumbled from his chest and the small sound sent a shockwave of need through her. She pulled his head up and their gazes locked;

the smoldering lust in his eyes sent shivers down to her toes.

"Olivia," he growled then pressed his mouth to hers.

I have to stop this. But that rational thought flitted out of her head the instant his hand slid over her hip and rested on her thigh. She briefly acknowledged that she was in trouble—*big* trouble—when his fingers inched away from her thigh and cupped her pulsing sex through her jeans. The thought slipped away on a moan as she arched into him, feeling his hard dick pressing against her.

"Fuck, baby, I bet you're real wet." His words smothered on her lips.

The loud ringtone of a cellphone made Olivia jolt. At first she didn't move and simply clung to Animal, who also remained still, but the phone kept ringing, urging someone to answer it.

"Fuck it to hell," he muttered under his breath as he pulled away from her a bit and jammed his hand in the back pocket of his jeans.

Olivia watched as he glanced at the screen, and she saw a frown pull his brows together just above the bridge of his nose.

"Yo," he said as he broke away from her and walked over to a large evergreen tree. The volume of his voice dropped, and she could barely make out any words.

Mental clarity replaced the sexual haze that had enveloped her. Olivia breathed in the cool pine air, felt it rush into her lungs, and puffed it out with a cloud of frost. *Saved by the ringtone.* She smoothed down her hair, snapped closed her jacket, and ran her finger over her lips, still swollen from Animal's lethal kisses.

The car door opened with a click, and Animal looked over and held up his hand to her as if gesturing her to wait. Olivia knew what waiting would bring, and she couldn't go there *again*. Animal was a hard man to resist, and despite her best intentions, it seemed like she was always caving in. If she wasn't careful, she'd fall hard for him then be nursing one of the biggest heartaches of her life when he kicked her to the curb. *Like Dad did with Mom. He destroyed her—broke her into a million pieces so she gave up on living.*

The door slammed shut and she turned the ignition. Animal strode over to her and knocked on the window.

"What the fuck? I *had* to take that call. Don't take it personally," he said.

"I didn't." She smiled.

Confusion rolled over his face. "Do you wanna fuck in the car? I thought we'd go to my old room—it's more comfortable."

Ah … there's the biker. "That was so romantically put, but I think I should go."

Animal scratched his head. "Why? I know you want some, baby."

"It's late. I'll see you at school on Monday, and we can talk about Lucy's reading assessment."

He shoved his hands into the pockets of his leather jacket. Anger plastered against his face, and his look went through her like an icy blow.

"I'm sorry. It's just—"

"Forget it, baby. You don't know what the fuck you want. Well, I'm dropping out of your goddamn schoolgirl games. Getting pussy's no problem." He looked over his shoulder in the direction of the clubhouse. "Plenty of chicks wanna play in there."

"I've had some bad experiences …" Her voice trailed off.

"Save it." He shrugged. "You don't owe me any explanations. As a matter of fact, you and I don't owe each other shit." He stomped his feet on the ground, puffs of steam streaming from his mouth. "Go on—I'm not gonna stop you."

She looked up and their eyes met, then Olivia turned away from him, backed out of the parking space, and drove away. In her rearview mirror, she saw Animal watching her until she turned onto the road and the trees and darkness filled in the distance between her and the club.

"I did the right thing," she said aloud.

Then why in the hell did it feel so wrong?

CHAPTER THIRTEEN

ANIMAL STOOD OUTSIDE the door, listening to Lucy's muffled cries and hoarse gasps, and he didn't move. Each sob was like a stab to his gut and his heart. Not knowing what to do or say to his daughter, he almost retreated until he heard something crash on the floor. He knocked softly before he opened the door.

Lucy sat cross-legged on a pink and green striped comforter, clutching her worn out rainbow llama—Cuddles. The room was a complete mess. It looked like a cyclone had just struck. All of the throw pillows and the window seat cushions were on the floor. Broken pieces of a white dresser lamp littered the floor along with video games, books, and several LEGO designs. A bent and twisted dark pink lampshade laid next to one of the lime-green painted walls, and Lucy's beloved musical ballerina jewelry box was perched precariously on the edge of the dresser.

For a few seconds, Animal stood at the doorway watching as his daughter's head hung disconsolately on her chest, her fingers digging into Cuddles.

He crossed the room and moved the jewelry box to the middle of the dresser then sat on the edge of the bed.

"What's going on, kiddo?" he asked.

Lucy sniffled then wiped her nose with her hand, but she didn't answer.

Animal pressed his lips together and reached out and touched her knee. Lucy jumped and scooted away. He slowly rose to his feet and began picking up the chaos on the floor, and from the corner of his eye, he saw Lucy watching him.

After he finished cleaning up and vacuuming the floor and rug, he pulled out the desk chair and sat down. Leaning back, he laced his fingers over his chest and let out a long sigh. The room was quiet like a tomb, and Animal sat waiting for his daughter to acknowledge him. After several long minutes, she looked over at him and they locked gazes.

"Do you want to tell me why you're upset?" he said in a low voice.

"I want to go home," she mumbled, tugging her braid with her free hand.

Animal scrubbed his face with both hands. "I know," he replied.

"I miss, Mom." Lucy's voice quivered.

He wiped his palms on his jeans. "I'm sorry that you feel bad, and I bet it's hard not having your mom around."

"Why doesn't Mom call me?" She wiped her nose again with her hand.

Animal pulled out a tissue from the box then walked over to the bed and handed it to her. Lucy took it without looking at him, and he perched on the bed next to her.

"I'm not sure, kiddo, but sometimes parents get caught up in their lives and forget about their kids. It doesn't mean she doesn't love you, it's just that she's settling down."

Lucy looked up, a small frown forming on her face. "That doesn't make sense."

He nodded. "You're right. I wish I could make this easier for you."

"Why doesn't Mom love me?"

Animal placed a tentative hand on his daughter's shoulder and when she didn't flinch away, he drew her to him.

"Your mom loves you. She's just having a hard time right now."

Lucy buried her face in his chest. "I must've been really bad." Her small sob muffled into his shirt.

Hot anger pricked his skin and his mind. "You're not bad, kiddo. I think you're great, and so does Aunt Jada, Grandma and Grandpa, Jax, Cherri, Hawk, Smokey ... Damn, I could go on for a long time, just telling you how many people think you're pretty awesome." She leaned silently against him. "I can also tell you how glad I am that you're with me. I tried to reach out to you so many times over the years."

"Mom told me you didn't care. You never called me."

He placed two fingers under Lucy's chin, tilting her head back so she had to look at him. "I called you, sent you cards, presents on your birthday and Christmas—the whole nine yards. Your mom and I didn't have a good relationship, and I'm afraid you were caught in the middle. I'm sorry about that, but I want you to know that I'm damn happy you're with me." He bent down and kissed the top of her head. "I love you, kiddo, and I'm not ever leaving you."

"Promise?" she whispered.

"Promise." Animal hugged her close and she wrapped her arm around his waist. He wished he could glue back together Lucy's broken heart or give her a potion to erase away her pain, but he couldn't.

She pulled away and climbed off the bed then padded over to the dresser and opened one of the drawers in her jewelry box. Then she took something out and walked back to the bed.

"Here," she said, handing Animal a feather.

"Where did you get this?" he asked as he took it from her.

"I found it the other day at school after some of the kids were saying I don't have a mom. Ms. Mooney said that my feather meant that an angel was near."

Animal rolled the soft feather between his fingers. "She said that?"

"Uh-huh. Do you believe in angels?"

"I guess. I never really thought about it, but it's not common to find a feather in the winter."

"That's what Ms. Mooney said."

Warmth spread through him. "Did you feel better after you found it?"

"Uh-huh. Ms. Mooney said that a white feather is one of the best."

"She said that?" The memory of how Olivia felt in his arms flooded his senses with pleasure.

"Yeah."

The thought of her voice whispering in his ear, the scent of her perfume curling around him, the softness of her lips pressing against his, and the feel of her tits in his hands were all playing havoc on him at that moment.

"Dad?"

Animal jerked his head back and scattered away the images. "Yeah?"

"Do you like it?"

He looked down at the palm of his hand. "I do, but it's yours."

"I want you to have it."

Heat radiated through his chest and his finger closed around the feather as he stood up. "Thanks, kiddo." Animal brushed the back of his hand across Lucy's cheeks. "What about going out to get some barbecue at Big Rocky's? Afterward, we can get some ice cream at Red Spot Creamery unless you think it's too cold for it."

Lucy shook her head. "No, I don't think it's too cold for ice cream."

Animal laughed and embraced her. "I don't either. Why don't you wash your face and then meet me downstairs."

She broke away from his arms and scurried to the bathroom. He walked out of the room, his jaw clenched. Animal had every intention of calling Emerald and telling her to give Lucy a call. *She's such a fucking, selfish bitch!* He strode over to the living room window and looked through the blinds at Olivia's house. Several lights were on and he pictured her lying on the couch wearing sexy lingerie while watching television and thinking of him. Well … it was *his* fantasy.

"I'm ready, Dad," Lucy said behind him.

Animal turned away from the window. "Let's get going." He smiled at his daughter and made his way toward the garage as she followed close behind.

BLACK T-SHIRTS, DENIM, and leather filled the main room, as a cacophony of music, shuffling feet, clinking glasses, and loud voices merged into a roar. Church had been particularly heated that morning, and Animal needed a double whiskey, pronto. Skinless, one of the three prospects scrambling to make sure the brothers were taken care of, placed the tumbler in front of him. Animal tipped his head back and let the amber liquid slide down his throat.

"We shoulda gotten rid of the traitorous bastard back when we dealt with Tigger," Wheelie said, slamming his beer bottle on the counter.

Animal shook his head. "Yeah—we fucked up."

Rags turned to Bones, who'd been unusually quiet. "You guys are tight. Did you know he was a fuckin' turncoat?"

Bones held his hands up. "Don't fuckin' get on my damn case because a friend of mine—a brother of *ours* is a goddamn rat. I didn't know shit. I knew he was pissed as hell about Tigger. He thought the club abandoned Tigger and had a double standard when it came to Wheelie." He jerked his head in Wheelie's direction. "But he made amends with it, or that's what I thought. I mean, it's been almost two years since all that went down, right?"

Animal nodded. "Yeah, just about." He clasped his hand on Bones's shoulder. "I'm not blaming you, dude. I think that goes for most of us here." The other men tipped their chins at Bones. "It's just been a while since we had a brother betray the club."

"And to fuck around with Metal's old lady? They're together, not getting a divorce or any shit like that. Asshole!" Rags pounded his fist on the table.

"Skeet just opened himself up to a whole lot of fuckin' grief," Hawk said as he joined the group. "Metal doesn't deserve to be treated like this by a brother or a bitch wife."

Metal was an inactive Insurgent who'd stepped down due to medical issues. He'd been with the club for over thirty years, and he, Banger, Rob, Buffalo, Ruben, and Itchy were all good friends that went way back. They were old-school bikers who remembered the brutal turf wars between the Insurgents and the Deadly Demons MC. After years of bombings and dead bodies, Reaper, the president of the Deadly Demons, and Banger met and struck up a truce that brought peace to both clubs over the past nine years.

Even though Metal was no longer an active member, he was very much an Insurgent for life. A member didn't stop being a brother when he stepped down. Even if a fellow Insurgent died, he was still a brother, and if he had an old lady and kids, they were taken care of and treated with respect.

Metal had stepped down five years before, and he'd taken up with a woman half his age, and at fifty-five years old, his wife, Thea, was just under twenty-eight. Banger warned him that marrying a woman so young would spell disaster, but Metal had just laughed and ignored his friend's warning. In the beginning it was all good, but after four years of marriage, Metal started having medical issues, and the things he could once do were a thing of the past. His young wife didn't want to slow down, so she looked elsewhere for some fun.

The bond of an Insurgent was almost stronger than that of blood with a dedication to each other's lives that most people would never understand. A brother's problem was everyone's problem, and vice versa. So a member fucking another brother's old lady was very much a club problem.

Skeet and Thea had been screwing around behind Metal's back for quite some time, but if he suspected it, Metal didn't mention it to Banger or anyone else in the club. The whole affair came to light after Skeet and Thea took off, leaving a note that simply read: *"Fuck off, old man."* Metal had been crushed, and when Banger found out about it, he went through the roof.

To add insult to injury for both Metal and the club, Skeet had joined up with a group of bikers up in Northern Colorado who had started a club. They called themselves the Rising Order and were gaining a lot of members in the past year or so. The Insurgents watched them carefully, and as long as they didn't put Colorado on their bottom rocker, the club was okay with them, but the minute they claimed the state as their territory, the Insurgents would have to shut them down.

Skeet's betrayal was the worst thing a member could do to his club, and it was something that would ostracize both Skeet and Thea. The animosity the members felt toward him was off the charts, and it simmered beneath the surface of the club, always at risk of boiling over.

"What're we gonna do about it?" Animal asked.

"For now, not much, but if Skeet has the fuckin' nerve to show his traitorous ass in Pinewood Springs, he'll get the beatdown he deserves." Hawk took a long pull of beer. "If the damn pussy club he's with now puts Colorado on their bottom rocker, it'll be war, and Skeet will be history."

"Why the fuck didn't he just leave the club after Tigger?" Wheelie said. "What a dumbass." The other men chuckled, but anger showed in the taut lines on their faces and the way they stood: legs planted wide and chests thrust out.

Banger raised his fist in the air as he approached the group and they responded in the same fashion. The president gripped Hawk's shoulder and said, "How's Cara and the baby doing?"

The mention of his old lady and new baby made the vice president's face soften. "She's doing real good, and Neo's got a fuckin' pair of lungs on him. He's already demandin' and commandin'—perfect biker material."

Banger guffawed. "Glad to hear it. Belle's available to help out if you need her too. Having three young ones can't be easy."

Hawk nodded. "Thanks, bro. Cara and I will keep that in mind."

"Sofia's down for it too. Damn, since Macy was born, she wants another kid so bad," Wheelie said.

"Then what the fuck are you waiting for?" Animal asked.

Wheelie lifted his shoulder in a nonchalant shrug. "Nothing. It'll happen." He took a pull from his beer bottle. "How's is going with Lucy?"

"Real good. We kinda had a breakthrough the other night. Anyway, I got in touch with her fuckin' mom and told her to give Lucy a call. Can you believe the bitch hasn't reached out to Lucy since she abandoned her. I could fuckin' strangle her." Hot anger burned through Animal.

"Fuck, bro," Wheelie replied.

"That's damn tough," Rags chimed in and Bones nodded.

"Some moms can be a real piece of shit," Hawk said. "I know 'cause mine was. That's tough on Lucy. You gotta be there for her, man, and be damn patient."

Animal bumped fists with Hawk. "I know, bro. I'm trying, but damn, if this parenting shit isn't hard as hell."

Banger and Hawk laughed, then the president winked at Animal. "Wait 'til Lucy's a teenager—you're gonna wish she was seven again. Tough doesn't even begin to describe what's ahead of you."

"Ah, shit. I need another drink," Animal said.

Smokey walked up to Animal and handed him a bottle of Coors. "Here you go, bro."

The men laughed and Animal's fingers curled around the beer. "How the hell did you hear me?"

"What?" Smokey took out several joints and passed them around to the group.

"He said he needed a drink, and then you showed up with one. Fuckin' eerie," Rags said as he took out his lighter.

"You just looked like you needed one," Smokey said, clinking his bottle against Animal's.

"He did," Hawk said. "Banger just told him what to expect when Lucy becomes a teenager."

"Yeah ... that's gonna be tough. Remember how we were, and our sisters?" Smokey said, putting the bottle to his lips.

"I'm so fucked," Animal replied, and the men all busted out laughing.

Soon the conversation turned to motorcycles and the upcoming rally in Loveland. After a while, the only ones left were Animal, Bones, and Smokey. Banger had gone to his office to work on club business, Rags had left with Throttle to attend to their landscaping business, and Wheelie had to return to the carwash.

"You don't got shit to do?" Bones asked as he followed Animal and

Smokey to a table.

Animal shook his head. "I'm free until I have to pick up Lucy. I took today off."

"Doesn't it kickass to be your own boss?" Smokey stretched out his legs. "No orders from anyone, you can do whatever the hell you want, and most importantly—*you* make the fuckin' rules."

"Fuck, yeah," Animal said.

"I'm good with just working at the different club businesses," Bones said.

"But it's still not like working for some tight-ass boss. The time you spend is not only for the club but for your own share of the income too." Smokey gestured Rosie over.

"That's true. I got fired from every job I had before becoming a patched member. I couldn't stand no one telling me what the fuck to do," Bones said.

"Whatcha want?" Rosie said, running her hands over Smokey's broad shoulders.

The club girls had stayed away after church had let out based on the loud and angry voices of the members. Most of the time they were waiting in the main room to either serve the men their drinks, get them something to eat, or give them pleasure—but whenever the climate was hostile, they stayed away until the mood lifted.

Smokey smacked Rosie on her nice, plump butt then drew her to him and kissed her hard. "I want what you're offering a little later on, but first we need some food. You got any burritos in the kitchen?"

Rosie ran her glitter-tipped fingernails down Smokey's neck. "I think so. Is that what you want, baby?" She pressed his head against her ample tits.

"You're killing me," Smokey said in a thick voice.

"I'll take a couple of burritos," Bones said, rubbing his hand over her ass.

Rosie looked over her shoulder at him and winked. "Okay." She glanced at Animal and licked the top of her lip. "You want the same thing, baby?"

"Sure, why not?" Animal glanced at his phone to see if Olivia had responded to his text. He'd sent it to her the night before, asking her what times would work for tutoring Lucy. Olivia had mailed him a copy of Lucy's reading assessment along with a note that she'd shared it with the principal at Slavens. Mr. Lorry agreed with Olivia that Lucy was in need of extra help and gave his approval for her to spend a few hours a week after school to help the young student.

At first Animal was pissed that Olivia hadn't walked the damn report over to his house, but the more he thought about it, the more smug he became: Olivia didn't come over because she couldn't trust herself with him.

His pride quickly turned to irritation, because no matter how hard he tried, Animal couldn't get her out of his mind. If he were *that type of guy*, he'd probably admit that he might even be obsessed with her and that irked the hell out of him, especially since Olivia had been avoiding him at all costs. Even now, as he briefly closed his eyes, the image of her nipples hardening under his touch as she kissed him filled his mind. *Dammit!* Animal wanted her in the worst way.

He knew he should just forget about her and concentrate on hanging out more at the club, but the women were too easy for him. Sure, they loved to have a good time, but there was no pursuit. All Animal had to do was snap his fingers and point at Tania and Charolette, who were currently sitting on the couch, and they'd be all over him like flies on sherbet. But Olivia was a whole different story; she played hard to get, and it got his blood boiling and made his mind fucking screwy.

Animal leaned back in the chair, a smile lifting his lips. There was no doubt that his sexy neighbor was driving him crazy, but he liked the challenge of winning her over, as he knew he eventually would. So he'd just bide his time and wait.

"Here you go," Rosie said as she brushed up against Animal before setting the plate down. "Do you need anything else, baby?"

"I'm good. Thanks, Rosie." Animal picked up the fork and dug into the smothered shredded beef burrito.

"This is fuckin' good," Smokey said as he cleaned his plate. "I heard Kristy made them."

"Kristy can cook." Animal pushed the empty plate away from him. "I wonder if it's hard to make these."

"Becoming domestic?" Bones sniggered.

"Not by fucking choice. Lucy's getting sick of pizza, takeout, and frozen dinners," Animal replied.

"You need to get a club girl over to your house and let her cook for you and Lucy. Then when the kid's in bed, you can have some fun." Smokey bunched up his napkin and put it on the plate. "It's been a while since you've seen some action with one of the club women."

"Are you getting it from a citizen?" Bones asked.

"Maybe that cutie who lives next door to you?" Smokey said.

"I told you I'm not interested in her. She's just helping Lucy with her reading." Animal stretched out his legs, crossing them at the ankles.

"I heard she showed up at the party last Saturday," Bones said.

"Yeah—she came with a friend," Animal replied.

"Kennedy." Smokey snorted. "Fuck, that chick's wild."

"Olivia isn't. I think she got in over her head, so she left early." Animal glanced at his phone again. Nothing.

"I can't believe Kennedy didn't warn her." Smokey took out a joint and lit it.

"Me neither. Anyway, I got her out of here. Just thinking about her being at a club party makes me bust up laughing. She's so fucking green," Animal said.

"So, are you gonna go to the Loveland rally?" Bones asked, changing the subject.

"If Jada can stay with Lucy for the weekend. What about you?"

Bones nodded. "I got a chick waiting for me there. We meet up a couple of times a year. She's fuckin' insatiable." He laughed.

"I'm going this year too," Smokey said as a cloud of smoke rose above him. "I think most of the brothers are going to this one. The winter was so fuckin' brutal this year that it'll be good to do a road trip."

"If it doesn't snow," Bones said.

"Yeah, but the rally's in a few weeks, so we should be okay," Smokey replied.

Before Animal could put in his two sense about the crappy springs in Colorado, his phone rang. Rusty's name flashed on the screen.

"I wonder why the fuck the prospect's calling me," Animal said as he brought the phone to his ear. "Talk to me."

"There's a chick here who says she knows you. Her name is"—Rusty paused for half a second as if trying to read the print on the woman's driver's license—"Olivia Mooney. You know her?"

Olivia? "Yeah, send her through." Animal clicked off the phone and slipped it into the inner pocket of his cut. His mind whirled, trying to figure out what the fuck she was doing here.

A part of him wanted to meet her outside so he'd have some private time with her, but the other half of him was just a bit too self-satisfied that Olivia had come to him. *I knew you couldn't stay away, baby.*

The soft scent of vanilla and caramel reached him, and Animal knew she'd just entered the room. The perfume lingered in the air, conjuring up images of holding and kissing her.

"Fuck, that's *her*," Smokey said under his breath.

Bones's eyes looked like they would pop out of their sockets at any moment.

Animal casually looked over his shoulder and ran his gaze languidly over her wickedly curvy body. He groaned inwardly at her short black skirt, deliciously tight around that sweet, soft ass, and then at the form-fitting top, which accentuated her squeezable tits. *Fuck.* He shifted in the chair when his dick twitched.

"Hiya, Teach," he said, barely able to contain a smirk.

"Hello, Mr. Walsh," she answered as she approached the table.

"Are we back to that?" He winked at her, but Olivia ignored him.

"Hey, who's the chick?" Bones asked.

Before Animal could utter a single word, Olivia extended her hand to Bones. "Olivia Mooney."

Bones looked at her outstretched arm and laughed. "So, are you applying to be a club girl?"

Her face fell and crimson streaks colored her cheeks and chin, and Animal almost felt sorry for her … *almost.* He chuckled and kicked out the chair next to him.

"Have a seat," he said. He overheard Bones ask Smokey who Olivia was and he whispered something inaudible to Animal. Then Bones nodded and settled back in the chair, his gaze fixed on Animal and Olivia.

She slid on the chair and kept her hands in her lap, clutching a small purse.

"I was in the neighborhood, so I thought I'd take a chance and see if you were here. I want to talk to you about scheduling Lucy's tutoring sessions."

In the neighborhood? What a load of BS. "You coulda just come over to the house or called … or maybe answered my damn text." Animal bit back a smile when he saw her squirm and the streaks deepen. Yeah … he was *really* enjoying this.

"I could have, but I was in the neighborhood—"

"Yeah … that's what you said." Animal picked up his beer and took a long, slow drink, his gaze fixed on hers.

Olivia looked away. "Anyway, we need to set up a schedule. I work at the dental clinic two days a week—today is one of them, so it would be better for me to help Lucy on the days I'm at school. I'm thinking two days a week?"

Animal kept staring at her.

Olivia smoothed down her skirt then tightened the grip on her purse; Animal saw her fingers turn white. Oh yeah … he was loving every second of Ms. Mooney's discomfort. She'd been teasing the fuck out of him for far too long now, so it was about time he gave her a taste of own her medicine.

"Are you in agreement with that?"

He didn't answer and his gaze never wavered from her face.

She inhaled deeply, and Animal wondered if she was aware how her tits stood out more when she did that. Out of the corner of his eye he saw Smokey and Bones drooling, and he wanted to punch both of them in the face. Hard. Then Olivia exhaled.

"Stop acting like a child. The intimidation and mind games you're trying to use on me aren't working. We're talking about your *daughter*, okay? Do you want me to tutor her or not?"

"Yeah, I do." Irritation pricked his skin as his two friends looked over at him. "You're pretty feisty today, aren't you?"

"Not really, I'm just tired and don't want to play your BS biker games.

Bones's snigger pissed Animal the hell off and he turned and glared at his brother. The grin on Bones's face fell and he cut his gaze back to Olivia.

"I can do whatever's convenient for you. I just want Lucy to get the help she needs, so you decide," Animal said.

Olivia took out a pencil and a monthly planner and chewed on the eraser while she glanced at the calendar. "Monday and Wednesday afternoons will work for me. I usually have street duty, and then some paperwork, but I can meet with Lucy in my classroom at three forty-five. The sessions will last forty-five minutes, so we should be finished at four thirty. I'll make sure Lucy is in the after-school care program until I come get her. Does this work?"

Olivia was being all professional and businesslike, but she didn't fool Animal one bit. There was no fucking way she just stopped by the clubhouse to go over Lucy's schedule. *Maybe she wants me to invite her to one of the rooms.* Animal wasn't sure what her deal was, but he was 100 percent positive that she wasn't "in the neighborhood." He wanted to yank her to him and kiss those soft lips of hers while her tits pressed hard against him.

"Is that acceptable?" Her lips drew into a thin line, an exasperated sigh escaping from her nostrils.

Animal sliced his eyes to hers. "Yeah, that sounds fine. When do you wanna start?"

"Next week." She broke contact with him and busied herself with unzipping her briefcase and placing the planner and pencil into it.

"If Lucy can't make it after school sometimes, then we can do it at my house … or yours." Animal looked for those crimson streaks to appear on her cheeks.

Olivia slowly brought her eyes to his, her face clear of any red markings, and said, "I don't think that would work out. If Lucy misses a class, then we can make it up on another day."

"Don't flatter yourself, *Ms. Mooney*. My interest here is helping my daughter."

She didn't flinch or turn away; she held his gaze steadily. "We're definitely on the same wavelength, *Mr. Walsh*. It always helps when a student has the support of her parent." She glanced over his head at the clock on the back wall. "I have to get going. Thank you."

Animal watched her walk away, admiring those long and sexy legs in sheer black stockings and high heels and her swaying hips causing her short skirt to swish. He imagined her standing before him, naked except for those stockings and shoes, and his dick twitched as his mouth went dry.

Smokey pushed a bottle of beer into his hand and slapped him on the back.

"You so wanna fuck your neighbor, dude."

Bones guffawed, then wiped the back of his neck. "Shit … you're screwed, bro."

Animal ignored them. What the hell could he say? They were right: he did want to fuck Olivia *and* he was screwed.

The scent of her perfume still lingered in the air, and he stared at the door far longer than he should have, in hopes that she'd come back in, but she didn't. Animal took out his lighter and lit a joint, took two deep drags and stubbed it out. He then rose from his chair, bumped fists with Smokey and Bones, and walked out of the club.

CHAPTER FOURTEEN

INSIDE THE EMPLOYEES' lunch room, Olivia stood patting Ivy's hand, feeling helpless by the sorrow confronting her friend. Tears streamed down Ivy's face. Her shoulders shook.

"I was such a stupid fool," she said, her voice quivering.

"Shh," Olivia whispered. "It's not your fault. Kennedy and I didn't know either ... It'll be okay, Ivy," Olivia said, brushing her friend's bangs away from her face. "It's just going to take some time ... heartaches always do," she soothed, although her stomach churned at the words.

"I know," Ivy stammered as she patted her eyes with a tissue. "I just can't believe he lied to me. I'd never have gone out with a married man." She sniffled.

"I know that. Brady is a total jerk. He's an asshole at school too. What he did was despicable."

Tears welled in Ivy's eyes again, and she threw her arms around Olivia's neck. Olivia patted her back, anger burning through her. Brady Sickles was lower than scum, and he'd hurt Ivy very much. When Ivy had come back from lunch sobbing, Olivia couldn't imagine what had happened. She grabbed her friend's hand and took her back to the lunchroom, then listened in disgusted disbelief as Ivy recounted how she'd bumped into Brady in the drugstore. He'd seemed super nervous and kept trying to get away from her until a woman appeared with two boys in tow. The woman stared at Ivy, who stared at Brady, and when the jerk introduced the woman as his wife and the boys as his kids, Ivy had rushed out of the store. Olivia couldn't even imagine how humiliated Ivy must've felt, but then the image of Kory banging the butterfly-tatted woman flashed into her mind. Yeah … that was pretty bad, but Olivia didn't love Kory the way Ivy loved Brady. Ivy was really suffering right now.

"How did I miss the signs?" Ivy asked.

"When you're in love, the signs aren't as obvious." Olivia broke away and pulled a chair out for Ivy, who sank down into it. "If something bugs us, we ignore it or rationalize it away, because being in love feels so good."

Ivy nodded as she wiped her nose repeatedly. "I love him so much it hurts. He was weird with the sex stuff, but if I told him to stop, he would; outside of that, he was wonderful. I still can't believe it."

"Men can be real liars," Olivia muttered. "I'm an expert in lying men. I never seem to get one who doesn't hide shit from me." Animal popped into her head. *He's probably the biggest liar of all. Dad sure was and all of the guys from his club just cheated and denied it to their wives and girlfriends.* Then the way Animal's eyes lit up when he heard Lucy read after a couple of weeks of tutoring seeped into her mind. *A man who loves his daughter that much can't be all bad, can he?*

"Isn't your lunch break over?" Dr. Canty asked.

Olivia looked over at the doorway and saw the dentist standing there, arms crossed and face taut. Most of the employees at the dental clinic avoided Dr. Canty because he always went out of his way to criticize or find fault in whatever any of the staff was doing.

"Ivy's upset about something, and I was just helping her out with it," Olivia said, her chin lifted up in defiance. Dr. Canty just rubbed her the wrong way, and she refused to be intimidated by him or rendered into a quivering nervous wreck. He had that effect on Ivy as well as the two dental hygienists, Polly and Meg. The clinic's administrator, Lisa, didn't seem to let anything fluster her.

Dr. Canty narrowed his eyes. "This isn't a counseling clinic. Dr. Linney needs you to help out, Ivy, and it isn't fair to the patients to keep them waiting. You and Olivia can talk after work hours."

Ivy wiped her face with her hands, rose up from the chair, and smoothed down her multi-colored tunic. "I'm sorry," she mumbled as she rushed out of the room.

Olivia turned away and pushed her chair out.

"I'm disappointed in you, Olivia. You should know better."

She stood and threw the dentist a hard smile. "I was helping a friend. I'm sure Dr. Linney *and* Dr. Mitchell would understand." Satisfaction wove through her when she saw the dentist's face pale momentarily upon mentioning the partners' names.

Recovering quickly, Dr. Canty met her gaze head-on. "I'm not saying I *don't* understand, but the patients always come first, and I know Dr. Linney and Dr. Mitchell would agree with me 100 percent. Now, don't you have some work to do?"

Biting back a snide comment to the dentist's condescending demeanor, Olivia walked across the room. The dentist stood in the doorway and she looked up at him.

"Excuse me," she said. He didn't budge. "You're blocking the doorway."

"Am I?" Sarcasm dripped from each word.

"Yes. Do you want me to go back to the front desk or not?"

"I'm not stopping you." He moved to the side, but not out of the doorway. "Ladies first." He gestured for her to pass.

Sucking in a sharp breath, Olivia squeezed by him and refused to acknowledge the shit-eating grin on his face. There was something about him that gave her the heebie-jeebies, and the less contact she had with him the better. Ignoring his chuckles, she hurried down the hall and slipped into the swivel chair behind the front desk.

The next few hours flew by, and she didn't see Dr. Canty for the rest of the afternoon. She'd sent a quick text to Ivy, asking if she wanted to go out for dinner after work, and to her relief, Ivy agreed.

"Did you call Dr. Werner's office for Mrs. Losa's x-rays?" Dr. Linney asked as he stood beside her, a folder in his hands.

"I did. Her receptionist said that Dr. Werner sent them by courier this morning. As of yet, we haven't received them."

His forehead crinkled. "If we don't get them by the end of the day, I'll call Amy in the morning." The dentist shifted in place and seemed a bit nervous. "Uh"—he looked around the room—"is something wrong with Ivy?"

Olivia swiveled around and faced Dr. Linney. "Why?"

"She seemed distracted and upset during Mr. Riley's procedure."

"Did you ask her what was wrong?"

"I did, but she just shrugged it off." Dr. Linney scrubbed the side of his face.

"She's going through a rough spot with a personal problem," Olivia said.

"Okay. I was wondering about it, that's all. Carl asked me about it too."

"You and Dr. Mitchell don't need to worry. Ivy had just learned something upsetting today," Olivia replied.

Dr. Linney smiled. "I hope she gets through it okay. I'll let Carl know. Thanks." He turned around and walked back to his office.

Alan Linney and Carl Mitchell had gone to dental school together and had purchased the clinic from an older dentist whom Dr. Linney had worked for. The clinic had one associate dentist: Dr. Lyle Canty. The office was very busy, and most of the time Olivia worked nonstop from morning to the end of the day. She liked all the people who worked there except for Dr. Canty. Most of the staff didn't care for him, but his patients loved him, and Olivia suspected that was the reason why Alan and Carl kept him on.

Five o'clock couldn't come fast enough for Olivia. Holding down two jobs was exhausting even though they were both part-time. The hours Olivia put in as a teacher's assistant at Slavens far surpassed the thirty-two hours a week for which she was paid, but she loved working with the students so much that most of the time it didn't feel like a job. The receptionist job at the dental clinic was another story. On the two days a week she worked there, she couldn't wait until the doors closed, but the money was good, and it helped pay her mortgage and school tuition.

"Ready?" Ivy asked when she came into the bathroom.

"Just a sec," Olivia replied as she fluffed her hair then swiped a coat of lipstick on her mouth.

"I love that color. What is it?"

"Urban Decay's Crush. It's my favorite right now. I love the warm orange color," Olivia replied, looking at her friend's reflection in the mirror. She took out a tube of crystal clear gloss and dabbed it over her lipstick "I love this—it's like a hint of sunshine on my lips. God ... I wish the weather would get warmer."

"I do too." Ivy brushed out her short blonde hair. "Which restaurant did you want to go to?"

"Burgers & Beer Joint—it's in West Pinewood Springs. I've heard about it ever since I moved here but never checked it out. Alice keeps telling me that the burgers are the best she's eaten anywhere. Have you been there?"

Ivy shook her head. "I don't eat meat, remember?" She smiled.

"I do, but I checked out the menu online and they have several vegetarian dishes—even a veggie burger. It's also a brewery, and if anyone needs a cold beer tonight, you do."

"Well, you sold me." Ivy paused and caught Olivia's gaze in the mirror. "Thanks for being such a good friend. I dreaded going home right after work and thinking about Brady."

"Don't mention it—that's what friends are for." She squeezed Ivy's shoulder. "I can't tell you how many times Alice and Harper have been there for me after a breakup."

A small smile whispered on her friend's lips. "Brady was the first real relationship I'd had. I usually never got past a few dates."

"You'll find someone else. My problem is I fall too fast, then everything blows up when I get to know the guy. I kind of do it ass-backward, you know?"

Ivy sighed. "Who's to say what's the right way?"

"Well, dating a guy a couple of times, falling in love—or thinking that you're in love, and moving in with him after only a month, is definitely *not* the right way. I know because that's been my MO for like *ever*." Olivia zipped her lipstick and gloss back in a compartment of her purse then slung it over her shoulder. "Ready?"

Ivy pulled the sides of her hair back, securing them with rose-colored barrettes. "Let's go," she said.

The two women walked out into the parking lot to their cars. Ivy would follow Olivia since she wasn't the best at directions. Olivia started the car and pulled out into the traffic.

Spotting the bright yellow sign with the black lettering, Olivia turned into the strip mall and scanned the lot for a parking space. She glanced in her rearview mirror and saw Ivy's car right behind hers. She turned into a space, grabbed her coat on the passenger seat, then got out of the car. The air was chilly, so Olivia shrugged on her wool coat and leaned against the car as she waited for Ivy to find a parking spot.

Several people milled outside the restaurant, and Olivia figured there was probably a wait for a table. *As long as we can get a place to sit, I'm good.* She'd worn her high heels to work—something she'd never do on teaching days.

"It's packed," Ivy said as she approached Olivia. "I didn't think I was going to find a place to park."

The two women entered the eatery through the oversized glass doors, and the heat from a fireplace on the back wall surrounded them.

"I think those two people are leaving," Ivy said pointing to a long wooden bar.

Olivia rushed over and secured the two bronzed barstools and settled down on the rust leather cushions.

"I'll give the hostess our name," Ivy said.

Olivia peeled off her coat and adjusted her pale-green angora top as she looked around the restaurant. The glossed oak floors and red brick walls lent an urban feel to the place. Large planters filled with greenery, dried branches, and berries added warmth to the restaurant. The faint strains of classic rock tunes blended with the din of chatter, clanging pots and pans, and raucous laughter.

"Twenty minutes—not too bad," Ivy said as she sank on the barstool next to Olivia's.

"I thought it was going to be longer since there're so many people waiting."

"Tables for two aren't so bad. The larger ones are being told thirty to forty-five minutes. Are you going to have a beer?"

Olivia looked at the ten taps and the lengthy list of bottled beers and shook her head. "I'm not much of a beer drinker. I think I'll go with my usual white wine, if they have it."

"May I help you?" a pleasant-looking bartender asked as he placed cocktail napkins in front of them.

"I'm hoping you have something other than beer?" Olivia said.

The man laughed. "We do—red and white wine." He handed her a wine list.

As she perused it, Ivy ordered a local brew on tap.

"I'll take a glass of Domaine LaRoche Chablis, please."

"A very good selection," he said as he took the wine list from her. "I'll be right back with both your orders."

"I love it here," Ivy said as she took off her jacket. "It's got a real modern feel but a comfy small-town vibe."

"I like it too. I actually didn't expect it to be so nice," Olivia said.

"Me neither. I think it's the name—Burgers & Beer *Joint*." She giggled.

Before the women had finished their drinks they were ready to be seated, so they followed the hostess to a small table nestled in a corner near a window that looked out to the street.

"Your server will be with you soon," the cute hostess said as she handed them menus.

A fruity aroma mingled with the smells of roasted coffee and hickory, making Olivia's stomach growl.

"It smells so good in here," she said, reading the menu.

"The fruity scent is from the beer, and the one I ordered is delicious.

I'm really hungry, too, so I guess that's a good sign, right?" Ivy said.

"Do you normally stop eating when you're nervous or upset?" Olivia asked.

"Definitely. I can lose five pounds easily when I'm down in the dumps."

"Then it's great that you're hungry. I'm the opposite—I'll gain your five pounds when I'm feeling down. My breakup with Kory packed seven on me. Ice cream, brownies, and cookies, especially Oreos, are my go-to breakup foods."

"Hi, my name is Bridget and I'm your server. Are you ready to order?"

Olivia glanced at the menu. "I'll have the spicy guacamole burger with cheddar cheese and extra jalapeños."

"Fries?"

"Yes, and a side dinner salad with balsamic dressing." She handed the menu to Bridget.

Ivy ordered the veggie burger with swiss cheese, caramelized onions, and sun-dried tomatoes with a side of fries and fried pickles.

Soon they were chowing down the most delicious burger Olivia had ever eaten. As they talked, Olivia heard someone call her name. She looked around and saw Lucy rushing toward her. Her stomach clenched, and she put down her burger.

"Hi, Ms. Mooney," Lucy gushed, her face glowing.

"Hi, Lucy. How are you?"

"Good. Do you like your food?"

"It's very good, thank you."

"My dad's club owns this." Lucy waved her arms around as she spun in a circle.

"Really?"

"Really." His voice spilled over her.

Olivia kept her gaze on Lucy until Animal filled her field of vision. He looked amazing in his body-hugging dark blue turtleneck sweater and tight jeans. Swirls of ink on defined forearms peeked out from pushed up sleeves, and his pants highlighted the long, muscular shape of his legs.

"Hi," he said in a low voice. His eyes darted to the *V* neckline of her top.

"Hi," she whispered, her stomach fluttering as she recalled the feel of his hands on her breasts, the touch of his lips against hers.

"Ms. Mooney says she likes the burgers." Lucy spun around again.

"I'm glad Ms. Mooney likes them. So they're juicy enough for you?"

Flushed, Olivia nodded and looked away.

"Are you gonna have ice cream? My favorite is the chocolate chip."

"I like that too." Olivia smiled and looked at Lucy, but she was very aware that Animal was staring at *her*.

Ivy cleared her throat and Olivia's gaze cut over to her, and she placed her hand against the side of her face. "I'm sorry, I forgot to introduce you," she said. "Ivy, this is Lucy—she's a student of mine at Slavens, and this is her father." Olivia kept her focus on Lucy and Ivy, but Animal's presence took over the space around them.

Ivy smiled at the young girl and began to ask her questions, which seemed to please Lucy immensely. The girl wandered over to Ivy, and the two of them began chatting. Animal squatted down on his haunches beside her chair, and smiled.

Mouth dry all of a sudden, Olivia reached for her water glass and took a big gulp.

"Am I making you nervous?" he asked.

"No," she answered.

"Look," he said in a low voice, "let's stop playing games here. I'm sure you know I'm attracted to you, and I *know* you are to me, so let's do something about it." He glanced over at Lucy who was still chitchatting away.

Olivia's racing heartbeat drummed in her chest, but she refused to give any indication that she was even remotely flustered. She took another sip of water, then met his gaze. "I'm a very busy person, and I—"

"You're out tonight, so that means you have *some* time. You went to

Blue's Belly and the clubhouse. You got more time than you think."
Animal brushed his knuckles across the back of her fingers, and the
touch was electric. "I'm asking you out to dinner."

Okay ... *that* was surprising. She'd thought he was proposing a wild
night of sex so they could get each other out of their systems, but he was
asking her out on a date instead. She wasn't sure what to make of it.

"Okay," she muttered before her brain could stop her.

"Awesome." Another brush across her skin, then he rose to his feet.
"I'll call you," he whispered before turning to Lucy. "We gotta get back
to our table, kiddo. Grandpa and Aunt Jada are gonna wonder if we got
lost. Anyway, I'm pretty sure there's a bowl of ice cream waiting for
you."

Lucy jumped up and down. "Goodbye, Ivy. Bye Miss. Mooney."
She dashed away with her sexy-as-all-hell father following her.

"Who was that guy?" Ivy said, her head still turned as she watched
Animal over her shoulder.

"My next-door neighbor ... and the father of one of my student's,"
she groaned.

"Oh, wow." Ivy straightened out and picked up a fry and nibbled on
it.

"It gets worse. I just accepted a date with him. I'm totally insane!"
Olivia pushed her half-eaten burger away from her.

"Is that allowed at your school?" Ivy asked.

"Yes and no. I mean, if I was Lucy's actual teacher in her grade, it
would be a major no-no, but since I'm just tutoring her in reading and
she's not getting graded or anything like that, it's probably okay." She
crumpled her napkin and put it on the table. "I don't know. Anyway,
I'm not supposed to be going on a date with anyone—I've sworn off
men."

"A good-looking guy like him would make any woman break her
resolution. He's rugged and dangerous looking, don't you think?" Ivy
briefly glanced over her shoulder again.

"Yeah," Olivia begrudgingly agreed. "He's in a motorcycle club."

Ivy's eyes widened. "No shit."

"It gets even better—it's an *outlaw* club. When I fuck up, I fuck up big." She shook her head and motioned the server for another glass of white wine.

"Aren't you scared to go out with him? I'd be petrified to date a biker." Her friend shuddered.

"Not really. He's actually a decent guy, and the way he tries with Lucy melts my heart."

"Is his ex in the picture?"

"I don't know. I've never seen any woman at the house." Olivia should know since she'd spent far more time spying on her neighbor than she'd ever admit. "Lucy never talks about her. I really don't know what the deal is with all that." *But I'm sure as hell going to find out on our date. Date. I can't believe I agreed to go out with him. What was I thinking?*

"Considering what happened to me with Brady, you better find out exactly what the situation is, you don't want any surprises, believe me."

"I don't plan to go out with him more than once." Olivia reached over and patted the back of Ivy's hand. "I'm sorry you had such a jerk in your life. Let's forget about Animal and—"

"*Animal?* That's his name?" Ivy's fingers rested against the base of her throat.

"It's a road name—bikers have them. I'm sure he got his from partying too much with the ladies." Olivia rolled her eyes. "His real name is Raxton—I saw it in Lucy's records."

"I like *that* name. I don't think I could call a man Animal and do it with a straight face." Ivy giggled.

"You should hear some of the road names that bikers have, Animal isn't that bad." Skull Crusher—her father's name, and Torturer—her dad's best friend's name came to mind.

"I guess. I think I'm just too square, that's why I liked Brady—he was pretty conservative. He was also very meticulous and liked everything in its place." Her voice hitched.

"But he wasn't too nice during sex, remember?"

"I know, but that was a small part of us. I can't believe he lied to me."

For the next couple of hours, Olivia listened to her friend vent, cry, and lament over the breakup, and by the time Olivia locked the door to her house, she was exhausted to the bone. She kicked off her heels, unzipped her dress pants, and lifted her sweater top over her head as she trudged into the bathroom to wash off her makeup.

Fresh-faced and her dark brown hair in a half, pulled-through ponytail on the top of her head, Olivia sat in the desk chair with one of her legs tucked under her bottom, scrolling through the multitude of messages posted in her dating account. When Olivia had set up her profile, she'd used her middle name and a fake last name. As she read the messages, she scribbled notes in her writing pad. She already had half a notebook of research for her psychology paper, and she'd only had her profile up for a little over two weeks.

A bell chimed indicating that someone named "Hunter" had sent her a Real Time message, and she opened it.

Hunter: *You sound like an intriguing lady.*

Olivia scratched the side of her nose, then picked up her pen and jotted down what the person had sent her. She messaged back using "Rose," her alias name.

Rose: *I am.*

She groaned as she clicked the *SEND* button.

Hunter: *Now you've really piqued my curiosity. I wish I could see more of you.*

Olivia shook her head. "No way, buddy," she whispered under her breath.

Rose: *Maybe when we get to know each other better. Your picture is a bit vague too.*

She opened a bottle of water on her desk and took a sip.

Hunter: *It wouldn't be fair if I shared and you didn't. How many men are you talking to?*

Rose: *Not many. You're the first to reach out to me in Real Time.*

Hunter: *That's because I'm serious. A lot of men just want only one thing.*

Olivia scribbled in her notebook and took another drink of water.

Rose: *And you don't?*

Hunter: *I'm not vulgar like that. I want the right woman for a real connection. What do you want?*

Rose: *The same. I'd love to share my life with someone, but that special person is hard to find.*

Hunter: *I totally agree. Do you live with your parents?*

"That's an odd question," she muttered under her breath while writing it in her notebook.

Rose: *No. Why?*

Hunter: *Just wondered. Your profile said you were twenty-five. A lot of people in their twenties, even thirties still live at home because of the expensive rents. I guess you must have roommates.*

"Okay, buddy, you're just getting weirder," Olivia said out loud.

Rose: *Nope. What about you? I see you're thirty-seven.*

Hunter: *I don't live with my parents, if that's what you're asking. Just joking. I own my home and live alone.*

Rose: *That's cool.*

Hunter: *It can be very lonely sometimes. Do you ever get lonely, Rose?*

Rose: *I do.*

For the next half hour, Hunter kept messaging her and they talked about a lot of different subjects and topics, but never anything racy. Olivia could see the way he was trying to play on her emotions, especially on her professed loneliness. "He's definitely trying to reel me in," she muttered as she leaned back against the chair and stretched her arms high above her head. Olivia had decided that Hunter Lewis would be the star in her research paper. She'd have to dig up a photo to send him, then see how far he would take this. She didn't believe for one minute that he was as unique as he claimed to be. Even though he acted like a gentleman, Olivia wasn't really buying Hunter's act. Maybe he'd surprise her and be exactly what he claimed to be: an old-fashioned man, who respected women and wanted to make a soulful connection. The only way she'd find out was to meet him, and with her paper due in less than six weeks, Olivia had to make sure to move things along quickly.

There was one thing for certain: Hunter Lewis was different from any of the other guys who'd contacted her. A part of her was more than curious to meet him, and another part of her was terrified. Hunter set off small alarm bells inside her, but she chalked that up to him being a stranger in cyberspace, where so many people weren't who they claimed to be.

Rose: It was nice getting to know you, but I have to go now.

Hunter: I want to get to know you better. Let's talk tomorrow night at around nine?

Rose: Sure. Nite, Hunter.

Hunter: I look forward to continuing our conversation. Nine o'clock can't come fast enough. Goodnight, Rose.

Olivia clicked out of her profile and shut down her computer. Hunter seemed fascinated by her and anxious to move things along. A thread of apprehension wove its way along her spine. She stood and switched off the floor lamp, then walked around the house and double-checked all the doors and windows to make sure they were locked. "Can I get any more paranoid?" she mumbled while slipping the chain on the front door. Olivia pulled aside the sheet covering her living room window and looked out at the empty street. The evergreens stood erect in the front yards across the cul-de-sac. The tops of the neighboring maple trees swayed slowly in the nighttime breeze. She shifted her gaze to a window at Animal's house. Slits of light filtered through its shutters, casting thin threads of gold onto the frost-covered bushes on the side of the house.

Olivia pictured Animal sitting on the couch with his feet propped up on the coffee table as he watched television, and a cozy feeling spread through her. As silly as it sounded, just seeing a light on in his house made her feel safe.

She let go of the sheet and crossed the room to her bedroom. Tucked under the comforter, Olivia drifted off to sleep as thoughts of Animal floated through her mind.

CHAPTER FIFTEEN

ANIMAL SAT AT the kitchen table and leaned back in his chair, watching his mother dice carrots for dinner. The window was ajar, and an early spring breeze rustled the maple leaves outside and carried the sweet scent of wildflowers mixed with pine.

He picked up his mug of coffee, took a drink, put it back on the table, and stretched his legs out. His mother threw him a sidelong glance but never stopped chopping the pile of vegetables on the wooden cutting board.

"Whatcha got on your mind?" she asked, picking up three stalks of celery.

Animal drew the mug to his mouth again without answering her.

"I know you got something on your mind. You didn't come over here to watch me make beef stew. Is something going on with Lucy?"

"Lucy's okay. I'm worried about *you*."

She turned toward him. "There's no reason for you to be worrying about me." She laid the knife on the board, reached into the pocket of her housecoat, and took out a pack of cigarettes.

"Why the hell do you have an online profile on a dating site called *Discreet Passion*? The name alone is bad enough."

"You were snooping? It's none of your business what I do. Does that sound familiar? It should—you've told me that a couple of thousand times over the years." Smoke rose as she drew on her cigarette, her gaze fierce and challenging.

"I wasn't snooping, and what you do that affects the family *is* my damn business. What the hell's the matter with you?" Animal looked through the doorway to the family room and saw his dad sitting in the wheelchair, his head supported by his arm, which was rested on the end table. The way his head hung down to his chest, it was obvious that he'd fallen asleep.

Animal tipped his head in the direction of the family room. "And what about Dad?"

His mother threw back her head and let out a deep, throaty guffaw, then she lifted the cigarette to her lips, took a drag, and slowly exhaled, the smoke drifting up through brown eyes the color of sun-dried beechwood.

"If you'd talked about this with your dad, you'd have known that it was his suggestion that I go out and look for a little fun."

A sudden coldness hit his gut, and Animal jerked his head back, words failing him.

"Does that surprise you?" Again, she laughed way too loudly and glared at him. "You don't know shit." She stubbed out the cigarette and turned away from him, then began chopping again.

The rhythmic *thud* of the knife hitting against the wooden board was the only sound in the kitchen. Animal ran his gaze over his mom as he tried to understand what she'd just told him. He couldn't believe that his dad would let his wife openly screw around with other men. Maybe it was because his dad thought of himself as less of a man because he'd lost his legs in the war, or maybe it was because he was no longer interested in anything sexual. *Dad knows?* The question kept running through his mind like he'd hit the rewind button on a tape recorder.

His stared at his mother. She was an attractive woman with dark brown hair to her shoulders and very well-fit. At fifty-five, she had maintained herself nicely, and always took the extra effort to dress and look good before she left the house. Animal suspected that most men would find his mom—Rena Walsh—to be quite pretty. *But you're married to Dad ... and he's okay with you whoring around?* Anger clouded his mind, and regret stabbed his heart. He hated thinking ill of her, but all he could remember was how going out with her friends, getting her hair and nails done, and shopping took precedence over him and Jada when they were younger.

"So you don't feel guilty at all?" Animal asked, breaking the tense silence between them.

"Not anymore." Rena pivoted toward him. "I never thought my marriage would be like this. Before your dad went to Iraq, we had a wonderful and thriving marriage, but he came back broken in so many ways. His legs were gone, but so was his spirit, his desire, his will to adjust. I could live with his disability, but how do I repair a shattered soul? It was real tough for a long time. You were too busy with your club to notice or care, and Jada was still a teenager."

"So you're putting *this* on me?"

Rena placed her hands on her hips, a scowl deepening the lines between her brows. "You weren't around very much, that's all I'm saying. I was overwhelmed and you weren't around."

"And *you were* when I was young?"

Redness crept into his mother's face, and Animal could hear her breath through her flaring nostrils.

"Don't give me that shit! I did the best I could. You weren't the easiest kid to raise."

"Dad didn't seem to have a problem with it." Memories of his father's kind patience filled his mind.

"I was always the bad parent when it came to you and him. Did you ever once try to understand what I was going through?"

"Being out all day with your friends and Dad having to cook dinner after a long day at the plant was kind of a clue to me that you didn't give a shit." Animal lifted one shoulder in a nonchalant shrug. "Maybe you didn't like boys—Jada says you were a little better with her."

"You ingrate," Rena gritted.

"Yeah … I could say the same about you." Animal held up his hand to halt any retorts his mother may have. "This is going nowhere—you and I have never gotten along. I just want to make sure you're not hurting Dad. If he's down for you strutting around town like a …" he caught himself before he said something he'd regret.

"Like a what?" Staring at him, her eyes brimmed with tears.

Fuck! He shook his head. "Just be careful, okay? There're a lot of fucking crazies out there. Harmless flirting online is one thing, but meeting up with these guys you know nothing about is another."

His mother bit the corner of her trembling lip and nodded.

Shit. He hated to see any woman cry, and watching his mother on the verge of doing so broke his heart. His relationship with his mother had always been strained, but he loved her in his own way. They were two very different people and they came together like oil and water. Ever since he was a kid, he'd butted heads with his mom, but he was attached at the hip to his dad. Theirs was a relationship of love, mutual respect, and admiration. His father loved him and his sister unconditionally, but he could never say that about his mother. No matter what their differences or recriminations, Animal didn't want anything bad to happen to his mom.

"Just be smart, and if you go out with one of those assholes, tell someone about it so we know the who and the where." While Animal talked, he saw his mom fidgeting with different items on the kitchen counter. "I don't want anything to happen to you. I know Jada feels the same way and, of course, Dad."

Opening one of the cupboard doors, his mom nodded then took out several small spice bottles.

Animal cleared his throat. "I'm gonna visit with Dad for a few."

An awkward silence stretched between them before he walked out of the kitchen and went into the family room. The chopping of vegetables resumed as Animal went over to the fireplace and stoked the logs. Turning back around, he looked at his father and his heart squeezed: his dad looked so frail and old with his head tilted back and his mouth cocked open.

Once the weather gets warmer, I'll take him fishing. His father loved to fish for rainbow trout in the rivers around the county, and every spring and summer Animal made it a point to go fishing with him several times a month.

"Dad?" he said in a low voice. His father's mouth closed and his head lolled from one side to the other. "Dad?" he said again.

His father's eyes snapped open, and he blinked at the light and wiped the drool from his chin. He straightened up in the wheelchair and his bleary gaze stared at Animal.

"When did you get here?" he asked.

"A while ago." Animal walked over and sat next to him. "You were snoozing."

"Oh." He shifted in the chair and looked over his shoulder. "Is your mom still home?"

"Yeah." A huge smile filled up his dad's face, and it hit Animal like a punch to his gut. "She's making dinner."

The smile grew bigger. "Then she'll be staying home tonight." His dad turned back and looked at Animal. "Are you and Lucy coming for chow?"

"No, Lucy's got tutoring after school and then homework."

"Have your mom pack you up a care package so the little one can eat something decent. Your mom's a great cook ... but you already know that."

The warmth in his dad's eyes when he spoke about Rena slayed Animal. He really couldn't wrap his head around his dad being okay with his mom cheating on him, but then if his dad knew about it and encouraged it, was it really cheating? Animal raked his fingers through his hair in frustration.

"Are you and Mom good?" he asked in a low voice, his eyes darting to the kitchen. His mother was still at the counter preparing the stew, her back turned to them.

His dad laid his hand on Animal's. "We're great."

"I mean, you're good with her going out and meeting new ..." his voice trailed off. It felt strange as fuck to say *men*, but isn't that what they were? The truth was that his mom was hooking up with men to have sex. *Fuck!*

"I'm the one who suggested it. I'm not the man I used to be, and your mother is still young and has needs. It works for us."

Animal searched his father's face to see if there was any pain, but he found none. *If Dad's cool with this then it's none of my business.* "I just wanted to make sure."

"Always looking out for your old man." His father patted Animal's hand. "You're a good son, but you don't have to worry about your mom and me—we love each other, and I'm happy that she's happy."

"Okay then," Animal whispered.

For the next couple of hours, the two men talked up a storm about everything and nothing, and when the clock hit 4:15 p.m., Animal couldn't believe how fast the time had flown.

He stood and clasped his dad's shoulder. "I gotta pick up Lucy at school." His father nodded. "Poker night is at Ryder's house this month. You should come."

"Sounds like something I'd like to do. I haven't seen Ryder in a while. He mentioned wanting to go fishing with us when the weather warms up."

"Yeah, he said the same thing to me. We'll make a day of it."

"There's nothing like fresh pan-fried rainbow trout. I can taste it already." His dad chuckled. "You gonna bring Lucy over here on poker night?"

Animal fished out his car keys from the front pocket of his jeans. "No. Belle's having the old ladies and the kids at her house. Savannah and Timmy will be going there too, so it'll just be us guys at Ryder's."

"That's good. Is Lucy adjusting better?"

"Seems to be. Making friends with Paisley has helped a lot, and now she's spent a few times over at Chas and Addie's place playing with Hope. It seems like those three—Paisley, Hope, and Lucy are getting real tight. I wish she had some friends from her school, though."

"She will—it takes time. She's gone through a lot in the last several months. It's never easy for a kid when her mom walks out on her. We'll all help her along the best we can."

"Thanks, Dad. I better go. I don't want Lucy thinking I forgot about her."

"Throw another log on the fire before you go."

Animal did as his dad had asked, then walked into the kitchen. "I've got to pick up Lucy," he said to his mom.

With her back to him, she nodded. Animal could tell by the way her body stiffened and how she slammed the pot down on the stove that she was still angry at him. He stood there for a couple of seconds, and when she didn't acknowledge his presence, he opened the back door and walked out without uttering a single word.

A SOUND LIKE a car backfiring brought Animal to his feet and reaching for his 9mm in the pocket of his leather jacket laying on the chair. He crossed over to the window and peered through the slats of the blind. A man in jeans and a red hoodie slammed the door of a silver sedan parked in front of Olivia's house. The guy hurried up the sidewalk and pounded on the door as he kept looking over his shoulder.

The coppery glow from the setting sun shone on Olivia's face as she opened the door. Animal noticed her facial muscles tighten, and she didn't look too pleased to see the man. She closed the door slightly and hugged the doorframe with the side of her body.

A sudden uneasiness punched through Animal as he watched the two of them talk. Olivia's face looked strained as the man took a few steps closer to her and started to wave his hands around.

"That's it, asshole," Animal muttered as he backed away from the window. The dude was yelling at Olivia and it was scaring her, and Animal was going to shut that shit down. Now.

"Lucy," he called out at the bottom of the stairs. "Come here for a sec."

The girl appeared at the top of the stairs. "What do you want?"

"I'm going over to Olivia's for a minute, okay?"

Lucy shrugged.

"I'm locking the doors and I don't want you going out or opening the door to anyone."

Her eyes widened. "What's wrong?"

"Nothing. I just want you to be safe. I'll be back soon. Now go back to your room and finish what you were doing."

"Okay." She turned around and disappeared down the hallway.

Animal stepped onto the porch, making sure the front door locked behind him, then glanced over at Olivia's. The sound of angry voices rose suddenly to a shout, and Animal sprinted across the lawn and up the sidewalk.

"What the fuck's going on here?" he said.

The man turned around. "This isn't any of your business," he gritted. His eyes flashed like an angry bull, and red blotches spotted his face.

"The fuck it isn't." Animal looked at Olivia. "You want this fucker to leave?"

She grasped the collar of her turtleneck and nodded.

The man snapped his gaze back to Olivia. "We're not finished here."

In one smooth movement, Animal had the guy by the neck, dragging him down the sidewalk to his car. The guy took several punches at him, one that landed on the side of his face. The asshole was a strong fucker, he'd give him that, but Animal quickly bounced back and threw a few punches that seemed to calm the jerk down.

"Get the fuck outta here, and I don't want to see you back in this neighborhood. You will not bother Olivia again, got it?"

The jerk fumbled with his keys then opened the door and quickly closed and locked it. Animal stood with arms crossed, watching until he drove away. He smelled Olivia's enticing scent before he saw her approach him.

"Are you all right?" she asked, her fingers gently brushing his bruised skin.

"I'll live. Who the fuck was that?"

"Brady Sickles—he's the gym teacher at Slavens. He's blaming me for my friend Ivy breaking up with him." She gave him a weak smile. "The creep conveniently forgot to tell my friend that he was married."

"What a fuckhead. Why's it your fault?"

Olivia wrapped her arms around herself. "Good question. The guy's weird, and I never understood what my friend saw in him. I say she's lucky he's out of her life. Sickles gives me the creeps."

"If he comes around again, let me know."

"Thanks for coming to my rescue," she said softly.

"Anytime." He looked over at his house then back at her. He wanted to pull her into his arms and taste her lips, but he wasn't sure she'd want him to do that, and he didn't want to piss her off. Instead he stared at her. Damn … she captivated him in a way no other woman had before.

"Is Lucy at home?" Olivia asked.

Animal saw her shaking from the cold and he tilted his head in the direction of her porch. "Yeah, and you should go inside—it's damn chilly out here. I gotta get back to Lucy."

"I am freezing." She laughed and rubbed her hands up and down her arms, trying to warm them.

"Are you free for dinner on Saturday?"

"I am." Her green eyes sparkled like a bright, clear emerald, and in the fading light, they looked as though they were deep enough to hold a galaxy. He just stood there intoxicated with their depth. "What time?"

"Uh …?" he replied, his gaze still boring into hers.

"The time you want to meet for dinner on Saturday?"

Animal dragged his eyes away from hers and looked back at his house. "Oh, yeah. I'll pick you up at seven o'clock. Does that work?"

"That's perfect."

"You better get outta the cold. I'll see you around." He turned away before he did anything stupid like yanking her close to him and running his hands down to her ass, or telling her that he couldn't get her out of his damn mind. Shit … the woman had him spinning in circles.

"Bye," she cried out behind him.

He held his hand up in the air as he walked toward his house. The last rays of the sun faded behind charcoal clouds as darkness crept in. Animal heard her front door close before he jumped up on his porch and went inside the house.

He took out the gun from the waistband of his jeans and went over to the wall safe and put it inside, then he crossed the room and glanced out the window, noticing light seeping through the damn sheets on Olivia's windows. "When the fuck's she gonna get rid of those?" he muttered under his breath as he turned around.

Animal walked into the kitchen and opened the refrigerator, then took out a beer, a package of red leaf lettuce, and a large plastic container of food—courtesy of Jada. He unsnapped the lid on the food and put the chicken and dumplings into a pan that was on a burner, and then popped open the beer can.

He was going on a date with Olivia on Saturday. The thought scared and excited him at the same time. If his brothers knew about it, they'd have a heyday with all their joking. The truth was, Animal had never worked so hard to hook up with a chick.

He took a long drink and leaned against the granite counter. The thing that scared the shit out of him was that even though he wanted Olivia in his bed in the worst way, Animal also wanted to get to know her better—to talk to her and share ideas. Yeah ... that was fucked up.

He crushed the can and tossed it into the trash, and then ripped open the packaged salad and emptied the contents into a bowl.

CHAPTER SIXTEEN

ANIMAL WOULD BE here before long to take her out to dinner. At the thought of that, Olivia's hands trembled and her insides lurched for the umpteenth time that day. Ever since that morning, her stomach had gone crazy: coffee tasted bad; her favorite almond biscotti tasted worse.

"This is insane," she said as she tossed the latest outfit on the bed to join the four already discarded ones. "Ugh!" She flopped down on the rocking chair and slowly moved back and forth to try and calm her frazzled nerves.

What was wrong with her? Was it the date with Animal? Ridiculous. Olivia had started dating when she was fourteen and she'd had a steady supply of boyfriends or casual dates until her breakup with Kory when she'd put herself into the deep freeze. So what was the big deal with Animal? She closed her eyes and the memory of the way he held her and kissed her filled her mind. Her lids snapped open. So he was a good, no, great ... no, *fantastic* kisser ... so what? And then there was the way he treated Lucy with such love and tenderness.

"Stop!" Olivia pressed her hands against her stomach. "It's just a fucking date. No biggie. I just have to remember to not make it into anything more than what it is. That shouldn't be too hard since he's a biker and I know *exactly* how those guys are. Right. Just remember that and get over it." When she was nervous, she talked to herself like a madwoman.

One time when she'd gone on a job interview, Olivia had been so edgy that she talked aloud the whole ride up in the empty elevator, and when the doors opened, the people waiting couldn't hide their apprehension when no one else exited the car but her.

Olivia leapt from the chair and went into the bathroom once more to check her reflection in the mirror. "Too much eyeshadow," she murmured as she took a Q-tip and blended some of it away. Satisfied, she padded over to her closet *again* and stared at her clothes trying to figure out what to wear. Animal hadn't mentioned the restaurant to which they were going, so she wasn't sure if jeans would be appropriate. She flipped through her clothes, the metal hangers scraping lightly on the bar. Maybe something ultra conservative. That would keep everything in perspective.

A crimson top with lace along the *V*-neck collar and sleeves caught her eye. She'd bought it a couple of months before and hadn't worn it yet. She slipped the top over her head and grabbed a short black pleated skater skirt and shimmed it up her legs. Olivia looked at her reflection in the full-length mirror hanging on the back of her closet door. The crimson color accentuated her flawless complexion and made her wavy brunette hair darker.

"Not exactly conservative," she said, rolling up her thigh-highs before sliding on her black high-heeled pumps.

Olivia put several different sizes of gold hoops into the three holes in her right ear and the two in her left and pushed a few gold and silver bangles onto her right wrist.

"Not bad," she muttered as she inspected herself in the mirror. "Not bad at all." She tugged down on the hem of her skirt, then swirled around and looked over her shoulder to make sure her butt and upper thighs were properly covered. The skirt fell mid-thigh, which was just perfect. Olivia was shooting for an elegant look with a hint of sexy, and she thought she'd accomplished it.

Just as she finished spritzing her perfume, the doorbell rang and her gut clenched. Grabbing her purse and coat, she switched off the bedroom light and walked slowly toward the living room, her nerves winding tighter with each step.

Olivia paused to look through the peephole and found Animal filling the small space. She unlocked the door and swung it open to let him in, an unsteady smile plastered on her face.

"Hi," she said as her eyes skimmed over him. The way he was dressed surprised and warmed her. He wore a button-down gray shirt with thin black pinstripes, the sleeves folded back to his elbows. The pants were black, straight-legged with a small cuff, his belt, black leather with light gray stitching, and his boots were polished. Only his black jacket, adorned with patches and buckles, gave any indication that he was a biker.

Something inside her stilled, then simmered, calming her nerves and quieting the churning in her belly.

"Hey," he said, taking a step back. His eyes slowly teased over her, all the way down to her pumps, and she blushed when they moved up and met her gaze. "You look beautiful," he murmured.

"Thanks," she said lightly, then added, "You dress up pretty well yourself."

His gaze skimmed over her again, then Animal cocked his head toward his SUV and said, "Are you ready to go?"

"Let me just grab my things." She turned away to put on her coat that she'd quickly tossed on the couch, then picked up her purse and locked the door after they both headed out.

As they strolled down the walkway, Animal leaned enough that their shoulders brushed, and his subtle touch brought far more tingles skating along her spine than Olivia would've liked. When they got to the car, she went to open the door, but his hand landed on hers and the tingles intensified. If her body was reacting this way before they even started their date, she was totally screwed. Drawing in a deep breath, she released the handle slowly as her hand dropped to her side.

Animal opened the passenger door and stood aside, and Olivia stepped onto the running board then slid into the seat. The door slammed shut and she fumbled with the seatbelt, trying to ignore the scent of his cologne wisping around her as he climbed into the driver's side.

"Let me help you with that," he said, leaning over.

His hand brushed against hers as he secured the belt into the buckle, and she had the overwhelming urge to bury her fingers in his thick hair and take a deep breath of his spicy, earthy smell.

"I made a reservation for us at the Buckhorn Steakhouse. Have you been there?"

"No, but I heard it's very good." *And expensive. I couldn't justify going there on my own, especially since I still have sheets for curtains.*

"It kicks ass." He looked over at her and winked then switched on the engine.

"Speaking of kicking ass, the burger I had at your club's restaurant was one of the best I've eaten. I'm surprised that an outlaw club owns such a ..." she struggled to find the right word without insulting him and the Insurgents.

"Is *nice* the word you're looking for, or maybe chic or urban?" He laughed. "We got a lot of businesses in Pinewood Springs."

"Do you have the requisite strip bar?"

"We do—Dream House, but we also have a barbecue restaurant and some other investments. We're gonna build some apartments with stores on the ground floor. Axe's old lady is working on the designs."

"One of your brother's old lady is an architect?" *That's a first for me—an outlaw that is secure enough to have a woman with a career as his partner. Dad and his club preferred the ones who only knew two words—yes sir.*

"Yeah—Baylee. The club's planning a family grill when the weather warms up, so you can meet some of the old ladies."

A trill of pleasure skipped through her at his words; he was planning on sticking around until the warm weather, at least. She leaned back against the headrest and looked out the window; dusty pink and indigo clouds stretched across the sky, and houses and streetlights blurred past as the car sped down the road.

"Where do you usually hang out?" he asked.

"My friends and I do a lot of dinner parties at each other's place, or we go to My Brother's Bar off of Decatur Street. They have trivia night, and taco Tuesdays, karaoke, and a bunch of other things going on there. It's fun."

"I've never been."

She laughed. "It's not a biker bar, that's for sure."

Animal chuckled. "Yeah—it doesn't sound like my thing. I'm not into karaoke or shit like that."

"Besides the clubhouse parties, what do you do for fun?"

"The clubhouse is basically where it's at, you know. My buddies are there and other brothers from different chapters show up—it's good times. If we go outside the club, Belly's Blue is cool, but our go-to is Steelers. We have family night there at least once, sometimes twice, a month."

"I figured Steelers was a biker bar. I always see a ton of Harleys in the lot when I go by," Olivia said.

"Citizens go there too 'cause the food's decent and the drinks are cheap."

By the time they arrived at the restaurant, the sun had dipped behind the horizon, and the shadows of the trees and bushes melted away into the blackness of night. Animal led the way into the steakhouse, and Olivia's stomach fluttered when he pressed his hand to the small of her back.

The restaurant was packed, and Olivia looked around as the hostess guided them to their table. Linen tablecloths and napkins, rich burgundy leather booths, cherry hardwood floors, lavish Karastan rugs, and two wood-burning fireplaces created an elegant ambiance. The aroma of wine and grilled meat wafted in the air, and her stomach gave an audible growl. A cacophony of cutlery on china, clinking glasses, and chatter filled the air.

"This is perfect," Animal said as he pulled out a chair for her at the table for two.

"Thanks," Olivia said, sitting down.

He sat down opposite her and took the menus the hostess handed him. Smiling at Olivia, he handed her one. She put it down on the table and looked through the window. Floodlights shone on evergreen and aspen trees, accenting the foliage, and in the distance, the jagged peaks soared into the night, the stars casting navy blue light upon their silhouettes.

After the waiter took their drink order—whiskey for him, a vodka martini for her—Olivia spread the burgundy linen napkin across her lap, took a deep breath, and raised her eyes to look at Animal. "I bet the view is spectacular in the daylight."

"It is." His gaze penetrated hers.

"Do you come here often?" she asked, looking away.

"Not really. Are you nervous?"

Her eyes snapped back to his. "No," she replied too quickly. *Real cool and casual.*

"You don't need to be. I don't bite." Animal chuckled. "Unless you want me to." He winked at her and her insides melted.

"I'll keep that in mind," she replied, grateful that the waiter had arrived with their drinks.

"Do you have any questions about the menu?" the server asked.

Neither of them had looked at their menus yet.

"Give us a few minutes, okay?" Animal said as he picked up the tumbler of whiskey.

"Very good, sir." The waiter turned away.

Animal leaned back against the chair. "Where're you from?" he asked Olivia.

"San Diego."

His eyebrows raised slightly. "You're a ways from home. How did you end up in Pinewood Springs?"

"I stayed with a friend of mine in Denver for a while, but I wanted to get away from city living, so I applied for the teaching assistant job at Slavens."

"Why did you move from San Diego in the first place?" Animal asked.

"Just needed a change." The memory of her brother's funeral flitted through her mind, replaced by the rough face of Iceman—her dad's idea of the ideal man for her.

"From what?"

"Everything." Olivia fiddled with the napkin in her lap, smoothing out the creases with her crimson-tipped fingers. "Are you from here?" she asked, diverting the attention off of her.

"Yeah, and so are my parents. I've been to San Diego. The Insurgents got a charter club there."

Damn, if I don't know that. "That's nice. Do you have any siblings?"

"A younger sister. What about you?"

"I had a brother." She plucked the olive from the toothpick as she drained her glass. "He was killed in a fight." Popping the olive into her mouth, she looked away.

"Fuck, that's tough. Were you close?"

"When we were younger, but we sort of drifted after he joined ..." Her voice trailed off.

Animal sat still, fixing her with those dark piercing eyes, which made him seem even more handsome and ... dangerous.

Olivia clasped her hands together. "I still miss him a lot. I probably always will."

"Are you ready to order?" The redheaded server glanced earnestly at each of them.

Olivia picked up her menu and scanned it quickly then looked up at the waiter. "I'll have the garden salad with balsamic dressing, the six-ounce filet mignon—medium—and mashed potatoes."

The waiter took the menu from Olivia. "And you, sir?"

"Porterhouse—rare—loaded baked potato and give us an order of asparagus and sautéed mushrooms." Animal handed his menu to the server and the man scurried away. "I hope you like asparagus and mushrooms."

"I do. It smells so good in here that I can't wait to try the food." She buttered a piece of warm French bread.

"I want you to tell me why you came to the clubhouse a couple of weeks ago, and I'm not buying that BS that you were in the area. And for the record, I was shocked as shit to see you at the club party a few weeks ago. You're the last person I ever thought I'd find there. I know your friend parties sometimes at the club, but why were you really there that night?" Animal grabbed a piece of dark bread from the basket and slathered on a thick amount of butter.

Olivia drew in a breath and locked gazes with him. "I had no intention of going to the party, but I was missing my brother so much that I just wanted to immerse myself in the club life again, you know ... the smells, the loud music, all the guys in denim and leather, and *feel* my brother again. That's why I came by looking for you at the clubhouse. Ever since the party, I've had the urge to go back and feel Leo—my brother, for a second time." She turned away and brushed the crumbs off the table. "It's hard to explain." Olivia purposely left out the fact that she also wanted to see *him,* but why muddy the waters?

Animal jerked his head back. "Your brother was a biker? He was in an MC?" Olivia nodded, her gaze cast downward. "What about your old man?"

She groaned inwardly. "A biker too," she mumbled.

"I'll be damned—you grew up in the life. What's your dad's MC?"

Her mouth immediately went dry and Olivia took a big gulp of water. She blinked rapidly and folded and unfolded her hands too many times.

He cocked his head to the side, his brow furrowed. "What's the name?"

"East Bay Dogs," she mumbled, watching Animal as he digested the words.

A silence fell between them, and his dark eyes looked directly into hers as seconds stretched into minutes. Olivia's heart pounded so loudly, she was positive Animal must've heard it.

Finally he glanced away, breaking their contact, and stared out the window. "The East Bay Dogs are our rival," he said in an even tone.

"I know," she whispered. "But I don't have anything to do with any of that. My dad pulled my brother into the MC, and I'll never forgive him for that. My dad's whole life was building up my brother, forgetting that I existed, and cheating on my mom. Instead of his life revolving around his family, it rotated around the club, the brothers, and the club girls." Olivia gulped down more of the water. "My dad finally dumped me and my mom for a club whore. My mom's life crumbled and blew away like dust in the wind. She was nothing without my dad, and even though he treated her worse than shit, she was the ever-forgiving wife until he left for good. So am I involved with the East Bay Dogs? No. Do I give a rat's ass about them? Double no. I left all that far behind me." A lump the size of a golf ball formed in her throat, and she blinked, trying to stave off the tears.

Animal shifted his gaze back to her and reached out and took her hand. "Don't sweat it. It just took me by surprise, that's all. I didn't figure you were a biker chick, but I should've guessed it by your sassiness." A deliciously wicked grin spread across his face.

She pursed her lips and shook her head. "I didn't think bikers liked sassy. My dad and his cronies adhere to the women-are-there-to-please-and-not-be-heard school."

"I know quite a few who believe that, but not all bikers are like that. I like sassy and challenging, and you are both."

"I have to warn you that I'm not very fond of outlaws based on what I've seen over the years, and I'm tainted like hell on men and loyalty since every guy I've been with has cheated on me. For some reason, I keep getting mixed up with guys who are like my dad. Go figure."

"You're the psych major." Another quick wink and a squeeze of her hand.

Olivia busted out laughing. "I think that's why I majored in psychology—to figure out me and my fucked-up family."

"Good luck with the family part. We all got some fucked-up shit going on with our past and present. The thing to focus on is leaving that shit behind. And to set the record straight—I'm not at all like your dad, and I believe cheating is a fucking betrayal and the worst disrespect in a committed relationship, even if the other person is cool with it." Animal slipped his hand away from hers and downed the rest of his whiskey.

"What do you mean if the other person is cool with it? You mean like swingers or something? I'm totally not into that."

"Me neither. Anyway, forget it."

Olivia was about to say something when the waiter returned with their food. She wasn't sure what he meant by his comment, but she gathered he was upset about someone's relationship. Maybe a friend's or his sister's? Surely not his parents'. From the expression on his face, she knew *that* discussion was over, so she cut into her steak and took a bite. It was cooked to perfection and the taste was superb. It had been eons since she'd had such a good quality cut of beef.

"This is fantastic," she said, picking up her wineglass.

"It's the best steakhouse in the county," he replied.

Olivia set her knife and fork down and licked her lips. "May I ask you something?"

Animal looked up at her. "Sure—anything but club business." He scooped up a forkful of potatoes. "But you know that."

"Where's Lucy's mom?"

His hand froze in midair, hovering just in front of his mouth for a split second before he lowered it to his plate. "In Illinois somewhere."

"So, you've raised Lucy yourself?"

"Not exactly." Animal's chest moved up and down as he sucked in a deep breath and exhaled. "Lucy came about after a one-night stand. Her mom—Emerald—and I were both drunk, and she got pregnant. She wanted a relationship—you know the husband, the house, the two cars in the garage. I didn't even know her—we just hooked up at one of the club parties, so I told her no. I tried to be a part of Lucy's life, but after she turned one, Emerald took off and moved away from Colorado. I always paid child support, sent gifts and cards, and called to talk with my daughter when she was old enough to speak, but Emerald made it real hard. She was a vindictive bitch and kept Lucy away from me. Anyway, about four months ago, she showed up at the clubhouse and left Lucy in my care. Seems like the guy she took up with didn't like kids."

Olivia's skin crawled while she listened to Animal. She wrinkled her nose and shook her head. "That's unconscionable! How awful. I feel for Lucy."

"Yeah ... it's been real tough on her. I try hard, but I'm no substitute for a mother." Animal motioned the waiter for another whiskey.

"Don't short change yourself. You're showing Lucy that you're there for her and that's huge, especially since her mom abandoned her. It's going to take her a long time to trust again because she doesn't want to be hurt. Lucy's afraid that you may leave just like her mom did. For her, trusting and getting too close to a person—another parent, a teacher, a friend, grandparents—means risking getting hurt all over again."

"So what the fuck do I do? I'm never gonna walk away from her. I'm happy she's with me even if I'm still struggling with being a parent."

Olivia placed her hand over his and smiled. "Parents struggle their whole lives. No one is born knowing how to be a good parent. There are so many stumbles along the road, but the important thing is that you're there for Lucy emotionally as well as physically. She needs to feel safe and to know you love and care for her. Believe me, I know. All I ever wanted was for my dad to love me and pay attention to me."

"And he fucked up big time?"

"Oh yeah." Olivia took a sip of wine. "And so did my mom, but this isn't a pity party, okay?"

"That works for me. Have you ever hooked up with a biker?" Animal asked.

"No—the whole thing with my dad turned me off to the lifestyle. One of the guys in my dad's club—Iceman—wanted to hang with me, and my dad and brother were all over that, but I was *so* not interested. He was one step above a Neanderthal."

Animal chuckled. "I know some of those." He placed a morsel of steak in his mouth and chewed, staring intently at her.

"I bet you do," she muttered, breaking off a corner of her bread.

"If you hate bikers so much, why the fuck are you out with me?" He wiped his mouth with the napkin.

Taking her time to answer, she held his gaze then leaned forward with her elbows on the table, resting her chin in her hands. "Because I like you. You're not at all like the bikers I knew back home. I love the way you care about Lucy and her education."

"Is that the only thing you like about me?" Animal's mouth tugged up at the corners, his ebony eyes watching her steadily.

Olivia felt her cheeks grow warm as memories of his kisses and his body pressed against hers rushed through her mind. Thinking about it made her grow hot all over.

"Well?" The faint smile hovering on his lips sent shivers right to her core.

"There might be some other things I like about you," she replied, looking down at her plate.

Animal let out a deep laugh. "There's a lot I like about you, and I don't say that to many women." He pushed his empty plate away. "As a matter of fact, I don't say it at all." He rose up from the chair and stood next to her.

Olivia sat transfixed, watching him as he wrapped strands of her hair in his hand then tipped her head back.

"You do something to me, woman," he said, his voice low and sexy. His eyes zeroed in on her lips as he bent his head down.

Olivia's mind told her to pull away, but she didn't budge; there was no way in hell she was going to stop him. His lips pressed against hers, soft and tender, and she raised her arms and entwined them around his neck, pulling him closer. The kiss deepened. Someone at a nearby table coughed loudly, but Olivia simply tightened her grip and he slipped his tongue between her lips, which she met with her own. The world dissolved around her and it was only the two of them, pressed together, sharing so much more than this one kiss.

Flicks of desire swirled inside her, burning her body, stimulating every nerve ending. A small moan rose up from her chest, and he slowly pulled up, his gaze smoldering with unsated lust.

"I'll be right back," he said, his voice husky.

With her body still throbbing in places she didn't even know existed, Olivia nodded and sank back in her chair. She watched him swagger away, his firm ass moving oh-so-right, and noticed how several women gave him a double-take when he passed their tables.

What's wrong with you? You're doing exactly what you weren't supposed to. No ... she couldn't be trusted with him. Her body misbehaved in the most deliciously wrong way. *But is it wrong if it feels so good ... so right?* Animal was unlike any man she'd ever known, and even though she knew he wanted to sleep with her, Olivia didn't feel like that was the only thing he wanted from her. None of the men who'd littered her past gave a shit about who *she* was—they only cared about having sex like ... all the damn time. They'd all been shallow and she'd been sucked into their world because of her damn neediness to have a man pay attention to her. But Animal seemed different.

"Do you want another drink?"

His deep voice startled her out of her thoughts. "If you want." *Stop psychoanalyzing yourself. You're having a great time with him, and it's been a long time since you've been with a man.*

"I thought we'd go to Jimbo's for some drinks and dancing. They got a cover band on Saturdays."

"I'd love that." Olivia couldn't remember the last time she went dancing while on a date. Kory wasn't into music, and the guy before that, Nathan Rogers, didn't like to dance. *Nathan.* She hadn't thought of the police officer in quite a while. Every once in a while she'd see him drive by Slavens, but he didn't stalk her with the frequency he had before she moved into her home. *He probably found himself a girlfriend.* Olivia shuddered at the memory of going out with the possessive, overzealous cop.

Animal paid the bill and grasped Olivia's hand as he guided her out of the restaurant. Bright stars sprinkled the inky sky and there was a slight chill in the air. He slipped his arm around her shoulders, drawing her close, and she rested her head against him. Two electronic beeps rang out and the car's headlights flashed as they approached his SUV. Opening the passenger door, Animal helped Olivia into the car then walked over to the driver's side and slid into the seat. He leaned sideways and brushed his lips against hers in a light kiss. Then, without a word, he sat up and turned on the ignition, gripped the steering wheel, then threw the SUV into gear and drove out of the lot.

Jimbo's was on the other side of town, and when they arrived, the place heaved with people. Animal held her close to him as he pushed their way through the labyrinth of patrons and tables until they reached the counter.

"Dude!" A bartender with a shaved head, full sleeve tattoos on both arms, pierced brows and nose, and a plug in each ear grinned from ear-to-ear.

"Titus," Animal said, high-fiving him.

"Where the fuck have you been?" Titus poured a glass of dark beer and set it in front of Animal. "What does your girl want?"

Animal leaned into Olivia. "What're you drinking?" he said in her ear.

His warm breath fanned over her neck and a single shiver rode down her spine straight to her core. "A vodka cranberry."

"Cran vodka," Animal said, and Titus nodded.

"You must be a regular," she said to Animal.

"Yeah—some of the brothers and I like coming here to listen to the live music. One of the brothers—Gopher—has a sister who's in a local band. She's a great fucking lead guitarist."

"Is that who's playing tonight?"

"No—tonight's a cover band. Leila's band plays original music. They're real good. Do you like metal and hard rock?"

"I love them both."

He pressed her closer and dipped his head down. "Awesome." He kissed her quickly then reached for his beer.

Her lips tingled from his touch, and she murmured her thanks when he handed her drink to her.

"Can you get us a table?" he asked Titus.

"Hang on." The bartender rushed away.

"Is it always this packed?" she asked before taking a sip of her drink.

"Yeah, especially on the weekend. Titus owns the place. We go back to high school."

"That's cool. How long has he owned it?"

"About five years or so. He and his brother started it, but he bought his brother out three years ago, and now he's flying solo." Animal nudged Olivia with his elbow. "Titus got us a spot—let's go."

Olivia sipped her drink while he guided her to a table near the stage. She plopped down on the chair then shrugged off her coat. The band was on stage setting up their equipment while hard rock tunes played from overhead speakers.

"I'm having a good time," he said.

"Me too," she said, looking up at him.

Her breath caught as the feral look in his eyes seared her. A shiver raced down her spine, and arousal flashed hot through her system.

Animal scooted his chair toward hers, closing the space between them. An influx of butterflies danced inside her as his gaze melted over her.

Curving his hand around the back of the her neck, he drew her to him, bent down and crushed his lips to hers. His tongue invaded her mouth, flicking across her teeth, entwining with hers, and she looped her hands around his corded neck. She'd never been kissed like that; it was wild, consuming, and addictive all at once, making her senses come to life. Their mouths meshed with escalating hunger.

"Fuck, Olivia," he murmured on her lips.

Hearing him say her name between kisses sent static sparks from her hardening nipples straight to the pulsing between her legs. She never wanted to pull away; she wanted to stay forever cocooned in his arms with their lips fused together. Moaning, she ran her fingers through his hair, and he yanked her closer against him. At that moment, all her notions about bikers faded away, and she wanted nothing more than to feel him inside her.

The first few beats of Whitesnake's "Here I Go Again" filled the bar, and Animal broke away and glanced over at the band.

"Let's go," he said against her ear as he grasped her hand in his.

As always, his touch caused a small jolt through her, and she rose from her chair and followed him onto the dance floor where he pulled her into his arms. Olivia rested her head against his hard chest and heard the erratic thud of his heartbeat. As they danced, Animal sang the lyrics softly into her ear as he ran his hands down her back, stopping just before her ass. The scent of him surrounded her and his warm breath teased her skin into a carpet of goosebumps. Animal's hand on the small of her back pressed them together and her breasts rubbed against his chest. A low growl stopped the flow of the lyrics as he ground against her, his firm erection sending sizzling shockwaves shooting through her. Olivia clenched her legs together in the vain attempt to stop the throbbing between her thighs.

"You feeling it too, baby?" The hoarse timbre of his voice sent sweet lust coiling tighter.

Olivia tilted her head back and met his intense gaze, which skated over her face and stalled on her lips. The music and the chatter disappeared. The only thing she was acutely aware of was Animal: his arms touching her, his hardness rubbing against her, the bar's blue lights falling over his strong face, a lock of wavy hair falling across his forehead, and his sexy full lips coming very close to hers. Desire, lust, and sweet electricity ran through her, and then his lips hungrily covered hers as he kissed her frantically and deeply for the rest of the song.

After the song ended, she pulled away, smoothing down her hair.

The rest of the night flashed by and before Olivia knew it, the overhead lights flickered several times, indicating that "last call for alcohol" was upon the customers.

"Do you want another drink?" Animal asked as he pushed his empty beer bottle away from him.

"No thanks, I'm already tipsy." She giggled and brushed against him.

He wound his arm around her shoulders and tugged her to him. "I like you this way." He nuzzled her neck, his stubble scratchy, his breath warm and soft.

"Do you?" She stroked the side of his face with her fingers.

The overhead lights turned on and people began to file out of the bar.

"Oh yeah, baby. Are you ready to go?"

Olivia glanced around and noticed all the empty tables. "Where did everyone go?"

Animal chuckled. "The place is closing." He broke away then stood up and reached out his hand to her.

After she grasped onto his, he pulled her up and helped her on with her coat, then led her through the bar, raising his fist to Titus as they walked out.

On the drive back to her house, Olivia leaned her forehead against the passenger window; the coolness felt good against her skin.

"You okay?" Animal asked, looking at her sideways.

"Yeah, my head just feels a little fuzzy. You know, I'm surprised you picked me up in a cage."

He laughed. "I wouldn't have if I knew you were a biker chick."

She reached over and lightly punched him. "I'm not a biker chick. I just had a dad and brother who were bikers."

"You weren't interested in any of the brothers?"

"Not at all. Like I mentioned before, my dad and brother tried to push Iceman on me, but ... no ... just no." She shuddered.

"That bad?" He grinned.

"Yeah."

"Now that I know you're used to the life, I'll have to take you for a ride."

"I haven't been on a motorcycle since my brother died." Olivia snapped her eyes closed, trying to squeeze out the images of Leo.

"Do you miss the ride?" Animal grabbed her hand and kissed it.

Her lids fluttered open as memories of the wind rushing around her and the sun warming her face filled her mind. "Very much."

"I'll fix that for you. I can't wait until Lucy's old enough to go on her first ride. She's gonna love it."

Olivia smiled and laced her fingers through his free hand. "She's got a lot of fire in her."

"Don't I know it."

"I'm pretty sure she has a lot of *you* in her. I suspect that once Lucy gets on the back of your Harley that she'll be addicted to the ride." She looked over at him and admired his strong jaw, his high cheekbones, and a stubborn chin that dared anyone to try and mess with him. "I wouldn't be surprised if, at some point, Lucy will want her own motorcycle. How would you feel about that?"

A long pause stretched between them, and she watched the muscles in his jaw clench and twitch, and then he breathed out an audible sigh.

"I hope I'll be cool with that. I mean, if I had a son, I'd want him to have his own bike, but a daughter?" He pulled his hand away from hers and scrubbed the side of his face. "Shit, I don't know. I'd be scared as hell that some fuckers would mess with her 'cause she's a girl and all that. Kimber's got a bike—a pink Harley." He chuckled. "She can really ride. At first Throttle was wacked out about it, but now she's his old lady and they ride all over the damn countryside."

"Throttle's an Insurgent?" she asked.

"Yeah, and Kimber works in Hawk's—he's our VP—bike repair shop. She's a mechanic."

Olivia playfully swatted Animal's bicep. "Get out of here."

He laughed. "I'm not bullshitting—Kimber's a mechanic who rides a pink Harley, and Throttle was so fucking old school that the brothers still can't believe it's for real. I mean, the dude did a complete one-eighty—it was the damnedest thing."

"I'm actually shocked. I never thought I'd hear about an outlaw having an old lady who not only is a bike mechanic but rides her own

Harley. I guess your club isn't as primitive as I thought it was."

"That's what I was saying earlier; you can't judge all clubs by your dad's and his standards. Most of us are pretty damn decent." The corners of his mouth lifted.

Olivia rolled her eyes. "Now comes me stroking your ego …"

"I don't need the ego shit. Your tongue twistin' with mine as you moaned took care of that." He tweaked her chin and chuckled.

Olivia felt a slight flush heat her skin, and she looked away, grateful that they'd turned into the cul-de-sac. They stopped in front of her house, and Animal switched off the engine and climbed from the car. She shoved open her door before he came over and hurried up the sidewalk to the front porch. The moonlight shone down weakly, and she rummaged through her purse for the keys, stiffening when she heard his footsteps behind her.

Olivia's fingers grasped the keys at the bottom of her bag, and she quickly inserted the right one into the lock. She had to get inside fast to stop the thoughts of Animal that were whirling in her head. She'd had a nice time … okay a *great* time. *One of the best times I've ever had with a guy. He makes me feel so alive, so sexy, so special. Stop. Right now. This is foolish. This can't go anywhere, but so what? Don't I deserve a night of great sex? I've had more than my share of bad ones. After one night we'll both be sated, and we can move on without hormones zigzagging constantly through our bodies. No. Don't—you like him too much. You fall too hard too quick. Remember your pattern. You can't afford—*

Before she could turn the lock, Animal came up behind her and slipped his arms around her waist, pulling her tightly against him. He moved her hair to the side and his fingers lightly swept across her skin. He kissed around her ear and briefly licked her lobe with the tip of his tongue, then continued feathery pecks and nips down her neck. Each caress of his lips left a trail of goosebumps in its wake. She trembled with desire and her taut nipples pushed against the lace fabric of her bra and her thighs quivered.

"I don't know what it is, but you do something to me," he said against her skin.

"Animal," she gasped.

He reached over her and turned the key in the lock, then pushed open the door and walked her inside; the front door closed itself.

Olivia pivoted in his arms until she faced him, and he crushed his mouth to hers. She lost herself in his kiss, blocking out all worry or recriminations, only allowing herself to *feel*.

"I've been wanting you for a long time, baby," he whispered as his hands slid down her back and landed on her behind.

Damn, it felt so good being in a man's arms again, especially a man who was taking the time to please her. No fast, sloppy kisses followed by a cock buried in her; just slow brushes of lips that made her toes curl.

"What about Lucy?" she murmured.

"She's at Chas's house having a sleepover with Hope," he replied, his mouth still on her lips, her neck, her throat.

Oh man, does he turn me on.

"Who's Chas?" *Really ... that's the best you could come up with?*

"A brother. He and his old lady have a daughter Lucy's age." His tongue swept across her collarbone then dipped into her cleavage.

Olivia groaned and curled her fingers in his hair, urging him closer, then gasped when he nipped her playfully with his teeth. *Oh fuck!*

Then his phone rang.

"Fuck," he muttered as he pulled away, shoving his hand inside the front pocket of his pants. He glanced at the screen. "Double fuck." He caught her gaze. "Sorry, babe, but I gotta take this—you know the score." He crossed the hallway into the kitchen, and she heard the low murmur of his voice.

Yeah ... Olivia knew the score; it had been played out a million times during her growing years, and now she'd let herself get pulled right back into *that* world. Shaking her head, she let out a ragged breath and raked her fingers through her messy hair.

She heard his footsteps before she saw Animal walk back into the foyer. A frown pinched the space between his brows as he approached her.

"Club business," he said as if that made everything crystal clear and all right. He moved over to her and snaked his arm around her waist. "Now, where were we?"

Olivia stiffened under his touch and he drew back, a quizzical look etched in his face.

"What the fuck?" he said.

A few heartbeats passed before she spoke. "It's late and this isn't really a good idea. The phone call brought me to my senses." She rubbed her hands down her skirt.

"Are you fucking serious? You're upset because I got a call from my club? *You* of all people?"

"It's not that ... it's just that I'm Lucy's teacher and—"

"Don't start that bullshit up with me. You're not her teacher, and if tutoring her after school is the problem, I'll pay you privately for the lessons. Don't stop something that you know we both want. Stop being afraid of your feelings."

"I'm not afraid of my feelings." Well, maybe a little, but he didn't need to know that.

"Yeah, you are. You're the psych major and you can't even figure yourself out. You've been living on shallow feelings for so long that you've buried all the true emotions inside you."

"No, I haven't."

Animal held up his hands. "Be in denial—you're the one who's going to be sorry. Run to some pansy-ass who doesn't know how to treat a real woman. Whatever, babe ... What. The. Fuck. Ever."

He whirled around and flung open the front door then stepped out onto the porch. She watched as he stalked down the walkway, each footstep like a stab to her gut. Animal was right—she was so afraid of admitting that she liked him, of recognizing the starved, feral side of her because she'd been hiding it for so long. For the first time in her fucked-up dating life, she had a *real* man, who, no doubt, could please her like no one ever had, and she was letting him walk away from her.

"Animal!" she cried out as she stood in the doorjamb.

He stopped and looked over his shoulder.

"Come back."

Animal turned around and stared at her. "You sure about this, because I don't go in for regrets and shit like that."

A smile danced across her lips. *Damn, I like him.* "I'm sure." *But don't get carried away. This is a night of great sex, not a love affair or happily ever after. Don't let that happen.*

A magnetic grin spread over his face as he swaggered back up the sidewalk, and she stood to the side, waiting for him to enter.

CHAPTER SEVENTEEN

OLIVIA SWITCHED THE floor lamp near the cushy chair by the window to low then slowly walked over to Animal who stood by the bed. His gaze teased up her body then locked on hers; lust heated his eyes, and the look sent a bolt of fire between her legs. A low growl rumbled from his chest, fanning the desire inside her.

"Get over here," he gritted as he unbuttoned his shirt.

She shook her head. "If you want me, come get me."

A wicked glint lit up his eyes, and he threw his shirt on the floor before walking toward her. Seeing him shirtless for the first time made her knees shake, and it took every bit of strength to stay rooted to the spot when all she wanted to do was run over and collapse in his arms.

"Like what you see?" he said in a low, deep voice that made her panties damp with want.

"Oh, yeah," she whispered as her gaze tracked his body up and down. He was superb—a work of art. Every muscle was taut, lean, and so sinfully enticing. A smattering of dark hair dusted his chest and trailed down his flat stomach then disappeared into the waistband of his pants. Oh man, she wanted to see what he kept hidden below that waistband.

Animal's abs rippled with each step until he stopped in front of her. Without warning, he reached out and jerked her into his arms, crushing his mouth on hers. His kiss was hot and hungry. Her mind reeled out of control as he thrust into her mouth, touching her body and making it burn.

Olivia pulled back slightly and ran her fingertips across his chest; it was something she'd wanted to do since that day he'd come over to help move her cupboard into her home. She bent down and traced the swirling ink pattern with the tip of her tongue and smiled when Animal threw his head back and groaned. Softly, she ran her fingernails over his nipples while she continued to forge a trail with her tongue down his chest and toward his navel.

Suddenly, he yanked her to him, his hands squeezing her ass hard. "I want to see your body. Now. All of it."

Her fingertips slipped into his waistband, brushing against the softness of his hair and the sharpness of his muscles, and he grunted.

"What the fuck are you doing to me, baby?" he rasped, pulling her hand away.

"Don't you like that?" she asked. Her tongue swiped at his Adam's apple before her teeth nipped his skin.

"Damn, woman," he gritted.

The vibrations of his groan against her lips and tongue burned through her. She leaned her head back, and he showered airy kisses down her throat to the creamy swells that her top's neckline exposed. Her hardened nipples strained against the thin fabric of her blouse and she rubbed them against his muscled chest, burying her moans against his shoulder. Everything about him sent her reeling: his scent, his look, his touch. Her vow not to become involved with him shattered; she wanted Animal to take her rough and hard, and do things to her she'd only dreamed about.

In one smooth movement, Animal broke away slightly, grasped the hem of her top, and yanked it over her head. He bent down and lavished a trail of kisses and bites over the tops of her breasts as his hands traveled up to cup them. His thumb grazed over her nipples, then flicked them teasingly until they ached for his mouth. He jerked her bra down, and her breasts popped out revealing dusty-pink taut buds. Leaning back on the heels of his boots, his gaze devoured her, stroking her with dark intent.

"Damn, your tits are fucking beautiful," he rasped as he dipped his head.

Tilting her head back, Olivia closed her eyes, her body tingling in anticipation for his touch.

"Open your eyes. I want you to watch what I'm doing to you."

Fluttering them open, she caught his stare as he slowly licked the tip of her nipple. *Damn!* Sparks snapped through her, and she arched her back, thrusting her breasts closer, hoping he'd take them in his mouth. Animal leaned back again. *Dammit!* With his eyes boring into her, he pinched both of her taut buds between his fingers and pinched them, softly at first, then harder. It was exquisite and tormenting at the same time.

"So good," she moaned, sliding her hands into his hair, her nails scratching along his scalp before her fingers tangled in his strands.

"Fuck," he said, backing Olivia up and slamming her against the wall. His mouth assaulted her neck with hard, biting kisses—the kind that left deep red marks for days. It then moved down to her breasts, and he sucked one of her aching buds into his mouth while tweaking the other until she thought she'd explode.

"Oh fuck!" Heat flooded between her legs and she pressed closer to him, humping his leg. Harder and faster he sucked, and her low moans turned into cries. When he slipped his hand under her skirt and placed his palm on her damp panties, shivers rushed up her spine.

"You're so sexy, baby," he rasped, rubbing her aching sex.

"That's so good," she muttered as she ground against his hand.

"What do you want me to do?"

Swallowing hard, she looked into his eyes. "Fuck me," she moaned.

Suddenly, Animal scooped her in his arms then threw her down on the bed and she bounced. Barely able to catch her breath, he grabbed the sides of her skirt and yanked it down, sliding it past her legs and ankles then throwing it on the floor. She sat up and reached down to take off her shoes, but he gripped her hand and shook his head.

"The heels and stockings stay on. I'll get rid of those sexy-as-fuck panties in a minute," Animal said. There was a feral, predatory look in his eyes as he pushed her back down on the mattress.

Her arousal surged through her senses, screaming for him to take it further, to release the built-up tension that made every one of her nerve endings crackle. Her breath caught in her throat when he grasped one side of her panties and ripped them at the seam. A wicked smile spread across his lips and he ripped the other side easily.

"Fucking amazing," he muttered as he pushed off the bed and stripped off the rest of his clothes until he stood naked before her.

Her gaze landed on his pulsing dick, which was so thick and long that she almost feared it may rip her in two. Animal climbed back on the bed, and dug his fingers into her soft flesh, spreading her bent knees wide until she felt a small stretch down the insides of her thighs. He stared at her pussy, and Olivia could feel her juices dampening the small strip of dark hair on her engorged lips.

"Fuck, woman, you're so wet," he said in a low voice as he slid his hands under her and cupped her ass cheeks. His shoulders kept her opened wide as he lifted her. Olivia raised her head and flattened her hands on the mattress and captured his piercing gaze. Holding her breath, she watched as he slowly licked the length of her, his lips soon glistening from her arousal.

Her body jolted from the sheer pleasure of it, and her synapses sparked and sizzled as he shoved his tongue into her slippery slit. Over and over, he licked, nipped, and feasted on her until she didn't think she could take it anymore. As Animal shoved his fingers in and out of her, he steadily licked her hardened nub while his penetrating gaze watched her. Never in her life had she been so aroused, and never had a man taken this much time with her before plunging into her. Everything around her blurred; the only thing Olivia was aware of was the tangy scent of her arousal and the sound of his warm, soft tongue swishing in and out of her, coaxing her to orgasm. And then the tight coil deep inside her unfurled with such ferocity that it rocked her entire body as her climax tore through her. Thrashing on the bed, she came hard, raw, and completely.

"Oh shit ... that was just incredible," she panted.

Animal leaned over and kissed her passionately; his lips were wet from her juices and she tasted her salty-sweet self on him. "There's more to come, baby." He pinched her nipples then bent over and picked up his pants.

As Olivia watched him slip on a condom, all kinds of shivers danced over her skin. In the past, she'd been lucky to have one true orgasm, but possibly two … unheard of.

"How do you like it, baby?"

"All kinds of ways," she said, her hands cupping her breasts.

Animal grunted and bent down and pulled her nipples into his mouth again, alternating between sucking them hard then gently.

"So, it's my choice?" he asked, straightening out.

"Yeah."

A devilish smile twitched on his lips, and Animal leaned back and stared at her wide-spread legs. "Get on your knees," he ordered.

Olivia flipped over and knelt down, spreading her thighs and resting on her forearms.

"Perfect," he muttered as he caressed her rounded ass cheeks. "You've got the most amazing ass," he said.

Before she could answer, a sharp sting cracked against her butt and she cried out.

"Too hard?" Animal peppered the sting with soft kisses then tenderly stroked the area before another crack sounded but not as hard as the previous one.

"You like that?" he said against her skin.

Her moan was her only answer.

Animal placed his finger against her small puckered opening and ran his other hand down her ass to her slick pussy. Slipping between her folds, he played with her clit while she whimpered and writhed against the mattress.

"Feels so damn good," her muffled voice said.

He kept up the rhythm for a long while: smacking her ass, kissing and licking away the sting, stroking her sweet spot. Then, with his knee,

196

he spread her wide, pushing her head down more so her ass was sticking high in the air. He cupped her wet pussy and smeared her juices over her ass.

"Your tattoo is real sexy and such a turn-on."

She felt his tongue tracing the flowering vine from the middle of her shoulder blades all the way down her spine.

"You've got some sexy tats yourself," she replied.

His breath blowing over the wet trail he'd just made pebbled her skin and a tremor vibrated along her body.

Olivia felt him rub the tip of his dick all over her wetness before gliding it deep inside her. A contented moan escaped through her parted lips, and Animal moved his hands up and down her back, throwing in painfully sweet kisses.

"You feel so fucking good, baby. Tight and warm and just fucking perfect."

One hand holding her shoulder, Animal pulled all the way out then pummeled into her while the other hand pressed on the small of her back, pinning her in place so she was completely at his mercy. And she fucking loved it. With each thrust, her body jerked back and forth until they were going at it at such a frenzied pace that Olivia thought for sure the bed would break. Grunts, moans, and skin slapping on skin were the only sounds in the room. When he reached under her and tugged at her swaying breasts, sparks went off behind her eyelids and she exploded with a yell. One last, hard thrust and feral sounds came from Animal as he stiffened and dug his fingers in her ass.

Still buried inside her, he collapsed on top of her, and for several minutes, they lay panting until he pulled out and climbed off the bed. Olivia rolled onto her side and watched him dispose of the condom before coming back to her. He drew her close to him.

"Fuck, babe. Just ... fuck," he murmured, running his fingers through her disheveled hair.

Olivia was so overcome with emotion she almost cried, but she didn't think Animal went in for crying women.

"You are amazing," she said, pressing her lips against his chest.

"You are too," he replied, squeezing her shoulder.

Olivia watched the moonlight spill into the room while listening to the soft sounds of Animal's breathing. Warmth radiated through her chest as she snuggled closer to him. *I can't believe how wonderful it was with him.* The familiar tugs at her heart surfaced and she pursed her lips. *Now don't go and make what happened into a bigger deal than it is.* Olivia had to watch herself because if she didn't, she could easily fall head over heels in love with him. *You can't lose your head. Remember, he's a biker and you're definitely not the only woman in his life.* But Animal had made her soar to heights she'd never been to, and it had been glorious. *I don't need to think about any of that now.*

All she wanted to do was bask in the afterglow before she drifted off to sleep.

MORNING SUNLIGHT POURED in through the kitchen window, making bright rectangles on the gleaming wood floor. Olivia stood at the counter, squeezing oranges in the new electric juicer she'd bought on sale the week before. A breeze stirred the curtains of the window and rustled the leaves in the budding trees in her backyard. She loved the gingham and colorful floral pattern on her newest purchase: curtains for the window above the sink. The country chic pattern was perfect for her white farmhouse kitchen, and it hadn't cost her an arm and a leg.

Olivia added water to a clear vase that held the bright yellow daffodils she'd bought earlier that morning at the flower market before she rushed to the grocery store to pick up staples for breakfast. Earlier that morning, when she'd woken up cocooned against Animal with the heat of his skin seeping through hers, happiness engulfed her, and the usual morning-after regrets were absent—a first for her.

Animal had stirred and pressed his hips against her and a wave of arousal flooded through her as she reached back and felt that he was hard. She ran her hand up and down his dick and gave it a little squeeze, and he grunted and placed his hand on her breast and began flicking her nipple to a stiff peak. She'd moaned and he'd whispered her name and pushed a little closer. Olivia had wiggled her hips and shifted so that his dick was pushed directly at the crack of her ass then she raised her leg and bent it at the knee. Animal nuzzled her neck, covering it and her shoulder with wet kisses while playing with her breasts. She wiggled some more, then he mumbled for her to grab a condom on the nightstand and hand it to him. After sheathing his dick, he'd draped his arm over her chest and yanked her closer and thrust inside. He'd pushed in and out, his thumb stroking her special spot until she shattered into a million pieces, crying out his name. He soon followed suit, and they both lay panting heavily as the early morning sun filtered slivers of lights through the thin sheets over the windows.

Olivia clenched her legs together and fed the juicer another orange. Animal was so different from any man she'd ever known, and he made her feel things that were new to her. Deep, dark, and exciting things. And damn did the guy know how to please her in ways no man ever had. No more faking an orgasm like she'd done with Kory just so he'd stop pounding into her and finish up his damn business already. Animal brought the sexy Olivia out. She'd always known that part of her existed, but none of the men in her past life had a fucking clue.

The timer on the oven beeped, and Olivia grabbed a set of oven mitts and opened the door. The ham and cheese quiche bubbled as she pulled it out and set it on one of the burners to rest. Then, she threw a handful of blueberries, strawberries, and raspberries into a hand-painted fruit bowl she'd picked up on one of her visits to Tijuana a few years back. She and her friends used to go over the border to party at some of the bars and clubs on Avenida Revolución. *Fun times. I really miss Karla, Colleen, and Maria.* She sighed and sprinkled some sugar on the berries and mixed them with a wooden spoon.

"Morning, babe," Animal said in a low voice as he wrapped his arms around her waist and held her.

"Morning," she whispered, leaning back into him and lifting her chin as his lips nuzzled the curve of her neck, sending shivers skipping through her whole body. She inhaled her citrus body wash and shampoo and smiled. "You smell good."

He chuckled. "I smell like a fuckin' woman, but next time I'll bring my own stuff."

A thread of joy curled around her spine. *Next time. Oh, Animal.* "That would be good."

"What're you making? It smells awesome." He reached around her and plucked out a blueberry and popped it in his mouth.

"Is it sweet enough?"

"It's good—not as sweet as you taste, but then I've never tasted anything like you before. Try one." He picked out another berry and she took it between her lips. "Good, right?" Animal turned her around and slowly licked the granules of sugar off her lips before pressing his mouth to hers in a deep kiss.

She broke the connection and rested her forehead on his chest. "If I don't get over to the oven, we're going to have burnt croissants for breakfast." She tilted her head to look at him.

Animal kissed the tip of her nose. "We wouldn't want that." His smile widened into a grin that was both boyish and seductive.

Olivia turned away. "I hope you're hungry."

"I am, but I'll eat breakfast first." He swatted her butt playfully, and when she looked at him over her shoulder, a pink flush colored her cheeks. He winked, and her insides melted on the spot.

"I have fresh squeezed orange juice on the counter and coffee in the pot. Help yourself," she said, taking out the sheet pan.

Olivia put the quiche, croissants, fruit salad, pitcher of juice and coffee on the table and sat down. Animal glanced down at his phone when it pinged, a crease forming across his forehead.

"Is everything okay?" she asked, placing a generous portion of food on his plate.

"Yeah." He picked up his fork and took a bite. "This is really good, babe."

"Thanks. What time do you have to pick up Lucy?"

"In a couple of hours. Addie took her and her daughter Hope to the mall."

"Lucy told me she loves going to the mall. She showed me what her aunt bought her the last time they went together. It's the cute panda purse and matching sweater."

"She told you that? I figured she liked going out with my sister, but she's never told me that. I'm glad Jada loves to shop 'cause I wouldn't know what the hell to do at the mall with Lucy."

Olivia smiled and tossed her hair over her shoulders. "If Jada can't make it sometime, I'd be happy to take Lucy to the mall. I love to shop, so it would be a pleasure."

A funny look crossed his face and Olivia froze, wishing she could take back the words. *Why the hell did I say that? It's like I'm trying to throw myself into his family. Great move.* Not.

Animal nodded then picked up the glass of orange juice and took a drink. For a long while, they ate in silence but for the clatter and scrape of silverware against yellow stoneware plates. Olivia concentrated on the sounds filtering through the open window: a train passing by in the distance, children laughing, birds singing, dogs barking. She glanced over at Animal, who had his head down as he scrolled through his phone.

She cleared her throat, set her knife and fork down on her plate, and asked him what model his motorcycle was; being around bikers her whole life, she knew none of them could resist talking about their babies.

Animal's head popped up and a grin spread across his face before he launched into a discussion of best and worst models and years for Harley-Davidson motorcycles. The ice had been broken, and Olivia let out a sigh of relief as she listened intently to him.

After their meal was long over, she stood up from her chair and gathered the empty plates from the table and walked over to the sink.

"Let me help you," he said, carrying the rest of the dishes to the counter.

"Thanks, but I can handle the cleanup on my own." She rinsed the plates and giggled. "The dishwasher is going to do all the work."

Animal dipped his head down and kissed her softly. "Thanks for the food." His hand slipped down to her butt and he squeezed it gently. "When you're finished we can have some fun before I have to pick up Lucy."

Her body hummed with arousal caused by the heat radiating from him. She wiped her hands with a dish towel then pivoted toward him, entwined her arms around his neck, and kissed him hard. "I'd love that," she murmured against his lips before pulling away.

"Are you sure you don't want me help you stack the dishwasher?"

"I'm sure. Just go into the living room and make yourself comfortable. I'll be done in bit."

"Do you have a computer I can use? I wanted to look something up and I hate searching shit on my phone."

Olivia giggled. "I know what you mean. I prefer a larger screen and my phone is so painfully slow sometimes that it drives me crazy. You can use the laptop on the desk in the corner of the room."

"Thanks, babe." Another playful swat to her ass then Animal walked out of the room.

A huge grin crossed her face as a warm and cozy feeling spread through her. If Kory or any of the other guys she'd dated had smacked her butt, she'd been infuriated and insulted, but with Animal it was different. It wasn't like he was trying to demean her or show her he was the superior one in their dynamic. Unlike Kory, Animal didn't judge her or try and belittle her; he was just so different from all the others, that part of her kept thinking there had to be a catch.

"What the fuck?" Animal yelled.

Olivia closed the door to the dishwasher, dried her hands, and hurried into the next room.

"What's wrong?" she asked. The anger plastered all over his face stopped her in her tracks. His look went through her with an icy blow, and she stood there wringing her hands.

"Why the fuck do you have a profile on this bullshit site—*Discreet Passion*?" he asked his eyes narrowed and flashing.

Relief washed over her and she laughed softly. "That's research for my psych paper, and why're you snooping on my computer?"

His lips turned downward. "I'm not *snooping*. This shit came up when I clicked on."

Olivia tilted her head back slightly. "That's right—I forgot to close the window when I logged off yesterday." She smiled and walked over to him and placed her hands on his shoulders, kneading them. "Sorry for accusing you of being a snoop."

Animal reached up and grasped her hands bringing them both to his mouth and kissing them. "So, this is for *school*? You're not looking for a dude online?"

"Hell no. I'm not into that, and anyway, I had a moratorium on dating after a ridiculous breakup a while back." She bent down and kissed his cheek. "You're the one who broke my no-dating streak."

"What can I say? I'm fucking irresistible." He chuckled when she smacked him lightly on the arm.

Actually he is, but he's confident enough without me telling him that.

"So what made you pick this site?" he asked, scrolling through her profile.

"My friend recommended it. She's on it for real. You act like you know it, so I should be asking what the hell are *you* doing on the site?"

Animal jerked his head back and pulled her around so that she fell into his lap. "Why the fuck would I need to be on an online dating site? I find plenty of women without some damn dating app."

"I'm sure you do." Her stomach clenched tight. It shouldn't be a surprise that he was a womanizer and had plenty of women who'd drop their panties for him in a second.

He pressed her closer to him. "But no one's been like you, baby."

Olivia wanted to ask him if he was talking about sex or other things about her. Being the best in sex wasn't exactly what she was looking for; she wanted him to see beyond her breasts and butt, to see the person she was. *No man ever has taken the time to get to know me. They only see my big boobs and never get beyond that.*

"Your pretty face is way too serious, baby. What're you thinking?"

It was way too soon for them to have the conversation about *them,* so she shook her head and poked her finger into his chest. "You never answered why you know about *Discreet Passion.*"

His face darkened for a split second then went back to normal, and Olivia thought she'd imagined it.

"I know someone who's on the site for real." His eyes flicked back to the screen.

Before she could probe any further, the small bell chimed telling her a Real Time message had just come in. *Hunter, of course.* He was the only one who "talked" exclusively to her through messenger.

"Who the fuck is that?" Animal stiffened.

"This guy who's been my—or should I say *Rose's*—number one fan. He's the main subject I'm using for my paper."

"Open it up," Animal ordered.

"I'm not in the mood to 'talk' to him, but I am in the mood for you." She dipped her head down and kissed him and he responded, but she could tell that his mind was still on Hunter's message. "Okay," she said, pulling away from him. "I'll see what he wrote, but I don't want to spend more than a few minutes with this."

Animal nodded. "Sounds good to me."

Hunter: *How's my beautiful Rose doing today? I missed talking with you last night.*

"How the fuck does he know what you look like? You didn't send him your picture, did you?" Anger laced Animal's voice.

Olivia shook her head. "No. The guy's just saying stuff to try and reel me in. He's trying so hard to make me think I'm the most special woman on the whole site, and I bet he's chatting up a storm with at least five or six other women."

"This guy could trace your computer's IP address. You need to be careful with this. What kind of a class are you taking?"

She swept her lips across his. "Your protective side is sweet, but you don't need to worry about me. First off, I have an IP blocker so it can't be traced, and second of all, my prof is totally down with what I'm doing. Dr. Davison is real excited about my research up to this point and has even checked out the site himself."

"He sounds like a fucking nut," he grumbled.

She laughed. "He isn't. He's totally obsessed with his field and a great teacher." The bell chimed and she focused her attention back to the screen.

Hunter: Are you there? I hope you're not chatting with another man. I've grown very fond of you. Did you get your flowers I sent you?

"Flowers? What the fuck, Olivia?" A scowl buried deep in his face.

"Electronic ones. On this crazy site, a man can send pictures of bouquets with notes, just like the real thing. Hey, you're the one who wanted me to open his messages, so just chill." She took a screenshot of the messages thus far then typed her response.

Rose: I'm here. I'm multi-tasking. Sorry. The flowers were beautiful. I love roses.

"Pretty lame, huh?" she asked Animal, clicking the *SEND* button. "The whole thing is lame as fuck," he huffed.

Hunter: I think it's time for us to take our relationship to the next step, my sweet.

Animal growled and held her tighter.

Rose: I'd love that.

Hunter: I thought you would. We need to exchange photos, then if we like what we see, we should talk on the phone. I want to meet you very soon. I promise our meeting will be romantic and full of tenderness. Nothing is too good for my sweet woman. I have a small confession to make: I think I could fall in love with you and hope you have some feelings for me.

"What a fucking asshole," Animal said. "And there's no fucking way you're giving out you photo, phone number, or meeting this nutcase anywhere."

"Will you calm down? I don't plan to meet him privately—only in a public place, *if* I even meet up with him." She placed her fingers on his lips. "Don't start with me. I'd be better to meet him for my paper, but I'll admit I'm starting to feel sorry for him. I mean, what if he's sincere and is really falling in love with Rose? I'm basically cat-fishing him and it's starting to feel wrong."

"How the fuck can he be in love when he hasn't even met or seen you? The guy's bullshitting. He's got an ulterior motive going here."

"Maybe … maybe not. Loneliness makes people look for relationships and then try and make them fit. I'm really starting to feel bad about this now."

"This dude's not lonely, he just wants to fuck."

"I'm not so sure," she said as she began tapping the keyboard.

Rose: *Falling in love is pretty serious. I'm not there yet. Sorry. We can talk on the phone, though.*

"Why the fuck are you telling him *that*?" Animal said.

"A burner phone. I'm going to end the conversation now." Olivia needed time to think about what she was doing. A part of her was drawn to Hunter—she felt his loneliness and his pain, and another part of her felt terrible in stringing him along like this. The other guys she'd communicated with were in it only for the sex, and several of them admitted they were married and just wanted a fling, but Hunter was different, even though Animal would disagree with her. But then, he hadn't been talking to Hunter for the past several weeks. Hunter truly did seem like he needed *her*, and that could be a powerful aphrodisiac for a woman. She wondered how many other women he'd met on the site.

Hunter: Being in love is absolutely serious, my sweet, and I don't expect you to feel it now. I'm just hoping that you feel something for me. I want us to get to know each other, and when we do, I know we will love each other—body and soul. Let's start first with a phone call.

"No dude talks like this except some pansy-ass trying to get fucked or a damn psycho. I don't have a good feeling about this, babe." Animal rubbed his hands up and down her back.

"He's just lonely, and I think what he's saying is sort of romantic. I mean, I can see how a woman would fall for him, *if* he's sincere."

Rose: I do like you, but I need to think about everything. I have to go now.

Hunter: Did I offend you? Please tell me you still want to talk to me.

Rose: You didn't offend me. I do still want to talk with you. It's just that I have a lot to think about, and a friend of mine is here.

Hunter: A friend? I thought you had no one.

"That's strange," Olivia said.

"I told you the guy's a psycho. Why the fuck does he want a woman who's all alone? My radar's going off big time, baby."

"Maybe he doesn't have any friends and thought we were kindred spirits."

"Bullshit."

Rose: I do have friends—just not any family. I do have to go. Bye.

She clicked out of the site and closed the lid to her laptop. Animal was right: something *did* seem off with Hunter. Maybe she should just make her own assumptions and wrap up the paper. It seemed like she was getting in over her head, but then just one phone call with Hunter wouldn't really hurt. Olivia could get a better sense of him after talking on the phone.

"I don't like you talking to this guy, but if you're ever gonna get together with him, you need to tell me and I'll come along with you. There's no way you're meeting him alone—public place or not."

She rested her head against his shoulder and he held her tight. "Agreed. I've got to admit, he's creeping me out a little. I just want to forget about all that now." Olivia tipped her head back, and his lips captured hers possessively. The kiss sent the pit of her stomach into a wild swirl.

Standing up with her in his arms, Animal made his way to her bedroom, his lips still fused to hers.

CHAPTER EIGHTEEN

DUCT TAPE COVERED the victim's body as she lay naked on her back with her arms and legs tied in a spread eagle position to the posts of the bed. She was covered in blood and it looked as though multiple stab wounds had been the cause of death. Detective Ed McCue noticed bruising around the woman's neck and noted it in his report.

"Her name is Samantha Paulson," Officer Levi White said.

The detective cocked his head in the young officer's direction. "You know her?"

White nodded. "Her son, Daniel, was one of my mom's students at Slavens a few years ago. My mom teaches second grade at the school, and I volunteer to coach softball in the summers. Daniel's a great player. I can't believe she's dead. This is going to be tough on him."

"Was she married?" McCue jotted down everything White had told him in a small spiral notebook. He was old school and refused to use the handheld notebooks the department had given all law enforcement two years before.

"Divorced, but my mom suspected she was having an affair with one of the teachers at the school—a *married* teacher."

"You got a name?"

The officer shook his head. "No. My mom wasn't 100 percent sure about the affair, so she didn't tell me that name."

"Sounds like that's where I'm going to have to start. Let me know if you hear anything about the murder through the school's grapevine." He turned away and stared again at the young woman. "White?"

The policeman stopped at the door of the hotel room and looked over his shoulder. "Yes?"

"Do you know how old she was?"

"Thirty-three."

"Gotcha." McCue scribbled the number on the piece of paper.

"Older than the other one in our county and the other five in the neighboring counties," Detective Ibuado said as he approached the bed.

"Yeah, but it's the same sonofabitch doing the killing. This murder is similar to the last one and the others in Chester and Valley Pine counties." He looked around the room. "An out-of-the-way bed and breakfast or boutique hotel, the woman registers alone, duct tape across the mouth, tied up, stab wounds and the bruising around the neck. I'll bet she was raped too."

"And the sheets are gone." Ibuado blew out a long breath. "Seems like we got a serial killer in Pinewood Springs."

McCue ran his hands over his face. "Fuck! We gotta find this madman fast."

"We need to alert the papers so women can be careful."

"Yeah, but let's not jump to conclusions until we get the reports back from the coroner. We've got to find a connection between these murders. Something is tying them all together, but what?" McCue tapped the cap of his pen against his mouth.

"I'll order copies of the case files on the women in the other counties. Maybe we can see something in them that they don't." Ibuado slipped his electronic notebook into the inside pocket of his jacket.

"That'll be a start. Let's hold off with the press for a bit—I don't want this killer going underground or moving on."

"Agreed," Ibuado said as he walked away from the crime scene.

The squeaky wheels of the gurney drew McCue's attention away from the body and to the corner's crew as they entered. He nodded to the men then trudged out of the room and down the stairs to the lobby. A growing number of hotel guests stood in the lobby, speaking in hushed voices, their gaze fixing on him as he walked over to the manager.

"I'm going to need the guest list for the past two days. Do you have security cameras? I didn't see any when I walked around the property."

A flush crept across the cheeks of the thirty-something woman. "No." She pulled at the collar of her lavender blouse. "The owner of the hotel hasn't installed them yet, but I'll have one of the desk clerks print out that list you wanted. Can you tell me anything about the"—she glanced around and lowered her voice—"*murder?*"

"At this time I'm not at liberty to say anything. I'll be in touch."

The detective walked away and paused at the large glass front door and watched as the gurney rolled by. The black body bag wiggled from side to side as the crew navigated it across the terra cotta tiles.

The detective sucked in a breath through his teeth and followed the techs out into the bright sunlight. His next stop was the one that he hated the most: death notification. Even though he'd been in law enforcement for twenty-five years, there was never a right way of telling a family that their loved one had been murdered.

Putting on his sunglasses, McCue plodded over to his car.

CHAPTER NINETEEN

ILES, RECEIPT BOOKS, orders, and manuals littered the large wooden desk. A framed photograph of Lucy's school picture sat on the left corner of the work surface; her face was glum and red ribbons intertwined with her dark hair. Jada had come up with the idea to braid the fabric with Lucy's strands, and the young girl loved it so much that she refused to wear her hair any other way.

Glancing at the picture, Animal muttered, "Thanks a fucking lot, Jada." He'd had a particularly shitty morning trying to remember what the hell Jada had told him about the damn ribbons and braiding Lucy's hair. After three failed attempts—even though Animal thought he did a pretty damn good job—he had called Olivia to rescue him.

Animal shook his head and narrowed his eyes. "You're gonna take me down, kiddo," he said under his breath. And if his daughter didn't, Olivia most certainly would.

Since their date, they'd gone out one more time, but having a young daughter at home with him made it somewhat difficult to get together more often with Olivia. Hands down, Lucy came first, and Animal wasn't sure how she'd feel if he brought Olivia into the mix. Lucy seemed to have taken to the cute teacher's assistant, and her reading was improving greatly, but he didn't know if Lucy would freak out if she knew he was going out with her tutor.

Animal swiveled around in his chair and gazed out the window at the snowcapped mountains in the distance that glittered in the sun. Forests of pine, aspen, and evergreen dotted the mountainside, their leaves and branches swaying gently in the breeze. A few birds flew across a crystal blue sky; there wasn't a cloud in sight. It was a perfect day to ride around the mountain roads, feel the rush of wind, the smells of wet earth, fresh pine, and sweet hay.

Animal looked back at his desk and groaned. He had too much work to justify taking off on his Harley. He tilted back in his chair and closed his eyes and imagined Olivia, in tight as sin jeans and a clingy top that barely touched the top of her jeans, on the back of his bike with her tits pressed against him and her arms wrapped snugly around his waist as they sped around the countryside.

His dick stirred and his lids snapped open. *Fuck!* Animal sat up straight and swiveled around to face his desk. *I gotta stop thinking about her. What the hell?* Plain and simple: Olivia had gotten under his skin in a way no woman ever had. Normally, he'd have some fun with a chick, then he'd move on when the desire started to wane, but with Olivia, he couldn't imagine moving on and that was what surprised him.

"I just have to think rationally about this," he said aloud as he picked up a book of receipts on the desk.

But how could Animal think *anything*? His senses were too clouded by her. He'd fallen under her spell, but in fairness, her laughter and sassiness along with her wit and her generous heart had blindsided him. Olivia was so much more than just a good time. Everything about her enticed him and he couldn't walk away even if he wanted to, which he didn't. How could he? He already knew so much about her: how the skin around her waist was taut and satin smooth, that he made her tremble when he licked her sweet pussy, and when they kissed, her lips were soft and so fucking demanding.

Whenever he was at the clubhouse, Rosie, Wendy, Charlotte, and the other girls would rub up against him and shove their tits in his face, and he could control his libido just fine, but he couldn't be near Olivia for ten seconds without getting steamed up. It'd been like that from the first day when he'd seen her trying to take apart her cupboard. She'd hooked him with her dark hair, her stunning green eyes, and her feisty attitude.

Animal flipped open the receipt book and stared at the numbers.

Olivia was still wary of him because he was a biker. She didn't tell him that, but he could sense it in the way she'd study him when she thought he wasn't looking, or the way she'd wince when Animal told her something was club business. Her fucking dad had done a number on her when Olivia was growing up, and now Animal had to figure out how to put the pieces back together and make them all fit.

"Fuck!" He threw the book at the door just as it opened.

"Whoa, dude," Smokey said as he bent down to pick it up. "Having a bad day?" His lips twitched and Animal was pretty sure Smokey was fighting a smile.

"What gave you *that* idea?" He motioned for his friend to take a seat. "I gotta get a damn bookkeeper. I'm sick and tired of dealing with the numbers, the payroll, and all that other shit."

"Put an ad in the paper and online—I'm sure you'll get some applicants." Smokey thumbed through the receipts.

"I'd rather hire someone who comes recommended. Maybe I'll ask Throttle or Rags. They finally had to get someone to help out with the books."

"That's the price you pay for running your own business. I got my niece doing my stuff. I could ask her if she knows anyone." Smokey shut the book and pushed it toward Animal.

"That'll work. Let me know what she says. What're you doing around here?" He leaned back in the chair.

"Doing a basement remodel. The fuckin' place is covered in black mold which I didn't see because it was painted over. I got a crew over there taking care of it, but we can't get back in until tomorrow. I haven't seen you at the clubhouse in a while."

"Been busy with work and Lucy."

"Is that all?" One corner of his mouth hitched up in a cocky smirk.

Animal glared. "Just tell me what the fuck you mean. I don't have time for this shit."

"Bones, Rock, Puck, and Shadow saw you out with a hot chick a few nights ago. They were at ... damn ..." Smokey snapped his fingers, tilting his head as if trying to remember the restaurant.

There was no way Animal was going to help him out, so he just sat there with his hands folded on his stomach, watching Smokey struggle to remember.

"You know, dude. Fuck, it's right on the tip of my tongue." Smokey tapped the left temple of his head.

"I'm kind of busy, bro. When you think of it, text me." Animal turned toward his desktop and opened the inventory screen.

"El Tecolote!" Smokey yelled. "How the fuck couldn't I have re- membered that? We go there all the damn time. Shit ... I'm getting old."

"Yeah, you just hit thirty, and it's downhill from there. I oughta know—I'm thirty-two, and I can't remember shit, bro."

Smokey's eyes widened. "Fuck ... that's not good."

"You're telling me—it fuckin' sucks." He bit the inside of his cheek to keep from laughing, and failed at it. Loud guffaws filled the room, and Smokey's anxiety morphed into anger.

"Fuck you," he gritted while Animal continued to laugh. "So who was the bitch you were with?"

Animal's merriment stopped abruptly and needles of fury pricked at the back of his neck as he clenched his fists.

Smokey shook his head. "You started this, dude. So who was the chick?"

"How is any of this your damn business?"

"It was your neighbor, right?" The fine lines around his eyes crinkled when he smiled.

For several long seconds, Animal sat there, breathing deeply, trying to control his heartbeat while waiting for his ire to subside. *No one* said shit about Olivia, but none of his fellow brothers knew how he felt about her, so he decided to give Smokey a free pass from getting Animal's fist in his fucking face.

"Yeah. Her name's Olivia, and before you say something's that gon- na really piss me off, I gotta tell you that she's not just a sweet piece—I like her."

Smokey threw him an incredulous stare, then a bark of laughter escaped his lips. "Never thought I'd hear those fuckin' words from you."

Animal shrugged. "Me neither, but now you know."

Smokey didn't have to answer: there was an unspoken code in the brotherhood that all the members treated their brothers' women with respect.

"Do you want to join Helm, Shadow, Wheelie, and me for a ride after work?" Smokey asked.

"I'd be down for it in a minute, but I gotta take Lucy to the dentist. Another time, dude."

Smokey pushed up from the chair. "Sure. I'll ask my niece if she knows anyone who can help you out."

"Thanks. Tomorrow I'm meeting up with Hawk, Bones, Klutch, and Shadow for lunch at Ruthie's around noon. Do you wanna come along?"

"Sure. I'll see you then, dude." Smokey lifted his chin then walked out of the office.

Animal figured that in less than an hour, the news that he had a woman would spread like wildfire among the brotherhood. There was no way he could be pissed about it. Animal had his fun ribbing Wheelie with Sofia and Ryder with Savannah, and all the other members who ended up having their women wear their patch.

He and Olivia had a long way to go before he'd ever ask her to wear his patch, and there was a real possibility it would never happen, but for now, Animal just wanted to get to know her and spend more time with her.

Animal picked up the receipt book again and started plugging the numbers into a spreadsheet.

LUCY AND A blonde-haired girl with several colorful barrettes in her hair skipped over to the SUV. His daughter opened the passenger door, and the two girls giggled between pants as Lucy pushed herself up on the running board.

"Can Aria come over for dinner tonight?" Lucy asked.

Animal's gaze darted to the young girl standing on the grass in front of the car, her blue eyes sparkling, and red blotches dotting her cheeks and chin.

"You got a dentist appointment," he replied.

Lucy slumped her shoulders and threw her book bag on the floor. "I forgot. Can we change it, please?" Her whole face crumpled up.

Animal shook his head. "We can't. It took more than a month to get the damn appointment. Sorry. Maybe your friend can come to dinner another time."

"Her name's Aria," Lucy snapped as she flopped down on the passenger seat.

"Whatever." His jaw hardened.

"Aria," a woman's voice called.

"I'm over here, Mom," the young girl replied.

A striking woman with long blonde hair came into view. Animal glanced at the car's clock glaring out the time in its blue numbers: 3:18 p.m.

"Hi," a cheerful voice said.

Animal averted his eyes from the clock to the door and nodded at the blonde. "Hey."

The woman ran her eyes over his face, then down his body and back up. She placed her hands on the young girl's shoulder and said, "I'm Aria's mom." Licking her lips, she extended her hand. "Elise Griffin."

Animal took her hand and Elise squeezed it lightly before he pulled it away. "I'm Lucy's dad."

"Does Lucy's dad have a name?" Elise fixed her gaze on his.

"Animal. We gotta get to a dentist appointment."

"Mom," Aria said, tugging at Elise's cardigan. "Lucy asked me over to her house for dinner. Can I go?"

Elise drifted her eyes back to Animal. "I think Lucy has an appointment."

"She does—I just told you that. Dinner won't work for tonight, but another time's okay." Animal switched on the ignition.

"I normally don't let Aria go to people's houses unless I go with her for the first time." Elise placed her fingers over Aria's mouth as she tried to say something. "I guess I'm just over protective, but you can't be too careful, you know?" She chortled.

"I get it." He suspected that wasn't her rule with Aria's other friends. Animal caught the look Elise gave him—he'd seen it more times than he could count. The mother was coming on to him, and if Lucy had any chance of keeping Aria as her friend, he'd have to humor the mom and have them both over for dinner.

"Maybe tomorrow night?" Elise said.

"Let's set something up for next week," he replied.

"Dad!" Lucy protested.

"Why don't you give me your phone number and I can call and set it up?" Elise asked.

"I'll see you around the school. We gotta go now." Animal turned to his daughter. "Close the door and buckle up."

Mumbling something under her breath, Lucy waved at Aria then slammed the door shut. Animal helped her with the seatbelt then pulled away from the curb, noticing that Elise stood watching until he hung a left turn.

"You don't want me to have any friends." Lucy's lower lips pushed out and she turned away from him and stared out the passenger window.

"Don't start with me. If I didn't want you to have friends, why in the hell would I arrange for you to hang out with Paisley and Hope? Aria can come over, just not this week. I got a lot going on at work."

Lucy kept staring out the window.

"Now, you're mad at me? Fine. You have to learn that you can't always have what you want."

"I already know *that*. I don't have Mom, remember?"

"How can I forget—you keep reminding me."

For the rest of the drive neither of them spoke, and when Animal killed the engine, Lucy leapt out of the car and dashed into the small three-story building.

"Wait up!" Animal strode over to the entrance and saw his daughter leaning against the wall, shuffling her feet. "Don't ever fucking do that again. If you're pissed at me, your mom, or the damn world, that's fine, but you don't run off like that. Something can happen to you in a blink of an eye."

Lucy looked up her eyes shimmering. "So what?"

Animal dropped to one knee in front of her. "*So what?*" He grasped her chin with his hand and tilted her head up until her eyes met his. "So *everything*. There's no way I want something to happen to you or lose you. You mean everything to me."

Several tears spilled down her cheeks, and he wiped them away with his fingers then pulled her into a tight hug.

"I know you're disappointed about Aria not being able to come over tonight, but I promise you can have her over next week. And I know you're real pissed at your mom. I am too, but it's not because she left you with me—hell, I'm thrilled about that; it's because she's hurting you and I can't fuckin' fix it."

Lucy buried her head in the crook of his neck, and Animal held her for a long while, then he pulled back a little.

"We better get upstairs or you'll lose your appointment. Do you wanna go out to eat tonight?"

Lucy nodded.

"How about Ruthie's?" Animal knew that his daughter loved the double chocolate milkshakes there.

Lucy's head jerked up and there was a small light in her eyes. She nodded again.

"Then that's what we'll do, kiddo." He tucked her hand in his as they made their way to the dentist's office.

When they entered the reception room, Lucy made a beeline to an elaborate wire bead maze on a low table. For a few seconds, Animal watched her nimble fingers run the beads over the complex wire design, and he tried to bury the rage he felt toward Emerald. For the past three weeks, he'd tried to get a hold of her to no avail. She hadn't called Lucy at all, and the only reason Animal was reaching out to the fucking bitch was because he thought it would make Lucy feel better, but now he wasn't too sure about that. Animal didn't want Emerald to upset Lucy and say something mean to her, and he certainly didn't want her spiteful ass to take Lucy away to punish him. If she even attempted to do something like that, Animal would fight her with everything he had; there wasn't a chance in hell that he was going to let Lucy go.

He turned away and walked up to the front desk to check in and his gaze landed on Olivia's rounded ass encased in a sexy-as-fuck pencil skirt. As if sensing his presence, she whirled around and her smile shone like stars in the sky with no city lights to dim them. Animal smiled back.

"Hi," she said, coming over to the counter.

"Hey. So this is your other part-time job?"

She nodded. "Who are you seeing today?" Olivia sat down and looked at the computer screen.

"Lucy has an appointment with Dr. Linney."

"He's nice, and very good with children. You just need to sign in and if you have insurance, I'll need the card."

"No insurance." Animal scribbled Lucy's name. "How've you been?"

"Good. And you?"

"Itching to go for a long ride. Are you free on Saturday afternoon? Lucy's going with Jada to the mall and a movie."

"Saturday's perfect."

Animal leaned over the counter. "I've missed you, baby." He inhaled her clean, citrusy scent. "And your perfume right now is driving me fucking wild. Maybe you can sneak over tonight and we can have some fun when Lucy's asleep."

"I'd love that, but I'd be worried Lucy would wake up. It'd be horrible if she found us. She'd feel like you betrayed her or something."

"I know. I just need to be with you again, baby."

"Me too."

Olivia brushed her fingers over his hand, and he grabbed and kissed them, his gaze fixed on her heated one.

"Fuck, babe."

"Olivia, I needed those files ten minutes ago. Get a move on." A tall man in his early thirties wearing a white coat stood by the printer, glaring at her.

Olivia jumped up from her chair and turned toward him. "I had to tend to something Dr. Linney needed, Dr. Canty. I was just ready to bring you the files," she said picking up several folders from the desk.

The dentist cut his eyes to Animal, and he stroked his throat and grimaced. "It seems like you're neglecting your duties." His gaze averted back to Olivia.

"I'm sorry—" she began.

"What the fuck's your problem, *Doc*?" Animal's lip curled.

Brows lowering and pinching together, Dr. Canty leaned back against the wall. "Excuse me?"

"There's no fucking excuse for the way you're disrespecting Olivia."

Red blotches mottled the dentist's face. "Stay out of this or I'll have to ask you to leave."

"You'll do no damn thing because I'm sure you like your pretty-boy looks and want them to stay like that. Do you get my meaning?"

"Animal, please," Olivia whispered as she clutched the files against her chest.

Dr. Canty just stood there glaring, and a woman in bright pink scrubs came into the area. She glanced down at the sign-in sheet and said, "Lucy Walsh."

"That's my daughter," Animal said, his hard gaze still fixed on Dr. Canty.

"Let's go on back," she said, darting her eyes from Animal to Olivia to Dr. Canty, and then back to Animal.

"Lucy," Animal said, without moving a muscle.

His daughter went over to him and the friendly lady in pink opened the door wide.

"Hi, Lucy, I'm happy to see you again. Remember we met at the burger restaurant a while back? I'm Ivy."

"I remember. Hi," the young girl mumbled.

"Hi," Ivy smiled at Animal. Did you want to come too?"

With clenched jaw, Animal nodded then tore his gaze away from the dentist. "I'll talk to you later," he whispered to Olivia as he pushed away from the counter and followed Ivy down the hallway.

As Animal sat on a metal chair, all he could think about was rearranging the fucking dentist's face. When he saw the way Dr. Canty was treating Olivia, it was like a hot poker stabbing him, and Animal couldn't just stand there and let it happen. He was pretty sure Olivia would call him on it, but no matter what she'd say, Animal would never just stand by and watch someone disrespect his woman.

He glanced over at Lucy and her hands clutching the sides of the dental chair so hard that her knuckles were white. Animal stood up from the stool and crossed over to her.

"There's nothing to be scared about, kiddo," he said, placing his hands on top of hers. "I heard this doc is really nice and gentle. You know who works here?"

Lucy met his gaze and shook her head.

"Olivia—Ms. Mooney."

His daughter's eyes widened, and he could feel her hands relax under his. "Really?"

"Yep. She works the front desk, and she's the one who told me that you're so lucky to have Doc Linney as your dentist."

"Really?"

"Really. When you get done here, you can say hi to her."

"Okay."

The door opened and a tall and slender man in his late thirties walked in with a folder in his hands. A wide smile crinkled the lines fanning out from his eyes, and he walked over to Lucy and held out his hand.

"Hi there, Lucy. I'm Dr. Linney. How are you?"

Lucy glanced over at Animal, who lifted his chin at her, and then she took the dentist's hand, a small smile spreading across her lips. Animal leaned back on the stool, happy that Lucy's dentist wasn't the fuckface who'd berated Olivia, and smiled at his daughter.

An hour later, Animal and Lucy—a glittery unicorn sticker in hand—walked into the reception area, and the young girl rushed up to the counter.

"Hi, Ms. Mooney," she said. "Look at my sticker."

Olivia smiled. "You picked an awesome unicorn. I love the way the rainbow shines. How'd you like Dr. Linney?"

"He's nice. My teeth are real good."

Every so often, Olivia would glance over at Animal, her eyes sparkling, and he wanted to take her in his arms and kiss the hell out of her. He watched as Lucy and Olivia chatted, and beneath his cool exterior beat a warm heart.

"Dad, can Ms. Mooney come to dinner with us? Please?" Lucy asked, tugging on his jacket.

Animal looked over at Olivia. "What do you say?"

"*Pleeeeze*," Lucy said as she stood on her tiptoes. "We're going to Ruthie's Diner and they have the bestest chocolate milkshakes."

"I've heard that," Olivia said, smiling. "I'd love to go. I've never been there, so you'll have to teach me the ropes."

"I will. We go there a lot." Lucy craned her neck. "Don't we, Dad?"

Animal ruffled the top of her head. "We sure do, kiddo." He swung his gaze back at Olivia. "What time do you get off work?"

"I have to stay a little later tonight because Dr. Linney has a couple of patients coming in after hours. I should be out of here by six thirty. Is that too late?"

"No," Lucy said.

Animal laughed. "That works. Lucy can do her homework before we go."

"I'll just meet you there."

Lucy covered her mouth and laughed while she shook her head.

"You don't want me to meet you at the diner?" Olivia asked.

"You have to come with us," Lucy said. "You live next door."

Out of the corner of his eye, Animal saw Dr. Canty starting to come into the reception area, but then turn around when he saw the biker. *That's right, asshole. Stay the fuck away.*

"Okay, Dad?"

Animal quirked his lips. "What did you say?"

"Ms. Mooney lives close." Lucy shoved her sticker into the front pocket of her corduroy pants.

"Lucy was saying that we should all go together since I live next door." The warmth of her smile made her green eyes electric, her face radiant.

Desire pumped through his veins. *Damn she's so fuckin' sexy and beautiful.* "That makes sense." He winked at her.

"Then it sounds like a plan." Olivia looked at Lucy. "Thanks for asking me. I have to get back to work now. I'll see both of you later." She smiled slyly at him.

The whole ride home, all Animal could think about was Olivia and how much he wanted her. At first, Olivia was a challenge and he loved the pursuit, and in his mind, he figured once he'd gotten her between the sheets, he'd hit the road. Damn, was he wrong about that. He craved everything about her: her taste—dark and sweet, her touch—soft and warm, her kisses—hot and sexy. Olivia was an escalating addiction, and Animal was quickly becoming hooked—like a junkie pining for the lost high.

"Will Ms. Mooney want a milkshake?" Lucy's voice took him out of his thoughts.

"Maybe. You seem real happy she's coming with us."

"I am. I really like her," Lucy replied.

"That's good. What're you gonna do with your sticker?" he asked.

"Put it on my notebook."

"Sounds good. When you get home, you have to do your homework, then we can play a video game while we wait for Olivia to come home from work."

Lucy bobbed her head. "Okay."

Animal was pleased as fucking punch that Lucy liked and got along so well with Olivia. Lucy needed good female role models, and she had that in Jada, and now in Olivia, and since he was crazy as hell about his sexy neighbor, it was working out better than Animal could've imagined. The only thing that made him hesitate was Olivia's aversion to bikers, although she didn't seem to have much of a problem with him when his face was buried into her tempting, wet pussy. Animal tried to block out the image of Olivia walking naked across the room, ass wiggling, hips swaying, tits jiggling. *This woman.* He exhaled a ragged breath and felt his chest tighten.

"Dad?"

Fuck. Dammit. Had he missed a question while he'd been fantasizing about his daughter's tutor?

Animal gave Lucy a sidelong glance. "Sorry, kiddo, I was thinking about work."

"Do you think Ms. Mooney can read me my bedtime story tonight?"

Fuck, yeah. Good idea. "You can ask her."

"Okay." Lucy turned away and looked out the passenger window.

Turning on the radio, Animal concentrated on the road and the music as he headed toward their house.

After a dinner of chicken-fried steak and mashed potatoes for him and Olivia, and mac 'n cheese and a milkshake for Lucy, Animal sat on the couch waiting for Olivia to come back downstairs after reading a story to his daughter.

Lucy had been so animated at dinner that he'd just sat back with this silly-ass grin on his face most of the night. Olivia had been great with Lucy, and each laugh she shared with Lucy, endeared Olivia more to him. Animal laced his fingers behind his head and leaned back, staring at the ceiling. He liked being with her in a way he'd never felt with anyone else. Olivia was warm, witty, and smart. It kind of scared him how quickly he was falling for her, and not much scared Animal. There was something about Olivia that drew him to her.

A light footfall behind him brought him out of his reverie as the scent of spiced oranges and sunlight teased his nostrils. Olivia's hands slipped down his chest, her long tresses brushing across his face and throat, as she nuzzled her face against his. Animal tipped his head back and her lips covered his. And then his fingers were in her hair, gently moving over her warm scalp as he pulled her closer to him. She slid her hot tongue into his mouth, dancing against his own. Fuck, Olivia sure knew how to kiss, and her mouth was amazing. She tasted delicious too—warm and like hot fudge.

"Olivia," he gritted as his fingers dug into her hips.

"You like that?" she whispered over his lips.

"Fuck, yeah, baby. Come here." Animal lifted her up a bit and she giggled as she climbed over the top of the couch and landed next to him. "That's better," he growled, crushing her against his chest and claiming her mouth.

His hands slipped under her blouse and spread across the satiny skin of her back, and she moaned, rubbing against him. Heat tore through him, and he cupped her tits in his hands, kneading them as he deepened their kiss.

Olivia moaned again, this time more guttural—more raw. The noises she made fueled his lust and wildly intoxicated him. No woman, and he meant *no woman*, even came close to Olivia … *ever*. She was the blood in his veins, and Animal had a constant desire … a craving for every inch of her.

"Fuck, woman." His mouth trailed down her throat, and he swallowed her soft moans as his thumb and index finger pinched her nipples hard.

Olivia arched her back and he pushed up her blouse and pulled her bra cup down to tease her stiff bud.

"I love your tits, baby." He lowered his head and bit the pebbled nipple before tugging it into his mouth.

She laced her fingers through his hair, pulling him closer. "Animal," she whispered.

"Baby," he smothered against her skin, gliding his hand down her belly and into the waistband of her jeans. The snap popped open, the zipper hissed down, and his fingers grazed the lace fabric of her panties.

Animal smelled her desire—wet and sweet. A low grunt rumbled from his throat "You soaked right through your panties." Olivia whimpered and ground into his hand. He couldn't remember wanting—*needing*—a woman more. His cock was so damn hard that he had to press against her for some relief.

His fingers moved to the edges of her bikini panties, and before he could slip inside, she gently pushed his hand away then pulled back a bit.

Wild with desire, he yanked her back to him, but she wriggled out of his grip.

"What the *fuck*, baby?" He slumped back against the cushion, frustration rushing through him.

Olivia leaned over and kissed him tenderly. "I want nothing more than to have you inside me, but this isn't the right time and place. Lucy's upstairs."

An audible sigh escaped his parted lips as Animal scrubbed his face with his fists. She was right—he knew that, but his cock didn't like it one fucking bit.

She rested her head on his shoulder and put her hand on top of his. "I'll make it up to you on Saturday when we go for our ride."

He kissed her hand and placed it against his heart. "You're right, babe. I got carried away. You just turn me the fuck on."

Olivia chuckled. "You do a pretty good job of getting me going too. I'd hate it if Lucy came down and saw us."

"Me too." Animal smiled.

"I better go," she whispered.

Damn, he hated to see her leave. "I'll walk you."

"I'm good."

"There's no way I'm letting you walk alone at night to your house."

Olivia pushed up from the couch and he stood up and walked her to the door. After locking it, they strolled over to her house and kissed passionately on her porch, then she unlocked her door and waved goodbye.

Animal hurried back to his house. His dick was still hard and aching for release. He flopped down on the couch and switched on the television to the local cable channel that ran replays of town meetings—that should do the trick.

Now all he had to do was forget about her hot breath on his lips and the sound of her moans as he teased her tits.

Yeah ... right.

CHAPTER TWENTY

"I CAN'T BELIEVE what happened to Mrs. Paulson," Alice said as she stirred the creamer into her coffee.

"I just found out about it," Olivia said. "How's Daniel?"

"I don't think it's sunken in yet. Poor kid. His grandparents have come in from Iowa and are staying with him." Harper sat down on the cushioned chair in the teachers' lounge.

"Where's his dad?" Olivia asked.

Harper shrugged. "I don't know. I heard that he hasn't been involved in Daniel's life since the divorce a few years ago."

"What a creep." Alice frowned.

"Hey, what's happening?" Kennedy asked as she entered the room and walked over to the refrigerator. "Is there any orange juice? I feel a cold coming on, or it could be my damn allergies. The warm weather feels good, but the pollen is wreaking havoc on my sinuses." She pulled out a carton of juice and grabbed a glass from one of the cupboards. "Why the glum faces?"

"We're talking about Daniel and what happened to his mom," Olivia replied. "It's just so terrible, I can't even imagine. The paper said it's similar to two other murders that happened in our county."

Harper's eyes widened. "Are they saying we've got a serial killer in our town?"

"Not exactly, but the article I read is sure intimating it." Olivia shuddered.

"I still can't believe it," Kennedy said after taking a sip of orange juice. "Have the police talked to Thurber? You know they had a thing going."

Alice darted her eyes to the shut door, then to Kennedy. "Don't say things like that so flippantly, especially now," she whispered.

"Why not? It's true." Kennedy sank down into the chair.

"How do you know for sure? I've heard rumors, but ..." Olivia's voice trailed away.

"I saw them at the Lake Pine Motel. I thought I recognized Marcus's car, and then I saw them kissing up a storm in front of room 17. I mean, if you're going to be a douchebag and cheat on your wife, at least you should wait until you get into the damn motel room instead of flaunting it in the open." She took another sip and looked at each of her friends. "Am I right?"

Olivia nodded, wrinkling her nose. "He's despicable. I've never liked him, and the way he acts all lovey-dovey when he's with his wife is sickening. I wonder if she knows?"

"Probably suspects it, but doesn't want to find out," Kennedy answered.

"Or she may be clueless." Harper broke off a piece of her blueberry muffin and wiped her fingers on a napkin. "He can be very charming, and he plays the role of the guileless man quite well."

"How do you know how he treats his wife? I've only seen them together at some of the school's fundraisers, but I've never noticed him over the top with his affections," Alice said.

"I tutor one of his boys at their house. Marcus is so polite and caring toward his wife—very different from the leech he is at school," Olivia replied.

"I forgot that you help his son with his reading. Is Marcus always home when you go over?" Alice asked.

"Most of the time. I only do it once a week because I'm so damn busy with school. However, having that extra money, I bought curtains for the kitchen, and after work on Friday, I'm gonna put down a deposit on the cutest shutters for my living-room window. I can't wait! I'm so sick of that damn sheet." Olivia laughed.

"Speaking of being so busy, how's your sexy biker?" Kennedy asked.

Harper and Alice giggled and leaned forward in their chairs.

Olivia felt her cheeks flush, which was a dead giveaway that she was totally into a guy. The way Alice and Harper looked at her told her they knew—they were her best friends and nothing got by them. "Good." She picked up her can of Dr. Pepper and took a long drink.

"That's not going to cut it," Kennedy said.

"You're over the moon about him!" Harper said as Alice clapped her hands.

Olivia rolled her eyes and shook her head. They knew, so why should she fight it? The truth was, she was so in love with Animal despite all of her good intentions not to be. *The road to hell is paved with good intentions.* She groaned softly. *So true.*

"So?" Harper's eyes sparkled.

Olivia covered her face with her hands. "I'm crazy in love with him."

"I *knew* it!" Harper cried.

"I'm happy for you," Alice said.

"Are you fucking serious? Do you know what those Insurgents are capable of?" Kennedy said.

Her hands dropped down to the table and she splayed her fingers on it. "Animal is different," she replied, looking at Kennedy.

"Oh, please. You're not going to be one of *those* women, are you? These guys are players. You're in over your head—you have no clue about the biker lifestyle." Kennedy pushed her empty glass away from her.

"Leave her alone," Alice said. "I've never seen Olivia happier."

"But don't you fall in love too fast? I mean that's what you've told me. I'm just trying to be the voice of reason here. I'm all for partying and having a good time with the Insurgents, but fall for one of them? That's just crazy." Kennedy pushed up from the chair and took the glass to the sink.

Before Olivia could respond, Harper jumped in. "I've been through the ups and downs of your love life, but I've never seen you glow the way you have for the past month or so. You've got a serenity about you that has never been there with any of the guys you've been involved with. Whatever Animal has, it complements you."

Olivia smiled at her friend. "Thanks, Harper. I've never been happier with anyone else like I am with Animal."

"And the way he treats his daughter tells me he's a good man. I say, good for you," Alice said.

Kennedy turned around and leaned against the counter, her hands up in the air. "I'm not saying I'm not thrilled that you're having a good time, I'm just saying watch your heart. Outlaws know how to shatter them. A guy can be great with his kids but shitty to the woman in his life. Take Marcus Thurber as an example—lovey-dovey with wifey and screwing women right and left behind her back, but he's a great dad."

Olivia nodded. "I agree with you. A guy can adore his kids but not be the best husband or boyfriend, but Animal isn't like that. Believe me, I'm an expert on cheaters and louses, and Animal hasn't checked any of those boxes." She held her hand in front of her face, fixing her gaze on Kennedy. "And before you say anything about him being a biker and all the free sex he can get, I know that, but just because it's there doesn't mean he wants to take it. Several of the Insurgents have old ladies who they treat with love and respect, and they're not screwing the club girls or hangarounds at all."

"True, but I think you're just being naïve, that's all." Kennedy shrugged.

Olivia took a deep breath and slowly blew it out. "I'm not naïve about the life. As a matter of fact, I know it too well." Her friends' eyes bored into her. "I grew up in the lifestyle—my dad, and then my brother were bikers—outlaw bikers."

"Are you serious?" Kennedy asked, her hand flying to her mouth.

"Yeah, that's why I was cool with going to the club party."

"I thought you were pretty comfortable when we got there. I was shocked you even wanted to go. Why didn't you tell me?"

"I've tried for so many years to forget that part of my life that I pushed it away and tried to invent a new identity devoid of my past. My dad was a SOB and the stereotypical biker who treated my mom like shit and didn't pay any attention to his kids until my brother was old enough to prospect for the club. My brother embraced the lifestyle, but he was still decent to my mom and me, and he was a biker through and through. He died because a guy disrespected him and his club in a barroom fight, a fight that proved to be fatal for my brother and left the other guy paralyzed from the neck down. The other guy was a biker, too, just not from the same club."

"I'm so sorry," Harper said. "You should've told us."

Olivia shook her head. "I wanted to forget all of it, but I've realized that I can't. I miss motorcycle rides, I love the smell of leather and oil, and I love a tatted, tough, take-charge guy who has a heart of gold under all the roughness." She sat back in the chair. "I love Animal, and it surprises the hell out of me. From the first day we met, I felt the spark but fought it for so long. I held his biker lifestyle against him, and when I finally put my prejudices aside and looked at him as just a man, I saw all of his layers, and now I've fallen head over heels in love with him. The problem is that I don't know if he feels the same way about me. I know he likes me a lot, but love? I don't know."

For several seconds the lounge was quiet, and then Harper cleared her voice, breaking the silence.

"You're an amazing woman. You've been through so much, and if Animal doesn't see how awesome you are and fall madly in love with you, then he's crazy as hell."

"I agree with everything Harper just said," Alice said.

"The fact that you guys have been dating for a while speaks volumes. Since you've been around the biker world way more than I have, you must know that these guys don't date unless they're serious about a woman. I bet Animal is totally in love with you. He's probably so shocked by it that he doesn't know what the hell hit him." Kennedy laughed.

Olivia chuckled. "I think you're right. Sometimes he has this dazed, what-the-fuck look, and I have to dig my nails into the palms of my hands to keep from laughing. I just want to hear him say it, that way I'll be sure. I'm also scared because I think I've fallen for him too quickly, but it feels right, and I'm so comfortable around him. I've never felt that way with a man."

The lounge door opened and Marcus Thurber strolled in, his gaze running up and down each woman's body before he crossed the room and plopped down on the couch.

"How're you ladies doing?" he asked.

"Okay. We were just talking about Mrs. Paulson. Her murder is so awful," Kennedy said.

He pulled out an apple from his briefcase, took a large bite and chewed for several seconds, then smiled. "It is a shame, but what was she doing at that hotel anyway? The old saying 'If you play with fire you get burned' seems to apply here." Then he bit into the apple again.

Olivia stared at her friends and they stared back at her as chills ran up her spine. How could he be so callous, so cold, about the mother of one of his student's? And about a woman with whom he was having an affair. He must have had *some* feelings for her.

"Olivia, we'll have to reschedule next week. The boys and Marie will be out of town for spring break."

"Sure," she mumbled.

"Aren't you going with them?" Harper asked. Her eyes then widened as if she was shocked she'd been so bold to ask him that question.

"No. I have too many things I need to take care of. They're going to my in-laws, and I'm not that fond of them anyway." Thurber chuckled.

A tense silence descended over the room, growing more acute as alarm bells starting ringing in Olivia's head. She crushed her can then rose from the chair and crossed the room to throw it into the recycle bin.

"I better prep for the afternoon," she said.

"Me too." Harper jumped to her feet with Alice quickly following suit.

"I've got a lot to do before recess is over," Kennedy said.

The four women began moving toward the door, and a low laugh rumbled from the corner of the room.

"I hope I didn't drive you pretty ladies out," Marcus said.

Olivia looked over her shoulder, pinning her gaze on him. "Not at all."

The fellow teacher's brown eyes were cold, distant. "That's good. Maybe we can all go out for lunch or dinner sometime."

"Will your wife be there?" Kennedy asked.

There was a split-second pause. His eyes narrowed, but Olivia couldn't mistake the evil glint sparking from them. And then it was gone and a smile filled his face. "Of course. Why wouldn't she?"

A tremor ran through Olivia and she couldn't get out of the room fast enough. She closed the door behind them, and as they walked down the hall toward their respective classrooms, an audible sigh escaped from her parted lips.

"What the hell was *that* all about?" She ran her hands up and down her arms. "I'm chilled to the bone."

"I wonder if he killed her," Harper whispered.

"God! Don't say that—it's too frightening to think about," Alice whispered back.

"That jerk's got some real problems. He basically said that Daniel's mom deserved what she got. Bastard," Kennedy said.

"You should tell the police what you saw at the motel. As far as I know, you're the only one who's actually seen them together—the other stuff is just rumors," Olivia said.

"I was thinking the exact same thing," Kennedy said. "Even if he didn't do it, it would serve him right to have to explain it to the cops and to his wife."

"What were *you* doing at the motel?" Harper asked.

Kennedy's eyes twinkled. "Having some nasty fun."

"Oh ... I guess I should have figured that." Harper looked down at her phone and smiled. "Darcy," she said out loud.

"Still hot and heavy?" Olivia joked.

Harper looked up from texting. "Very. He's so sweet. I never thought I'd meet a nice guy in a bar."

"Just like I told you—when you least expect it. Like me and Jonathan," Alice said.

"I'm still liking the uncoupled life too much, but I guess I'm the only one in our group who is." Kennedy chuckled. "How's your psych paper coming along?"

Olivia paused at the door to her classroom. "Pretty good. I'm sort of feeling guilty about leading this guy on, and when I talked to my prof about it, he said not to be. Dr. Davison is actually encouraging me to meet the guy. I don't know if I feel comfortable with that."

"That's kind of strange that your professor would want to put you in a potentially dangerous situation. I mean, you don't really know anything about this guy," Alice said.

"I know, but if I do meet him it'll be in a public place, but I'm struggling with the ethical and moral dilemma of it. I bought a burner phone, so I think I'll just talk to him on the phone and see if he's for real or just some guy wanting to score."

"Maybe your prof's into you. Did you tell him your profile name?" Kennedy asked.

"I told him, and no way is Dr. Davison into me—he's got a wife and kids. That's just crazy. Also, he'd never do that and screw up the data. You're way off base with that one," Olivia replied.

"Maybe, but stranger things have happened. What's the name of the guy you're talking with? I may have connected with him on the site," Kennedy said.

"Hunter."

"Hunter? Is he tall with brown hair and nicely built but keeps his face blurred?"

Olivia nodded. "That's him. So you've talked to him?"

"I wasn't his type. He didn't seem to like that I was playing the field. It seemed like he was looking for a relationship with a very special woman. Since you're at the almost meeting stage, I'd say he likes whatever you're feeding him."

"See, that makes me feel even more guilty. I'm cat-fishing him big time and he thinks it's for real. I should just end it now."

"Isn't your paper due after spring break?" Harper asked.

"Yeah." Olivia rubbed the back of her neck. "What a mess. Why did I think this was a good idea? I still can't believe Dr. Davison doesn't see the moral dilemma with this situation. After I talk to Hunter on the phone, I'm calling it quits. I'll just tell him I got back with an old boyfriend of mine. I won't meet him."

The school bell rang, and the doors slammed open as throngs of children rushed in, scurrying to their classrooms. The children yelled, locker doors slammed shut, and hundreds of feet pounded the shiny linoleum floor. The sounds bounced off the walls, echoing and making them louder.

Olivia waved to Kennedy and Alice, and walked into the classroom with Harper. Soon the desks would be full of students, and the afternoon session would begin. She went over to the cupboard and pulled out the reading material for the students she'd work with in the class.

Standing by the window, she looked at the small park across the street and smiled when she saw the white and cherry-red blossoms on the trees swaying slightly in the breeze. A shiver of excitement about the upcoming ride on Saturday with Animal shot through her. She couldn't wait to be behind him on his Harley, breathing in his clean scent and holding him tightly.

Olivia slid out her phone and dashed off a quick text.

Olivia: *Hiya sexy. Just thinking bout u.*

Immediately a ping sounded.

Animal: *That's fucking weird. Just ready 2 send u a text. Thinking bout u 2.*

She looked up and saw a few students walking in.

Olivia: *I miss having ur arms around me.*

Animal: *Fuck, baby, I need u so fucking bad right now.*

She squirmed a bit and shifted from one foot to the next.

Olivia: *Sat seems so far away.*

Animal: *Yeah. Damn I need to be inside ur pussy.*

"Ms. Mooney?" Billy said. "Can I read the fire engine book today?"

Olivia looked up at the freckled-face boy. "If we have time, but we're going to start a new book, and it's about a boy your age who takes a journey under the city he lives in."

Billy's mouth fell open. "How can he live under a city?"

"I don't know—we'll have to read the book to find out." She smiled.

"Can we read it now?"

"In about an hour. I have to work with Sara, Emily, and Andy first."

"Are they reading the same book?"

"No, they're reading the elf book that you and I read last fall, remember?"

"Uh-huh. I liked that one."

"Me too. Now go take your seat because Ms. Colter is about to start class."

Billy dashed over to his seat, and Olivia looked down at her phone.

Animal: *R u still with me, babe?*

Olivia: *Class is starting. Gotta go. Sending u a big, deep, wet kiss for now.*

She switched her phone to silent, slipped it into her pocket, and took a seat at one of the small tables in the back of the classroom, waiting for Harper to begin the afternoon session.

OLIVIA SLAMMED HER hand against the steering wheel, cussing up a storm after her fifth attempt to turn on the ignition resulted in nothing but a low grinding sound. The dashboard lit up like a Christmas tree, then groaned. Leaning back against the headrest, she rubbed her eyes with the heel of her hands. The last thing she could afford was a pricey car repair.

"There go the shutters," she said out loud. "Dammit!"

Olivia pulled the hood lever then slid out of the driver's seat and walked around to the front of the car. She glanced around the parking lot and saw that there were a couple of cars parked over on the east side, but she didn't recognize whose they were. Olivia pulled up the hood and looked inside even though she didn't know a damn thing about cars. The jangle of wires and hoses looked like a bunch of snakes crawling in different directions.

"Shit," she muttered under her breath as she continued to stare inside.

Why the hell did she think it was a good idea to stay late that night? If she'd decided to take the students' workbooks home to grade, she'd have hitched a ride from Harper and would be nestled on her couch watching a movie. Instead, she was alone in the parking lot, looking at the inside of a broken car, and feeling a bit spooked, especially after what had happened to Samantha Paulson.

The trees she'd admired earlier that day now looked ominous and threatening in the encroaching darkness. The rustling of the branches sounded like whispering voices, and fear tore through her from the inside out. She pulled out her cellphone and quickly tapped in Animal's number.

"What's up, baby?"

Olivia latched on to his familiar voice like a drowning person grasping a life preserver. "My car won't start." Her voice trembled even though she tried to steady it as much as she could.

"Where are you?" Concern laced his words.

"In the school parking lot. I stayed late to do some grading." The afternoon breeze had grown into a stronger wind that blew clouds of dust and leaves across the parking lot. "I'm starting to think that was a bad idea."

"Why?"

"It's silly, but I'm a little spooked. It's the damn trees and wind." A low moan echoed in the distance.

"Hang on," Animal said, and she could hear him telling Lucy to put on her coat because they were going to help Olivia out. Warmth spread through her and she leaned against the front bumper of her car. "Babe? We're on our way. Get inside your car and lock the doors. We'll be there soon."

"Okay," she replied weakly, not ready to disengage the call.

The sound of gravel on tires made her heart leap into her throat. She peered around the raised hood and saw a car slowly approaching her. Her temples throbbed and blood rushed through her veins as she took a few steps backward as if trying to use the hood as her shield.

"Are you still with me, Olivia?"

"Yes." Her lips had suddenly become parched and she licked them several times. "A car's coming."

"Get inside your car. Now."

"I don't think I can make it in time." Her heart was beating so hard, so wildly, she feared it would tear through her chest. "It stopped," she croaked.

"Olivia," Animal said, but his voice faded away as fear seized her.

The passenger window slowly rolled down and a man leaned way over. The glow from one of the streetlights partially lit up the man's face—Marcus Thurber. Olivia had thought she'd been the only employee left in the school after five o'clock had passed. Knowing that Thurber had been inside as well made her shiver in spite of the warm evening air.

"Having car trouble?" His eyes traveled up and down her body before landing on her face.

"I'm good," she replied.

"Who the fuck are you talking to?" Animal yelled out.

"A teacher," she replied, but she felt no comfort in Thurber being there with her.

"Do you need a ride?" The passenger door popped open.

Olivia shook her head. "Thanks, Marcus, but a friend is picking me up."

"*Friend* my ass," Animal growled over the phone.

"Is that your friend on the phone?" Thurber's gaze fixed on hers and his casual smile wiped off his face.

The hair on the back of her neck stood up, and an icy chill raced down her spine.

"Yes." Olivia inched her way to the passenger side of her car. "He's almost here."

"I am, babe."

The sound of tires squealing against the asphalt sliced through the night as Animal's car approached. Relief washed over her as the bright headlights illuminated the area around her. Thurber glanced behind him, then pulled the door shut and rolled up the window, and sped away.

Animal jumped out of the idling SUV, dashed over to her, and drew her to him. Safe in his arms, her knees grew weak and she collapsed against him as he walked her over to the SUV. Lucy climbed out of the passenger seat and ran over to them.

"Are you okay?" she asked Olivia.

Olivia smiled weakly and tugged Lucy into Animal's embrace. He scooped Lucy up with one arm and held Olivia tightly with his other one as they made their way to his car.

"Both of you stay inside. I'll check out your car," he said once Olivia was settled in the front seat with Lucy in the back.

"Is your car broken?" Lucy asked, propping her elbows on the console and resting her chin on her hands.

"It is. Do you want to trade places? I can sit in the back."

"No, it's okay. What's Dad doing?"

Olivia glanced over and saw Animal shining the flashlight on his phone under the hood.

"Seeing what's wrong."

"I want to help," Lucy said.

"Your dad told both of us to wait in the car, remember?"

Lucy sighed as she kept watching her father.

Soon Animal walked back to the SUV and swung into the seat. "I'm pretty sure the problem is a bad alternator." He threw the gear in Drive and headed out of the parking lot.

"Is that a major repair?" she asked, crossing her fingers.

"Major? Nah. Necessary? Yeah."

"Do you know how much it'll cost?"

Animal glanced at her then put his hand over hers. "Don't sweat it. I have a buddy who can do it for free."

"*Free*? Why would he do that for me? I don't even know him," Olivia asked.

"'Cause he owes me a favor."

"My dad knows lots of people. Is it Uncle Hawk, Dad?"

"Nope—it's Hank. Remember, he came with us a couple of weeks ago when we went to the Pancake House with grandpa?"

"The one that looked like Santa Claus?"

Animal chuckled. "That's the one."

"He's nice," Lucy said to Olivia.

Olivia smiled. "Should I trust him with my car?"

Lucy's head bobbed. "Yes!"

"Then, I will." She glanced over at Animal. "Let me know how much the tow will be."

"I told you not to worry about it," he replied.

"Even so, please let me know."

Animal lifted up his chin and kept his eyes on the road ahead of them.

Olivia pivoted in her seat and looked over at Lucy. "You did an excellent job with your book report. I was very impressed and so was Mrs. White. Do you like to read a bit more now?"

"Yes. I liked the book. The dog was funny. Can we get a dog, Dad?"

"You gonna take care of it?" Animal looked in the rearview mirror at Lucy. Olivia saw his mouth twitch as if he were fighting a smile.

"Yeah, I will. Please, Dad?"

Animal threw a sidelong glance at Olivia. "You started this," he said, merriment lacing his voice.

"Guilty as charged." She giggled.

"When I get you alone, I'm gonna smack that sweet ass of yours real good for this," he whispered.

"I'll have to remember to do bad things more often if that's the punishment I get," she murmured.

One corner of his mouth hitched up into a smug grin, and he swept his fingers over her hand.

"Are you whispering about my dog?" Lucy asked.

Olivia inched closer to the passenger window and stared straight ahead. She'd let Animal answer this one.

"Sorta. I'm thinking a dog may make a great addition to our family."

Lucy laughed and clapped her hands. "Can we get him tomorrow?"

"Let's wait until school lets out so you have more time to be with him. If we get a puppy now, he'll be home alone too much. You wouldn't want that, right?"

She shook her head. "No. Ms. Mooney, how many more days until school is over?"

"A little over two months. Let's see," Olivia closed her eyes as she figured out the dates. "Sixty-seven days, but there are some half days in there and spring break."

"That's a long time." Her voice sounded … sad.

"It'll go by real fast because you have field day, the talent show, the school fair, and a couple of school trips. Mrs. White said that one of your class trips is to the candy factory. I heard they give a sucker to each kid. What's your favorite flavor?" Olivia said.

"Grape. Can you come with us?"

"I'll ask Mrs. White if I can be a chaperone. I've never been there before, but I heard it's a really fun tour."

While she and Lucy chatted about school activities, Olivia felt Animal's hand on her knee. She cut her gaze to him, and her stomach fluttered: Animal's dark eyes glowed with warmth … and *love* as he looked at her.

At first shock rushed through her, then a moment of doubt until disbelief set in. Olivia couldn't believe it, and maybe she was reading way more into it than she should, but—to her—the look in his eyes was love. *Was it? I can't believe it. Really? Probably not ... yes ... it was. I'm sure of it.* Elation swelled in Olivia's heart, and she scooted closer to him and discreetly held his hand. He squeezed hers and gave her a wink, then averted his gaze back to the road. Olivia didn't want to let go of his strong hand. Not now when love filled his eyes and heat radiated from him. *Not ever.*

Before she knew it, they'd arrived home, and a thread of disappointment wrapped around her. Olivia loved spending time with Animal and Lucy and didn't want the evening to end, but Lucy had school in the morning, and Olivia had to work on her research paper. Her plan for that night was to call Hunter on the burner phone she'd purchased.

"Can you come in to play a game with me?" Lucy asked Olivia.

She hugged the young girl then held her at arm's length. "I'm sorry but I still have some work to do. Can we do it another time?"

"Okay. Maybe on Friday?"

"Or Sunday," Animal said.

"We're going to Grandma and Grandpa's."

Animal nodded. "Maybe Olivia wants to join us."

Lucy's eyes sparkled and she jumped up and down. "Do you? Aunt Jada will be there, and she has a little bird. He sings."

Taken aback, Olivia just nodded.

"Is that a yes?" Animal asked, nudging her side with his elbow.

"Yes, I'd love to meet your family." *He's asked me to meet his parents. I can't believe it. I'm so damn glad my car broke down.*

Lucy jumped up and down like she was on a pogo stick, giggling and singing alternatively. Shaking her head, Olivia laughed, and Animal placed a hand on his daughter's shoulder as if to calm her down a bit.

"Let's walk Olivia to her door, kiddo."

Olivia reached out her hand and Lucy took it, and Animal grasped

Olivia's other one, and she leaned against him as they crossed over to her house.

She unlocked the front door and light from the hallway spilled onto the porch. Animal stared intently at her, and she craved for him to take her in his arms and kiss her deeply. She ached with want for him, and from the way he looked at her, Olivia was pretty sure he was feeling the same way.

"Thanks for helping out," she said.

"Anytime." Animal's gaze dropped down to her mouth.

"Bye!" Lucy cried as she twirled around in circles with her arms outstretched.

"I'll call Hank in the morning and let you know what he says." Animal took a step closer to her, and their fingers brushed. Hot shimmers ran up her arm and she locked her gaze with his. "I'm feeling it too, baby," he said in a hushed tone.

"I miss you."

"Yeah ... fuck."

"Aren't we going, Dad?" Lucy gripped the iron railing with one hand, the other one clutched her belly.

"Did you get too dizzy?" Olivia chuckled.

"Yeah." Lucy gulped in big breaths then held them before sputtering them out.

Animal puckered his lips lightly, winked, then moved over to Lucy. "Let's go, kiddo."

He glanced back a few times as father and daughter walked toward their house. When they reached their porch, Animal opened the door and Lucy rushed inside. He turned to Olivia and said, "Go inside and lock up."

"Yes, sir." She giggled and brought her hand up in a mock salute before blowing him a kiss and closing the door.

Sighing loudly, Olivia padded into her bedroom and changed into her comfy nightshirt, then went into the kitchen and poured herself a large glass of white wine. Settling down on the couch, she took a big gulp. Her body pulsed with desire for Animal. *Saturday is only two days away.* Her phone pinged and she dug it out of her pocket.

Animal: I'm sitting here with a fucking hard-on.

Olivia: I'm horny as all hell.

Animal: Can u meet for lunch? I can pick u up.

Olivia: Yes! I'm at the dental clinic tomorrow. I have an hr. Noon works.

Animal: Fuckin' awesome. Do u need a ride to work in the a.m.?

Olivia: Ivy will pick me up. If not, then I'll let u know.

Animal: Ok. Damn ur so sexy and beautiful. I fuckin' need u.

Olivia: I need u too. Looking forward to tomorrow!!!

Animal: Fuck yeah!

Olivia: I need to work on my paper.

Animal: Yeah. Lucy wants me to play a video game with her.

Olivia: That's great!

Animal: She's gonna beat my ass, for sure.

Olivia: Hehe. Have fun. Nite.

Animal: Nite, darlin'.

Olivia hugged the phone to her chest and let the rush of his words flow through her brain again and again. Her car needed repairing, her paper was due in less than two weeks, final exams were looming, she was juggling two jobs, extra tutoring, and full-time school, and Olivia had never been happier in her life.

She pushed up from the couch and went into the kitchen to warm up a frozen burrito and refill her glass of wine. With plate and glass in her hands, Olivia plopped back down on the sofa and munched away. After a bit of television, she'd call Hunter on the burner phone. He'd asked her to call him at nine thirty that night. She glanced at the clock: 8:35 p.m. Olivia switched on the television, settled back against the cushion, and cut into her burrito.

CHAPTER TWENTY-ONE

THE ONLY LIGHT in the den was from the small lamp covered with a red shade beside the wingback leather chair. There were two books stacked on the lamp table and he reached for one, changed his mind, then curled his fingers around the wineglass. The room was quiet except for the soft ticking of the grandfather clock in the corner of the room; the hands on the face read 9:16 p.m. In fourteen minutes Rose would call, and he'd try and lure her in some more so she'd agree to meet him.

Hunter *knew* Rose was the one he needed to make his world feel back in balance. From their conversations, he had grown to care very deeply for her, and his hunger for her had grown exponentially with each conversation. She had begun to consume his thoughts, and he desperately needed her to feed the hunger which had become harder to contain.

He picked up the burner phone and engaged the voice changing app in anticipation of the call. Since Rose lived in Pinewood Springs, he had to be especially careful in case she wasn't who she said she was and may recognize his voice. A bit paranoid? Perhaps, but the articles that had appeared in the *Pinewood Springs Tribune* had contributed to his suspicions. After Rose, he'd start hunting again outside of the county.

Hunter rested his head back against the chair and his latest victim flashed through his mind, bringing a smile to his face. *Pretty, sexy Samantha.* He tapped his index finger against his lips. *Her fear was exquisite.* Normally, he didn't go in for women who had children—he liked his victims pure, but he'd made an exception with Samantha.

It was true that he hid his real self like a snake covered in leaves, and some people might have said he was evil, like that ridiculous journalist who'd penned the article about Hunter's lovely Samantha and Katie, but Hunter would say that he was just wired differently. To him, the most important thing was that he *knew* who he was, which was something that most people couldn't say about themselves.

A small sigh passed his lips, and he rested his chin on a hand, his elbow propped up on the arm rest. When he'd reached adolescence, he'd realized he was different from the other boys. Where they craved carnal pleasure, he craved sensual connections. They'd sit around talking about women as if they were nothing but body parts, but Hunter had seen the female sex—and still did—as beautiful creatures with hearts and souls. Of course, the hormones inside him craved their luscious bodies, but he saw so much more than breasts, hips, and butts.

As he grew older, all the men around him just wanted to fuck as many women as they could—it was like some sort of contest, but he sought that one perfection—the blending of body, soul, and mind with him. The only way Hunter could achieve the ultimate balance was through fear, pain, and the mixing of primal sex with sheer terror. It was dark, perhaps a bit disturbed, but very necessary. He had known the darkness dwelled inside him from the time he'd come of age.

Had he wanted that?

Yes. Very much so.

The sound of the burner phone snapped him out of his thoughts, and Hunter looked at the time: 9:30 p.m. A slow smile spread over his face as he picked up the phone.

"Thank you for being so punctual, my sweet. This is your ardent lover." He chuckled. "How are you?" He picked up his glass of wine and took a sip as adrenaline pumped through him.

"Good. How're you?"

"Perfect, now that I can finally hear your voice, which I knew I'd love."

"I wasn't sure if you'd pick up. The last few times I was online, I saw that you were too, but you didn't message me—I had to do it first. Are you talking to other women?"

My sweet Rose is jealous. That's perfect—it means she cares.

"No worries, my sweet. I'm very busy with my job. Sometimes I'm online for work and don't have time to chat with you, but that doesn't mean that you aren't on my mind. You're always in my thoughts, you know." Hunter loved the cat-and-mouse game they were playing; he loved to be in control and the one who set the pace.

"I wasn't really jealous. I just want to make sure you're not a player since that's not what I'm looking for, you know?"

It sounded as though she were trying to disguise her voice. Disappointment ran through him. "I'm not a player, and I'm very hurt that you'd think that of me." He took another sip of wine and waited.

After a few seconds, a small audible sigh. "I'm sorry. I didn't mean to hurt you, it's just that so many men are looking to just hookup on this site."

Hunter didn't respond. He wanted Rose to sweat for a bit.

"Are you still there? Are you mad at me?"

After another pause he spoke, "Not mad ... just terribly disappointed. I thought we trusted each other. If you don't trust me, then we have nothing. Don't you think believing in each other is paramount?"

"I do. I guess I've been burned too many times." A soft giggle.

His heartbeat suddenly raced. *I know that laugh.* A pause.

"I understand," he said in a low voice. "Please don't accuse me of something like that again. Now tell me what you did today." Hunter had to get her to talk longer—he had to place the voice.

As Rose spoke, Hunter listened carefully without interruption, and the longer she did, the clearer her voice became until realization jabbed him right between the eyes. *Olivia! Rose is Olivia.* He felt small beads of perspiration form near his hairline as a jolt of excitement rushed through him. At the sound of her voice, desire flooded through him—the beast within fighting for control.

How many times had he wanted to bury his fingers into her lush dark hair? And her eyes ... so beautiful ... were anything but ordinary: the kind of green that revived dull grass from the harshness of winter.

He had to admit that her eyes were never more beautiful than when she cried. He'd caught her once, and even though she'd tried to pretend that she had an allergy, he'd known better. Hunter had loved seeing the tears in them and the anguish they held, and he'd wanted to hold her close and feel those tears on his shoulder. He couldn't wait to see her cry again.

Very soon, my sweet.

Hunter focused back on the present; Olivia wasn't talking anymore.

"My sweet?" he said, hoping she hadn't hung up.

"Did I lose you? You weren't responding."

"I was so taken with your words, your voice, and my feelings for you, that I couldn't speak. I have to confess that I've fallen in love with you." *Dammit! Too bold. Too soon. Olivia isn't like the others. She's not so naïve or desperate.* "Or at least what I think is love," he quickly corrected. "All I know is that I have strong feelings for you and would like to meet you." Hunter drew in a breath and held it.

For a long while Olivia didn't respond, and he cursed himself for his lack of patience. He'd wanted Olivia for such a long time that he let his desire speak instead of his intellect.

"I think meeting would be the next logical step, right?" Another cute giggle.

He let out his breath slowly. "Only if you're ready," he said cautiously.

"I am."

A bolt of desire ran straight to his groin.

"When do you want to meet?"

The doorknob jiggled, and Hunter looked over.

"Daddy?" Aaron's muffled voice came from the other side of the door.

"I'll let you know the details soon, my sweet. I have some business I need to attend to right now. I hate saying goodnight, but I have to." His gaze stayed fixed on the door.

"Okay. Goodnight."

The phone went dead and a grin broke out over his face. *I have her.*

Pushing up from the chair, he said, "Daddy's coming" then switched off the lamp and unlocked the door.

CHAPTER TWENTY-TWO

THE MOTORCYCLE WOUND around the twisting road that led to the summit of Mount Estes.

The sun shone bright and warm in a brilliant blue sky dotted with wisps of white clouds while red-tailed hawks performed magnificent aerial displays.

The wind whipped Olivia's dark hair around her face, and she inhaled deeply, loving the sweet scent of pine and wildflowers infusing the air. With her arms wrapped around Animal's waist, and her body pressed tight against his back, Olivia took in the view: glacier-carved valleys, meandering creeks, and forests of bristlecone pines. All of it was like a slice of heaven on earth.

"You good?" Animal yelled, shifting gears as the bike climbed up farther.

The vibrations of the engine rippled through her and she leaned closer and kissed his neck. "Great," she replied.

Sitting on the back of a Harley again thrilled her, but being so close to Animal sent her senses into overdrive. It seemed like a luxury to have the whole day to spend with him instead of the lunchtime quickie from the day before. Recalling their rabid coupling in the back of his SUV made her stomach flutter.

Olivia leaned with the bike as Animal took several sharp turns, finally turning on a dirt road. She secured her hands tighter around him as the motorcycle bumped and bounced for the next couple of miles then came to a stop in front of a crystalline lake. She waited until his feet were firmly on the ground, then got off the bike and stretched out her legs.

"You know how to ride," Animal said as he swung his leg over the seat of the Harley. "You sit still and know how to lean with me when I make turns." He snapped open one of the saddle bags.

"Have you taken a lot of women on your bike?" She finger-combed her tangled hair.

"No, but the few I've taken squirmed and moved around the whole fuckin' time." Animal pulled out a blue plaid blanket and a paper bag from the saddlebag. "Come on."

Olivia grasped his hand and he led her to a grassy area where he laid down the blanket. The reflection of snow-capped mountains was painted onto the diamond-clear lake. The only sounds were the soft lapping of the ripples upon the shore, an occasional splash of the speckled-fish in the water, and the low buzzing of flies hovering over the deeper parts of the lake.

"It's so peaceful here," she murmured.

Animal came up behind her and hooked his arms around her waist and nuzzled her neck. "I wanted to share this with you, baby."

"I love it," she said, leaning back into him. A delicious tingle traveled through her: she loved feeling his hard body around her.

Olivia craned her neck and his mouth covered hers, the touch of his lips sending her senses into a frenzy. Animal's tongue thrust deep into her mouth, and she slid hers against his and moaned.

"Baby," he muttered.

Olivia broke away and rested her head against his chest, and he buried his face in her neck as he cupped her breasts and squeezed them in his hands. Arousal flashed hot through her system.

"Oh, shit," she moaned as his nimble fingers teased her nipples, making them grow rock-hard. The pulsing buds pushed against the knit fabric of her top, craving for him to take them into his mouth.

"Olivia," he whispered.

His hard dick ground against her and she moved in rhythm with him as he bit the nape of her neck. She shivered as one of his hands moved down past her belly, then unbuttoned her jeans and pulled down the zipper. He pushed her pants down and she wiggled a bit until they pooled at her ankles.

His fingers skimmed along the edge of her silk panties.

"Animal," she rasped.

He rubbed harder against her and slid his fingers under the elastic lace. "So fucking wet," he growled, burying a finger between her folds.

Olivia took a step to the side, and Animal plunged one of his digits deep inside her. "Yes," she muttered, her eyes closing.

"You like that," he said against the skin on the back of her neck, biting then licking it.

"Oh, yeah …"

His finger pulled out then plunged back in even deeper, and his thumb was doing wickedly delicious things to her sensitive spot. Olivia writhed against him, pushing back on his erection, loving the way he grunted each time she did it.

Between the in-and-out action with his finger and that skilled thumb, some serious sensations were burning through her. Damn, the man knew how to push her buttons in the best and most seductive way.

"I fuckin' love your pussy, baby. I can't wait to taste you." His free hand cupped her chin and tilted her head back. "Olivia," he whispered before pressing his lips to hers. He kissed her deeply as his tongue thrust into her mouth, matching the movement of his fingers.

Olivia gasped into his mouth, the pulse of desire throbbing deep and low in her body, every nerve tightening in awareness caused by the most delectably wonderful things he was doing to her.

Pulling away for a split second, Animal locked his heated gaze on her. "Come for me, baby." Then his tongue plunged back into her mouth.

She began to unceremoniously fuck his finger, bucking and jerking hard, and then a mind-numbing, shattering climax rocked her body. Animal held her close, murmuring softly in her ears, but Olivia was still riding the wave of euphoria, and his voice sounded distant and muffled. She collapsed against him, almost sliding down to the ground, but he held her up; then threw her over his shoulder as she squealed, and walked over to the blanket, his strong hand rubbing her ass.

Animal gently put her down then fixed his heated gaze on her as he fluidly stripped off his clothes, socks, and boots. His dick stood straight and hard, and Olivia sat up and reached out to grab it, but he shook his head while throwing her a devilish grin.

"I'm gonna make you wait," he said, stroking his cock. Slow and even movements that went down his shaft and pinched the tip until he hung his head back and groaned. "Although, your mouth would be fucking perfect right now."

"Yes," she agreed breathlessly.

"Take your top off and don't look away from me," he said.

Gazing at Animal with a seductive smile, Olivia put a finger in her mouth and sucked it slowly. She looked at him and saw pure desire in his intense gaze, and it nearly took her breath away. Olivia withdrew her finger and trailed it down her throat to her cleavage, her body flashing with instant heat at the way Animal stared at her.

"Fuck," he muttered as he fell to his knees.

Olivia grasped the hem of her top and lifted it up and over her head. Animal's jaw clenched as his gaze fixed on the swell of her breasts, and she reached behind and unhooked her bra. The straps slid over her shoulders and down her arms before she discarded the black lacy fabric on the blanket.

A low growl rumbled from his chest, and then Animal was right there—next to her, kissing her deeply while cupping the weight of one of her breasts in his palm and grazing the swollen nipple with his thumb until it beaded. Pure white heat crackled through Olivia, and she curled her arms around his neck and arched into him, driving their kiss deeper.

He broke away and dipped his head lower then gently bit the rock-hard tips of her breasts. She moaned while he teased and tortured her nipples.

"It feels so good," she murmured, burying her fingers in his hair.

Animal gently pushed her down on the blanket then trailed feathery kisses over her breasts, down her belly, and to her inner thighs. A few nips on her sensitive skin had her squirming and gasping, and he reached down and pushed off her jeans, socks, and boots and trailed his mouth up her legs. She cried out when he tugged off her panties then buried his face against the smooth skin at the juncture of her thighs.

Olivia felt the soft, warm movement of his tongue caressing her clit, arousing her into the edge of ecstasy. She bucked hard but he placed his hands on her hips and pinned her down as he kissed, nipped, and licked her from front to back. When his tongue poked into her wet heat she writhed beneath him and bit the corner of her bottom lip to keep from going over the top.

"You taste and smell so fuckin' amazing," he said as he clasped her thighs and spread them open farther.

Animal's fingers stroked her pussy lips then he pressed one of them into her hot hole. While he pushed into her, his thumb stroked the outer flesh. A moment later, his finger pressed against her mouth and she could smell the scent of her own arousal. "Taste yourself," he whispered. She opened her mouth and let his finger enter, sucking and licking her own salty-sweet juices from his digit. Smiling at her, he removed his finger from her mouth.

"I need you," she whispered.

Animal leaned over and picked up his jeans, but Olivia grabbed his arm, stopping him. A quizzical look spread across his face as his gaze locked on hers.

"I want to *feel* you," she said. "I'm on birth control and I'm good."

The corners of his mouth lifted up. "I'm good too, babe." He tossed his jeans aside then cupped her breasts and kneaded them while he scooted between her parted legs.

Hovering over her, his mouth was back on hers, bruising and wild, sending fiery sparks through her. She dug her hands into his ass and gripped the firm muscles.

"Are you ready, baby?" he rasped.

"Always," she replied as Animal pulled away.

Dark hunger filled his eyes as he lifted one of her legs and draped it over his shoulder. Shivers of delight tingled through her as he kissed her ankle and inner calf. He glanced down and smiled.

"I love your pretty pussy. It's all pink and wet and just waiting for my cock," he said, swiping a finger through her slick folds.

Olivia groaned and shifted her hips, and he gripped her other leg and placed that one over his shoulder as well. The head of his dick lightly pressed against her entrance, and with intense eyes fixed on hers, he shoved into her.

"Yes!" she cried as her warmth molded around him.

"Fuck," he hissed before pulling out and plunging back in.

Her fingers clutched onto his shoulders as he fucked her hard and rough, and she quaked and shook under his relentless pummeling—over and over. As she lifted her hips, their two bodies met like claps of thunder and her inner walls clenched around him tightly with each stroke. Animal gripped her hips so hard she knew there'd be bruises. Olivia loved it when he marked her, as she already wore a steady supply of love bites over her body.

"You feel so fucking good and tight. Fuck, Olivia," he panted.

Then he reached down and rubbed his finger over her sweet spot in that swirling motion she loved, and it sent her over the edge. She shuddered violently as waves of bliss washed over her.

"Babe," he grunted before stiffening, and then Olivia felt his cock spasm inside her. The muscles of her walls hugged him and he dug his fingers deeper into her skin. "Fuck, baby," he rasped as her pussy greedily milked every drop from his dick.

As a delicious warmth spread through every nerve and muscle in her body, Olivia opened her eyes and met Animal's sated gaze. She curved her arms around his neck and brought his mouth to hers and kissed him wildly.

"So good," she murmured. "Oh ... Animal."

Pulling up a bit, he eased her legs off his shoulders then leaned over and traced her bottom lip with his thumb.

"That was fantastic, baby." He kissed the side of her neck then rolled over and drew her close to him.

For a long while they lay in each other's arms listening to the sounds of nature and enjoying the warm breeze caressing their sweaty bodies.

"You're great with Lucy," he said, playing with a few strands of her hair.

"It's not hard to be—she's a wonderful girl. I have a soft spot for her. She reminds me of the way I was at her age."

Animal kissed her softly on the temple. "She's crazy about you too."

Olivia squeezed her arm around him tighter. "I'm happy to hear that."

"Her old man's fuckin' crazy about you too."

She paused, warmth spreading through her. "And I'm crazy about him."

Animal put a finger under Olivia's chin and tilted her head up so their gazes met. "I love you, baby," he whispered. He said it so low and soft that, at first, Olivia wasn't sure she'd actually heard it. "I really do. You're the first woman I've said that to." He pressed his lips to hers and kissed her gently.

"I love you too. At first I was terrified to admit it because I thought it was too soon, but now I can't even remember how my life was without you." She ran her fingertips down the side of his face.

He laughed and held her closer to him, his arms curling even tighter around her. "No problems with me being a biker?"

"None at all. I can't believe how hanging on to that prejudice for so many years only led me to a bunch of creeps. I had nothing in common with them, either." She poked his ribs lightly. "But then you came along, and how could I resist?"

"Good point." He chuckled.

"I'm just so happy."

"Me too, and that's huge for me."

Another poke to his ribs. "Yeah, it's a shock for the big, brooding outlaw, huh?" She giggled.

"Actually ... it is." He rolled her over and peppered kisses all over her face. "Let's go for a swim."

"Isn't the water like freezing?"

"I'll keep you warm." He sat up then pulled her with him.

"If I get pneumonia, I'm blaming you." She joked as they walked toward the lake.

After spending time swimming, kissing, and fooling around in the water, they made long, slow love for the rest of the afternoon. By the time the lake and surrounding valley was all in shade and the tops of the mountains were bright with sun, the two of them shrugged on their clothes. Olivia shook out the blanket and folded it while Animal tossed the paper bag filled with empty water bottles, beer and soda cans into a large receptacle. He wrapped his arm around Olivia as they walked back to the motorcycle.

Twigs and leaves crunched under the weight of their feet, and branches swayed and rustled in the late afternoon breeze. Animal stowed the blanket back in one of the saddle bags, then straddled the bike as she put her boot on one of the foot pegs and climbed on behind him.

The sound of the engine revving seemed out of place in the idyllic surroundings, and Olivia looped her arms around Animal's waist before he turned the bike around and headed back to town.

Later that night, Olivia made tacos for the three of them, and after dinner, Lucy kicked both of their butts—which neither would admit to anyone—in the New Super Mario Brothers video game. Of course, Lucy reminded them several times that she was the champion, and Olivia thought the way Animal pretended to be bothered by it was super sexy … and cute. Yeah … cute, but she'd never tell him that.

When Olivia switched off the nightstand lamp later that night, the last thought on her mind was that Animal loved her. The thrill of it pulsed through her body, and she snuggled deeper into her pillow as her lids fluttered shut with the memory of him seeped into her soul.

CHAPTER TWENTY-THREE

THE MORNING LIGHT struggled through clouds scudding across the leaden sky. Mountain tops peeked through gauzy veils of mist, and a sweet, earthy smell permeated the air. Pulling up the collar of his leather jacket, Animal took a sip of his coffee as he walked out of the Mugs and Things shop.

Trees lined Main Street on both sides, standing so tall that their branches touched high in the sky. Shops and restaurants were bustling with activity, and several people strolled on the sidewalks, looking in the store windows.

Animal had one more stop to make before meeting up with Hawk and Throttle at Ruthie's for an early lunch. Bones had told Animal he'd meet up with him at the Shade Store since he'd be in the area, and then they'd both head over to Ruthie's together.

Animal pushed open the door to the small store filled with bolts of fabric, several types of blinds, shutters, and shades, and stacks of books filled with design ideas. A forty-something-year-old woman dressed in a tailored suit smiled as she approached him.

"May I help you?" she asked.

Animal glanced around the store, wondering why the hell he thought coming here was a good idea. "I need to get some stuff to cover some windows."

The woman's smile widened. "In that case, you're at the right store." She gestured at the various items in the shop.

He wiped the corners of his mouth with two fingers. "I wanna buy some shit for my woman's windows."

The saleslady's face fell slightly. "Okay." A buzzer sounded and she looked over Animal's shoulder and her face paled.

"Dude," Bones said. Animal turned around and bumped fists with him. "So remind me again why the fuck you're in this place."

The woman took several steps backward.

"Buying shit to put over Olivia's damn windows. She's had those fuckin' sheets up since she moved in." He glanced at the sales clerk. "Olivia Mooney has an order here for one of her windows. I wanna pay for it."

The woman nodded. "Okay—let me look that up." She scurried behind a counter, a look of relief washing over her face.

"What the hell do you know 'bout decorating, dude?" Bones laughed.

"I didn't do half bad at my place," Animal answered.

"As I remember it, Jada did most of the decorating."

"I found it," the woman said. "White shutters for the living-room window. She also picked out treatments for the bedroom, bathroom, and sliding glass door, but only put a deposit on the shutters."

"Damn, this is gonna be easy. I'll pay for the whole damn thing." Animal took out his wallet.

"*Everything?*" the woman asked.

"That's what I said, didn't I?" Animal walked over to the counter.

"Yep ... that's what you said," Bones answered.

Flustered, the woman shuffled some papers around on the counter. "I was referring to you paying for the installation as well as the treatments."

Animal's jaw tightened. "Yeah. *Everything*. Fuck, lady." Her tight expression emphasized the lines around her mouth. "When can you get all this delivered and installed?"

She touched the base of her throat and glanced back at the computer screen. "The shutters she put the deposit on can be done right away, but the Roman shades for the bedroom, the sheer shade for the bathroom, and the white shutter panels for the sliding door will have to be ordered."

"That's cool. Let's do the shutter thing this weekend, and order the rest." Animal glanced at his phone. "Write it up quick 'cause we gotta get going."

"Certainly. There'll be an extra charge for installation on a Saturday."

"Okay." Animal turned to Bones. "You wanna help me fix a stove today? I gotta pull it out and it's a cast-iron motherfucker. It's the woman's great-great grandma's stove, and I'm gonna need help dragging that thing away from the wall."

Bones shrugged. "Sure—I don't have any plans. So, you just being in this damn store means you must really like this chick."

"Fuck, dude. How the hell did you figure that out all on your own?"

"Asshole," Bones grumbled.

"For Saturday, we have morning and afternoon openings, which do you prefer?" the saleslady asked.

"After 10:00 a.m. is good," Animal replied.

"I'll put it down for the ten-to-noon spot."

"I never thought I'd see you go all mushy and shit about a chick. Buying fuckin' curtains for her? Fuck." Bones shoved his hands in the pockets of his leather jacket.

"Olivia's not just a chick," Animal said.

"It's just that you never wanted to go out with citizens that much. What the fuck? Aren't you missing the club girls and all that easy pussy?"

One long, loud choking cough drew Animal's attention back to the saleswoman, who was grabbing for a bottle of water on a table behind her. He turned away and shook his head at Bones.

"I can't explain it." He laughed. "I guess she reformed me. It just happened, dude."

Bones scrunched up his face. "I never fuckin' thought you'd be the next to fall."

Animal clasped his hand on his friend's shoulder. "You talk like it's a fucking death sentence."

"For me, giving up easy pussy is worse than death."

Animal guffawed, then looked back at the woman. "You got that set up yet?" She nodded and brought the water bottle to her mouth. "How much do I owe you for all of it?"

After Animal finished the transaction, he and Bones left the store and headed down the sidewalk, talking about the newest motorcycle that Bones was aiming to buy at the end of the month. Out of his peripheral vision, Animal caught sight of Skeet across the street. Animal looked over with more intent, noticing the fucker walking down the sidewalk in Insurgents' territory wearing his cut with the Rising Order patch.

"Fuck *that*!" Animal yelled and ran across the road.

"What the hell?" Bones's voice floated behind him.

"You fuckin' asshole," Animal said to Skeet.

The ex-member didn't respond, and just stood there staring into Animal's eyes. Thea tugged on Skeet's hand, seeming to sense the building tension.

"Let's go," she said, her gaze darting from Animal to Skeet then back to Animal.

Bones sidled beside Animal. "We got a fuckin' traitor in our territory."

"Yeah," Animal gritted, his muscles growing tight.

"Come on," Thea pleaded, her lips trembling slightly.

"Okay, babe," Skeet said, turning away from them. When he did, his shoulder collided with Animal's. Hard. Too hard for it to be an accident.

Animal just looked over at him and didn't say a word nor changed his stony expression.

"Watch where you're going, honey. Animal's gonna think you did that on purpose." A nervous giggle spilled from her lips. Thea glanced over at Animal. "We're going." Another tug on Skeet's hand.

Skeet flicked a cursory glance at Bones, then settled his blue eyes on Animal. He stood still: feet spread, hands at waist level.

Animal rocked back on his heels, his gaze never leaving Skeet's face. Bones muttered obscenities under his breath and took a couple of steps toward the biker. Tension crackled in the air, and Thea kept pleading with Skeet to move on.

The ex-Insurgent threw the first punch, but Animal was already coming at him and knocked Skeet off balance so that he missed Bones's face. Animal slammed Skeet against the brick wall of a novelty shop, then leaned back far enough to throw a punch at the asshole's jaw. Before he made contact, the fucker landed a kick in Animal's groin, and pain shot through him, sizzling every fucking nerve in his body. He stumbled backward, almost losing his balance, and lowered his head, avoiding Skeet's fist to his face.

"You good, bro?" Bones asked.

Rage burned through Animal, and he kicked out his leg and slammed the tip of one of his steel-toed boots against Skeet's shin. The traitor groaned and bowled over, and Animal landed an uppercut flush on the jerk's nose.

"Fuck!" Skeet yelled as blood leaked over his lips then dripped off his chin.

Thea screamed and rushed Animal, scratching and kicking him. "You asshole!" she yelled. People on the sidewalk quickly crossed the street, and shop employees closed and locked the doors.

"Don't fuckin' disrespect an Insurgent, bitch!" Bones yelled, pulling the woman away from Animal, who had landed a few sharp kicks to Skeet's ribs.

"Let me go!" She struggled in the Insurgent's arms.

"You're a fuckin' skank! You're lucky I'm not kicking your ass after the shit you did to Metal," Bones said.

A deafening roar filled the air, and Animal looked toward the street and saw Hawk and Throttle pull over to the curb and jump off their bikes.

"What the fuck's going on?" Hawk asked as he rushed over to Animal.

"This fucker's in Insurgents' territory," Animal said.

Skeet glared at Hawk.

"His ma's sick," Thea said, jerking away from Bones. "We rode down to see her."

Hawk glowered at her. "Don't fuckin' talk to me." He turned to Skeet. "You didn't turn in your rocker, asshole."

"It's at my ma's," he gritted.

"What a fuckin' jerk." Throttle spat on the sidewalk.

"I'll get Rock, Jax, and Puck to go get it. You shoulda turned it in." Hawk landed a hard blow to the traitor's stomach. "That's for fuckin' around with Metal's old lady."

"Seems like you're owed a beatdown," Throttle said. "Metal gets the first punch."

"Metal's okay now," Thea whined. "I talked to him and he told me he's over it. He—"

"Didn't Hawk tell you to shut the fuck up? You're nothing, bitch. Don't talk to us," Animal said. Thea crossed her arms and glared at them.

"What's going on here?" a deep voice said.

Animal turned around and saw a damn badge walking up to them. *Fuck!* "Nothing," he replied.

"That's not the way it looks." The badge's gaze fell on Skeet, who lay on his side; dried blood crusted the biker's lips and chin.

"It's personal business," Hawk said. "Move on."

The cop jerked his head back. "*Move on?* You don't tell me shit like that." He huffed.

The vice president visibly stiffened. "I just did. There's nothing here for you. Call Chief Landon—he'll tell you." The Insurgents and the police chief had a tacit agreement: the MC kept hard drugs out of the county and law enforcement would look the other way in most instances.

The badge didn't move an inch, just stood there scowling, looking like he was debating with himself on what to do. After a few long seconds, he shook his head. "I'm taking the whole lot of you in."

"No … you're not," Hawk said.

"Call Landon. We don't have time for this shit," Animal said.

"Or we'll call him. Your choice," Throttle added.

The badge walked back to the patrol car and Animal watched him pull out the radio.

"The fuckin' badge must be new," Bones said.

"Yeah, I haven't seen him before," Hawk said as he bent over and dragged Skeet to his feet. "You're one stupid fucker to have come back."

"His ma's sick," Thea said.

The Insurgents glowered at her, and she placed a hand over her mouth. Hawk turned away and looked at Animal. "Tell Skinless to get his ass over here with the SUV. We got an asshole he needs to pick up."

Animal pulled out his phone, stepped away from the group, and tapped in the prospect's number. He told him what Hawk wanted, then Animal ended the call and sent out a group text telling the membership that Skeet's beatdown was imminent and to get their asses to the clubhouse pronto. Animal glanced over at the badge and chuckled: he was red-faced, his eyes narrowed into slits, his lips pressed into a thin line. Animal slid his phone into the inner pocket of his jacket and ambled over to the group.

"Skinless is on the way, and I sent the brothers a text."

Hawk nodded as he, Throttle, and Bones crowded Skeet against the wall. Thea leaned her head against it and watched them, her chest rising and falling rapidly.

"You," the badge said, pointing at Animal. "Come here."

Animal lifted his chin up. "Fuck, no."

The man in uniform slammed the car door and strode over to him.

"Did Landon set you straight, big boy?" Animal said, and Throttle, Hawk, and Bones guffawed.

"Just fuckin' remember what you were told," Throttle said.

"I'm watching you. If you assholes cross the line by even one inch, I'll be all over your asses," he said.

"And we'll be watching *you*," Animal replied.

"Like Hawk said, 'Move on.' We got shit to do." Throttle turned his back.

The badge glared at Animal. "Leave Olivia alone," he gritted.

Taken aback by the mention of his woman's name, Animal just stood there, his mind reeling. The cop sneered at him.

"What the fuck's your name?" Animal growled.

"Nathan Rogers." A satisfied smirk spread across his face.

"There's no way my woman's into fuckin' badges."

"*Your* woman?" A dry laugh. "She's *my* girlfriend. From the dumb look on your face, I'm guessing you didn't know you were just biker cock."

White-hot rage burned through him, and Animal clenched his hands and stepped closer to the fucking badge. He raised his arm, but before he could throw a punch at the smug fucker's face, Hawk grabbed his wrist and stopped him.

"If you do that, it'll cause all sorts of fuckin' problems, bro. Just let it be. The fucker's just talking out of his ass to goad you."

Jerking away from Hawk's hold, Animal breathed heavily through flaring nostrils as he stared at Rogers. Of course Hawk was right: if he hit Rogers, Landon wouldn't look the other way. The smug badge was just dying for an excuse to haul Animal's ass in, but how in the hell did *he* know Olivia? There was no damn way she was two-timing him by going out with this idiot. Was she? Doubt mixed with fury coursed through Animal.

"Let's take care of business," Hawk said, gripping Animal's arm and leading him toward Skeet.

Animal looked over his shoulder and saw Rogers march back to the patrol car, slam the door, and speed away. He still couldn't figure out how in the hell the jerk knew Olivia, or better yet, about Olivia and him.

Skinless pulled up in the SUV and he and Rusty jumped out and promptly handcuffed Skeet, then dragged his sorry ass back to the vehicle and took off. Thea—tears streaming down her face—stood on the curb watching ... well after the car had disappeared.

Hawk and Throttle jumped on their bikes and switched on the ignition.

"See you at the clubhouse," Throttle said as he peeled away from the curb with Hawk following behind.

"You shoulda shed some tears for your old man, not for a fuckin' traitor, but then again, you're a whoring cheat," Bones said to Thea.

She spun around. Black trails of mascara stained her cheeks, and she dabbed them with the corner of her sleeve. "Are you gonna kill him?" She sniffled.

Without answering, Animal and Bones stalked away toward their motorcycles, and then headed to the Insurgents' clubhouse.

ANIMAL DELIVERED SKEET—HIS face a bloody pulp, his body, battered and broken—on the front lawn of the ex-Insurgent's mother's house. He saw Thea peeking through the curtains as if waiting for him to leave. The moment Animal threw his SUV into drive, she scurried outside and bent over the biker.

Animal swung a U-turn and made his way to Slavens to pick up Lucy. Skeet had been taught a lesson by the club he forfeited and by the member whom he'd disrespected by fucking his old lady. Metal had decided that beating the shit out of the sonofabitch was all the vindication he needed, and had declined to exact any vengeance on Thea for her betrayal of their marriage vows. The members respected their fellow brother's decision, and the whole incident was laid to rest.

Animal parked in a spot right in front of the school and slid out of the car. He was a few minutes early so he leaned against the hood, hoping that Olivia would come out with the children once the bell rang.

Soon the final bell of the school day rang out, and children poured out of various doors around the building. He lifted his chin when he saw Lucy and Aria bouncing toward the car, and pressed his lips together when he saw Aria's mother approaching him. The only woman he wanted to talk to at that moment was Olivia. He had to find out how she knew the fucking badge, and why the asshole said that she was his girlfriend.

"Hi there," Aria's mom said.

For the life of him, he couldn't remember her name. "Hey," he replied, his gaze darting around for Olivia.

"How've you been?" she asked.

"Good."

"Do you have a day in mind that Aria can come over to play? She's been talking about it nonstop. Remember, I said I'd fix you dinner." A warm smile spread over her face as her gaze ran up and down his corded arms. "By the way, I love your tattoos. Did you get them done in town?"

"Yeah. I'm pretty busy for the next couple of weeks. So ... yeah."

"That's okay. I'll just touch base with you again and you can let me know. I'm real busy too with my real estate business and raising a child on my own. My husband walked out on us two years ago and ..."

She talked and talked and Animal just wanted her to shut the hell up; he didn't feel like engaging in any conversation. He rubbed the back of his neck and tuned out Aria's mother and continued looking for Olivia. Finally he spotted her dark hair gleaming under the bright sun, which had finally decided to make an appearance. He looked over at the playground and saw Lucy and Aria on the swings.

"I gotta talk to one of the teachers," Animal said.

Aria's mother looked like he'd slapped her in the face or something. "Oh," she said weakly.

"Later." He walked away and watched Olivia as she crouched down on her haunches and zipped up a young boy's jacket. She then ruffled his blond hair and gave him a quick hug. Animal never thought she looked sexier than at that moment, and he wanted to yank her to him and press her close while he rubbed against her soft body. Then the damn badge's smug face upstaged his desire, and he jammed his hands in the front pockets of his jeans and stalked over to her.

"Hey," he said when he reached her.

"Hi," Olivia answered as she rose to her feet and held her hand above her eyes to shield them from the sun.

"Can you talk?" Animal glanced again at Lucy, who was squealing with laughter as she swung higher.

"Sure. Is something wrong?" Worry etched her face.

Animal grasped her by the elbow and nudged her toward the wall so that their conversation wouldn't be heard, yet he could still keep an eye on Lucy.

"How the fuck do you know Nathan Rogers?" he said without any preamble.

Olivia's eyes widened. "Nathan Rogers? Why're you bringing up *his* name?"

"I'm the one asking the damn questions here. So, you *do* know him. Are you fucking him?"

Olivia's hand flew to her mouth, and she let out a loud gasp. "No! Why the hell would you ask me something like that?" Her eyes brimmed with tears. She seemed genuinely shocked and hurt, and a dull pain stabbed at his gut.

Rubbing his face, he drew in a ragged breath. Animal didn't mean to upset her or to make her think that he didn't trust her. He ran agitated fingers through his hair, sorry that he caused the tears in her eyes. *What a fuckin' mess. Dammit!*

"Animal?" she whispered. "Why did you ask me that?"

He tilted his head back and watched the clouds moving across the sky. After a brief few seconds, he looked down at her. "I got crazy in the brain." He'd never been jealous over a woman before, but now he felt almost crazed with it like a lovesick adolescent who'd just become aware of girls. One thing was for certain: Olivia was in his blood. He had a gnawing need for her that never left him, that made him ask stupid pansy-assed questions to the woman he loved. Fuck, this shit was complicated.

"About what? I love you—I'd never cheat on you." Olivia ran her fingertips lightly over his forearm. "I dated Nathan for a short time way before I met you. I ended it because he was creeping me out and getting way too possessive. Anyway, he started stalking me, but ever since I'd moved into my house, he seemed to have left me alone. However, by your question, I'm guessing I may have been wrong in assuming that."

"I ran into him this morning when I was downtown. The fucker said you were his girlfriend."

"And you believed him? Don't you even *know* me?"

"Okay—I acted like a pussy. I own that. I just ... I don't know ... Just the thought of you with him or any dude is hard to take, you know?"

"I get that, but you know I wasn't a virgin hiding out in a tower. I have a past, but it shouldn't affect our present or future. And talk about a past—how many women have you been with." She held up her hand in front of his face. "Don't answer that—I'm already sorry I asked. I know what goes on in the biker clubs, and you don't think that sometimes it makes me feel a bit insecure or jealous?"

"You don't have anything to worry about, baby. I only want you."

"That's the way it is with me too—I only want you."

He pulled her close to him and hugged her tightly. "I didn't mean to accuse you. Hell, I'm new to all this relationship stuff."

Olivia giggled as she broke away from him. "Just so you know, it never gets easier."

"Fucking great." He moved closer to her. "I wanna kiss you, babe."

"Not here in front of all the children."

Animal looked around and saw some of the teachers and the angry eyes of Aria's mother aimed right at him. "Fuck," he muttered. "I forgot about her."

"Who?" Olivia said looking over her shoulder.

"Aria's mom. She's been coming on to me since Lucy and her daughter became friends."

"You mean Elise Griffin?"

"Yeah, that's her name. She's using her kid to get close to me."

Olivia looked over her shoulder again. "Like how?"

"Saying that the only way Aria can come over to play with Lucy is if she comes too. She gave me some bullshit about doing it with all of

Aria's friends. She wants to fix dinner for me."

"I'm the one who'll fix dinner for you and Lucy. She's attractive though. One of the eighth grade teachers, Marcus Thurber, has chatted her up numerous times."

"She can't even begin to compare to you, baby. I want you to come out with Lucy and me for dinner. We're going to Luigi's for pizza."

Her eyes sparkled. "I'd love to, but will Lucy be okay with it? I don't want to butt into her time with you."

"Let's ask her." Animal waved Lucy over.

"I think Aria's mom's mad. She made her get off the swing and leave."

"She's probably just having a bad day," he replied. "I was telling Olivia that I'm taking you to Luigi's for pizza."

"Yay!" Lucy twirled around. "Are you coming, Ms. Mooney?"

Olivia smiled. "Do you want me to?"

"Uh-huh. Have you been there?"

"I've never eaten there—I've only done takeout."

"I've been there a lot. I really like it." She tucked her hand into Animal's and looked up at him. "Are we going now? I'm hungry."

"I'm not sure." Animal glanced over at Olivia.

"I won't be able to go until about six o'clock. I have an online class that starts at four," Olivia said. "Will six work for you, Lucy?"

His daughter cocked her head to the side and scrunched up her face as if deep in thought, then said, "That's good."

Animal laughed and squeezed her hand lightly. "You sure about that?"

"Uh-huh." She bobbed her head up and down.

"We'll pick you up then," he said to Olivia.

"Sounds good. I have to get back and straighten out the classroom. Remember to practice the passages I marked for you," she said to Lucy. "See you later."

On the drive home, Lucy chatted about the upcoming school trip to the candy factory. She told him Olivia was going to come with her class on that day.

"Sounds like you really like Olivia," he said.

"Yeah, you like her too." Lucy blew a bubble with her gum and popped it.

"I do."

"I've seen you kissing." Lucy giggled.

Surprise ran through him. "When did you start spying on me?" he asked, which only made Lucy laugh harder.

"Does Ms. Mooney have a mom?" she asked after her laughter died down.

"Yeah, why?"

"Does her mom live here?"

"No. She lives in California, but Olivia's not that close to her."

"Does her mom love Ms. Mooney?" Lucy fixed her gaze on Animal.

For the thousandth time, Animal wondered how Emerald could desert her daughter in the way in which she had. "I don't think they get along. Her mom was not really there for her and neither was her dad."

"She was all alone?" A small frown formed on his daughter's forehead.

"Pretty much."

"She's happy now."

"Yeah, she is." Animal shifted in his seat. He hadn't wanted to tell Lucy about Olivia and him before because he wasn't sure if what they had was going anywhere. The last thing he'd wanted was for Lucy to get attached to Olivia if she wasn't going to stick around. But ever since their day at the lake, Animal knew he wanted her in his life, and he knew she wanted that as well.

He looked sideways at Lucy. "How would you like it if Olivia became part of our family?"

Lucy's eyes widened. "Like marry her?"

Animal almost choked. "Whoa … I didn't say that. I was just asking if you'd like to include her in stuff that we do. Sometimes you and I will do things alone, but we can start asking her to hang with us. You know, come over and watch TV with us, have dinner, and other things."

"I'd like that. If you marry Ms. Mooney, will she be my mom?"

"I'm not marrying anyone, kiddo. Get the marriage thing outta your mind." That's all he needed was for Lucy to say something to Olivia. Wouldn't that be a fucking mess?

"Oh … why not?"

Animal let out a loud sigh. "I don't know. We're not there yet, and I never thought about it." Marriage was a dirty word for him, like a deadly diagnosis or something.

"Can Ms. Mooney be my mom?"

His heart lurched. "Do you want her to?"

"I don't know." Lucy turned away and looked out the window.

"You don't have to know, kiddo. I just wanted to ask you if you're cool with Olivia spending more time with us. What do you want on your pizza tonight?"

While Lucy talked, Animal made a mental note that he'd call the child psychologist Olivia had told him about. Even though Lucy seemed better than she'd been a few months before, he knew her mother's abandonment had scarred her. All Animal wanted was to give her the best life he could, and helping her heal and work through all the anger shit that her fucking mother had caused was the first step in the right direction toward his daughter's well-being.

He pulled into the garage and Lucy jumped out of the car and ran to the back door.

"Can I have a cookie? Please?"

Animal unlocked the door and followed her to the kitchen. "You can have two, kiddo." He smiled and walked over to the cupboard and took down a bag of iced animal crackers.

CHAPTER TWENTY-FOUR

THE PLACE RENA Walsh found for her rendezvous with Hunter Lewis was the Ramble Hotel, nestled in the mountains among the pine trees, studded with balconies overlooking the valley. To the north was the Colorado River meandering through the valley. In the distance, lights from the town twinkled like fireflies against the darkness of night.

The first thing Rena noticed when she entered the hotel room were the chocolates on the overstuffed pillows on the bed; each of the truffles were brightly covered in pink, orange, blue, red, and purple shiny wrappers. She placed her overnight bag down on the mahogany dresser and then walked over to the bed. Picking up one of the chocolates, she unwrapped it and popped it into her mouth. Rena slowly walked over to the balcony doors and stepped onto the terrace. A light wind had begun to blow, and with it came the fragrant scent of wild roses growing along the gravel roads.

A twinge of guilt wove through her as Animal's opinionated eyes flashed across her mind. Her son was the last person who should judge her. Over the years, she'd heard plenty of stories, and watched enough documentaries on television to know *exactly* what went on in that outlaw club of his. Animal had a lot of gall to think she was a slut. Oh, he didn't say it, but Rena knew he thought that about her, and she hated like hell that her son had found out about the extracurricular activities she'd been engaging in *with* her husband's permission.

Rena inhaled the clean mountain air and blew out a long breath. The truth was, she hated hooking up with different men, and she and Jay had agreed upon no more than two dates with the same man. She gripped the railing on the balcony. Rena loved her husband, but he couldn't satisfy her needs. For the first few years after his injury, they'd tried different things, but the reality was that Jay had lost the feeling for sex. He knew that and it killed him, so he'd proposed that she find pleasure outside their marriage. At first Rena had balked at the suggestion, but after a couple of years of celibacy, her body craved release, so she took the first step. Now, years later, Rena still wished she and Jay could go back to the way they were before the war, but that would never be. At fifty-five years old, she still looked damn good—people thought she looked forty at the most—and she still loved sex.

Rena sighed and pushed away from the iron railing and went back into the room. She'd have to turn the lights way down before Hunter arrived since she'd fudged her age and had sent him a photo of her when she was twenty-five. Animal had only been five years old then, and Rena remembered that she couldn't wait until he was in school full-time because he was a handful. If she were being completely honest, Rena really wasn't very good mother material. She'd never wanted children, but Jay had so desperately wanted a family that she decided one kid wouldn't be too bad, but Rena had been so wrong. She just wasn't into the whole maternal thing—some women weren't—and that was just the way it was. When Jada came along ten years after Animal, she'd been devastated. The whole baby-cycle had started up again, and it had been years until she was finally free.

Jay always got along great with both of their kids, but from very early on, she had locked horns with Animal and still did. He was so hardheaded and just didn't try to understand her. And what did he know about relationships anyway? The man never had a girlfriend who Rena knew about, and she rarely saw him twice with the same women, when she *did* happen to see him around town.

Rena glanced at the clock on the nightstand and her heart skipped a beat. Hunter would be here soon, and she was pretty sure he'd love the look of the room with the midnight blue velvet headboard and the antique rug spread over dark wood floors. The look and feel of the space was luxurious and elegant, and from their many conversations, Rena gleaned that it was something Hunter would appreciate.

The man intrigued her, hence the reason for the lies. Normally, she'd never rendezvous with a man who seemed interested in a relationship rather than a hookup, but the way Hunter talked, his sophistication and boyish charm had reeled her in enough that she was willing to meet up with him for a romantic night of lovemaking. She hadn't made love in years, not since Jay had been injured. All of her meetings with men were strictly sex, nothing more. This night with Hunter would be very different, and while they enjoyed each other, Rena could close her eyes and pretend she was with her husband again.

A slight jiggle of the doorknob pulled Rena out of her reflections, and she rushed over and switched off the floor lamp and dimmed the small one on the nightstand. She drew in a ragged breath and waited. She'd left the keycard under the door, barely visible just as Hunter had instructed. He'd been very detailed with what he wanted: she was to find the hotel; it had to be away from town and not a big place; she was to check in alone without any mention of him, and she was to pay for the room with the prepaid Visa card he'd sent her in the mail. When she'd read all his instructions, Rena had laughed and figured he was married, but she didn't judge him because she didn't know anything about his home life.

The door swung open and a small rush of air from the hallway curled around her legs.

"Rena, my sweet?" His deep, sexy voice washed over her.

Without turning around, she nodded.

"Why is it so dark in here?" he asked. She heard his footfalls approaching.

"I thought it was more romantic," she replied.

"Turn around, my sweet ... I want to look at your pretty face."

Rena hesitated. "I wasn't 100 percent truthful about my age."

The footsteps stopped.

"How old are you?" The edge in his voice was clear and sharp—like a knife.

"Thirty-nine," she lied, hoping that in the dim light she could get away with it.

The sound of his shoes on the wooden floor echoed behind her. A shiver rippled through her, but it was from fear, not excitement.

"That isn't too old, my sweet. You could have told me the truth."

His words should have sounded reassuring, yet they made her skin crawl. A chill ran up and down her spine and she shuddered. Rena had to get out of there—something was off-kilter with this man. Before she could do anything, Hunter was behind her with both hands on her shoulders, pulling her until her back tucked against his chest. There were no thrills from his touch, instead, she found it repulsive.

"Sweet Rena," he whispered. He draped a hand across her upper chest. "You shouldn't have lied to me."

She swallowed and licked her dry lips. "I was afraid to tell you the truth because I liked you so much." Rena was now cursing herself for even agreeing to meet up with Hunter.

"*Love*—you love me, right?" His arm inched up toward the base of her throat.

"Yeah—I love you. Let's sit down and talk."

"I haven't forgiven you for lying to me. Your lie has spoiled *everything*."

Rena stiffened, not daring to move a muscle. "What do you mean?"

"I love a certain type, that's all. Age is very important. Now my mindset has been altered, and I don't like that."

"I'm sorry. I just thought—"

"You thought wrong." His voice was frost.

"Okay. I'll just go."

He pulled his arm away. "You're not going anywhere, bitch."

Hunter's strong hands tightened around her throat, squeezing and pulling her back further into him. Rena tried to scream but only hoarse croaks escaped through her parted lips. Clawing at his hands, she tried to loosen them from around her neck, but he was too strong. Dark spots floated before her eyes, and her lungs felt as though they were going to burst. Hunter squeezed tighter.

Panic set in and she became feral. With waning strength, Rena lifted her leg, bent it at the knee, and pushed it backward with all her might. Hunter cried out and loosened his hold on her for a couple of seconds, but in that brief time span, her arms reached above her and she scratched his face with her long nails. Rena aimed for his eyes, and Hunter let go of her as he tried to grab hold of her hands.

"You fucking bitch!" He screamed.

"You bastard!" she yelled back as she twisted around and saw him for the first time. Before she could even take all of him in, he lunged for her, but Rena's pointed-toe shoe landed a perfect shot right on the jerk's balls, and he howled as he doubled over.

Taking the window of opportunity, she dashed for the door, not stopping for anything.

"Get back here, cunt!"

Rena turned the knob and jetted out the door, rushing to the stair-well without even a glance backward. She kicked off her high-heeled shoes and scrambled down the stairs as the sound of her panting bounced off the concrete walls.

As she flung the door open to the lobby, she just stood there, gasping in an attempt to catch her breath while tears trickled down her cheeks. Rena glanced around but there was no sign of Hunter, so she hurried over to the front desk and leaned against it.

"May I help you, ma'am?" the reception clerk asked.

"No, I'm fine," Rena responded as she slid her phone out of her dress pocket. She tapped in Animal's phone number.

"What's up, Mom?"

She hated calling him, but there was no way she wanted the police involved in this. The car keys were in her purse in the room upstairs, and there was no chance in hell Rena was going to go back up to get it. Animal was her only choice.

"I'm in a bit of trouble."

"Whaddaya mean?"

"I don't want you to lecture me, okay? The guy I hooked up with just tried to kill me. I made—"

"What the fuck?" Where are you?"

"At a small hotel near Aspen Grove Valley. I'm scared shitless." Her voice hitched.

"I'll be there soon. I gotta call Olivia to see if she can come over and stay with Lucy. I'll have some of the guys get to you now. Text me the name of the hotel, okay?"

"All right. Thanks. Who's Olivia?"

"Really, Mom? You were almost murdered and you're asking me that?"

"I was just curious. Who is she?"

"My woman. Gotta go. Don't leave the lobby."

Rena stared at the blank screen then looked around the reception area. She doubted Hunter would come after her with people around. Had he intended to kill her regardless of the fib about her age, or did that set him off? She wrapped her arms around herself and shivered. Now it was beginning to make sense as to why he wanted her to make all the arrangements in *her* name: he didn't want to leave a paper trail. "The bastard planned to kill me," she muttered under her breath. Hunter was probably waiting for her to come out of the hotel so he could finish off the job in the dark of night.

"Are you sure you don't want anything?" the fresh-faced young clerk asked again.

"Yes, I'm sure. I'm waiting for someone." A dry cough seized her, and she struggled to breathe. "Some water," she managed to croak out.

The clerk rushed over to a table holding paper cups and a large glass container of water and poured her a glass. Rena gulped it down and pressed her hand to her sore throat; there would no doubt be some bruising. She padded over to a wingback chair, and the marble floor felt cool beneath her feet. Maybe when Animal arrived, he'd go to the stairwell and retrieve her shoes. She'd paid more for them than she normally did for a pair of high heels, and Rena hated to lose them.

Sinking down in the chair, Rena stared out the large glass doors into the night. *So Animal's got a woman.* That surprised the hell out of her, and she wanted to meet this woman who'd finally reformed him from his carousing ways.

The glass on the sliding door rattled as five motorcycles rode up to the entrance. The loud roar ended all at once, and five men clad in denim and leather strode into the lobby. Rena sprang up from the chair, and a good-looking man with dark hair and the stormiest gray eyes she'd ever seen walked over to her.

"You Animal's mom?" His voice was gruff like sandpaper.

"Yes," she said looking at the other four men. The only one she recognized out of the bunch was Bones. He'd been to the house numerous times helping out with Jay. He lifted his chin to her and came over.

"Where's the fucker?" Bones said.

She shook her head. "I don't know. I just ran out of the room."

"He's probably gone by now," the handsome gray-eyed guy said.

"We need to check." Bones turned to her. "Do you have the keycard?"

"No. I just took off. I'll get one at the desk." Rena walked over to the counter. "I misplaced my key—I need another one, please."

The young man looked over her shoulder at the group of bikers then turned around and grabbed another card. "Here you go. Are those men sharing the room with you?"

"No." She took the card and gave it to Bones.

"We'll be right back." The biker jerked his chin toward a very muscular man. "Helm will stay with you while we check out your room." He turned away, and he and three of the men disappeared in the stairwell.

For the next ten minutes, Helm stood watch over her while Rena sat in the chair wishing she were soaking in her deep tub at home. A low rumble came from the distance, and at first, she thought it was thunder until it grew louder, and she recognized Animal's bike. He stormed into the lobby, then bumped fists with Helm before saying anything to her.

"What the fuck happened?" he asked, concern etched on his face.

"Can we talk privately?" she asked, her eyes darting to Helm.

"Helm, smoke a joint," he said, and the fit biker swaggered out of the hotel. Animal looked at her. "So?"

"I met this guy online, and we made plans to spend the night together. I lied about my age and when he found out, he just flipped out."

"You were going to spend the whole night with him?"

"That was the plan, but when I met him, he just gave me the creeps. I then decided I wouldn't, but I didn't tell him that."

"Did you meet him on that *Discreet* bullshit site?"

"Yeah." She held up her hand in front of her son's disapproving face. "I know—stupid. The thing that really freaks me out is that I think he met me with the intention to kill me."

"He definitely did."

"Yo, bro," Bones said as he walked into the lobby.

Animal turned away from her and bumped fists with Bones and the others. "Anything?"

"Nah—the room was spotless and the fucker's long gone." Bones handed Rena her shoes. "I found these on the stairs and figured they belonged to you." He glanced down at her bare feet for a second then looked back at Animal. "Rock, Jax, and I are gonna walk around the property just in case, but my bet's on the pussy being long gone."

"You need me to help you?" Animal asked.

"We got it. Stay with your mom," Rock said.

Rena watched the three of them disappear out the door and she looked at the gray-eyed biker and smiled. "Thanks for helping me out."

He shook his head. "No worries. Animal's my brother, and when he needs help, I'm there."

Rena watched as her son and the man talked in hushed tones, and she felt an understanding of Animal's lifestyle choice wash over her. Except for Bones, these men didn't know her or owe her anything, yet they dropped everything in a blink of an eye to make sure she was safe. The strong bond of friendship her son and his brothers had made her a bit envious ... and sad. She'd never had such an unconditional friend-ship like that before.

Animal walked over to her again and tilted his chin at the handsome biker. "Shadow thinks this sounds like that fucker who's been killing all those young women in the county. I haven't been following the story, but he's been reading about it in the papers. Do you know about it?"

An icy chill enveloped her. "It can't be." She gasped, swallowing air like a drowning person.

He gripped her shoulder. "You're safe," he said in a low voice.

"Have you been reading about it?" Shadow asked.

Clutching the base of her throat, she nodded. "If I hadn't gotten away, he would've killed me. Oh, God."

"But he didn't, Mom. You gotta focus on that. What the hell did this fucker look like?"

"I don't know. I mean, he was standing behind me, but I did turn around when I was fighting him, but my mind's a blank." A small sob escaped her lips.

"It's okay ... it'll come back. What's his name?" Animal said.

"Hunter Lewis."

His eyes widened, then anger crept across his face, dark and deadly.

"What's wrong? Do you know him?" Rena asked.

"Not yet, but I will ... and then I'm gonna fuckin' kill him." She could feel the ferocious fury growling through him.

All of a sudden an irrational fear seized her, and she grabbed him and hugged him tightly. He hugged her back, and in a tiny splinter of time, they came together as mother and son.

CHAPTER TWENTY-FIVE

A SHIVER TIPTOED up Olivia's spine as she stared at the computer screen reading Hunter's message. Could *this* Hunter be the same one who'd attacked Animal's mother the night before? Olivia had been in shock since the night before when Animal had come home and told her about the incident, but surely there was more than one man named Hunter on the site.

She tipped her head back and looked up at the ceiling fan then back down to the screen. The answer was clear: she had to stop talking to Hunter. A part of her wanted to call the police, but Olivia really didn't know that this man with whom she'd been communicating was, in fact, the serial killer who had every woman in Pinewood Springs on edge. She drew in a breath and shook her head. What if he was the guy? Any tip would be worth pursuing, right?

Olivia picked up her phone and dialed her professor's number. She'd ask Dr. Davison for advice on this because the last thing she wanted was to ruin a lonely man's life by having the cops breathing down his back for no reason. The phone went to voicemail and she left a quick message telling him to call her as soon as he could, then she looked back at the screen.

Rose: *Hey, Hunter. Sorry for the delay.*

Hunter: *I thought you were ignoring me, my sweet.*

Rose: *Just super busy. I gotta get going to work soon.*

Hunter: *We need to meet, my sweet. I'm tired of talking by phone and message. Does this weekend work for you?*

Olivia rubbed the back of her neck then took a sip of coffee. She had to end this, but what if the cops wanted her to keep talking with him to draw him out? Maybe they'd want her to go undercover. "Stop it," she chided herself. "Your imagination is running wild."

Rose: *This weekend doesn't work. I have to go now. We can talk later.*

Hunter: *Don't you want to meet me? I thought we had something special. I love you, my sweet.*

"What a fucking nut," Olivia whispered under her breath.

Rose: *I just can't do it this weekend. I'm going to be late for work.*

Hunter: *I hope you're not playing with my feelings and stringing me along. I hope you are who you say you are.*

Olivia took another sip of coffee. "Okay, buddy, this is just getting too damn creepy and ominous."

Rose: *Gotta go. Later.*

Olivia signed out of the site then closed the lid of her laptop. She was done; she had enough data to finish her paper. Olivia glanced at the time and gulped the rest of her coffee. If she didn't get a move on, she'd be late and Dr. Canty would be yelling up a storm if she wasn't there when his seven thirty patient came in.

Twenty minutes later, Olivia pushed open the door and hurried to the employee's room to throw her purse and sweater into her locker before taking her position behind the reception desk. At exactly 7:29 a.m., Dr. Canty strolled into the area, and Olivia threw him a sweet smile when she saw the look of disappointment crossing his face upon seeing her.

"When did you get in?" A twinge of annoyance laced his voice.

"A few minutes ago. How about you?" She pulled out the daily sign-up sheet and placed it on the counter.

"What difference does that make? I'm the professional, not you." He leaned against the desk and stared at her.

"I was just making conversation," she replied.

Dr. Canty didn't respond, he just continued to stare, and Olivia ignored him, refusing to play into his juvenile intimidation tactics. When the door chimed, she glanced up from the computer screen, glad that the first patient had arrived only a few minutes late.

"Good morning, Mrs. Jurist. How are you?" Olivia pushed the sign-up sheet toward the older woman.

"Very good, thank you. You're always such a ray of sunshine with that warm smile of yours," she responded as she picked up a pen.

Olivia heard Dr. Canty sigh then walk out of the room. *Good.* She looked up at Mrs. Jurist. Ivy will come get you in a minute. Would you like a glass of water?"

The woman shook her head, a small smile brushing across her lips. "If I have any water before my teeth cleaning, I'll have to go to the bathroom."

Olivia smiled then looked up as both Dr. Linney and Dr. Mitchell walked in, each holding a cup of store-bought coffee in their hands.

"Hi, Thelma," Dr. Linney said to the older woman. "I'll be with you in a few minutes."

"Hello, Doctor. Take your time." Mrs. Jurist focused her attention back to the magazine she held.

"Olivia, I have a patient who may go over a bit tonight. Can you stay?" Dr. Mitchell asked.

She nodded. "I'm staying for Dr. Linney's late patient anyway."

"Thanks," he said as he walked through the door, then headed toward his office.

"I'm sorry to keep you late again tonight," Dr. Linney said. "I asked Janelle if she could come in and cover, but she wasn't available."

"Don't worry about it, I'm good. I know Janelle has another job on her days away from the clinic like I do, so it's all cool. What time do you think we'll be done?"

"If Charles Piper's on time, then around six thirty, but no later than seven o'clock. I'm not sure what time Dr. Mitchell will be done."

"I'll ask him, but that should work," Olivia said, even though dread wove through her. She'd forgotten to bring home the reading test materials the day before, and now she had to go back to the school after work. No one else had the key to her desk but her, so there was really no choice. Olivia had hoped she could've left no later than six o'clock that night, but the clinic always seemed to have late-night appointments.

"Hey, Olivia," Ivy said as she scurried into the reception area and looked over Olivia's shoulder at the screen. "Seems like we're busy all day."

"And night. I have to stay until seven." Olivia craned her neck and looked up at Ivy.

"Ugh … that sucks. The dentists should really get someone else to help. One receptionist isn't enough. Janelle is always swamped and working late on the days she comes in, and so are you." She glanced toward the hallway. "They're just cheap," she whispered.

Olivia giggled. "I really don't mind because I make more money, but I have to go back to Slavens and pick up some stuff I forgot, and I hate going there that late. I know the custodian will be there, but I still get the heebie-jeebies. I need to do some things to prepare for the standardized reading tests the students are taking tomorrow."

"Why don't you ask Animal to go with you?"

"That's a good idea—I think I will."

"You guys still going strong? I mean, any man who surprises you with window treatments for your whole house is a definite keeper, outlaw biker notwithstanding."

Olivia laughed. "I keep running around the house like a wacko opening and closing all the shades and shutters. It's so awesome but also pathetic." Animal's rugged face flashed through her mind, and she felt a rush of love. "I still can't believe he actually went into that store. It's not really the type of place he'd ever go into."

"That was just so sweet of him. I better get back to work." Ivy smiled as she walked into the lobby area. "Thelma Jurist," she said before escorting the older woman to one of the rooms down the hall.

The morning flew by in a blur of paperwork, phone calls, and patient check-ins, and by lunch hour, Olivia couldn't wait to go outside and bask in the sunlight while she called Animal. She grabbed her purse and snuck away before any of the dentists or hygienists thwarted her plans.

Miner's Square was half a block away from the building and right in the center of the business district. Surrounded by banks, small restaurants, and Victorian architecture, this was one of Olivia's favorite places in town. Benches lined the brick sidewalks, and sprawling oak trees provided ample shade during the day. A large bronze statute of a miner panning for gold stood in the middle of the square.

Olivia plopped down on one of the benches and pulled out her cellphone while balancing a hotdog in her other hand. She took a big bite, wiped the corner of her mouth with a napkin then had a sip of Coke before tapping in Animal's number.

"You must've read my mind, baby. I was just ready to call you," he said.

"I'm sitting in Miner's Square eating a hotdog I bought from one of the carts, and wishing you were here with me, sweetie."

"Me too. I'm stuck repairing a fuckin' garbage disposal because one of the guys called off this morning. Let's get together for dinner."

"I'd love to, but it'll have to be later. We have some patients coming in late tonight, so I won't get done until around seven. I need to go to Slavens to get some stuff I forgot to take home yesterday. Can you come with me? I don't like going there that late."

"Sure—I don't want you going there at night. I'll get Jada to stay with Lucy, and I'll follow you there. I've got your back, babe … *always.* Have you heard from that fucker?"

"Yeah. He contacted me this morning before I left for work. He's trying to get me to meet with him this weekend. Are you sure it's him?"

"Damn straight. I talked to my mom this morning, and she remembered he used that fucking expression 'my sweet.' I recalled seeing that when I was reading the messages that morning at your place."

"It *is* the same guy," she whispered, shivering despite the heat. "I can't believe it."

"And I'm pretty sure he's the fucker who's been doing all the murders in our county and some of the neighboring ones. Shadow and I talked for a long time this morning and he's up on all that shit. Anyway, he's convinced—so am I—that this Hunter bastard is that fucking serial killer."

"I was thinking that may be the case this morning. Oh crap … this is scary as hell. I have to call the police."

"Not yet. Badges just complicate shit. The MC can take care of it, but it'll mean you making a date with the SOB. I'll be there the whole time, along with several of the brothers. Are you up for it?"

"Yes," she blurted out without thinking. "He has to be stopped."

"I doubt that he's using his real name, but Hawk's real good with computers—he's our IT guy. He wants to see if he can figure out this guy's IP address."

"Maybe he's using a blocker like I do."

"Probably is, but Hawk wants to try it out. Can you spare your laptop being outta commission for a week or so?"

"It's fine. I back everything up on an external hard drive so I can use my older laptop to finish up what I need for teaching and my psych class. I need to tell Dr. Davison about all this."

"Don't tell anyone anything," Animal replied.

"There's no way Dr. Davison's involved in this, or *anyone* I know."

"It's just better not to tell people your business. Anyway, the club doesn't want anyone knowing what's going down."

"The chance of me knowing this horrible bastard is so slim."

"Agreed, but still … *no one*. Okay, babe?"

"Yes, I promise. Did your mom tell you what Hunter looked like? I know you told me last night that she was just too freaked and shocked by everything to remember, but maybe now?"

"I'm swinging by the house after I get two jobs finished. She told me her memory is getting clearer. I'll arrange for an installation of an alarm system at your house."

Olivia took a sip of her soda. "I can't afford that."

"Don't worry about it."

"Animal, you've done enough for me already, and I'm starting to feel guilty. You put in all the window coverings, you made sure I didn't pay anything for the car repair, and now this? I can't accept it."

"What's the fucking problem? You're my woman and I want to take care of you. I'm not gonna worry about you when we're not together just because you can't afford a security system. Fuck that. I'll get it installed."

From the tone of his voice, she knew *that* discussion was over.

"I wish you were here right now, baby. I'd kiss you real good then shove my finger into your wet pussy."

Her cheeks heated and she glanced around the area then took another sip of Coke. "The dirty things you say get me going." She squirmed in her seat.

"And just thinking about you, hearing your voice, and remembering how sweet you taste, turns me the fuck on, baby. I want you to stay the night so fuckin' bad."

"Me too. Will Lucy be okay with that?"

"Yeah—she's cool. She knows we're going out, remember?"

"I know you told me that, but sleeping over is different and kind of a big deal."

"If you make a breakfast without eggs and bacon, she'll be good." Animal chuckled. "Lucy's cool. She really likes you and the therapy is helping her a lot."

"I'm so glad. Doesn't she like eggs or bacon?"

"She does but she's fuckin' sick of them 'cause that's all I know how to make."

"Then I'll make her homemade pancakes with link sausages."

"Okay, but I'm just warning you that she'll never let you leave." He laughed.

"Sounds good to me." The minute the words flew out of her mouth, she stiffened. Even though she and Animal had professed their love to each other, it didn't mean that they were going to live together, or even take their relationship to a higher level.

"Yeah, well … I gotta get going. I'll come to the clinic before seven."

Olivia's heart sank. *I shouldn't have said that.* "I'll see you then. Good luck with the installation."

She tucked the phone back into her purse and slowly finished her lunch. Animal was the perfect complement to her personality, and she wanted to be a part of his life for a long time—maybe even forever. He was a biker through and through, and she highly doubted that he wanted anyone to wear his patch. *But I'm not anyone—I'm his woman. For fuck's sake, he furnished my house with shutters and shades. Who does that?* Olivia crumpled up the paper hotdog carrier in her hand. *I'm being silly. I know he loves me, and what the hell do I want anyway? I love living alone and being free.* But when she thought about wearing his patch, a thousand tiny tingles shot through her body. Olivia stood up from the bench and threw the remnants of her lunch in the trash. She didn't have to think about any of that now.

Glancing at the clock on one of the buildings facing the square, she smiled: only six hours to go until she could fall into his arms and kiss him. Olivia slipped her purse strap over her shoulder and strode back to the office.

The afternoon proved to be as busy as the morning, and Olivia didn't have a chance to think about anything but insurance claims, appointments, patients, and a whole slew of other work-related things. When the clock hit five thirty, the door chime made her turn around from the filing cabinet and meet the cool stare of Marcus Thurber. *What the hell is he doing here?*

"Don't look so surprised, Olivia," Thurber said as he leaned against the counter, picked up a pen, and signed the sheet.

"I didn't know you had an appointment." She looked at the screen. "I can't seem to find your name. Who are you supposed to see?"

"I'm a walk-in." His brown eyes bored into her.

"We don't do walk-ins. Don't you have a dentist you go to?"

"If I did, I wouldn't be here." His gaze pierced her, and her heart raced.

"Let me see if someone can squeeze you in. What're you having problems with?" *Why the hell are you here? This is too weird.*

"My tooth hurts." He smiled. "Do you like working here?"

"Yes. I'll be right back." Olivia leaped from the chair and dashed down the hall toward Dr. Linney's office. There was no way she was going to ask grumpy Dr. Canty if he'd take a look at a last minute patient. She knocked on the door.

"Come in."

When she walked in, Dr. Linney smiled.

"I'm sorry to bother you, but there's a guy—actually he's a teacher at my school." She paused and took a breath. "Anyway, he wants to see a dentist because he has a toothache. I know we don't do walk-ins, but I thought I'd ask if you or maybe Dr. Mitchell can look at him."

"Maybe Dr. Canty can. I've got two patients that'll be here soon, remember?"

"I do, but maybe after them?"

Dr. Linney shook his head. "Don't you want to go home tonight?"

Olivia chuckled. "I do."

"Dr. Mitchell has a late-night patient as well. Ask Dr. Canty—he may be able to help out. If not, tell your friend to buy an over-the-counter pain medication for toothaches and to make an appointment for tomorrow after five. I'll squeeze him in."

"I'll go ahead and do that. Thanks." Olivia walked out of the room and stopped in the hall, hesitating about whether to approach Dr. Canty or not. Deciding that she didn't need his sarcasm or creepiness, she walked back to the reception area to make an appointment for Thurber for the following day.

When Olivia returned, the only one in the room was Mr. Dyer—Dr. Mitchell's appointment. She crossed the room and opened the door then looked down the hall, but Thurber was nowhere in sight. Figuring he stepped out to use the restroom, she went back to the desk and resumed what she was doing.

After fifteen minutes Marcus Thurber still hadn't returned, and Olivia walked over to the window overlooking the parking lot and peered out, scanning the area for the teacher's car. It wasn't there. *That's strange.*

"When you came into the office, was anyone in here?" she asked Mr. Dyer as she gestured around the room.

"No. I was the only one."

"How about in the hallway when you were coming to the room?"

"Nope. Why ... did you lose someone?" The man chuckled.

She smiled. "I think so."

"Maybe he changed his mind. No one likes going to the dentist." Another chuckle.

"Good point." Olivia turned back to the parking lot and saw a car that looked like Brady Sickles's vehicle. *What the hell? Is this too strange or what?* It seemed that all of a sudden her other life was crashing into this one. *Ivy. I bet the asshole's waiting for Ivy to come out.* Brady had still been calling and texting Ivy ever since she broke up with him after finding out he was married. The gym teacher also had the gall to try and approach Olivia at school so she'd relay messages to Ivy. One thing the dirtbag hadn't done was show up at her house again. She chuckled at the memory of Animal removing Sickles from her property.

Looking back at the car, Sickles just sat there staring at the window. She was pretty sure he saw her, but Olivia didn't care. If he started anything, she'd call the police in a second. Ivy had left an hour earlier due to a doctor's appointment, and now Olivia was so happy that her friend wasn't at the office.

It seemed that the minutes crawled by, and she was bursting at the seams to get out of there and see Animal. Olivia glanced at the stack of files she needed to copy for Dr. Mitchell and took out the metal desk bell and put it on the counter. The last two patients hadn't arrived yet, and she wanted to finish with the copying as soon as possible.

She ducked inside the room then placed a stack of insurance claims into the copier's automatic feeder. Olivia kept her ears pricked for the sound of the bell as she worked. An eerie feeling held her as she stared at the last six files. The bell hadn't chimed, but maybe the patients were late or blew off their appointments.

Olivia gripped the sides of the table and arched, stretching out her back. For some reason she couldn't shake the sense of impending doom which niggled at her. Instead of putting more documents into the feeder once the copy machine stopped, she listened, straining to hear any voices or movement in the office. The clinic was silent. The only sound was her own heavy breathing.

"I'm being paranoid," she whispered out loud as the anxiety inside her mounted.

Quickly Olivia picked up the remaining files and held them in her shaking hands, debating whether to finish the job or get out of there. She couldn't figure out why she was so jumpy and edgy, and certain that something bad was about to happen.

Opening a folder, she began stuffing the copied documents into it when she heard a shuffling sound behind her. Olivia froze, her breath caught in her throat.

The sound came again, as quiet as a whisper.

Maybe it was one of the patients. Maybe she didn't hear the bell. Maybe—

Suddenly, the lights went out, plunging the room into darkness.

"Oh fuck!" she yelled, the folder dropping from her hands. She heard the papers flutter down to the floor.

Olivia could sense a presence behind her, could hear steady breathing and the soft approach of footsteps. A cold, prickling fear crawled up her spine.

"Who's there?" she asked, hating the quiver in her voice.

No answer. Just breathing and shuffling.

"Is that you Marcus? This isn't funny." For some reason Olivia got it into her head that Marcus Thurber had hidden in one of the rooms and was trying to scare her. There was no explanation as to why he was doing it, but who else would be doing this? Then Brady Sickles' face popped into her head and she gasped. He'd come in to look for Ivy and was mad she wasn't there. *He's always blamed me for Ivy breaking up with him.* "Stop it now, Brady. We're not alone—people are still here."

Before Olivia could turn around, cool, smooth fingers gripped her arms and she screamed.

"Shh, my sweet," a low voice whispered next to her ear.

Fear paralyzed her and she couldn't move. Did she hear him correctly?

"Hunter?" she said as terror tore through her.

The soft heat of breath on her neck brought a new wave of fear crashing over her. "Yes." His lips pressed against her jawline.

How the fuck is Hunter here? What the hell is going on? I have to get out of this damn room.

"Do you like that?" Another kiss as his fingers dug deeper into her skin until it hurt. "You thought you could get rid of me. That wasn't very nice, my sweet."

Olivia felt the blood drain from her face. Her mouth went dry as a horrifying realization began to grip her. *Hunter is Dr. Linney.* The shock of it echoed through her.

His fingers had inched their way up her arms, now resting too close to her throat. Olivia willed herself to turn around. She focused and met his gaze, her eyes now fully adjusted to the dim light. Cold, brown orbs with a glint of evil bored into her; his nice-looking features had turned dark and sinister. She didn't know this man before her, and as she gazed upon him, she knew in her heart that *Hunter* was going to kill her.

"Dr. Linney, please. Your patients will be coming in soon."

"There are no appointments, my sweet. I lied to you. I'm sorry, but I had to. You forgive me, don't you." He lowered his head and moved his face closer to hers. Olivia turned her head, and his kiss landed on her cheek. He pulled back, anger etched on his face. "I'll let that one slide, but you won't turn away from the next one." His gaze pierced her like a knife.

"Dr. Linney, don't do this," she said softly.

"My name is Hunter, Rose."

He's a fucking psycho!

As his fingers tightened against her throat, Hunter pressed his mouth to hers. Olivia reached behind her, grasping for the large three-hole puncher as his hands squeezed her throat.

Small red dots floated in front of her eyes as she gasped for air.

I can't black out. I just can't.

CHAPTER TWENTY-SIX

"IS AUNT JADA going to do my hair again?" Lucy asked as she skipped down the sidewalk.

"I bet she will if you ask her." Animal opened the gate in front of his parents' house then followed his daughter to the porch.

"Are we having dinner over here?" Lucy opened the screen door.

Animal inserted his key and turned the lock. "I thought we'd have dinner with Olivia later on."

"But what if Aunt Jada's not done with my hair?" Lucy walked into his parents' house.

"We can wait, unless you don't wanna go out for chow, kiddo."

"I do. Can Aunt Jada come with us?"

"Sure—I'll ask her."

"There's my favorite granddaughter," Animal's dad said, his arms outstretched.

Lucy giggled. "I'm your only one, Grandpa." She rushed over and looped her arms around his neck.

"Hey, Dad," Animal said, lifting his chin.

"Hiya." Jay jerked his head toward the kitchen. "Your mother wants to talk to you."

Animal shoved his hands in his pockets and crossed the room to the kitchen. He heard his dad asking Lucy if she wanted one of his chocolates. His dad always kept a box of them stashed in one of the drawers of the small cupboard near the couch.

When he walked into the room, his mother sat at the table drinking a cup of coffee and staring at the wall. He went over to the counter and poured himself a cup of java then plopped down on one of the chairs.

"How're you holding up?" he asked, bringing the cup to his mouth.

"All right. Just sore as hell, but it's better than what could've been."

Animal nodded. "I don't need to tell you not to do this shit again, right? It's dangerous and stupid."

"I know. Your dad and I already talked about it. No more online shit for me."

"Do you remember anything more about the fucker?" Leaning back in his chair, he stretched out his legs, crossing them at the ankles.

"Yeah. Last night everything was a blur, but now I can see the asshole's face as clear as I'm seeing yours."

"Describe him."

"Are you going to go out looking for him?"

"Something like that."

Lucy scurried in and stood by Animal, her gaze fixed on her grandmother. He wished his mother would be more affectionate with her granddaughter, but he knew that wasn't her way. He grew up with little of that from his mom, so Animal figured he shouldn't expect anything different with Lucy.

"What's up, kiddo?" he asked snagging an arm around her.

"Grandpa said that I can have a cookie. He wants one too." Lucy leaned into Animal.

Rena chuckled. "You can have one, but your grandpa knows he can't have sweets. Hell, I'm constantly trying to stop him from eating too many chocolates, but he sneaks them in." She stood up and went to the pantry.

Lucy turned to Animal. "Grandpa really wants one. Is it bad if I tell Grandma I want two then give one to him?"

Animal laughed.

"I heard that," his mother said walking back to the table with a bag of chocolate chip cookies in her hand. "I can see that you're your father's daughter—you're just like him."

Lucy leaned further into Animal.

"You can have your cookie in here with some milk. When you're finished, you can take one to your grandpa—the old goat."

Even though his mom pretended to be annoyed, Animal saw warmth and love in her eyes when she talked about her husband. He didn't pretend to understand his parents' marriage or arrangement, but it was clear that they loved each other.

"Okay, Grandma." Lucy scrambled onto the chair next to his.

As his daughter ate her snack, his mother described the guy who'd attacked her. Animal took mental notes, and each time his mother remembered another characteristic or physical description, licks of angers burned through him.

"And that's about it." Rena reached over and took out a cookie then nibbled on it.

"Grandma's friend must look like Dr. Linney." Lucy took a sip of milk.

His head jerked back. "Fuck," he muttered as he took out his phone. He jumped to his feet then crossed over to the back porch while plugging in Olivia's number.

No answer.

Again.

Voicemail.

"Fuck." Every muscle in his body clenched with fury. The hackles on his neck rose and he sensed danger. He had to make sure Olivia was safe.

Animal called Hawk and told him what was going on, and the VP said he'd arrange for a group of brothers to meet Animal at the dental clinic stat.

Animal came back into the kitchen, ruffled Lucy's hair, and let out a long breath.

"I gotta go. I'll be back later," he said to his mom. "Be a good girl, kiddo. If I'm late and you get hungry, Grandma will make you some dinner."

"Okay. Can I bring Grandpa his cookie now, Grandma?"

"Yes," Rena said standing up. "You be careful," she whispered to Animal.

"Yeah. Later."

He walked out the back door and ran to the SUV then sped away.

When Animal arrived at the building, the parking lot was empty except for Olivia's car, a BMW parked in the far corner of the lot, and a small van with a sign that read "Sunshine Cleaning" on the both sides of it.

"Fuck," he muttered under his breath as he leaned over and popped open the glove box, then took out his 9mm and got out of the car. He dashed across the parking lot and as he tried the front doors, the rumble of several motorcycles were like music to his ears.

Animal pivoted and saw Bones, Shadow, Smokey, Throttle, and Rock glide into the lot.

"Hawk said your woman's in trouble," Throttle said as he came over to Animal.

"She's not answering her phone. I think her fucking boss is the serial killer." Animal tugged at the front door. "Fuck! It's locked."

"We gotta get in there quick," Shadow said taking out a small case filled with lock picking tools. "These glass entry door locks are a fuckin' joke."

Just then two women wearing bright yellow smocks and green plastic gloves appeared on the other side of the door.

"Open up," Animal said. "We got an appointment."

One of the women unlocked the door and smiled widely. "Hi, guys."

"Hey. I'm late for an appointment," Animal said brushing past her.

"I don't think anyone's in the building," she said. "You guys real bikers?"

"No, we just like to dress up like them." Shadow winked at her and she turned several shades of red as she giggled.

"We gotta get going," Animal dashed to the stairwell, flung open the door, and rushed up the stairs two at a time, with several of his friends right behind him. Their footsteps reverberated around the stairwell.

When Animal pushed open the door to the third floor, he heard

Olivia's scream. "Fuck!" he yelled, barreling down the hallway.

"Bro, cool down," Throttle said as he grabbed Animal's arm and pulled him back. "You're way too involved. We'll go in."

"No fuckin' way," Animal replied.

The rest of the members gathered around him, and Shadow nodded. "Throttle's right. You gotta cool the fuck down or this fucker's gonna kill your woman."

"If you can't detach yourself from it, you're gonna make the situation worse," Smokey said.

Animal knew they were right: emotions had no place in carrying out a plan. If he let his anger, his fear, and his love for Olivia rule him, she would be forever lost to him. He had to compartmentalize his anger from his love for his woman. Taking several deep breaths, he let go of his emotions and let steely, icy determination take root.

"There's a back door over there," Animal said pointing halfway down the hall. "Do your magic," he said to Shadow.

"I got my lucky pick," Rock said as he went to work on the front door lock.

Within seconds the lock clicked and Rock slowly opened the door. Animal looked over and saw that Shadow, Throttle, and Bones had already entered through the back way.

The office was quiet, and a fear like he had never known before sent an icy chill through his veins. If he was too late, Animal didn't know what he would do. *Calm down. Focus. Complete your mission.*

Animal motioned some of the men to check out the rooms down one hallway while he and Smokey walked quietly toward a closed door. Smokey pulled Animal back and pointed into a darkened room. Animal switched on the lights and saw papers and folders strewn over the floor by the copier. A large metal puncher laid near the wall where he saw a small spattering of blood.

"We gotta find her—fast," he said in a low voice.

Animal strained his ears and thought he heard mumbling coming from one of the offices at the far end of the hallway. As he came closer, the voice grew louder, and he heard a man saying, "We will soon be one, my sweet. Our body, heart, and soul will mingle together until …"

Animal tuned the voice out and slowly turned the knob and opened the door. White-hot anger seared through him when he saw Olivia tied up, her breasts exposed, her skirt pushed up, duct tape across her mouth, lying on top of the desk. The fucking bastard straddled her, his flat ass jiggling as he continued to murmur psychotic BS to her.

The light from the desk lamp made the blade of the knife gleam, and the psycho held it in both his hands, high above his head, ready to plunge it into Olivia's soft skin.

Without hesitation, Animal aimed his gun and shot the asshole in both shoulders. The man squealed and cried, and before he could collapse on top of Olivia, Animal shoved him to the ground and landed a forceful blow with his boot into the bastard's stomach. Smokey kicked the knife across the floor, and Animal ran over to Olivia's side. He drew her to him holding her trembling body as he carefully pulled the duct tape from her mouth.

"He—Dr. Linney tried to kill me," she said between sobs.

"I know, baby. It's all over. I'm here." He peppered her face with kisses then wiped away the tears on her cheeks with the hem of his T-shirt.

"He's the one who's been doing all the killings. The one who attacked your mom. How could it be him?" She buried her face into his chest.

"It's all good now, babe. The guy's obviously a fucking psycho." Animal cut off the zip ties from her hands then shrugged off his jacket and draped it over her shoulders.

"I feel so sorry for Mrs. Linney. And his kids. Poor Aaron. What am I going to say to him? How could Dr. Linney do this to his family?"

Animal rubbed her back, kissed the top of her head, and let her pour out her shock, grief, and anger.

"Here you go," Throttle said as he handed Animal a sheet.

He slipped his jacket off her, wrapped the sheet around her, then draped his jacket over her shoulders again.

"We better call the fuckin' badges," Smokey said.

"Or we can just waste the fucker," Shadow added as he kicked the killer in the ribs. Dr. Linney cried out. "You're not so tough now, you fuckin' pussy. You're only the hero when you're scaring women and carving them up."

"Let the fuckin' badges deal with that piece of shit," Animal said. He placed two fingers under Olivia's chin and gently tilted her head back. "You up for the bullshit tonight? The badges are gonna want to talk with you."

"I'm good. I want to make sure he's put away for the rest of his life." She curled her arm around his neck and drew him to her. "Kiss me," she whispered.

Animal crushed his mouth to hers and held her close to him. For a second there, he'd thought maybe they'd be too late. A mixture of emotions swirled inside him as he deepened the kiss. He could've lost her that night, and that thought was like a hot poker to his gut.

"I'm never letting you go, baby. I love you," he whispered into her ear. "You're a part of me; you ignite a fire deep in my soul."

"I love you too. I'll never stop loving you. I want every part of you."

"You have it, baby. Don't ever forget that."

"We're gonna take off, bro," Bones said, clasping his hand on Animal's shoulder. "You good?"

"I'll stay," Shadow said.

Animal shook his head. "No reason to deal with the fuckin' badges if you don't have too. I got this, bro." He bumped fists with his friends then they walked out of the room.

He looked down at the bastard who'd hurt his woman and his mother and rage burned inside him. If Olivia weren't in the room with him, the fucker would be a pile of blood, guts, and broken bones the badges would have to scrape up off the floor.

"Is he dead?" Olivia whispered.

"Nah. The badges will be here soon and they can patch him up so he can get his ass ripped open in the pen."

"I still can't believe Hunter is Dr. Linney. He must've recognized my voice when we talked on the phone. He obviously used a device to disguise his. This is so unbelievable."

"You never know what's lurking deep inside someone." Animal brushed his lips across hers. "Did he mess with you?" Anger seared through him as he asked her that question.

She shook her head. "No, but he would've if you hadn't come. What made you come? I kept trying to reason with him, stall for time until seven o'clock, but he was too crazy ... too evil. I hit him with the hole puncher in the copy room, and almost made it out of the office, but he grabbed me just as I opened the front door. He was so angry, so psychotic." Olivia shivered. "It was awful. I really thought I was going to die." Her voice hitched.

"When my mom described the fucker, Lucy said it sounded like her dentist. I tried calling you, and when you didn't pick up, I just knew you were in trouble. I'm damn glad I made it in time." He kissed the top of her head and held her tight.

In the distance, Animal could hear the wail of the sirens. They grew louder and closer until he could see the police car lights flashing red and blue pulses into the night. Soon a swarm of badges would fill the room, and the dance between cop and outlaw would begin.

"Babe, the badges will be here soon. Remember to just stick with me coming by. No need to say anything else."

She smiled weakly at him. "I know the score." Olivia lightly poked him in the chest. "I'm a biker chick, remember?"

He chuckled. "The best kind of woman." He held her while they waited for the badges to come in. Animal knew the guys had given the cleaning ladies a warning along with some bucks to make them forget they saw the bikers.

Flanked by three uniformed men, Detective McCue walked into the room. His eyes darted from Animal to the downed man then back to Animal. The biker didn't say a word, he just sat there holding his woman.

"Call the paramedics," the detective said. He looked at Animal. "Do you want to tell me what exactly went on here?"

"Just doing your job, *again*," Animal replied.

"That's not good enough," McCue said, taking out his notepad.

"That fucker's the serial killer you've been looking for." The look of shock crossing the cop's face brought an immense amount of satisfaction to Animal. More than once, the Insurgents had done the work the police should have.

"You're jumping to conclusions here." McCue wiped one of his hands on his pants.

"He tried to kill me. It's Dr. Linney—my boss. He meets women online," Olivia blurted out.

"I'm going to have to ask you some questions," McCue said as he walked over to her. "Let's go into another room so they can process the crime scene."

"The copy machine room is where it started," Olivia said as she pulled away from Animal to stand up, then immediately leaned into him again.

"Okay."

Animal and Olivia followed the detective to the reception area. Animal sank down in one of the chairs and settled his woman on his lap.

It was going to be a long night.

CHAPTER TWENTY-SEVEN

Three months later

TANGERINE, THEN AMETHYST emblazoned a sky broken by long trails of clouds. The sun, now a fiery orange ball, sank low behind the craggy mountain peaks.

The carnival's colored lights blinked in the encroaching darkness, and a warm breeze carried the tantalizing scent of freshly spun cotton candy.

"Can I go on the Ferris wheel with Paisley and Hope?" Lucy asked, pointing at a large wheel studded with yellow, blue, and green lights in the distance.

"Yeah, but you gotta hold on tight," Animal said.

Lucy reached for Olivia's hand, and a warm glow spread through Olivia as the three of them—Lucy in the middle—walked toward the entrance of the carnival.

"I used to love the roller coaster when I was a kid," Olivia said.

"I want to go on that too, Dad."

"Okay, but you gotta ride with us," Animal replied.

"I've never been to a carnival before," Lucy said, her eyes widening the closer they got to the flashing neon sign.

"You're going to love it," Olivia said. "I think they're all about the same."

The traveling carnival materialized in the same open field for the same three weeks every summer. During the day, the booths and tents looked a little worn and rusty patches were evident on some of the rides, but at night, everything was magical.

When they entered under the large archway, Lucy broke away from them and ran over to one of the booths where Paisley and Hope were trying to fish a prize out of a gigantic bowl. Olivia saw Cherri and Addie huddled together, talking while their husbands, Jax and Chas leaned against the counter watching their daughters.

As they walked toward the group, Animal's arm settled around her waist, and she moved closer to him until she could feel the heat of his body seeping into hers. When they reached the booth, Animal bumped fists with Jax and Chas, and Olivia crossed over to the two old ladies.

"Have you been here long?" Olivia asked Addie.

"Just about an hour." Addie looked over at the three giggling girls. "Lucy's come such a long way since she moved in with Animal."

Olivia beamed. "Yes, she has."

"So has Animal—he doesn't have that befuddled look on his face all the time," Cherri said.

Olivia laughed. "He's finally gotten comfortable in the daddy role." She looked over at him and a shiver ran through her. "He's such a wonderful person."

"And he's totally in love with you. To be honest, Animal was one of the last guys in the MC who I thought would be in a relationship. In the years that I've been around the club, I've noticed that when one of these guys falls, he goes down big time." Addie giggled. "I remember how hard Chas fought his attraction to me, and he was downright pissed about it."

"Jax was the same, but I have to admit that I wasn't the easiest one to catch," Cherri added.

"And now you're both happily married with families. When I first met Animal, I fought it and thought he was the last man I wanted to be with, but it turns out he was the one guy I couldn't live without." She glanced over at him again and found him watching her with hooded eyes that were alight with desire. Her body hummed as memories of late nights spent tangled up with him flashed through her mind. Reluctantly, she dragged her gaze away from his and back to the old ladies.

"I got a stuffed animal!" Lucy cried as she clapped her hands.

"Choose the doggie," Paisley said.

As Olivia watched Lucy decide between the small spotted dog or the white one with tiny hearts all over it, Animal came behind her, wrapping his arms around her waist. He pulled her back against the hard line of his body.

"Did I tell you how sexy you look tonight?"

The warmth of his breath on her skin made the prickle of electricity dance along her spine, sparking low in her belly. "Yeah, but you can tell it to me again."

"You look fucking hot, baby." Animal buried his face against her neck, lips nuzzling slowly … tantalizingly up to her ear.

Arousal surged through her senses and she wanted to drag him behind one of the outlying tents and throw herself at him. She wriggled closer against him, and a low growl rumbled from his chest.

"Fuck, baby, you feel good," Animal said, voice vibrating against her skin.

Olivia moaned softly and put her hands on top of his. What she wouldn't do to have those hands all over her, doing wicked things to her body.

"Look, Dad and Olivia." Lucy held up the prize she'd won—stuffed brown dog with black spots. "He looks like Patches … sorta."

Olivia broke away from Animal and ran her hand over the stuffed animal's fur. "He's so soft, and he does look like Patches."

Once Lucy had gotten out of school, she'd been relentless about getting a dog and had enlisted Olivia's help in convincing her dad to get one. Olivia smiled at the remembrance of the three of them at the shelter, checking out the dogs until a mutt with various hues of brown and black spots came up to the cage and nuzzled his wet black nose against Lucy's hand.

"You did good, kiddo." Animal tugged playfully on his daughter's braids. "You want us to hold him for you so you don't lose him when you go on the rides?"

"Yeah." She handed her prize to her dad. "Can we go on the Ferris wheel now?"

"Let's go!" Paisley said, tugging Jax's hand.

Jax laughed. "I guess our daughters have spoken."

The rest of the night was filled with rides, games, corndogs, cotton candy, and many stolen kisses as they strolled across the carnival grounds. The colored lights piercing the darkness, the melodic music from the carousel mingling with the din of the crowd, and the constant clicking and clacking of the roller coaster cars as they moved along the tracks lent to the wonderment of the evening. The times they spent as a family cemented the deep love they had for each other even more. Olivia couldn't imagine her life without Animal or his sweet daughter. He was all she ever wanted, and Olivia loved Lucy like she was her own.

On the drive home, the radio was turned down low, her hand was in his, and a warm breeze blew through the half-opened windows. Lucy slouched in the back seat, dozing, and Olivia's eyelids drooped as she stared at the passing houses and trees standing in silhouette against the moonlit sky.

"Lucy had a great time tonight," Animal said in a low voice.

"It was precious seeing her so happy." She leaned over and kissed his cheek then ran her fingers through his hair. "You're a very good dad," she whispered. "Lucy's lucky to have you."

He threw her a sideways glance. "I'm lucky to have her ... and you." He brought her hand to his lips. "I fuckin' love you, babe."

"And I'm crazy about you, sweetie." She tucked his hand under her chin and rested her head on his shoulder.

"You worried about the upcoming trial?" he asked.

"Not really ... sort of ... I don't know."

"The fucker should just plead." He spoke in a hushed tone.

"He won't. Dr. Linney is too egotistical to do that. I still can't believe how he turned out to be the psycho. I don't blame Mrs. Linney for taking the boys and moving back to Oregon. They could never live a normal life in Pinewood Springs—Dr. Linney forever tainted that for them."

"I still say his old lady must've known he was a fuckin' nutcase. How can you not know something is wrong with a dude you live with all those years?"

"I agree with you, but Dr. Linney could be a very charming man. I bet she picked up some strange vibes from him and either ignored them or rationalized them away."

Animal chuckled. "Your psych classes are paying off, babe."

"Dr. Davison still can't get over that the subject for my research paper turned out to be a serial killer. How's your mom doing with all this?"

Animal looked in the rearview mirror at Lucy. "She's pissed as fuck that she may have to testify."

"Is Lucy still sleeping?" Animal nodded. "Has your mom stopped having liaisons with guys online?"

"That's what she tells me. This shit scared the hell outta her, and she's been staying home more."

Olivia saw his jaw clench, and she kissed it softly. "I know this is hard for you, but from what you've told me, it's a mutual thing between your parents."

He shook his head. "It still sucks. I don't know ... I've stopped trying to figure it out. It is what it is."

"As long as they're happy and your mom's careful, I guess it's something you and Jada just have to life with."

"But not accept." His jaw hardened again.

"Dr. Linney was definitely a Dr. Jekyll and Mr. Hyde. He kept talking about a beast inside him that had to be satisfied. He said that the hunger was overpowering and he couldn't control it. You'd think he would've gotten some help over the years."

"Don't kid yourself, the fucker enjoyed what he was doing. He got off on the fear and the control he had over his victims. He should fry."

A comfortable silence stretched between them, punctuated by passing long-haul trucks. Animal veered the car off the highway, and the low hum of the motor soon lulled her to sleep.

The engine shutting off startled her awake, and Olivia glanced over at him as she stretched, her chest thrusting out. His gaze dropped to her breasts.

"I dozed off," she said, bending down to pick up her purse.

Animal tipped his head in the direction of Lucy. "She's out like a light. Once I get her settled, you and I can have some fun."

Anticipation flushed through her at the husky sound of his voice.

Olivia slid out of the car and crossed the garage to the back door. Animal cradled a conked out Lucy in his arms as he walked through the door Olivia held open for him. She followed him upstairs and watched as he disappeared down the hall into Lucy's room.

Olivia walked into the master bedroom and rushed over to the dresser where she'd been keeping a few personal items. She took out a package she'd stashed there earlier that morning and hurried into the bathroom.

Olivia slipped on the sexy, black lingerie and padded over to the bed. Sitting on the edge of it, she put on a pair of stilettos, knowing he loved fucking her with her heels digging into his firm ass. She fluffed her hair with her fingers, then got up and switched off the overhead light, leaving only the nightstand lamp on, then sat on the bed and waited. Short, uneven breaths escaped her as the seconds ticked by, wanting, needing him in the worst way.

A thin, silvery line of moonlight filtered in through the slatted wooden shutters and slowly crept along the floor almost to the door that had just opened. Animal stopped in the doorway, his gaze raking over her. Olivia saw the look in his eyes, and her heart thrilled at its intensity.

"Fuck, baby," he rasped.

Olivia cupped her breasts and squeezed them. "Do you like it?" She teased him.

"Fuck, yeah," he replied hoarsely.

Animal shut the door behind him then pulled his shirt over his head and threw it on the floor. Next came his boots and socks. Mesmerized by the revelation of each inch of his magnificent body, Olivia's hands dropped to her lap. The sound of him unbuckling his belt sent a shot of hot desire through her.

"Let me do it," she whispered.

Lust sparked in his eyes as he moved closer to the bed. "I'd like nothing better than to have your hot, pretty lips around my cock. Get on your knees, baby."

Olivia climbed off the bed and knelt down on the multi-colored rug, licking her lips in anticipation.

"Your look so fucking sexy. Did you just buy that?"

"Uh-huh." She cupped her breasts again and squeezed them. "I bought it just for you."

"Fuck, baby." Animal stood in front of her. "My dick's aching to get inside your mouth."

Olivia captured his gaze as she undid his belt then slowly unzipped his jeans. With both hands on the waistband, she pushed down his pants along with his boxers. His hard rod popped out and swept across her mouth. Animal stepped out of his jeans and kicked them away then he grabbed a handful of her hair and pushed her face toward his shaft.

"Make me feel real good, babe," he said in a low, husky voice.

Holding her gaze with his, Olivia smiled seductively then ran her tongue over the length of him, circling the underside of his head. She licked the bead of pre-come, then swallowed his thick cock while she lightly scratched and played with his balls.

"That's it," he rasped his eyes burning into hers. "You know how to please your man."

"I *love* pleasing my man," she said then pushed his dick back into her mouth again.

He held her head in place and thrust his hips in and out of her throat. "So fucking good," he whispered. "And I love seeing your tits bouncing and your ass wiggling as your hot lips wrap around me. What a fuckin' beautiful sight. Damn." He groaned and the small sound sent a shockwave of need down to the very base of her toes.

He shoved in and out faster and harder as he held her head tight, and the sparks of desire zapping through her were off the damn charts. Moving her hand between her legs, she slipped her finger under the thong and massaged her soaking sex. A sharp pull on her hair made her eyes water and she looked up and saw Animal's piercing gaze.

"No touching, baby. That's all for me. I'm gonna take real good care of you. I can't wait to peel you outta that fuckin' hot number you got on."

The swollen head of his cock pulsed in her mouth, and the ache between her legs throbbed. She hummed and she felt him jerk in surprise. She'd been wanting to try that tip she'd read about in one of her women's magazines. By the way his fingers gripped her head, Olivia knew that she was on to something. She grasped the sides of his outer thighs and kept humming a low, wordless tune that made her throat vibrate. Olivia increased the intensity as her tongue laved his hardness, and she took him in even deeper.

"Fuck, that's good. Shit … yeah …" His hand yanked her hair.

Her hand pumped the base of him in rhythm with his thrusting.

"Damn, woman," he rasped, easing her back a bit then withdrawing from her mouth. "I'm gonna blow if we keep this up, and I want your hot, sweet pussy wrapped around my cock, darlin'." He pulled her up and inched her backward toward the bed. When the backs of her knees hit the mattress, she sat down, pulling him with her. He lay on top of her, their lips fused together as his palms skidded down her skin before slipping under her ass and squeezing her cheeks.

"Oh, Animal," she murmured as he kissed a trail down to her breasts.

With his teeth, he untied the satin ribbons covering her tits and flicked her nipples with the tip of his tongue before drawing one into his mouth and pinching the other with his thumb and index finger.

Olivia moaned and arched her spine, stretching her arms over her head as coils of desire unfurled inside her. She knew she would never get enough of him; he was her lifeline, the blood that pumped through her, the lover she'd always imagined.

"I love unwrapping you, baby," he said huskily as his hands skimmed down to the throbbing between her legs. "I bet you're soaking wet," he whispered as his finger untied the ribbon covering her sex then encased itself between her swollen folds. His touch was like the spark of a match, igniting all her nerve endings. She groaned and his mouth was back on hers, swallowing all her cries of pleasure.

"Animal, I need to feel you inside," she said when he broke away.

"You will, but first I wanna taste and feel every inch of your beautiful body." Animal slowly peeled away the lingerie until Olivia had nothing on except for the stilettos. He knelt next to her reclined body, his heated gaze roving over her nakedness. "Fuck, baby ... just fuck."

She reached up for him but he grabbed her wrists and placed them above her head then bent down and kissed her hard, deep, and raw. Desire coursed through her, lacing around her nipples and sending jolts of pleasure to her throbbing sex. Animal always made her feel so alive, so cherished, so nasty. And at that moment, the only thing she wanted was to feel him inside her, move in rhythm with him, and soar to euphoric bliss with his name on her tongue.

"You look so fucking tempting," he rasped as he settled himself between her legs, spread them wide with his hands then lapped her in one long sweep from her puckered hole to the top of her hood.

"Oh fuck!" she cried out as he continued to lavish deep strokes over her most private part. She sucked in her breath and gripped the sheet, balling it in her hands. Animal looked up and caught her gaze, his lips and chin glistening with her juices.

"You taste so sweet and awesome, darlin'. I fuckin' love it," he said before burying his mouth in her folds and gently sucking her hardened bud. She thrust her hips up and his chuckle created the most intense vibrations against her clit. Then two of his fingers plunged into her and she moved in rhythm with them, trying to build enough friction to reach that place where her body would explode and all tension would melt away.

All of a sudden, Animal pulled back, and Olivia thought she'd lose her mind. Her gaze wildly sought his, and he smirked at her, his dick in hand.

"I wanna feel that warm, tight pussy clamped around my cock, baby." With one hard thrust, he buried himself inside her.

"That feels so good," she murmured as her walls molded around his hardness, coaxing him in deeper.

"Fuck, yeah," he growled as he pulled out all the way then slammed into her again.

She wrapped her legs around him, the heels of her stilettos digging into his taut ass.

"I love *that*," he rasped, then bent his head down and tugged her bottom lip into his mouth and sucked hard as he plunged back into her heat. He broke away a bit, his face mere inches from hers. "Do you want it rough, baby?"

"Oh yeah. I want it good and hard," she said against his lips as she threaded her fingers through his thick hair.

A wolfish grin crossed his face. "I'll really give it to you." He withdrew and before she could think, he shoved back into her then began hammering hard and fast, pulling all the way out with each thrust before slamming back in. With each thrust, her body moved up until her head hit the headboard. Leaning over, he placed a pillow behind her head and then continued his relentless, wild pounding of her dripping pussy. When his finger swirled around her sweet spot, the wound up spring inside her sprung in a burst of sensation, ecstasy and mind-numbing pleasure. Her entire body clenched and then unclenched from the waves of delicious deliria overtaking it.

"Animal! Oh ... oh ...," she moaned.

A feral growl came from him as he stiffened and came, his pulses throbbing against her warm walls. Placing her legs on the mattress, he wrapped his arm around her waist and placed his damp forehead between her heaving breasts.

"Fuck, woman," he panted.

Sweat misted over his body, and she gently kissed his shoulder. He breathed deeply and rolled over, then drew her close to him.

"I fucking love it when we come together," he whispered, lightly tickling her upper arm. "I can't get enough of you, babe. I want to fuck you all the time."

"That's a good thing, right? It means we're on the same wavelength because I always crave you."

Animal chuckled and kissed the top of her head. "We're a good team, babe."

Warmth spread through her at his words. "I agree," she said softly.

"I love you so damn much, baby."

"And I love you." She snuggled closer to him.

He held her tighter and soon his even breathing told her he was sleeping. For a long while, Olivia watched the moonlight seeping through the narrow slats of the shutters, casting moving shadows on the walls and ceilings. Feelings of happiness and love enveloped her; she loved Animal with a fire that could never be extinguished. For the first time in her life, she had found her home and it was safely in his arms. With thoughts of Animal filling her head, she closed her eyes and drifted off to sleep.

SUNLIGHT FILTERED INTO the room as Olivia nuzzled cozily into the crook of his arm. Animal was sleeping soundly, and she lay there mesmerized by the way his tattoos danced each time his chest rose and fell with every breath.

After a while, Olivia quietly slipped out of his arm and padded to the closet where she kept some of her clothes then crossed over to the bathroom. She wondered if Lucy was up yet as she closed the door and turned on the shower. Twenty minutes later, dressed in black biker shorts and a turquoise tank top, Olivia made her way down the stairs and into the kitchen. Lucy sat at the table coloring, and looked up when Olivia walked in.

"Hi, Olivia," she said.

"Hi, Lucy. What're you coloring?" Olivia stood behind the girl and looked down over her shoulders.

"A butterfly. I love them—they're my favorite insect. Are you and my dad going to get married?"

Olivia jerked up and took a step backward. "Uh ... I don't know. Why?"

"Because ..." She took out another crayon and showed it to Olivia. "This is a newer color. Do you like it?"

"Yeah ... it's really pretty. Carson's Grocery is having a contest for the best-colored pictures. I really think you should submit yours. They have it according to age. You've got a real artistic talent."

Lucy glanced up at her and scrunched her face. "Really? No one's ever told me that."

"You really do. Once you finish your picture, we can go over there and enter it if you'd like. I really think you should."

"I'm almost done with it." Lucy bowed her head and resumed coloring.

"What're you almost done with?" Animal's deep voice washed over Olivia sending tingles through her body.

"My picture." Lucy picked it up. "See? Olivia says I should enter the contest at Carson's."

"You're doing a damn good job, kiddo. I think you should go for it." Animal ruffled his daughter's hair and winked at Olivia. "Morning," he said in a low voice. "How're you feeling?"

She licked her lips and brushed her hair away from her face. "Pretty darn awesome. You?"

"Yeah ... damn good." He crossed over to her and snagged his arm around her waist and swept his lips across hers. "Fuckin' love you, babe," he whispered against her ear.

"I'm hungry," Lucy said. "And so is Patches."

"Did you change his water?" Animal asked as he shuffled over to the pantry.

"Yep. He was real thirsty too."

"Do you want French toast?" Olivia asked as she watched Animal pour some dog food in Patches's bowl.

"Yes, please!" Lucy's eyes lit up and Olivia laughed.

"French toast it is. I'll make a strawberry sauce too in case you'd like that with your powdered sugar." She crossed over to the refrigerator and starting taking out the ingredients when Animal came behind her.

"You're fucking fantastic." He nuzzled her neck, his lips soft, his stubble rough against her skin. "Lucy's real fond of you, just like her dad."

"I'm pretty crazy about the Walsh family myself." She leaned back into him.

"I wish I could bend you over the counter and show you how hard you make me, darlin'."

Olivia glanced over her shoulder at Lucy whose face was tight with concentration. "Me too, sweetie." She pulled away and walked over to the counter and began preparing their breakfast.

An hour later, Animal sat back in his chair, his legs stretched out in front of him, his hand on his stomach. "That was so damn good, babe. Did you like it, kiddo?"

Lucy bobbed her head and scrambled off the chair. "It was the best French toast I ever had." She ran over to Olivia and gave her a quick hug. "I'm going to my room to finish my picture then we can go to Carson's."

"For sure." Olivia smiled.

Lucy began to walk out of the room with Patches following behind her when Animal cleared his throat. "You need to help clear the table, kiddo."

Lucy groaned but turned around quickly and picked up her plate and brought it to the sink. After clearing the rest of the dishes, she turned to look at her dad. "Are you going to ask?"

Animal narrowed his eyes and jerked his head toward the stairway. "Didn't you say you were gonna finish your picture in your room?"

Grumbling something inaudible under her breath, Lucy stomped out of the room, the half-colored picture and box of crayons in her hands.

"What did she want you to ask?" Olivia said as she sat down with a steaming mug of coffee in her hand.

Animal shrugged and rose from the chair. "I'll be right back, babe. Why don't you pour me a cup of coffee?"

"Okay." She padded over to the counter and took out a cup from the cupboard. When she turned around, Animal was already back in his chair and had a funny look on his face.

"What's up?" she asked, putting the cup in front of him. "You look like you've got a secret you want to tell me."

He splayed his hands on the table. "It's more like I got something I wanna ask you."

Butterflies scurried about in her belly while her heart quickened and her cheeks warmed. Animal looked so earnest and serious that it scared, excited, and intrigued her all at the same time.

"What is it?" she said softly as she brought the mug to her mouth.

Animal bent down and put a box on the table. Green and orange ribbons decorated it in a haphazard fashion, and the big bow on top was a bit off center.

Olivia's eyes widened. "Is this for me?"

He nodded and pushed it toward her.

She figured it was some racy lingerie he'd ordered online for her again. Animal loved dressing her up then unwrapping her slowly. A wicked smile flashed across her lips as she opened the lid. For a couple of seconds Olivia just stared at the leather cut neatly folded in the box. She knew immediately what it was—Animal's patch. A shot of excitement sparked through her as she realized that he was asking her to be his old lady.

Olivia snapped her eyes to his then back to the box. She ran her fingers over the buttery, soft leather then took it out and saw the ivory-colored embroidery on the back "Property of Animal." Once again her gaze returned to his.

"This is beautiful and … so unexpected," she murmured, reaching for his hand. Tears formed in the corner of her eyes.

"I wanna see you with my patch on," he said standing to his feet. "Let me help you put it on."

Olivia rose from the chair, and Animal helped her put on the cut. He drew her back into him and ran his hands down the sides of her body, caressing and petting. "I love you, baby. Will you be my old lady?"

She tilted her head back and looked up at him, catching his gaze. "I'd be honored to be your old lady, sweetheart."

He crushed his lips to hers and stole her breath away in a wild kiss that had her twisting around, clinging to him, and craving more.

Breaking away a bit, Olivia ran her fingernail over the bottom of his lip. "I love you so much," she whispered.

"Me too, babe … me too." He stepped back. "You got inside pockets in the cut."

Okay … that was a change of subject. Olivia nodded and figured he wanted her to try out these pockets, so she shoved her hands in them and felt something square in one of them. She pulled out a navy blue box. Her heart pounding, she looked at him. "What is it?"

"Open it up," he replied.

With trembling fingers, Olivia opened it and held her breath as she gawked at the sparkling ring nestled in dark velvet. She let out a long breath, glanced up, and met his eyes.

"Oh fuck … Animal … it's beautiful." Her voice quivered.

Animal took the box from her and slid the ring onto her finger. "Babe, I can't live without you. Since you came into my life, no one exists but you. You made me believe in love and I want to spend my life with you. Will you marry me?"

She wiggled her fingers then paused to admire the ring. "I love it!" Olivia dabbed her eyes with the back of her hand.

"You haven't answered me, darlin'."

She laughed as a few tears trickled down her cheeks. "I know … this is crazy and wonderful, and I never thought this in a million years. Yes! I

will marry you. For the first time in my life, I know what love is. Oh …
sweetie." Olivia rushed over to him and threw her arms around him and
kissed him wild and deep. It was like she never wanted to let go.

"I never thought I'd be a one-woman man, but, darlin', your sassiness, your loving, and your fuckin' sweet ass reformed me."

Olivia giggled. "I'm so happy and lucky to have you and Lucy in my
life."

"Did you ask her?" Lucy's voice broke through the euphoria coursing through Olivia's body.

She pulled away from Animal and spun around. "You knew all
along," she teased the girl.

Giggling, Lucy nodded. "I wrapped the box. Do you like the ring?"

"Lucy helped me pick it out," Animal said, stretching his arm out to
his daughter.

She skipped over and Animal wrapped his arm around her shoulder
and Olivia did the same. The three of them embraced while Patches
stood next to Lucy, his tail thumping against the floor.

"I love you and your father so much," Olivia said, smoothing down
the girl's hair. "I can't wait to share a life with the two of you."

"I'm glad you're going to be my mom," she said, looking up.

Olivia's chest ached, and she swallowed back the lump forming in
her throat. "I'm beyond happy about having such a sweet daughter." She
bent down and kissed Lucy's head.

"When are you going to get married?" the girl asked.

Animal laughed. "I just asked her, kiddo. We got some time."

"I'd love for you to help me plan the wedding. I need a flower girl to
walk down the aisle."

"Me!" Lucy broke away and twirled a couple of times and Patches
barked.

"Of course. You can help me pick the dress color and the flowers.
We'll make it real special and a real biker wedding." She glanced
sideways at Animal, who leaned against the island with an amused smile
on his face.

"Can I tell Paisley and Hope now, Dad?"

"Yeah," he said.

"Yay! I'm almost finished with my picture. I'll be back soon." Lucy dashed away and Olivia heard her small footsteps echoing on the hardwood stairs.

Animal yanked Olivia to him and pressed her close. "After we drop off the picture at the grocery store, I arranged for Cherri and Addie to take the girls to the mall and to a movie. I wanna spend the rest of the day loving you everyway we can think of."

"I love that plan," she said, burrowing her face in his chest.

"The first thing I want to do is fuck you over my Harley with just your cut on, and then we'll take it from there." He cupped her bottom and squeezed. "You've ignited a fire deep inside me that no woman ever has. You're mine, babe. All of you." He rubbed his hardness against her.

"You are my heart and my life," she said.

"I'm all done," Lucy said as she entered the kitchen. "Are we going now?"

Animal nodded. "Let's do it, kiddo."

Lucy tucked her hand in her dad's and then in Olivia's and the three walked toward the garage.

Olivia looked over at Animal whose gaze was full of love, warmth, and a bit of wickedness, and she blew him a kiss. Her life had finally come together, and she had fallen in love with the most amazing, caring, sexy man who turned out to be a biker. He was the missing piece in her life. How wonderfully ironic.

Who would've thought it?

Olivia slid into the SUV, leaned over and kissed her man, then stared out the window at the clear blue sky and the colorful flower planters dotting the neighbors' yards.

She kissed his hand and tucked it under her chin as they drove away.

Make sure you sign up for my newsletter so you can keep up with my new releases, special sales, free short stories, and other treats only available to newsletter readers. When you sign up, you will receive a FREE hot and steamy novella. Sign up at: http://eepurl.com/bACCL1.

Notes from Chiah

As always, I have a team behind me making sure I shine and continue on my writing journey. It is their support, encouragement, and dedication that pushes me further in my writing journey. And then, it is my wonderful readers who have supported me, laughed, cried, and understood how these outlaw men live and love in their dark and gritty world. Without you—the readers—an author's words are just letters on a page. The emotions you take away from the words breathe life into the story.

Thank you to my amazing Personal Assistant Natalie Weston. I don't know what I'd do without you. Your patience, calmness, and insights are always appreciated. Thank you for stepping in when I'm holed up tapping away on the computer, oblivious to the world. You make my writing journey that much smoother. Thank you for ALWAYS being there for me! I'm so lucky you're on my team!

Thank you to my editor Lisa Cullinan, for all your insightful edits and making my story a better one. You definitely made this book rock. I couldn't have done it without you! As always, a HUGE thank you for your patience and flexibility with accepting my book in pieces. I never could have hit the Publish button without you. You're the best!

Thank you to my wonderful beta readers Natalie Weston, Maryann Becker, Sera Lavish, and Christina Spence. You rock! Your enthusiasm and suggestions for Animal's Reformation: Insurgents MC were spot on and helped me to put out a stronger, cleaner novel.

Thank you to the bloggers for your support in reading my book, sharing it, reviewing it, and getting my name out there. I so appreciate all your efforts. You all are so invaluable. I hope you know that. Without you, the indie author would be lost.

Thank you ARC readers you have helped make all my books so much stronger. I appreciate the effort and time you put in to reading, reviewing, and getting the word out about the books. I don't know what

I'd do without you. I feel so lucky to have you behind me.

Thank you to my Street Team. Thanks for your input, your support, and your hard work. I appreciate you more than you know. A HUGE hug to all of you!

Thank you to Carrie from Cheeky Covers. You are amazing! I can always count on you. You are the calm to my storm. You totally rock, and I love your artistic vision.

Thank you to my proofers who worked hard to get my novel back to me so I could hit the publish button on time. There are no words to describe how touched and grateful I am for your dedication and support. Also much thanks for your insight re: plot and characterization. I definitely took heed, and it made my story flow that much better.

Thank you to Ena and Amanda with Enticing Journeys Promotions who have helped garner attention for and visibility to the Insurgents MC series. Couldn't do it without you!

Thank you to my awesome formatter, Paul Salvette at Beebee Books. You make my books look stellar. I appreciate how professional you are and how quickly you return my books to me. A huge thank you for doing rush orders and always returning a formatted book of which I am proud. Kudos!

Thank you to the readers who continue to support me and read my books. Without you, none of this would be possible. I appreciate your comments and reviews on my books, and I'm dedicated to giving you the best story that I can. I'm always thrilled when you enjoy a book as much as I have in writing it. You definitely make the hours of typing on the computer and the frustrations that come with the territory of writing books so worth it.

And a special thanks to every reader who has been with me since "Hawk's Property." Your support, loyalty, and dedication to my stories touch me in so many ways. You enable me to tell my stories, and I am forever grateful to you.

You all make it possible for writers to write because without you reading the books, we wouldn't exist. Thank you, thank you! ♥

Animal's Reformation: Insurgents Motorcycle Club (Book 13)

Dear Readers,

Thank you for reading my book. I hope you enjoyed it as much as I enjoyed writing Animal and Olivia's story. This gritty and rough motorcycle club has a lot more to say, so I hope you will look for the upcoming books in the series. Romance makes life so much more colorful, and a rough, sexy bad boy makes life a whole lot more interesting.

If you enjoyed the book, please consider leaving a review on Amazon. I read all of them and appreciate the time taken out of busy schedules to do that.

I love hearing from my fans, so if you have any comments or questions, please email me at chiahwilder@gmail.com or visit my facebook page.

To receive a **free copy of my novella**, *Summer Heat*, and to hear of **new releases, special sales, free short stories**, and **ARC opportunities**, please sign up for my **Newsletter** at http://eepurl.com/bACCL1.

Happy Reading,

Chiah

Shadow's Surrender: Insurgents MC
Coming August 2019

The Crossroads of Destiny and Desire.

He's a hardcore biker who likes his women easy, his whiskey neat, and his Harley fast. Nothing complicated ... until a pampered beauty collides into his world.

Shadow is an **Insurgent**, one of the **largest outlaw MCs** in Colorado. Riding his Harley, hanging out with his fellow Insurgents, and enjoying the ladies, are his idea of the perfect life.

He likes things simple and free from drama, and that includes his women. Privileged princesses? Definitely not.

Then at his cousin's engagement party, he sees *her*. **Sexy, curves in all the right places, and a dangerous look in her dark green eyes.** Oh yeah ... his libido is starting to smoke.

All he wants is one long taste.

Scarlett Mansfield comes from one of the richest families in the county. Her life is perfect and well-orchestrated until she sets her eyes on **the chiseled biker across the room**. The intensity of his gaze makes her blush ... *almost.*

She knows in her world the rugged stranger is taboo, but she is drawn to him.

Scarlett has complication stamped all over her, but an undeniable desire sizzles between them, and Shadow can't stay away.

55562185R00186

Made in the USA
Middletown, DE
17 July 2019